CURTAINS FOR MISS PLYM

Previously published Worldwide Mystery titles by KATHLEEN DELANEY

DYING FOR A CHANGE
GIVE FIRST PLACE TO MURDER
PUREBRED DEAD

CURTAINS FOR MISS PLYM

KATHLEEN DELANEY

WORLDWIDE®

TORONTO • NEW YORK • LONDON
AMSTERDAM • PARIS • SYDNEY • HAMBURG
STOCKHOLM • ATHENS • TOKYO • MILAN
MADRID • WARSAW • BUDAPEST • AUCKLAND

Curtains for Miss Plym

A Worldwide Mystery/February 2018

First published by Severn House Publishers Ltd.

ISBN-13: 978-1-335-50646-7

Printed in U.S.A.

CURTAINS FOR MISS PLYM

ONE

Mary McGill stood in front of St Mark's community hall, staring at the black recess she knew held a door. Only, someone had turned off the outside light and, at this hour on an early spring morning, it was as dark as ink. How was she supposed to find the keyhole when she couldn't see the door?

'Blast.' Mary put down her overloaded tote bag, laid Millie's dog bed on top of it and pulled her phone out of her coat pocket. She'd downloaded the flashlight app but never used it. She hoped it worked. It did. 'See what a wonderful thing modern technology is,' she told the little black cocker spaniel who sat beside her. The dark had reduced Millie to a blurred outline, but she heard her whine.

'It will only be another second. I'll just…' She thrust the key at the now-visible hole but the door swung open before she inserted it.

'What on earth…' Mary stared at the door, along with the dog. 'I locked that door last night. I know I did. Remember? We were the last ones to leave, and I made sure it was locked. We left the light on, too.'

Suddenly the church hall, where she'd spent so many hours organizing all kinds of events, seemed very dark and not at all friendly. Had someone come back after she'd locked up last night? Who? She had no idea how many people had a key. Reverend Les McIntyre did, of course, and…she couldn't think who else. Had she given a key to someone on St Mark's annual spring rummage sale committee? Pat Bennington, maybe? Pat was organizing the dog and cat adoption center they were holding for the first time in conjunction with the rummage sale. Half the sale proceeds were to go to the no-kill shelter the town had recently built. The hope was that, with the number of people who always turned out for the sale, they could find a few good homes for some of the animals in need of a new family. Had Pat already come? Of course she hadn't. She would hardly wait in the dark.

Mary pushed the door open a little more and let her cell phone light up the doorway. That's all it lit. The inside was as black as a bat cave.

'Pat?' Mary's voice echoed in what seemed to be an empty room. No one answered. Mary hadn't really expected anyone to, but it seemed prudent to try. She waited another minute. There wasn't a sound. She must have left the door open last night. How could she have been so forgetful? Disgusted with herself, she pushed the door open wider, reached in and felt for the light switch she knew was there. Light flooded the room. No one moved; no one called out. The hall was empty.

Shaking her head in disbelief, Mary stooped to pick up her tote bag, tightened Millie's leash and started into the room. 'I'll come back for your bed in a minute,' she told the dog, 'after I've put on the coffee.'

Millie's only answer was a low rumble in her throat. The hairs on the back of her shiny black head stood straight up as she surveyed the room.

Mary watched her for a second, amazed. Millie didn't growl. At people, at least. Occasionally she told another dog walking down her sidewalk not to consider stepping on her porch, but she contented herself with a warning and then only when the screen door was secure and she was behind it. Something had to be wrong for the dog to act like this, but what? The hairs on the back of Mary's neck started to tingle as she looked around the room from the safety of the doorway, but everything seemed just as she'd left it and no one was in sight. The long tables holding the sale items looked undisturbed. The jackets, coats, blouses and shirts that hung on the clothes racks she'd borrowed from Target hung neatly. The three baby cribs were still empty. The imitation maple chest of drawers still stood next to them, its five-dollar price tag prominently displayed. Holding Millie's leash, she set her tote bag down by the door and took another step into the room, surveying every corner, trying to see what was bothering the dog.

Large pieces of furniture were grouped along one side wall. Tables holding just about everything from old toasters to computer screens to piles of children's clothes stretched out down the middle. Breakables, lamps, dishes, vases and even a rather lovely white porcelain clock had been placed on tables pushed against the other side wall. The back wall held the door to the kitchen, right next to a serving pass-through, its roll-down cover in place. Farther down the wall was a short hallway that housed the bathrooms and a door into the side parking lot where the dog crates and pens would be set up. The cats would be indoors. Next to the hallway Mary had rigged up, with the help of several committee members who didn't mind climbing on ladders, a makeshift dressing area. Old curtains and a bedspread hung rather precariously on round curtain rods to provide two makeshift dressing areas for ladies who preferred to try on clothes with a little privacy. She had dragged a couple of chairs behind the curtains as well as a free-standing mirror that, while not perfect, would do.

'I have no idea what you're making a fuss about,' she told the dog, 'but there's no one here. No thanks to me. I could have sworn I locked that door last night and was positive I'd left the light on over it as well.' She sighed. 'You don't suppose that means I'm getting old, do you?'

With a snort of laughter at her little joke, she let go of Millie's leash and turned to pick up her tote. 'Better get the coffee going before anyone else gets here. I'll get your bed… Where are you going?'

Millie headed through the tables toward the dressing area, but not with her usual brisk trot. She crouched down, almost slinking, the rumble in her throat audible as she dragged her leash. Mary watched her for a moment, the unease she'd felt before returning and building. She'd never seen Millie act like this. Where was she going? Toward the curtains. There was no uncertainty in the dog's destination. There was something behind those curtains she didn't like.

Mary set her tote down once more but held tightly onto her phone. She clicked off the flashlight and set her finger on the red button AARP had so thoughtfully provided for quick access to 911. Surely she wouldn't need it, but she didn't like the way Millie was acting. Was there really something behind those curtains? She slowly threaded her way through the tables, her eyes never leaving the dog.

Millie stopped in front of the faded green bedspread that closed off one end of the dressing area. She looked back over her shoulder at Mary then back at the bedspread, and the rumble in her throat got louder. Something stuck out from under the bedspread. Mary came to a halt and stared. Whatever it was hadn't been there last night. She stepped closer. Slippers. Pink furry slippers. Had someone come in here last night to try on slippers? Irritation wiped away the unease that had filled her. Of all the idiotic things to do. Why anyone would… How anyone could have… Puzzled, but no less irritated, Mary descended on the slippers, intent on putting them back on the correct table before everyone got here. She stopped.

The slippers had feet in them.

Her heart started to beat faster and her breath came out in little puffs. Holding her cell in one hand, she grabbed the bedspread with the other and pulled. They'd done a good job. It slid easily on the makeshift rod to expose the chair Mary had left in the dressing area. A chair that should have been empty but wasn't. A woman sat sprawled in it. An old woman with wispy gray hair, her feet encased in the pink slippers. The rest of her was covered with a long-sleeved pink nightdress. A blue corduroy robe had come loose from its tie and fell open on each side of her, covering the chair. The tie lay on the floor beside her.

Mary gasped loud and clear in the empty room. It couldn't be. It was impossible, only she was looking at her. Emilie Plym, poor little Miss Plym who wouldn't hurt a fly, who most of the time didn't know where she was or how she got there, but who never seemed to mind. Someone would gather her up and return her home, she was sure. Everyone was her friend, and she had a smile for them all. How had she gotten in here? Why had she? Mary made herself look closer. Miss Plym's face was an odd gray color, and her eyes were open and bloodshot. Her mouth was slightly open and her tongue… Mary started to blink rapidly in an effort to clear her vision and then staggered a little. Whatever had happened, Miss Plym had not come in, sat down and quietly died.

Breathe deeply. Deep breaths, that's right. She looked at Millie, who no longer seemed to want to growl. She stared at Miss Plym as if she, too, couldn't believe what she saw.

Mary sighed and hit the red 911 button. 'Hazel? Is that you? Yes, it's Mary. No, I'm not all right. Hazel, I'm at Saint Mark's, in the church hall. No, no. It's not on fire. I'm afraid it's worse than that. Miss Plym is here. No, I can't take her home and neither can anyone else. Hazel, she's dead, and I don't think from natural causes. Can you get Dan over here right away? Thanks.'

Mary hung up and slipped the phone in her jacket pocket before she addressed the dog. 'I don't know what happened, but I do know there'll be no rummage sale today.'

Millie whined.

TWO

Mary McGill set her coffee mug on the church kitchen counter and stared at Dan Dunham, chief of Santa Louisa's small police force and her nephew-in-law. 'You can't mean that.'

'I'm afraid I do.' Dan had never looked so glum. 'Miss Emilie was strangled.'

'Oh.' Mary let her breath out slowly, trying to come to terms with what Dan said. She thought back to the sight of Miss Emilie, sprawled on the wooden chair, and shivered. 'I saw her bathrobe cord on the floor but I never thought someone might have… I thought at first maybe she'd had a stroke, like her sister, Miss Eloise had. It wasn't until later I realized… Why would someone deliberately…' Mary's voice was faint and she knew it. She felt faint. Strangled. That harmless old lady. Who could have done such a thing? Why? Miss Emilie was no threat to anyone. 'Are you sure it wasn't a stroke or something?'

Dan looked uncomfortable. 'There are some other things that happen in strangulation.'

'Like what?'

'You don't want to know. Just rest assured, she was old, didn't struggle and probably died very quickly.'

Mary stared at him. So did Millie, who sat as close to Mary's side as she could get. Finally Mary picked back up her coffee mug and, with hands that still trembled more than she liked, lifted the coffee to her lips, took a sip and once more let the sight of little old Miss Emilie float in front of her. She'd never seen anyone who'd died of strangulation, but she'd never seen anyone who'd died from a stroke, either. Dan was right. She probably didn't want to know how you could tell. 'I can't get my head around any of this. Why was she even here? How did she get in? She must have been with someone, but who? And who could possibly want to kill her?'

'Good questions. Let's start with how she got in.'

'I've been thinking about that. Dan, the door was unlocked when I got here this morning and the light over the door was off. I left it on when I left last night, I'm sure I did.'

'I assume that means you were the last one out of here. Did you lock the door?'

'Yes. When I found it unlocked, I thought maybe somehow I'd forgotten, but I didn't. Forget, I mean. I remember having a hard time getting the key in the lock because I had Millie's leash and she wanted to...find a grassy spot. So we went over under that old oak before I got in the car. The light over the door was visible from there. I remember because I knew it would be dark when I got here this morning.'

'What time did you leave here?'

'It was a little after ten.'

'Who besides you has a key?'

'Les, of course. I don't know who else.'

'I'll ask him. Probably a lot more of them floating around than there should be.'

He walked over to the now-open counter window, leaned on the counter and looked out at the activity overflowing the church hall. Mary followed. The paramedics were trying to get Miss Plym onto a gurney, but she'd been on that chair awhile. Bending her was proving to be a bit difficult. Mary gulped, set her coffee down on the counter and turned to watch a couple of uniforms cordon off the room with crime-scene tape. A couple of people not in uniform, one a woman in jeans and a sweatshirt, were taking pictures of the chair Miss Plym had sat on, the old bedspread and the entire dressing area. Two uniformed officers, both members of the crime-scene team Dan had been training, set out what looked like miniature white cones with large black numbers on each one. The woman took pictures of each one as the officers scribbled something in a large notebook. One lone man stood in the doorway of the little hallway, seemingly staring toward the bathrooms. At what, Mary didn't know.

She didn't know what the police hoped to find, either. The hall had been full of people all day yesterday. It was a popular place to hold events, and the annual spring rummage sale was one of the most popular. It took a lot of volunteers a couple of days, all working in the hall, to put it together. Finding any useful forensic evidence wasn't going to be easy. She supposed they had to go through the motions. If this turned out like the *CSI* programs she sometimes watched, they'd come up with a vital clue.

'Dan. Dan Dunham. Mary. Will you please tell this young man we can come through?' Pat Bennington and her husband, Karl Bennington, the local small animal vet, and Dan's and Ellen's best friends. Pat was hailing him from the front door.

Dan waved at the young officer at the door and Pat walked into the room, closely followed by Joy Mitchell, Mary's most loyal and dependable volunteer. They had identical expressions of foreboding as they approached.

'What's going on?' Pat stopped in front of Dan, who

leaned on his elbows on the counter. He started to answer Pat but was interrupted by a loud gasp. The activity around Miss Plym was hidden from most of the room by the makeshift curtains still pulled across much of the dressing-room area. The curtains near the kitchen pass-through were pulled back, giving a full view of the paramedics and Miss Plym. They had finally secured her onto a gurney, almost totally encased in a large black bag which they were trying to pull up over her shoulders. Her face was in full view.

'That can't be Emilie Plym. Can it?' Disbelief, horror and a small gagging sound replaced Joy's usual slightly disapproving but monotone voice.

It startled Pat enough that she wheeled around, almost losing her balance. She was just in time to catch a glimpse of Miss Plym's gray face and white hair before the black bag swallowed her body entirely.

'Oh, my God.' Her hands flew to her face, covering her mouth as if to smother the gasp that escaped. 'It is Miss Plym. What happened to her?'

Mary stared into her white coffee mug which she held tightly with both hands. Joy's reaction had brought her eyes back to the gurney and the body bag on it. 'Someone killed her. In here. Sometime last night.' She managed to make her hands stop trembling by clutching the mug tighter but couldn't quite clear the tremor out of her voice. 'Come in the kitchen. Half the town is going to start pouring in here in…' she checked her watch, '…a little less than an hour, and we have to figure out how to stop them.'

Dan nodded. 'You're right. Half the town wandering through my crime scene isn't going to happen.' He pulled himself back from the pass-through and disappeared into the kitchen.

Mary picked up her mug and straightened. 'Coffee's ready. The kitchen doesn't seem involved, so Dan let me make it. That and it's early and he hadn't had any yet.'

'Coffee's essential at a crime scene,' he called out, his voice devoid of emotion.

Pat and Joy hurried through the doorway, firing questions at Mary and Dan as they went. 'You mean she was actually killed? On purpose? It wasn't an accident of some kind?'

The sight of poor old Miss Emilie leaving so ignominiously seemed to have shaken the usually unflappable Pat. Either that or she hadn't had her coffee, either.

Joy was more to the point. 'I'll bet she came back looking for her blasted dog.' She walked through the kitchen toward the large coffeemaker, pulled a white mug off the tray beside it, ladled sugar into the mug then filled it with coffee. She turned.

Three faces—four if you counted Millie—stared at her.

'What dog?' Mary glanced at Millie, who moved in closer and sat on her foot. 'Emilie didn't have a dog.'

'She used to.'

All eyes turned toward Pat.

'Willis. A Shih Tzu. I'm told she's had several over the years and they were all named Willis.'

'I'd forgotten that,' Mary said slowly, 'but the last Willis has been dead for years. Why would she come looking for him here, in the middle of the night?'

'Yesterday…' Pat took a sip. She made a face, put the mug back on the counter and fanned her mouth. 'Hot. She was in here yesterday with Lorraine Duxworth. You know, she and her husband, Caleb, work for the Plyms. Where that niece of hers was or why she allowed Lorraine to drag her down here when we've got so many of her family things her niece donated, things she might actually remember, I don't know.' She paused and looked at her mug as if considering whether to pick it back up before she went on. 'I can never remember her name.'

'Whose name?' Joy paused in her stirring and turned to face her.

'The niece. The one who came out to arrange Miss Eloise's funeral and wanted to put Miss Emilie in Shady Acres.'

'Cassandra, and we don't know that they were going to. Only that they were looking into it.'

'What do you mean "they"?' Pat turned toward Mary, a blank look on her face.

'Her brother came out with her. Richard.'

'I thought Richard was the twin's father, the original Mr Plym.' Evidently Joy's coffee was stirred enough because she set the spoon in the sink and leaned back against it to stare at Mary. Her hair was twisted into a severe bun, her dress faded from too many washings and her sweater bulky and shapeless. Joy's approach to life was one of no nonsense, good cooking and clean living. She had the clean living down pat, but Mary often thought she didn't need to put quite so much stress on the no-nonsense part. That said, she was one of Mary's most reliable volunteers.

'They're all Richard. The twin's father, their brother, and now their nephew.'

'That makes him Richard the third.' Pat grinned.

Mary ignored her. 'The Richard who was Emilie and Eloise's younger brother was in high school with my husband, Samuel. They were good friends. Why, I never understood. They had almost nothing in common. Richard went to college in the East somewhere and stayed. He married a girl from Baltimore and opened a furniture store, like his father had here, only I heard he was even more successful. He only came back a few times—once to be Samuel's best man at our wedding. I don't think he ever brought his family. The last time he came was for Samuel's funeral. He was a pall bearer. He had a heart attack and died not too long after. The first time I met Cassandra was last year at Eloise's funeral. She'd called and asked what she should do, said I was the only one in town she'd ever heard her father mention. I helped her make all the arrangements. Oh, dear. Now she'll have another funeral to arrange. Well, I dare say we'll all pitch in.'

'You'll see to it. You always do.' Pat smiled, but her smile faded as Dan spoke.

'What happened when they got here yesterday?' Dan had little frown lines across his forehead and around his eyes. That he wasn't interested in the Plym family tree was obvious, but what happened when Miss Emilie visited the rummage sale and why she was there interested him a great deal.

'I don't know,' Pat told him. 'I was leaving to meet one of the rescue people when they came in and I noticed Miss Emilie looked upset. She started walking up and down the tables, looking for something, but I had to go and don't know what happened.'

'Joy, you saw them?' Mary watched Dan out of the corner of her eye. He knew the Plym twins, of course. Everyone who'd grown up in Santa Louisa knew the Plyms. He'd been called out, along with the paramedics, when Miss Eloise collapsed in the grocery store a little over a year ago. It was Dan who'd gone to the old Victorian house on Cherry Street to break the news of Miss Eloise's stroke to her sister and Lorraine and Caleb Duxworth, who'd worked for the twins for years. Miss Eloise had lingered on, staying at home under the care of Gloria Sutherland, a home health nurse, for a couple of months before another stroke took her, leaving Miss Emilie all alone in that Victorian museum. Dan had returned her home more than once when she wandered into town, her big black purse over her arm, her stuffed dog under it. He'd laughed about it, but he'd worried about her. No wonder his face looked like a thundercloud. He must have felt protective of her—so had everyone who knew her.

Joy shrugged. 'Like I said, I think she was looking for something—that stuffed dog she carried all the time. For some reason, she thought it was here. Then she saw her little white clock and that really upset her. It was her mother's, and I guess it had been in her room. She couldn't understand why it was here. But it was Willis she was looking for. She was sure he was here somewhere.'

'I haven't seen her without that dog in her lap or under her arm for years. How could it have gotten here? Did anyone see it?'

Joy looked at her, then down into her mug, then up at all of them and stated in her usual brusque voice, 'I did. That blasted dog was in the box of donated items from the Plym house. I knew I had to get it back to her, so I took it out and put it in my car. Thought I'd drop it by her house and I forgot about it.' She paused and shook her head slightly. 'I was on my way to that meeting we had about the music for Easter Sunday when they came in, and I never even thought about the dog. It never crossed my mind they were looking for it. It was only later… If it had I would have gotten it for her right then.'

No one said anything for a minute. Mary couldn't. This was all so sad and so senseless. Who could possibility want to…unless someone was already in the hall looking for something when Miss Emilie came in? Only, what? There was nothing in that hall worth stealing and certainly nothing worth murdering someone.

'You're saying Lorraine brought Miss Emilie here yesterday, looking for her stuffed dog?' Dan's eyebrows narrowed and he shook his head as if this was an idea he was having trouble believing.

Joy shrugged. 'As I said, I was on my way to that meeting. I saw them come in but I was in such a rush it didn't register they were looking for the dog.' She paused. 'I never thought about it again until this morning.'

'They were looking for something,' Pat said. 'I came through the back door to fill my water bottle after getting the dog one of the rescue people brought settled and saw them. They were standing in front of one of the tables and Miss Emilie seemed distraught. I had someone else from animal rescue on my cell phone and two other people waiting for me in the parking lot, so I didn't stop. But it looked as if Lorraine had her hands full.'

Joy indicated one of the tables. 'Humph. One of those tables is full of stuff from the Plym house. I'll bet that poor little thing couldn't understand why her family things were here. I wondered about it myself.'

Mary looked toward the table and nodded. 'There must have been three or four boxes. But what I saw was mostly old clothes.'

'There was one box that wasn't clothes. Some of those things were old Mrs Plym's, and I wouldn't be surprised if some were her mother's before her. Antiques, I shouldn't wonder. Wouldn't the Plym trust have something to say about putting things like that in a rummage sale? Miss Eloise's clothes I can understand, but that pretty little clock… Why would she give that away?'

'The white porcelain one with painted flowers and a lot of gold on it?' That one had caught Mary's eye. It was pretty but hardly an antique. Her mother had one like it that Mary and her sisters had given her for Christmas one year. They'd bought it at Hallmark.

'That's the one. It was old Mrs Plym's. She had it in her room until she died. Then Emilie took it into hers. Or that's what Gloria Sutherland told me, and she should know. She took care of Eloise those last two months. I'm sure she was all over that house.'

Joy's look of disapproval wasn't nearly as severe as Mary's. Gloria was difficult and didn't always act…but she was a good nurse. At least, Mary thought she was. And even though Joy was probably right, and Gloria was known to go snooping, they didn't know she had.

'Where is it now?' Dan obviously wasn't interested in Gloria Sutherland's snooping or lack of it and only mildly in the clock.

Joy bobbed her head toward the big room. 'I put it on the table with the nicer things, the ones that might break. It's on the table up against the wall.'

Mary walked over to the serving opening and leaned forward a little to look at the tables with the breakables. They sat along the wall, just to the right of the window, close enough so she could see most of them clearly. She looked carefully before she turned. 'Where did you say you put it?'

'On that end table, in the back. I pushed it back there

so it wouldn't fall off.' Joy set her coffee mug down and got to her feet. 'It's right there.'

Mary shook her head. 'It's not there now.'

Joy gave Mary a look that plainly said she didn't know what she was talking about and marched out of the kitchen, followed by Mary and Pat. Joy stopped at the end table and her expression changed from irritation to puzzlement. 'That clock was there when I left. I know it was. I remember pushing it toward the back.'

There was no clock on the table.

'Do you suppose Miss Emilie took it?' Pat looked around the room at the other tables.

The clock wasn't on any of them, at least not on any table nearby.

'She didn't have it with her when I found her.' Mary spoke with certainty. Miss Emilie had carried no purse last night, and there was no place to put a clock in that nightgown.

'Maybe she took it home with her yesterday afternoon.' Joy sounded doubtful, but there didn't seem to be any other explanation.

'I'm not so sure.' Pat turned slowly. 'Lorraine seemed to be trying to get her out of here. She wasn't carrying anything that I remember.'

'Do you think she could have hidden it somewhere, meaning to come back for it?' Joy started toward the tables lined up down the middle of the room.

Many had piles of clothes that could easily hide a clock, or it could be behind a toaster, or even in one of the strollers. If Miss Plym had hidden it, it could be anywhere.

Mary doubted that's what happened. Lorraine had been with her the whole time. Surely she would have seen her if she'd tried to hide the clock. Besides, Miss Emilie couldn't always remember where she lived. She certainly wouldn't remember she'd hidden a clock and where. Or why. But where had it gone? Someone had taken it. Was it whoever had killed poor little Miss Plym?

Dan's voice broke her train of thought. 'Ladies, I hate to break this up, but this is a crime scene. I doubt the missing clock is important, but you not disturbing anything right now is.' Dan stood in the kitchen doorway, coffee mug in hand, watching them. 'Besides, Pat needs to get out in the parking lot and turn all those people with dogs away. You need to turn everybody away.'

Pat's cell rang. She fumbled for it, pulled it out of her pocket and answered. 'Tell them to wait. I'll be right out.' Her face was creased with worry lines and frustration as she hung up. 'Some of them just arrived. Now what do I do?'

'But we need to…' Joy's face was creased with anger. 'I don't like that things are going missing.'

'I'll tell my people we have a missing clock and make sure they keep an eye out for it. Right now, we've got dogs and cats coming with no place to put them and what are you going to do about all the people who'll be here in about…' he checked his watch and raised an eyebrow before resuming, '…way too soon. I really don't want half the town trying to get into this building to find a bargain, ruining what's already a pretty darn difficult crime scene. And as much as I'd love to see you place all those animals, they can't come in here and they can't go in the parking lot, either.'

'The basketball court.'

'What?' Dan and Pat stared at Mary.

'The basketball court. It's on the other side of the

church, next to the Sunday school building. It can't be part of the crime scene, can it?' She looked expectantly at Dan, who slowly shook his head.

'No, it's not.'

'Good. We'll set up the adoption center there. That way it will only be the rummage sale we have to postpone. But we better get busy.' She looked around. 'Where's Millie?'

'Right where she always is. Next to your ankle.' Pat smiled.

Mary looked down. Millie looked up at her. 'So she is.'

Mary, Pat and Millie left by the back door, stopping only long enough to pick up Millie's bed. Mary was already on her cell, talking to the radio station. 'Phil, I need you to put out a bulletin. Yes, it's an emergency. We've had a problem at Saint Mark's and the rummage sale is canceled, but we'll still hold the pet adoption. In the basketball court. Yes, please start announcing it now.' She listened for a moment. 'It's Miss Emilie Plym. She died in the church hall. No, I don't know any more than that. I have no idea how she got in, but the police are there now, trying to find out. That's all I know. Don't mention that on the radio until the police make the announcement. Just say there was an accident. I don't know when the rummage sale will be rescheduled but rest assured it will be. Can you announce that now? Thanks, Phil.'

That should stop an influx of early birds arriving to rummage through the tables looking for bargains. Everyone in town listened to WQXV in the morning. Hopefully it wouldn't keep people from coming out to find a new pet.

As for the clock, Mary thought she could put that out of her mind, at least for the moment. That it wasn't where Joy had left it was clear, and she was almost positive it wasn't going to be found anywhere in the building. Who had taken it and where it was now was a problem to be solved at a later time.

She hit speed dial on her phone and Bart's rentals answered. 'Is this Bart? Mary McGill here. We've had a change of plans. Can you bring the tent...?'

THREE

'MARY, CAN I talk to you for a minute?' Dan Dunham sat down on the picnic bench across from Mary and set his chief's hat in the middle of it.

He looked very handsome in his uniform, even if his tie was on a little crooked and his jacket only zipped up halfway. His gun was set much too easily on his hip for her taste, and all the other things hanging on his belt made her a little nervous, but then, even though Santa Louisa was a small town, it had its share of crime and she supposed he needed them. She let her hand drift down and touch Millie on the head. She'd been a little surprised when the dog had jumped up on the bench beside her, and a little worried she might fall off. She should have known better. Instead of thinking about the dog, she needed to concentrate on what Dan was going to say. From the look in his eyes, she wasn't going to like it.

'I need a favor. A big favor.'

She'd known she wasn't going to like it. 'What kind of favor?'

He ran a hand through his hair, just like he always did when he was trying to think how to put something, the look on his face troubled. 'I need you to go over to the Plym house and be there in case they hear before we arrive.'

Mary had no idea what she'd been expecting, but certainly not that. 'You want me to do what? Why?'

'A couple of reasons. One, I don't want them to wake up and find Miss Emilie gone. They'll panic. At least Lorraine will. I imagine the niece… Cassandra…will also. It's not quite seven, so you may be able to get there before they realize she's not in her room.'

Mary's mouth was slightly open as she stared at him, but it took a moment before she could make words come out. 'You want me to do what? Go over to the Plyms' and keep them from finding out that Miss Emilie's dead, strangled? I don't think so.'

'Don't get so upset. First, Ellen's going with you. She knows the Duxworths well and she's met the niece. I just called her. Got her out of bed.' There was a tiny smile under his tidy mustache as he said that. 'Second, I don't want you to tell them she's dead. Certainly don't tell them she was murdered. I'll do that when I get there.'

'Ellen and I are supposed to drop in for coffee at seven in the morning? Just a casual call?'

Dan sighed. 'No. Tell them there's been an accident. That Miss Emilie evidently wandered off during the night and that you wanted to tell them before they discovered she was missing. You don't need to say anything more, other than that I'll be there as soon as I can.'

'What's your other reason?' She didn't say it, but she thought it was the real reason he wanted them to go.

Dan's smile had disappeared. 'I want to know how they react. All of them. I understand Cassandra's brother arrived a couple of days ago and he's already been to see Glen Manning over at the bank. Glen says he's a cold fish if he's ever seen one, and I imagine he's seen a few. I haven't met him yet, although I will sometime today. I haven't met the niece, either, but Ellen likes her. I expect

Lorraine will be the most upset, but I'd really like to see how Caleb takes it.'

'Caleb?' Mary sat up a little straighter and quit stroking the dog's ears. 'Why Caleb? He wouldn't hurt Miss Emilie. He and Lorraine have worked for the twins for years. He might not have been as fond of her as Lorraine but he'd never hurt her. Caleb might rant and rave but he wouldn't hurt a fly.'

'He'd give one a nervous breakdown with all his yelling, though.' The voice came from behind Mary. Ellen, her niece and Dan's wife, slipped onto the bench beside her. 'Hi.' She gave her aunt a quick kiss on the cheek. She smiled at her husband and wiggled the fingers of her free hand at him. The other hand clutched a paper Starbucks cup.

'A latte?' Dan's gaze slid from her to the paper cup.

Ellen laughed. 'It's early. You woke me up and told me to get over here before I'd made the coffee, so I drove through.' She took a sip, looking at him over the lid. 'I got a large one so we could share.' She pushed the cup over toward him.

He grinned and took it. 'Thanks.'

'There's coffee in the church hall kitchen.' Mary looked with faint disapproval at the cup. She liked her coffee to be just that, coffee, with a little milk or cream and a small teaspoon of sugar, but no syrups, flavors or frothy stuff. How much might Ellen have paid for her drink? It was really none of her business.

'If we're going to do this, we'd better get a move on. They're all going to be up any time now, and if we're going to be of any use we'd better get there before they realize she's missing. Pat has everything under control, so Millie and I are ready.'

She leaned across Millie and picked up her tote bag, which was much lighter now the coffee, notebooks and cashbox had all been stashed somewhere else.

Ellen took her cup back from Dan and sipped. 'Do you want us to break the bad news to them?'

'No. Just say there's been an accident and I'll be there as soon as I can. I don't want them to hear it on the radio and panic. I want someone to be there as a sort of buffer.'

'And that someone has to be me. Me and my beloved aunt.' She sighed heavily and, it seemed, a bit theatrically. 'OK. I need to meet Richard Plym anyway, but I hadn't planned on doing it like this.' She set the cup down in front of Dan, said, 'You don't deserve that,' and eased herself off the bench.

He smiled and picked up the cup.

'Dan, you won't forget about the clock, will you? I saw it yesterday afternoon and if Joy says she put it somewhere then that's where it should be.' Mary paused. 'Unless Miss Emilie took it. She could have slipped it into her bag when Lorraine wasn't looking.'

'I'll find out.' Dan pushed himself to his feet. 'The county CSI guys just pulled up. I need to see them.' He started to hand Ellen back the Starbuck's cup but she smiled and waved it away. He grinned at her and left.

Mary set Millie on the ground and extricated herself from between the bench and the table. She gathered up Millie's leash in one hand, her tote in the other and looked at Ellen. 'Well?'

'What clock?'

'I'll tell you about it in the car.'

'We're really doing this?'

'Dan asked us to, and it makes sense. We don't want those poor people waking up and finding her gone.'

Ellen didn't look as if she agreed, but she yawned and then nodded. 'Are we taking the dog?'

'Of course. I always take her when I go to the Plyms'. Miss Emilie just loves…loved…her. Oh, dear. I still can't believe this is true. Let's get this over with.'

Ellen pointed to where she'd parked her car, well behind the line the police had strung across the front parking lot, and followed her aunt and the dog as they briskly headed toward it.

FOUR

THE DRIVE DIDN'T take long. The Plym house sat on a large lot on a side street not more than six blocks from St Mark's. There were four houses on the street, but only the Plym house was authentically old. The other three reflected various architectural styles over the last two hundred years but had all been built over the last twenty, all on land the Plyms had sold off. The original brick street had been carefully preserved, needing only a few new ones to make it drivable. Huge oaks pre-dated the Plym house and made a canopy of overlapping branches shading their front and side yards as well as the neighboring homes. The street lamps were the original gas lamps refitted to light with electricity. There had been some resistance to that from some of the newer residents who felt gas was somehow more romantic, but no one was left to light the lamps, so eventually the retrofit had been made. The Plym house, the only one with three stories, soared over the other three from its place at the end of the street. A brick chimney, actually three chimneys, rose against two sides of the house, the third peeking over the steep pitch of the roof at the very back. Fish-scale shingles were bright with fresh green paint. The window trim was white, outlined with a line of rose. The porch, adorned with curlicues on every post, wrapped around half the house. The white wicker furniture, obviously old but also freshly painted, sat protected by its overhang. Large potted plants guarded each side of the door. The walk was clean and the landscaping almost militarily neat. The round turret room on one corner of the house added to its rigidly formal look.

Mary sighed. 'Every time I come here I have the feeling I should have worn a corset.'

Ellen eyed her aunt. 'Do you even have a corset?'

Mary pulled her well-washed purple sweatshirt down over her navy sweatpants without dignifying Ellen's question with an answer. 'What are we waiting for? Let's get this over with.'

Mary had seen the heavily carved front door, its stained-glass insert and the elaborate brass handle many times and this morning scarcely noticed them. Her parents had brought her here with her sisters when they were children for the yearly Easter egg hunts the Plyms hosted on what used to be their huge lawn. They had come at Christmas to view the elaborate Christmas decorations the Plyms delighted in and to join in the caroling. There was always punch and cake served in the living room for everyone who came. Later, she'd attended parties here with Samuel. The Plyms' parties were always a bit dull, but they set a lavish table. In recent years, she had come to visit the sisters, especially after Miss Eloise was confined to her bed and Miss Emilie had settled into her faintly confused state. Emilie could no longer be trusted, if she left, to find her way home. However, Mary suspected she wasn't always as confused as she seemed. Getting a ride home in a police car just might have provided a little excitement in what must have been a fairly dull life. The last few times she'd visited, she'd brought Millie. Miss Emilie had delighted in her. Mary leaned over a little, gave Millie a pat on the head and rang the doorbell.

Lorraine answered, holding a crumpled tissue in one hand up to her nose. Her eyes were red and slightly swollen and her cheeks were stained with what looked like tear tracks. 'Oh, Mary, I'm so glad you came. You've heard? Miss Emilie's missing. I don't know what's happened or where she went. I can hardly believe it.' She burst into tears. From the look of her eyes, it wasn't the first time this morning.

'So much for being a buffer,' Ellen said softly in Mary's ear.

Obviously they were too late to soften the blow, but not by much. Lorraine still had on an orange-print cotton nightgown that stopped just above her ankles and a much-washed red plush bathrobe that ended at her knees. Her gray felt slippers were too big and in danger of being left behind when she picked up her feet. Her hair hadn't been combed and stuck out at those peculiar angles hair seemed to be fond of first thing in the morning. She appeared not to notice any of these things.

'Yes,' Mary murmured. 'That's why we're here. May we come in?'

'Please.' Lorraine opened the door wider and looked down as Mary advanced. 'Oh. You've brought Millie. How Miss Emilie would have loved to see her.' Tears started to flow once more. She dug a damp tissue out of the sleeve of her robe and dabbed her eyes. 'And Ellen. So good of you to come. Everyone's in the kitchen. Richard is on the phone to the police. No one seems to know anything. I just can't believe all this. I had to go up to her room to make sure. It was empty, of course, but I had to see…'

All of this came over her shoulder as she turned from the doorway and shuffled through the entry toward the back of the house. Mary closed the door and looked at Ellen, who rolled her eyes. Millie sat on the floor and looked around until Mary and Ellen followed Lorraine. She got up and trotted along beside Mary.

On their left, opening off the entryway, was a formal living room, probably originally known as a sitting room or parlor when the house was new. Mary ignored it, but Ellen seemed to find it intriguing. Heavy gold draperies that hung by the windows looked to be velvet. There was also a green velvet settee. Two large chairs were so overstuffed it was a wonder you could sit on them without sliding off. The heavily carved straight-backed chairs with lion-head feet were no more welcoming. A glass lamp with a fringed shade sat primly in the center of the table between them. Ellen hurried to keep up and found her aunt standing in the middle of a kitchen remarkably different from the rigid formality of the living room.

The kitchen was a somewhat jarring conglomeration of the thirties, forties and fifties. It looked like a larger version of the kitchen Mary had known as a child and not completely unlike the one in her own house. The cupboards were painted white, the drain board was well-scrubbed sixties' Formica and the floor a yellow pattern popular in the fifties. The stove was vintage forties, complete with a griddle on top, but there was a dishwasher by the old soapstone sink. An antique heavy mixer with large thick beaters sat in one corner and a stainless-steel slow cooker with a complex dial in another. It was an odd mix of periods, but the room was full of windows and early morning sunlight. It was also immaculate and smelled of fresh coffee. The table that sat in the middle of the room was stainless steel with a red Formica top. The chairs were bent steel with red vinyl seats. One was occupied by a man in the process of shutting off his cell phone. It was the sight of him that had caused Mary to stop abruptly.

'You must be Richard Plym. You look very much like your father.'

That didn't seem to please the man. He slipped his phone into the pocket of his silk burgundy robe and stood. 'So I've been told. And you are?'

Richard Plym ran a hand through thick brown hair as he glared at Mary, hair that hadn't been brushed yet. It made Mary think he might be a little more rattled than he wanted to let on. His father had been a man who always needed to be in control and only got rattled when a situation was one that refused to obey him. She suspected his son had inherited that characteristic, along with his long-lashed brown eyes.

'I'm Mary McGill. My husband, Samuel, and your father were best friends. I knew your father—well, most of my life.'

'Yes.' If one word had ever expressed indifference, it was that one. 'Is there something we can do for you, Mrs McGill?'

His eyes shifted away from Mary as he included Ellen in his abrupt remark then dropped to land on Millie. He stared at the dog. 'You brought your dog?'

Lorraine's voice was timid and exhausted sounding, but Mary thought it was better than the sniffing she'd been doing. 'Mary always brings Millie. Miss Emilie just loves Millie.'

Richard continued staring at the dog with a look of distaste. She hoped he wasn't going to ask her to put her outside, because she wasn't going to.

'Richard…'

The use of his first name seemed to startle him. He looked up at her and his glare intensified. Mary didn't care. He was being ridiculously pretentious. She'd known his father well and she'd gone out of her way to be kind to his aunts. She certainly wasn't going to start out what was going to be a difficult enough conversation by calling him Mr Plym. He, however, could call her Mrs McGill.

'Ellen and I have something to tell you, so perhaps we could sit down? Lorraine, I smell coffee. Maybe a cup…?'

'I can't find her anywhere. I tried Ellen as well, but she doesn't… Oh. There you are.'

Mary didn't think she'd ever seen such relief on anyone's face as on Cassandra Brown's. Like her brother, she also carried a cell phone, which she slipped into the pocket of her white terrycloth robe as she walked into the kitchen. She had at least made an attempt to run a comb through her deep brown hair, but it had done little to tame it. Her brown eyes looked wild, and her chin trembled as if she was on the verge of tears, or perhaps screaming in frustration. But relief had flooded her face as she caught sight of Mary and Ellen. 'Mary, I've been trying to find you everywhere. Aunt Emilie is missing. She must have gotten up sometime in the night and gone out, but we don't know where and don't know where to start looking. I knew you'd know what we need to do. I feel so… I can't believe this could have happened… We don't know… That's why you're here, isn't it?' There was foreboding in those last few words.

Mary nodded. 'Dan, Chief Dunham, will be over later to talk to you but asked us to come now. We wanted to break the news before you found she was missing. I guess we are too late.' She walked a little closer to the table. 'We found her at Saint Mark's.'

Lorraine gasped and her hands flew up to her mouth. 'Is she all right?'

'We don't have many details,' Mary said slowly. 'But we know she'd had an…accident.'

'Dan…my husband… Chief Dunham wanted to let you know he'll be here soon. He'll tell you…' Ellen broke off and looked at Mary a little uncertainly.

Clearly Ellen wasn't any better at lying, or in this case, avoiding the truth than she was. Mary tried to add something, but Richard interrupted her.

'You're Mrs McGill, the one my sister has been trying to find?'

Mary nodded and started again to say something, but Richard wasn't finished. He transferred his gaze to Ellen. 'You're the wife of the police chief ? The real-estate woman?'

Ellen nodded.

Richard went on: 'Would you mind telling me what you two were doing at Saint Mark's at this hour of the morning? How did you know she…our aunt…was there?'

A fair question. 'I didn't. I found her when I went to open the church hall for the rummage sale. I got there early. When I realized… I called nine-one-one. The paramedics were still there when Ellen and I came over here. We didn't want you to wake up and find her missing. Unfortunately we were a little late.'

Cassandra pulled out a chair and sank down onto it. She waved at the other chairs, an unspoken invitation for Mary and Ellen to do the same. Mary did, leaving enough room for Millie to sit beside her.

Richard frowned. 'Rummage sale. You start early. It's barely light. Where did you find her?'

'Inside the building.' Ellen walked over to the counter

where the coffeemaker sat and Lorraine stood, sniffling. She took Lorraine by the shoulders, turned her toward the table and gave her a small push. 'Go sit down.'

Lorraine slid into the chair farthest from Richard.

Cassandra folded her hands together so tightly her knuckles turned white and laid them on the table. 'How did she get into the building? Wasn't it locked?'

That was a question Mary could safely answer. 'Yes. I locked it myself. Who unlocked it, I don't know.'

'How did she make it all the way to the church by herself in the dark?'

Lorraine's timid question was one Mary had been wondering about, but she had no answer. She shook her head. 'I have no idea.' She leaned across the table, pulled a napkin out of the plastic holder and handed it to Lorraine. 'Who found she was missing? Did you?'

Lorraine had started to dab her wet eyes but abruptly stopped. 'No.'

'I did.' Cassandra looked up from examining her hands, worry lines outlining her mouth and eyes. 'I needed to use the bathroom and thought I'd look in on her on my way back to bed. I'm sleeping in what used to be Aunt Eloise's room when they were growing up. There's a connecting door between them. Aunt Emilie was gone and half her covers were on the floor.'

Ellen sucked in her breath. 'What did you do then?'

Cassandra twisted a little to look at her. 'I started to look for her. When I couldn't find her, I woke up Richard, then Caleb and Lorraine. We looked all over the house and grounds. Richard was on the phone to the police when you arrived.'

'They were singularly unhelpful.' Richard didn't seem too impressed with the Santa Louisa police department.

Mary wondered who he'd spoken to, but it didn't really matter, especially as he had turned his attention to Ellen.

'When did you say your husband would be here to give us a report?'

'As soon as he can get away.' Ellen's expression was neutral and so was her voice, but Mary had seen that look before. She was not impressed with Richard Plym.

'Hmmm. We have no choice but to wait for any factual information.' He pushed back his chair and got to his feet. 'We won't keep you any longer. I'm sure you both have things to do. Thank you for coming by…'

Richard didn't get a chance to finish. The sound of the front door opening and closing and fast footsteps coming down the hall caused every head to turn toward the front hallway.

'Who on earth…' Cassandra barely got the words out when Gloria Sutherland, a small woman, appeared, every short dark hair in place, makeup perfectly applied, gray knit pants without a wrinkle, lavender sweater sitting neatly around her hips.

'I came as soon as I heard,' she panted.

'Heard what?' Richard's voice was as cold as ice cubes. 'Who are you and why are you coming in my front door, uninvited?'

'Gloria Sutherland.' Ice cubes didn't clink in Cassandra's voice, but frost was evident as she spoke her name. 'She's the home health nurse who took care of Aunt Eloise before she died.'

'I've been helping Lorraine with Miss Emilie, and when I heard the news I thought I'd better get right over here.'

She didn't look like someone who had rushed out of the house when she'd heard bad news to Mary. She looked like someone who had spent some time on herself. But then, Gloria wouldn't be caught dead in a hurricane without a full face of makeup. 'What did you hear?'

'Why, that Miss Emilie was in Saint Mark's church hall early this morning.'

Richard addressed Gloria in a voice that had not warmed one bit. 'You rushed over here to make sure we'd heard the sad news or did you have another reason?'

Richard's nostrils flared and his eyes narrowed. Gloria took a step back, but only one. Her frown as she stared at him was impressive. The clash of the Titans was about to begin, but not if Mary could help it.

'Gloria, where did you hear Miss Emilie was in Saint Mark's?'

Gloria turned toward her, seemingly forgetting Richard for a moment. Something flickered across her face that Mary couldn't read, but her answer came readily enough. 'Someone who was at the church hall called me.'

'Who?'

Gloria never had a chance to answer. The kitchen door flew open and a tall, thin man stumbled through, his gray hair flying, his long thin nose practically twitching, his eyes wild. Caleb paused, hanging onto the door while he got his breath then blurted out, 'It's on the radio. Miss Emilie—she's dead. She's been murdered.'

No one seemed to be able to say a word but there wasn't one of them that didn't stare at the man in horror and disbelief. The silence was broken by Lorraine, who broke out into wild sobs, followed by Cassandra who kept saying, 'No, it can't be, no,' over and over.

Ellen leaned over and said softly in Mary's ear, 'I don't know about you, but next time Dan wants someone to be a buffer, I'm leaving town.'

FIVE

SILENCE FINALLY DESCENDED on the kitchen. Everyone, even Richard, looked at Mary and Ellen as if waiting for them to make sense of an increasingly terrible morning.

Mary looked at Ellen and rolled her eyes slightly. She had no idea what to say. This was not the way Dan had wanted things to go. It wasn't how she'd wanted them to, either. Leaving town sounded very attractive.

Finally Cassandra spoke. 'Did you already know…you came to tell us, didn't you? What happened?'

'Other than she didn't die of natural causes, we don't know much.' Mary looked around the room at the shocked faces and decided someone had to take charge. No one else seemed able, so it looked as if it was up to her. 'If you'll all sit back down, Ellen and I will tell you what we do know.' She paused and glanced over at Ellen, who nodded. 'Chief Dunham will be able to answer more of your questions when he gets here.'

'Who would want to kill Miss Emilie? She was frustrating, but that's hardly…' Gloria seemed uncharacteristically at a loss for words, but not for long. 'How did she get out of the house? I thought Caleb set up an alarm of some sort.'

'I did. It's a motion detector.' Caleb stared at Richard. 'He told me not to set it last night. He said he and his sister were right there, right next to her, so they'd know if she got up. Didn't quite work out that way, did it?'

The flush returned to Richard's face. It ran up the sides, onto his cheeks, turning his ears a vivid shade of red. His words came out razor sharp. 'That "motion detector" alerts you through a monitor set up in your apartment. It may be a good thing when no one else is here but we don't need you to monitor our movements. It was hardly unreasonable to think we'd wake up if we saw her light or if she left her bedroom. I certainly didn't think she'd slink down the stairs in the dark.'

'Miss Emilie didn't slink. She got…confused. She wanted her breakfast at midnight, decided to go for a walk and forgot to come back. If she woke up and worried about that blasted dog, it would be just like her to decide to go look for him again.' Lorraine reached into the pocket of her robe then pulled the remnants of a tissue from where she'd tucked it up her sleeve and tried to blot the tears that rolled down her cheeks.

Mary reached over the table, pulled another napkin out of the plastic holder and handed it to her. 'I'm not sure I understand. You…' she nodded at Cassandra, '…and Richard are sleeping upstairs?'

Cassandra had turned as white as Richard was red, but she managed to answer. 'Yes. As I said, I'm in what used to be Aunt Eloise's room. There's a connecting door between it and Aunt Emilie's. Richard is in his father's old room. Aunt Eloise took over my grandparents' room when they died. It's the largest room, but neither of us wanted to… It hasn't been cleaned out since she died, and I've been doing that the last few days. It's in a mess so no one—'

Her brother interrupted abruptly, 'Mrs McGill isn't interested in any of that.' What he probably meant was it was none of her business.

Maybe it wasn't, but Mary was quite interested. She asked Cassandra, 'Did you leave the door open between the rooms?'

Cassandra nodded. She reached for a napkin and blotted her eyes as well. 'Just a crack. I was sure I'd see if she turned on a light. The bathroom's down the hall, so I thought I'd know if she got up.'

Mary nodded. That made sense. 'But you didn't see a light?'

'I never woke up all night. I didn't hear her, and as far as I know she never turned one on. First I knew anything was wrong was when I peeked into Aunt Emilie's room. She wasn't there.' The last came out with a little sob. She pulled out a chair across from Gloria, who hadn't waited for an invitation to seat herself, and sank down on it. Lorraine immediately got up, went to the counter and poured a mug full of coffee. She added milk from a white pitcher and ladled in two heaping teaspoons of sugar, stirred and returned to the table, setting the mug in front of Cassandra, who smiled weakly.

'Good idea,' Mary said in a deliberately brisk voice. The one that had got everyone's attention when she'd taught home economics in middle school. She pushed her chair back, startling Millie in the process. 'Let's all have a little coffee. It will settle our nerves. Shall I get it, Lorraine?'

Without waiting for an answer, she headed for the counter. 'Are the cups in here?' She opened one of the cupboard doors but it held only plates and bowls and an old teddy bear cookie jar.

'Lorraine will take care of the coffee. Please come back and sit down, Mrs McGill. Tell us what happened to Aunt Emilie.' Richard gestured at the table.

Mary turned, barely avoiding Lorraine, who seemed intent on obeying Richard's instruction. Caleb, Lorraine's husband, stared at her back then walked over and took the chair at the other end of the table, opposite Richard. They glared at each other.

Caleb addressed Lorraine without taking his eyes off Richard. 'You know how I like my coffee.'

Richard said nothing. He continued to stare at Caleb.

Mary said, 'I like mine black and so does Ellen. Thank you, Lorraine.'

Richard blinked, apparently surprised she'd thanked Lorraine. Mary walked back to the table and pulled out a chair next to Cassandra and across from Gloria, leaving only one empty one. Millie, who was right beside her, gave it a thoughtful look but changed her mind when Mary tugged a little on her leash. She crawled under Mary's chair instead and settled down, her head on Mary's foot. Ellen raised both eyebrows at Mary and walked over to where Lorraine stood in front of the coffeemaker, seemingly unable to decide what to do next.

'Go sit. I'll handle the coffee.'

Lorraine did, dropping heavily into the only empty chair. Mary waited a moment, looking around the table. Gloria stared at her intently and Lorraine stared at the table, not looking up even when Ellen slid a mug of coffee in front of her. She put full mugs in front of Caleb, Mary and Richard and dropped a handful of spoons on the table.

'I'll stand,' she said.

Neither of the men made a move to get her a chair. It was as if neither of them heard her. They were too busy glaring at each other.

'So, what happened?' Richard snapped the words out as if asking for a report from a particularly inept aide.

What a joy this man must be to work for. Mary decided it was time—past time—to say what she knew. Her own questions could come later. 'I found her. Or, rather, Millie found her when I opened the hall this morning.'

Lorraine gasped and the tears started to flow once more. This time Ellen reached over her, pulled out a napkin and handed it to her.

Gloria looked up from staring at her hands folded around her mug with what Mary thought was a speculative expression. 'Of course,' she murmured. 'You'd be the first one there. You always are, aren't you?'

Mary wasn't quite sure how to take that, but like many of Gloria's comments it seemed best to ignore it. 'Millie headed right for the dressing-room area the minute we walked in. I followed her, and that's when I found her.' She paused, wondering how much she should tell them. They'd found out she was dead through no fault of Mary or Ellen's so she might as well tell them a little more. Dan could tell them how she died. She didn't think she could manage that in any case. 'She was sitting on a chair in the dressing area, in her bathrobe and slippers. There was no doubt she was dead.'

'What did you do then?' It wasn't just Cassandra's voice that shook. Her hand no longer seemed steady enough to safely hold her coffee mug. She set it unsteadily on the table and looked into it instead of meeting Mary's gaze.

'I called Hazel.'

'Who?' Richard's head jerked up and outrage sounded in his voice. 'You called a friend? I thought you said…'

'Hazel is nine-one-one. She's our emergency dispatch

officer.' Ellen's voice was mild but Mary knew that look. Richard Plym had not made a good first impression.

'Hmmm.' Richard took a sip of his coffee but it didn't warm his voice. His boardroom inquisition tone permeated the next question as well. 'And then what?'

Mary decided he wasn't making a good impression on her, either. 'Millie and I waited in the kitchen area for Dan and his troops to arrive.'

'I don't understand.'

Mary thought that was the first time she'd heard Gloria say she didn't understand something, but she simply said, 'What don't you understand?'

'How did she get in? Wasn't the door locked?'

'I don't know how she got in. I was the last one out last night and I locked the door behind me and left the outside light burning. I knew it would be dark when I got there this morning. But when I arrived, the light was off and the door unlocked. Actually, it wasn't even completely closed. Millie knew something was wrong right away. She led me right to poor little Miss Emilie.'

'How did she die?' Cassandra's voice was low, and this time she looked directly at Mary, her eyes misted. 'How do they know it was murder?'

Mary sighed. This was going to be the hardest part. Why, oh, why did they have to put that on the radio? She'd asked them not to. 'You'll have to ask Dan.'

A sob broke the silence—Mary thought it came from Lorraine. Then everyone started to talk at once.

'Oh, no,' moaned Cassandra with a quick glance at her brother. 'Why would anyone…'

Richard responded with, 'What the hell was she doing there at that time of night, anyway?'

Gloria replied with certainty, 'Looking for something.'

Caleb burst out, not bothering to soften his scathing tone, 'What would a feeble old lady who wasn't in her right mind be doing looking for something in a locked church hall in the middle of the night?'

Mary thought she couldn't have put it better herself. 'I don't know,' she told Caleb, but it was really addressed to all of them. 'I don't know how she got in or what she was doing there. Obviously someone was with her, but I have no idea who.' She broke off and turned toward Lorraine. 'You were with her yesterday, and Joy Mitchell said she was looking for something. What?'

Cassandra's eyes were dry but starting to mist. 'That was my fault. I've been cleaning out Aunt Eloise's room and made up several boxes to donate. Her bedspread, lots of her clothes, books, things like that. Somehow Aunt Emilie's stuffed dog got into one of the boxes. When she was having hysterics that she couldn't find it I remembered seeing it in Aunt Eloise's room and realized it must have gotten into one of the boxes. They went down to the church hall to look for it but, evidently, it wasn't there. I have no idea where it got to.'

Mary did, but she didn't think this was the time to relay that information. 'There was also a white clock—one that belonged to her mother. Did you mean to donate that?'

Cassandra responded somewhat faintly, 'I thought it was just some cheap little thing…pretty but that was all. I had no idea it was an heirloom and she'd feel that way about all that…'

Mary was almost positive the word she left out was 'trash.'

Lorraine seemed to shrink down in her chair, her arms crossed in front of herself as if something would come flying off if she let go. 'She saw it and picked it up. She kept asking me why it was there, saying we weren't in her room, were we? The clock belonged in her room. Then she got distracted and started talking about Willis again. She was working herself up to a complete meltdown.'

'Did she bring the clock home?'

Tears started down Lorraine's cheeks again. 'No. I wouldn't let her. I wish I had, but right then all I could think about was getting her home.'

Mary thought for a minute. 'Are you sure she didn't stick it in that big purse of hers?'

'Quite sure. She wasn't carrying the purse.'

Mary didn't think she'd ever seen Miss Emilie without her purse, an ugly big black thing with a huge old-fashioned clasp. If she didn't take the clock, who did? 'What happened when you got her home?'

'We finally got her to eat something, but she was so upset I gave her some of that sedative the doctor prescribed and she calmed down. I left the bottle here in the kitchen in case she got herself all worked up again in the night. See?' She pointed to the kitchen window. A prescription bottle sat in the middle of the sill. 'It calms her and helps her sleep, as well. Doctor Peterson prescribed it because she'd get so worked up when she couldn't remember something or lost something.'

Mary glanced up at Ellen, who was leaning against a counter, one hip cocked, sipping her coffee. She had a good view of almost everyone's face, Mary realized—everyone except Gloria's. All she would be able to see of her was the back of her head. But she could see the tightness in her shoulders, the way her hands clutched her coffee mug. Ellen straightened up as if she was about to say something but was interrupted by the doorbell.

The chimes sounded in the kitchen then sounded again. Someone wanted to make their presence known.

'Now who? Unless that's the police, please tell whoever that is that we can't be disturbed right now.' Richard gestured at Lorraine with a motion that couldn't be misinterpreted.

Caleb scowled, but Lorraine pushed back her chair and started out of the room. Millie raised her head off Mary's foot and began making little whiney noises. Mary wondered why but not for long. She forgot about Millie as Glen Manning, a tall, blond man dressed in a beautifully cut navy blue suit, a shirt so white it hurt your eyes and a discreetly striped blue and green tie walked into the room carrying a bulging briefcase and wearing a worried expression.

He pushed his glasses firmly back up on his patrician nose as he surveyed the room. He smiled at Mary and Ellen, let his eyes roll over Gloria and addressed Cassandra. 'Good morning, Mrs Brown. I'm so sorry we have to meet again under such tragic circumstances. Mr Plym, I know we had an appointment for later today, but when I heard the news I thought I should come over right away.'

'Why?'

Richard wouldn't get any prizes for good manners, but then, today was proving difficult. However, if he thought he could intimidate Glen, whom she knew well, he'd met his match.

'Because Miss Plym's death changes things and we need to talk. However, if you wish to wait… I believe the police should be here soon. We can talk after they leave, but you're going to have to tell them about the money, and I thought we should discuss that…' It was quite clear Glen was anxious to talk to them.

Cassandra stepped in. ‘I told you last night, Richard.’ Mary could have sworn she spoke through gritted teeth. ‘Things have changed and we need to… I assume Mr Manning is correct—the police will be here soon?’ She looked at Ellen, who nodded. ‘I think we should hear what Mr Manning has to say before they get here.’

Richard’s ears had turned red again; Mary was pretty sure with anger or perhaps frustration.

He nodded. ‘All right.’ He looked around at the rest of them and his scowl deepened. ‘We can go in my grandfather’s office, if you like. My sister and me and Mr Manning.’

Mary watched the effect this cryptic statement had on everyone in the room. Gloria’s head had snapped up at the mention of money. The sullen look she’d had since she arrived disappeared and a look of intense interest took its place. But Mary thought there was a trace of something else…what, she couldn’t tell, and she didn’t have time to explore her thought.

Lorraine burst into tears. ‘The police, oh, of course they have to come. My poor dear Miss Emilie. Will they have to search her room?’

‘I can’t imagine why.’ Richard’s voice was tight with anger. ‘She wasn’t killed here.’

Caleb didn’t look any less distressed but his reaction was anger and it was all aimed at Lorraine. ‘Don’t be a fool. What would they look for in her room? There’s nothing to find up there. Lorraine and I are going home.’

There was a heavy emphasis on ‘home.’ He grabbed Lorraine by the arm, almost tearing her out of her chair. There was no sound in the room except Lorraine’s sniffling as they left and the door closing with a bang behind them.

'I think we should leave as well.' Mary stood but Millie was ahead of her.

She'd been straining at the leash since she'd heard Glen Manning's voice and was determined to greet him. The strained atmosphere in the kitchen didn't seem to affect her as Millie stared at Glen, her stub of a tail wagging.

Mary let go of the leash and the little dog trotted up to him, jumping up against the side of his leg, waiting to have her ears rubbed.

He obliged. 'Hey, Millie. You're looking good but a little shaggy.' He quit stroking her and looked at Mary. 'Tell your mom you need grooming.'

'I know she does. I've been meaning to call you. Where should I take her?'

Glen Manning would know. He and his partner, John Lagomasino, had cockers of their own. They also owned the only pet store in Santa Louisa. They'd inherited it from Evan Wilson, who'd been cruelly murdered last Christmas. They'd also inherited Millie, Evan's dog. However, Mary and Millie had formed a bond while Mary helped find Evan's killer, and they'd had no wish to break it. Mary and Millie had stayed together. John, one of the county's most skilled surgical nurses, had insisted they keep the shop along with their regular jobs and Glen had agreed. The combination of John's enthusiasm and Glen's acute business skills seemed to be working. The shop was thriving. However, Glen's next announcement surprised her.

'John and I talked Krissie McDaniels, who's the best groomer in the county, into coming to Furry Friends. We've opened a new pet grooming area just for her. Of course, it was John's idea and I think it was a good one.'

He smiled, gently pushed Millie off his leg and looked at Gloria, who hadn't moved.

Ellen picked up her coffee mug and Mary's, walked over to the sink and set them down. 'If we can do anything, Cassandra, please let us know. I think you have both our numbers.'

Cassandra nodded. 'Thank you. I'll be in touch.'

But Cassandra didn't really seem to be paying any attention to them. Her attention was on Glen Manning, her need to hear what he had to say obvious.

Mary picked up her purse and Millie's leash and started to follow Ellen toward the door, then stopped. 'Glen, how did you hear about Miss Emilie? On the radio?'

'Not exactly. John had it on and when he heard there was an accident at the church he was afraid it was you. He knew you were going in early. So he called Hazel and made her put him through to Dan. When I realized who… anyway, that's why I'm here.' He smiled and started to turn back toward Cassandra, but stopped.

'Mary, before you leave—we're still on for tomorrow? Krissie will be in around noon, but we'll need you to open at ten. Did John go through everything with you? How to do the cash register and all that? The man from the zoo that's taking the Komodo dragon will be in to get him at about eleven. Be sure you don't go near that thing, and don't let Millie, either. I'll be glad to be rid of him. He may be a baby but he scares me to death.'

Ellen whirled around to stare at Glen Manning and then at her aunt. 'You're going to run the pet shop in the morning?'

Mary nodded. 'Only for a few hours. The hospital needed another surgery nurse and called John in. Glen has a meeting and can't be in the shop. John said they had someone coming in around one but I didn't realize it was a new groomer. Anyway, Millie and I said we'd do it. Should be fun. I've never run a pet store before.' She smiled.

Ellen sighed, shook her head and once more turned to leave.

Gloria sat where she was, not moving.

Ellen looked at Gloria and then at Mary, who shrugged. They both looked at Glen Manning. Before he could say anything, Richard took charge.

'Miss Sutherland…'

'Mrs.'

'What? Oh, yes. Mrs Sutherland, it was kind of you to come, but as you can see, right now we have things we need to take care of.' There was no mistaking the dismissal in his voice, at least Mary didn't think so. Evidently Gloria didn't hear it.

'I'm here to help. I took care of Miss Eloise all those weeks after her first stroke. I helped with Miss Emilie. I feel like family.' Gloria's eyes narrowed, her mouth closed tightly, her chin jutted out slightly. Mary had seen that look on Gloria's face before. At thirteen, Gloria had been in Mary's home economics class and had seen no reason to learn to make tuna casserole. They'd had quite a tussle. Mary had won. She wondered who'd win this one, but as stubborn as Gloria could be, and as much as she could wear down her opponent, this time Mary's money was on Richard. She was right.

'I appreciate your interest, Mrs Sutherland, but you are not family. Should we require your help sometime in the future, we will call on you. Good morning.'

Richard's polite rudeness had the desired effect. They

were all three out on the street, headed for their cars, almost before Mary realized what had happened.

Gloria looked a little dazed and very angry as she stood by her car, looking back toward the house. 'That is the rudest man I've ever met.' She seemed to be talking as much to herself as to Mary and Ellen. 'I gave that old woman the best care possible and gave the other one a lot of my time as well. For free.' Her face tightened and so did her fists. 'He'll be sorry.' With that she climbed into her car and drove off.

Ellen couldn't hold back her laughter as they watched her. 'Old Gloria's not used to being so neatly dispatched.' But her smile faded. 'However, I'm not so sure I want to list that house. It's not going to be an easy sale and Richard's going to rank right up there with the best sellers from hell.' She ground her teeth. 'Where do you want to go? Home?'

Mary came back with a start. She'd been watching Gloria's car turn the corner and been remembering how she'd reacted to snubs when she was in school. Richard just might want to watch his back. What Gloria thought she deserved from the Plyms, Mary couldn't imagine. She'd been paid for her care of Miss Eloise and had volunteered care of Miss Emilie over Lorraine's objections, but it was obvious Gloria thought she was owed something. Luckily, it was none of her business. She opened the back door, motioned for Millie to jump in, closed it and climbed in the front. 'No. Back to the church. I need to see what, if anything, needs to be done.'

'Are you really going to work the pet shop tomorrow morning? Don't you usually go back to the hall to do any final cleanup?'

Mary nodded. 'I had a whole crew staying to clean

up tonight. Ysabel has something scheduled tomorrow morning, so I thought I'd be free. It will be interesting, and John and Glen are paying me in dog food.'

Ellen started the car and slowly pulled out of the Plym driveway. 'You don't need to work for Millie's dog food.'

'I know that. But they needed someone and they trust me, and I can take Millie. After all, she used to go there every day when Evan was alive and owned it. It'll be fine.' Mary fastened her seat belt.

'Do you ever say "no"?'

'Of course,' Mary replied with dignity.

'When?'

Mary thought but couldn't come up with anything, at least not right then. Maybe she should say no to some of the things she was asked to do. Right now, she was feeling pretty wrung out. It had been a terrible morning and she didn't think the day would get much better. She thought about the conversation going on in the Plyms' study right now and wished she'd been able to sit in on it. There was something very odd about all this. Missing toy dogs, missing clocks, rude nephews and a murder. She wondered if Richard Plym was there because he thought he was going to get control of Miss Emilie's money. Could he? Even if he did, it didn't make him a murderer.

'I wouldn't have minded saying "no" to doing this. It wasn't fun.'

'No,' Ellen said as she turned into Main Street. 'It wasn't. I don't remember ever being in a room where there was more tension.' She turned into St Mark's parking lot and stopped. 'What was Glen talking about? What money?'

Mary had been wondering about that very thing. 'I don't know. Something about the trust?'

'I've heard...don't get yourself in a snit. I know you hate gossip but this comes from a friend whose mother had her money invested with Ed Kavanagh. She's almost broke because he did such a bad job these last few years. My friend told me Glen is trying to reorganize all their remaining investments and is doing a great job. Ed Kavanagh managed the Plym trust. I can't help wondering if it's in trouble too.'

Mary drew in a quick breath. Could that be true? Poor Miss Emilie. No. She would no longer be affected by it. Could that have something to do with her murder? She didn't understand how. Right now, she didn't understand anything. 'Dan will figure it out. Thanks for the ride.'

Ellen leaned over and gave her aunt a quick kiss on the cheek. 'I'm off to the office. I'll talk to you later this afternoon. Don't do too much and wear yourself out.'

As if she would. Ellen drove off, then Mary and Millie walked toward the church to see what needed to be done.

SIX

'WHERE HAVE YOU BEEN? We've been looking all over for you.' Les McIntyre, the pastor of Saint Mark's, looked more than a little frazzled as he grabbed Mary by the arm. 'We're having an emergency meeting to reschedule the rummage sale. We have to get it in before the Easter week services start. I think I can work around the girl scouts and the clog dancing class, but not any of the Holy Week events. Hurry. Everyone's waiting.' He practically pulled Mary toward the Sunday school building, the door of which stood wide open.

'I've been at the Plym house,' Mary managed to get out. 'Dan wanted me and Ellen, of course, to try to go to the Plyms' to be there before they discovered Miss Emilie was missing. Unfortunately they'd already realized it.' She couldn't get much more out as she grabbed onto Les' arm to keep from falling over Millie's leash.

Luckily he stopped and groaned. 'Oh, I should have gone with you. How could I have been so thoughtless? Of course, they would all have been distraught. I don't know Richard's children, but Lorraine and Caleb, oh, dear. Are they all right?'

The look of distress on Les' face appeared greater than on any of the faces at the Plym house. Except maybe Lorraine's.

'Horrified, but I think all right. Ellen and I left because Glen Manning arrived with a briefcase full of papers. Glen looked pretty upset.'

'I'm sure he was. He hasn't been handling the Plym sisters' trust fund very long, but I know he'd gotten pretty fond of them both. Especially Miss Emilie.' Les smiled. 'She was hard not to like.'

Mary pictured Miss Emilie: small, gray hair never combed quite neatly, sweater or dress never buttoned up correctly, but with a sweet, if somewhat vague, smile for everybody. She was impossible not to like. 'Yes, she was.' She had Millie's leash in one hand, her tote bag in her other and decided walking was once more safe. 'Who is at this meeting?'

'Ysabel, of course, Pat Bennington, Joy Mitchell and I think Leigh Cameron. She said she had to pick up her daughter at ballet class, but it seems early for that.'

Since this was a school day and not even halfway through the morning, Mary thought the ballet class improbable. Leigh often invented things to do when she didn't want to stay for a meeting or show up for a job she'd agreed to do. Mary couldn't help thinking they wouldn't miss Leigh if she skipped. Mary had thought, on more than one occasion, Leigh liked the *idea* of volunteering more than the actual jobs. 'Did I mention Gloria Sutherland arrived at the Plyms' unannounced and uninvited, not long after Ellen and I got there?'

Les had taken Mary's tote bag and started for the Sunday school building, but he abruptly stopped. So did Mary.

'Why? Why was she there at that hour of the morning? Why was she there at all?'

Mary didn't have an adequate answer. 'She said she heard about Miss Emilie on the radio and wanted to be there for them. She said she felt they were like family after taking care of Miss Eloise before she died.'

'Humph. She took care of her with Lorraine for what… a few weeks? Maybe more—a couple of months? That hardly makes her family. It was probably more she wanted to find out what was happening so she could somehow turn it to her own advantage.' Les' hand flew up to his mouth and he got a little flushed around the ears. 'Oh, dear. That wasn't a very kind thing to say.'

'It seems a true one. Come on. Let's get this rummage sale reorganized, and I want to know what's going on with the dog adoption.' She started toward the building but stopped again. 'Les, did Dan ask you who had keys to the community room?'

Les nodded.

'What did you tell him?'

'That you did.'

'I don't think I'm on his suspect list. Who else?'

Les sighed. 'Mary, I really don't know. There have been so many people using that room over the last few years, I've handed out a number of keys. I haven't gotten them all back. I try to unlock and lock up myself, but I'm not always available to do that, so I give out a key. I probably should have had the locks changed before now, but we've never had a problem…'

Les looked as miserable as Mary thought it possible for someone to look.

'Never mind. Let's go have our meeting.' Too bad. They'd just have to come at the problem of who had been with Miss Emilie and how they'd gotten in another way. What that way was, she had no idea.

It sounded as if everyone was talking at once, and no

one was listening. They all stopped as Mary walked in the room, closely followed by Les.

'It's about darn time,' Pat said, smiling.

Mary thought it looked more like relief than welcome.

'Where have you been?' Joy, of course, sounded aggrieved, but there was a little relief in her voice as well.

'At the Plyms. Ellen, Millie and I went over so they wouldn't wake up and find Miss Emilie missing. It didn't work out too well. They'd already discovered she was gone.'

Millie tugged a little on her leash. Mary let go and she trotted to Pat and sat on her foot.

Pat scratched her ears but looked at Mary. 'Oh, dear. That doesn't sound like fun. Was Lorraine in a complete panic?'

'More like a teary meltdown. And, no, it wasn't fun.'

Les set Mary's tote bag down beside the chair she had pulled out and took a seat next to her. 'All right, everyone. What are we going to do?'

'We're going to have to cancel the whole thing.' Joy glanced down at her watch. She was the only person Mary knew who still wore one. Everyone else consulted their cell phones. 'It's going to be too hard to reschedule all this. Newspapers, radio—they'll never get it all announced in time and no one will come.'

'Why wouldn't anyone come?' Mary ignored the impossibility of getting press coverage. That there would be a new date announced soon was already all over the local airways, and this rummage sale was eagerly awaited by half the town. Of course people would come.

'After what happened? Would you come to someplace where a crazed killer had strangled some little old lady?' Leigh asked.

Mary was surprised Leigh had actually stayed for the meeting, but she wasn't at her reaction. After all, this was Leigh, whose glass wasn't half-empty, it was completely dry. Joy also expected disaster but, if one occurred, was prepared to meet it head on. In the meantime, she briskly handled every task anyone asked of her, managing her family with a fist of iron and turned out food second only to Mary's. Miss Plym's murder was a tragedy, but she wouldn't make it into a disaster that meant calling off something as important as the rummage sale fund-raiser. She'd worked too hard on helping put it together. It would go on as close to schedule as possible, a sentiment Mary totally supported.

'Leigh, no one thinks there's a crazed killer running around town, and no one will think they're in any danger by coming to a rummage sale.' Mary tried to keep her voice neutral but she was getting tired. She was feeling rattled by all that had happened and there was still a lot to do. 'Dan says his people will be ready to release the building in a couple of days, so we can try again for next week. We have to have the building cleared out by… when?' She looked down the table at Les, who looked at his wife.

Ysabel opened the large engagement book in front of her. 'Easter is two weeks from this Sunday. We're booked starting…' She ran her finger down the page, nodded and looked again. 'It's either next Thursday or not again until May.'

'Then that's settled.' Mary gave Leigh the look, the one that dared anyone in her home economics class to contradict her.

Leigh settled back a little in her chair and said nothing.

'Now, Pat. What about the dogs and cats? Today wasn't

a huge success. Can we get them all back here for next Thursday?'

Pat Bennington shook her head, making her ponytail sway. 'Today was a disaster. The only people who came wanted to watch the police work. No one even looked at the animals. As for Thursday, I don't think so. The rummage sale people all live here, and they're organized. Getting the dogs and cats who were brought any distance back here would take a little doing.' She stopped as if she'd just had an idea. 'However, Furry Friends is having a special sale this Saturday—that's only the day after tomorrow. I'll bet I could get some of the out-of-town rescue people to leave their animals here if we promise to provide shelter for them. We can take a few at the vet clinic and I'll call Amber at the shelter and see if they can take some. We won't get them all, but I know John and Glen will let us do an adoption at their store. We can use the parking lot in the back for the dogs; the cats can come inside. The Komodo dragon will be gone tomorrow, so we won't have to worry about him.'

'The dragon.' The thought of it made her feel lightheaded. 'I'd forgotten about it.'

'He's leaving for a zoo tomorrow. John told me.' Pat started to laugh. 'It's tomorrow you'll be at the store, right? Well, you won't have to touch it or go near it. The guy from the zoo will take care of everything and we'll all be glad when that disagreeable thing is gone.'

'Yes. John told me not to go near him. Or is it a her? Anyway, I don't like it one bit, and I don't want Millie anywhere near it. When we were in the store while I learned about the cash register, she went up to that big glass thing it's in and it hissed at her.' Mary dropped her hand onto Millie's head, which was, as usual, right beside her knee. 'Anyway, why don't you call John right now? If he and Glen agree I'll call the radio station and Ben over at the paper and we'll start getting the word out.'

'Call Luke,' Joy said.

Mary looked over at Joy, surprised she hadn't thought of that. 'Great idea. I'll get him to put up a sign in the library and he can call his dog club and tell them we need to get people out for this.'

'Who's Luke?' Leigh looked up from doodling on her notepad.

'Luke from the library, of course. He's the head librarian.' Disgust dripped from Joy's voice. 'Don't you go to the library?'

'No.' At least this time Leigh's reply was short. 'He knows about dogs?'

Mary swallowed a sigh. 'Luke is president of the Pure Bred dog club of Santa Louisa. They put on the big dog show in the fairgrounds every year. They always help with adoptions, and he'll get people to spread the word.'

'Not all of them help.' Pat's eyebrows almost touched each other, her frown was so deep. 'There's still a contingent that wants nothing to do with any dog that's not a purebred of some kind.'

That was true but Mary was in no mood to worry about it. 'We'll get enough to help. Go call John.'

SEVEN

MARY LOOKED AT the three steps leading to the porch outside her kitchen door. Would she make it? She couldn't remember when she'd felt so tired. Millie, of course, was already on the porch, scratching at the door. It was dinnertime and her dish was inside.

'Let me take all that stuff,' Dan Dunham said as he got out of the car.

The 'stuff' was the once more heavy tote bag Mary carried, her purse, only a little less full, and Millie's dog bed.

'Give me your keys.'

She did.

Dan piled everything at the top of the stairs, unlocked the door and waited while Millie bolted inside then turned back to Mary. 'Do you need help?'

'You've brought me home. Walking seemed a good idea this morning but I'm not sure I'd have made it back carrying all this. I think I can climb these puny little steps just fine.' She grabbed hold of the railing and was almost immediately at the top.

Dan laughed. 'You'll be beating us off with a cane one of these days, still telling us you're fine and baking muffins. Let's go feed your dog.'

'I'll make coffee. Or would you rather have tea?'

Dan already had the broom closet open and the dog food scoop in his hand, Millie tight beside him. He poured a scoop into Millie's bowl before he straightened up. 'It's a warm afternoon and it's been a rotten day. I have to go back to work so I'll have a glass of water. But you look as if you'd benefit from a glass of wine. Is there a bottle open in the refrigerator?'

Mary smiled, set the tea kettle back on the stove and headed for the refrigerator. It wasn't long before they both sat at her kitchen table, Dan with a glass of ice water in front of him, Mary with a glass of her favorite Sauvignon Blanc. She slid off her shoes and sighed with relief. It was the only sound in the kitchen for a few minutes, except for Millie's enthusiastic crunching.

Finally Dan said, 'Tell me again everything that happened at the Plym house.'

'There isn't much to tell.' Mary took a sip of her wine, let it rest on her tongue for a moment, swallowed and set the glass back down. 'Richard Plym makes his father look like a kind, thoughtful human being. He wasn't. I never completely understood Samuel's friendship with him. Sam *was* a kind, thoughtful human being.'

'This Richard's certainly…terse.' A small smile appeared on Dan's face as he watched her.

'That's one word for him. I can think of another that wouldn't be accepted in polite society.'

This time Dan laughed. 'How about the rest of them? Why was Gloria there?'

Mary took another sip. 'I'm still not sure. She wasn't going to leave of her own freewill. Richard literally threw her out.'

'Why? Not Richard throwing her out—lots of people have wanted to do that, but few have succeeded. Why did she want to stay so badly? Any ideas?'

'Ideas? Impressions? Not facts? Because those I don't have.'

'Ideas.'

Mary let her fingers run up and down the stem of her glass while she thought how she wanted to put this. 'Gloria acted as if she had a right to be there. As if she really was part of the family. Until Glen came I thought it was just Gloria being her nosy, bossy self, but there was something more...she wanted to hear that conversation Richard, Cassandra and Glen were going to have, and it was clearly about money. Old Richard Plym set up a trust fund for the girls and the bank administered it. Everyone in town knows that. The house may be old but it's in good repair, and the land can still be split into a couple more lots, unless the planning commission changes the zoning to commercial. Either way, lots are scarce in downtown, so selling off a couple would bring in a considerable amount of money, and the trust fund seemed to support the twins in more than adequate comfort. I couldn't help wondering if they left a will and somehow Gloria thinks she might be mentioned in it.'

Dan didn't say anything for a moment. He set his water glass to the side and leaned his arms on the table, a troubled look on his face. 'How about Caleb and Lorraine?'

'What do you mean?'

'They've lived in that apartment for years. No rent to pay, no utilities. It was a good arrangement for all of them. The Plym twins got help, Caleb and Lorraine got free rent and Caleb could still hold down a regular job. I'm told Lorraine got a small salary as well. I'm sure they've made some plans for when this arrangement ended. But after Miss Eloise died, they stayed on and took care of Miss Emilie for a while longer. All this last year.

Now, suddenly, the Plyms show up, talking about possibly moving Miss Emilie to Shady Acres. No warning, nothing, just suddenly it's over. They weren't happy. At least, that's the word I got.'

'Killing Miss Emilie would hardly provide a reason for them to stay longer. Where did you get your information? Agnes?'

Dan smiled. 'Of course. How else would I know what's going on in this town? You, of course, but you don't gossip. Amazing how much information you pick up when someone does.'

'Most of it wrong.'

'That's why I'm asking you.' Dan picked up his water and took a sip, keeping a close eye on Mary as he drank.

Agnes worked at the police station as a clerk, but she thought of herself as 'law enforcement.' Which, in her eyes, meant she was free to gossip all she liked. Dan had threatened to fire her if she talked about anyone or anything she saw come through the station, but that didn't stop her from passing along other juicy tidbits about her neighbors to whomever would listen. Dan had listened to what she had to say about Lorraine and Caleb. Agnes was often wrong but, in this case, she might be right.

'I think they were planning on staying longer,' Mary said slowly. 'They'd never seen Richard, and Cassandra only for Eloise's funeral. I don't think they were prepared for them coming in and taking over. It was pretty sudden. I must admit, I wondered about it when Lorraine told me Cassandra was coming. She wanted to see how Miss Emilie was doing. I don't know why Richard came. Cassandra had talked to the people who run Shady Acres but I have no idea what she decided. I did hear she'd put the Duxworths on notice.' She took another sip. There was another little bit of information she'd heard—well, all right, gossip, but she didn't know how true it was. Dab Holt mentioned it. Dab and Lorraine worked together on the hospitality committee, so maybe she should say something. After all, this was murder.

'I heard…' That was as far as she got.

'You're going to tell me something you heard? Not something you know?' Dan looked surprised and definitely amused.

'This is something you can easily verify, and it may have some bearing on what's going on. Do you want to hear it or not?'

'Oh, yes. I want to hear it. What is it?'

'I heard that Glen Manning wasn't one bit happy about moving Miss Emilie to Shady Acres. Richard wants to sell the house, which makes sense if it's empty, but I don't think it can be sold as long as one of the sisters lives in it and Glen thought she should stay there. The trust can provide additional care if need be, but he said he'd hold up the sale of the house even if they moved her out.' She took another sip, watching Dan's face while he digested that bit of information. 'It just could be true. Cassandra had already started cleaning out things but mainly Miss Eloise's. Lorraine hadn't touched her room. That clock that's gone missing? Cassandra donated that but it hadn't been in Miss Eloise's room. It was in Miss Emilie's. She thought of it as hers.' She took another sip and went on in a more thoughtful voice: 'So, maybe she was getting ready to clean out Miss Emilie's room as well. I'd like to know why Cassandra was in such a hurry and if the trust had any say in this.'

Dan set down his empty water glass. The little smile

he'd had when Mary started was gone. 'I guess I need to pay Glen a visit at the bank.'

She nodded. 'I guess you do.'

'Do you really think they'll try to sell the house?'

'They've already talked to Ellen.'

'Do you know if Caleb and Lorraine think they're mentioned in the will? They've been working there a long time.'

'I have no idea. Lorraine never mentioned anything about that, but then she wouldn't. She never mentions anything too personal.'

'Hmmm. All right. Now, tell me your impressions of Cassandra Brown and her brother, Richard Plym.'

Mary didn't need to pause. Her opinion of them was already formed. 'Cassandra seems like a nice lady, but she appears to be a little overwhelmed by all that's gone on and what she's had to do, and a little sad. I think making arrangements for Miss Emilie to go to Shady Acres has been difficult for her, but she's had doubts about leaving a vague old woman all alone in that big house. Sure, the Duxworths take care of her, but I wonder if Cassandra thought that was enough. Gloria was underfoot a lot and I'm sure she would have loved turning taking care of Miss Emilie into a full-time job, with a good salary, of course, but I don't think Cassandra liked her very much. No, I really think Cassandra is—was—trying to do the right thing. What she told Richard and why he suddenly decided to come, I have no idea. Maybe she had no say in the matter. He may have simply thought he needed to come and take charge. Richard, he's...difficult.'

Dan burst out laughing. 'From what I've been told, that statement qualifies as the understatement of the year.'

Mary nodded with more enthusiasm than necessary. 'I

think Ellen agrees. They've asked her to handle the sale when they're ready to go forward but I'm not sure she wants to. She called him a seller from hell.'

A deep frown furrowed Dan's forehead. 'He's acting like he will be. I'm not sure I want her to take him on.'

'He won't be here when the house goes on the market. At least, I don't think so, and Cassandra's nice.' She paused and looked into her glass, the wine swaying as she twirled it a little. 'Richard is rude and doesn't seem to care, but I think there's more than that.'

'Meaning?'

'You wanted my impressions so I'll give them to you for what it's worth. I think he's worried about something. He seems on edge, frustrated and worried, as well as being bad-tempered.'

'You'd go out of your way to find good in the Devil.' Dan pushed back his chair, walked around and gave Mary a kiss on the cheek.

He squatted down and scratched Millie, who was stretched out beside Mary's chair, full of food and sound asleep. She raised one eyelid, realized who was scratching her, rolled over and put all four feet in the air, exposing her tummy. Dan laughed and obliged.

'Not a very ladylike position,' he said to Mary. With a final pat for Millie, he got up, reached for his jacket, which he'd draped over the chair, and started for the back door.

'Dan,' Mary called out. 'Wait.'

He turned.

'The clock. The little white clock. Did anyone find it?'

For a second, his face went blank. 'No. I told everyone to be on the lookout, but there hasn't been any sign of it. Why? Do you think it's important?'

'Miss Emilie did. She wanted to take it home when she saw it but Lorraine wouldn't let her. She made quite a scene. So much so Lorraine gave her some kind of sedative when they got home. The dog, and then the clock. They meant something to her. Something important.'

'Mary, I'll bet Miss Emilie dropped the clock in her purse on the way out.'

Mary looked at him with the 'you aren't paying attention' look she perfected while teaching middle-schoolers. 'According to Lorraine, Miss Emilie didn't have a purse when they were looking for the dog. Willis. What a ridiculous name. Anyway, there's no way she could have taken that clock without Lorraine knowing. But someone did, and I think we need to find out why.'

'It may not have anything to do with who killed Miss Emilie. It could be someone picked the clock up yesterday, decided they wanted it and put it aside.'

Mary didn't think he sounded convinced. She certainly wasn't, but she didn't say anything.

'Are you going to be all right?' Dan thrust one arm into his jacket, found the other one and shrugged it on.

'I'll be fine. I have Millie and I defrosted some chicken vegetable soup this morning. You go on and thank you for driving us home. Will I see you tomorrow?'

'More than likely.' He settled the jacket more securely on his shoulders. 'Next Thursday is set for the rummage sale? We should be done in plenty of time. There have been so many people in and out of that building over the last hundred years, any evidence we picked up is probably useless.' He went through the doorway, closing the door softly behind him.

Mary raised her eyebrows. A hundred years? The building had only been up ten, but the rest of Dan's gloomy statement was undoubtedly true. Finding Emilie's murderer was going to have to be done another way. She looked at her wine glass, still almost full, and pushed it away. She would drink it later but right now she needed something a little more stimulating. Coffee? No. Tea. A good, strong cup of tea. She pushed back her chair and, in her stocking feet, headed for the stove and the tea kettle.

Millie followed.

'One of these days I'm going to trip over you and then you'll be sorry you stick so close. So will I.'

The little dog looked up with sorrowful eyes.

Mary laughed. 'You know exactly what will happen when you do that, don't you.' She bent down to scratch the dog's ears.

Millie sighed in contentment.

The tea kettle whistled. Finally. Mary made her tea and took it into the living room. She settled down in her big reading chair with a sigh of relief.

'I've been thinking…'

Millie jumped up in the chair beside Mary and cocked her head to one side. Absently, Mary started to stroke her ears.

'Why do you suppose Richard Plym came out here?'

Millie looked thoughtful, or at least Mary thought she did.

'He didn't come for Miss Eloise's funeral. He didn't come to help Cassandra with all the details her death entailed. I doubt he came now because he wanted to meet his only living aunt. So, why did he fly out here now, leaving his family and his business?'

Millie whined.

'I don't know, either.' She paused to take a sip and to consider further. 'Why did Cassandra come back? Lorraine could have cleaned out Miss Eloise's room. I wonder why she hadn't already. It's been a year. There was no real need for Miss Emilie to go to Shady Acres. Caleb and Lorraine could have kept her at home, maybe gotten in a little more help. I wonder if Shady Acres was Cassandra's idea or Richard's. It all happened so suddenly. It seems…strange.'

Mary sipped little more and thought some more. Millie moved over and put her head on Mary's knee. Mary looked at the dog and smiled. 'Did anyone ever tell you how easy you are to talk to? No? Well, you are. So, what do you think of Gloria? She's acting a little pushy, even for her.'

Millie sat up, staring as if listening to every word.

'She couldn't possibly think she's named in the will. She's a home health nurse. They don't expect to be named in wills.' Mary sighed. 'Although, Gloria might. Time to get back to work. I've got some phone calls to make and I want to get to bed early. Before ten at the latest. We've got a big day tomorrow.' She reached for the phone she kept on the side table beside her chair. But before she could dial, it rang.

'Hello?'

'Mary? Is that you?'

Who was this? The voice was familiar, but she couldn't quite… 'Yes. This is Mary.'

'This is Joy. Oh, you're home. I was hoping you'd still be…busy with… I tried your cell but it went straight to voicemail. I think you've got it turned off… Oh, Mary. I've done something so stupid, and I need help.'

There was a pause. Mary sat up straight, waiting for what would come next. It wasn't like Joy to dither, so whatever it was she'd done, or not done, must be really serious. However, Mary was in no mood to guess. She was plain out of guesses, as well as energy, and she still needed to call Luke and make sure… 'What is it, Joy?'

'I've locked my purse in the church hall. I set it on the counter in the kitchen and when Leigh and I left I forgot it. She was driving, and it wasn't until I started out for the market… Oh, Mary. My car keys are in it, my wallet with all my cards, my cell phone, everything. Can you meet me there and let me in?'

'Joy, that's a crime scene. It's got yellow tape all around it. I can't do that. Call Dan. He'll send someone over.'

There was a long pause. 'I really don't want to do that. I'd be so mortified if I had to tell anyone I was that stupid. I'm sure he'd send someone and guess who that someone would be? I'd have Agnes making little remarks to me for months. Please, won't you do it?'

That plea had cost Joy something. The anguish in her voice told just how much. Mary thought about how she'd feel if Agnes had to let her in and how much she'd play up such a simple little thing. Anyone could forget her purse, especially on a morning such as they'd all had, but Agnes… She looked at her tea and sighed. It would still be there when she returned. This wouldn't take long. However, maybe…

'Joy, don't you have a key?'

'It's in my purse.'

There was no way out. 'All right, but I'm going in with you, and all you're doing is picking up your purse and we're getting out of there. I want to be able to swear to Dan we didn't touch a thing. If I have to, of course.'

'That's fine with me,' Joy said fervently. There was

a pause. 'And Mary, you'll have to pick me up. My keys are in my purse.'

It was with a great effort Mary repressed her groan. 'I'll be there in ten minutes.'

EIGHT

MARY DROVE INTO the parking lot by the Sunday school building and pulled into the area directly behind the church hall. It was empty. She'd hoped the police would still be there. Then all they'd have to do was ask for the purse and leave. No such luck.

She and Joy stared at the yellow tape wrapped around the building. It stated in bold black lettering: Crime Scene. Do Not Enter. Millie sat in the backseat and also stared at the building. What she thought, Mary didn't know. Why was she doing this? She knew why. She wouldn't like it one bit if Agnes was in a position to tell everyone in town she'd done something as stupid as letting her purse get locked in a crime scene. It could happen to anyone, but it wouldn't sound that way after Agnes got through embellishing the story. 'Well,' Mary said to Joy, through gritted teeth, 'at least the worst that can happen is Dan will be mad. It's not like we'll go to jail.' She paused, reflecting. 'At least, I don't think so.'

Joy got out and stood by the car, staring at the building. Mary got out on her side, closely followed by Millie, and joined her.

'How do we get under the tape?' There was a little tremor in Joy's usually decisive voice that Mary had never heard before.

'You hold it up for me. It's loose over the door, and

I'll unlock it. Then I'll hold it up while you come in. I don't want to break it.'

'No,' Joy fervently agreed. 'I'd just as soon no one ever knows we came here.'

'I wonder where they found all those stands they've got the tape run through.' Mary moved forward toward a line of short pillars, each with a ring on top and a large round plastic stand. They were designed to have a chain run through them and create a barrier or path so people could form a line. Mary had seen something similar at the movie theater when it first opened and a swarm of people had wanted entrance. There was no chain connecting these bright red pillars, only more yellow crime tape. Mary had to swallow several times before she could bring herself to lift the tape and duck under. Millie seemed not to share her qualms but trotted briskly up to the back door, ignoring the tape. Joy followed Mary, but at a distance. That she was shaking was obvious. Neither of them was very good at deliberately breaking the law, and although this was probably not a huge offense, Mary's heart was beating fast enough so she heard it.

'OK,' she whispered. 'Here we go.'

Joy pulled up the loose tape and Mary ducked under it and inserted her key. The door opened. She hurried in, Millie ahead of her, leaned out and grabbed Joy by the hand and pulled. Joy almost fell into the hallway.

'It's dark in here.' For some reason, Joy was whispering. 'Should we turn on the light?'

'We're going to have to unless you know exactly where it is and how to get to it in the dark.'

She felt along the wall for the light switch but her fingers felt nothing. Her cell. It was, of course, in the bottom of her bag. She flicked it on, found the flashlight app and turned it on. She'd missed the light switch by about an inch.

'That's much better.' Joy walked forward. 'We should have had this place designed with windows.'

Mary declined to comment. That was an argument settled ten years ago. She wasn't going to re-argue it now. They crept down the hallway toward the kitchen. The roll-top was back in place over the serving counter, the door to the kitchen closed. However, a light switch beside the door would flood the kitchen and the entire hall with light. Mary flicked it on. Light was what they needed right now. Shadows were more than she could bear. Joy pushed past her, opened the kitchen door and went in. Mary and Millie waited, surveying the tables. Nothing seemed out of place, Mary was glad to see. She had no idea how extensive the crime-scene investigation would be—if they'd just search the area where poor little Miss Emilie was found or if they'd search the whole hall. What they thought they might find, she didn't know, but all kinds of things turned up on those *CSI* programs on TV. She walked farther into the room, surveying it for evidence of disturbance and froze. There. On the breakable table. Sitting in front of that dreadful statue of what was supposed to be a nymph. It couldn't be. She walked closer and her breath caught in her throat. She must be imagining it. Her fingers reached out and touched it. It really was there. The white clock.

'Joy?' That didn't come out very loud. As a matter of fact, it wasn't more than a croak. But it didn't need to be. Joy was at her side.

'What's the matter? You're as white as a sheet.'

Mary said nothing, only pointed. The clock still sat on

the table, almost glowing in the light. She hadn't imagined it.

Joy saw it too. She gasped, her hands flew up to her face and her purse crashed as it hit the floor. 'It came back!'

'I think it had help.' Mary looked around once more, but nothing else seemed to be disturbed. No one else seemed to be in the building, only them. But someone had been, and recently. The police couldn't have been gone that long.

'What do we do now?' Joy started whispering again. It didn't seem necessary—there was no one there to hear them—but Mary understood the urge this time.

'I don't know. Someone had to have taken that thing and I assume the same person put it back, but is it evidence? Does whoever took it have anything to do with Miss Emilie's death or did they just want the clock?'

'Then why bring it back?'

Joy had a point. Instead of answering her, Mary took a step closer to the table, reached out and picked up the clock.

'What are you doing?' There was horror in Joy's voice. 'That might be evidence.'

'Of what?' Mary gently turned the clock in her hand so it faced her. 'It's not running. Maybe the battery is dead.' She tilted it slightly backward and heard a clunk.

'What was that?' That Joy didn't like any part of this was obvious from the fear in her voice, but Mary didn't think that clunk was something the clock was designed to do.

'I don't know. It came from…' The bottom of the clock slipped in her hand, twisting around enough to almost make an L. The only thing holding it on was one screw in one corner, which wasn't enough to hold what made the clunk. A long, narrow key, with numbers embedded in its top, fell onto the table.

'That looks like a safe deposit key.' Joy forgot to whisper in her surprise. 'What would a safe deposit key be doing in a clock?'

Mary set the clock back on the table, its bottom sticking out at an angle underneath it. She rubbed her forehead with one hand as she stared at the key. Joy's question was excellent and she could think of only one answer. She dropped her hand and rummaged in her jacket pocket. At first all she felt was her car keys, then the smooth dial of her cell phone. She pulled it out and turned toward Joy. 'As much as I hate to admit it, I think this might be evidence.'

'What are you going to do?'

Mary took in a deep breath but she really had no choice. She let it out slowly, then said, 'Call Dan.'

NINE

DAN STOOD IN front of the clock, staring first at it then at the key. 'Tell all that to me again.'

Mary started as Joy seemed incapable of speech. Joy had been very offhand about crashing a crime scene when no one was around, but now that the police were actually back she was a mass of quivering fear. Mary wasn't, but that didn't mean she was happy she'd been caught where she shouldn't have been.

'Joy forgot her purse in all the commotion, and when she realized she didn't have it, she also realized where it was. She couldn't drive because her keys were in it, so she called me. By the time we got here, all your people had gone.'

'I got that part. I also got the part about Agnes. Tell me about the clock again.'

'It was back. I couldn't believe it but there it was. I picked it up and the bottom almost fell off. It only has one screw holding it. Then I tipped it a little and the key fell out.'

'And that's it?'

'Should there be more?'

Dan sighed. 'You might want to tell me what you thought you were doing handling evidence.'

'Oh, for heaven's sake, Dan.' Exasperation was getting the better of her. It had been a long and terrible day, and she wanted to go home and have her tea. They should have called the station before letting themselves into the church hall but it had all seemed so easy, so innocent. It had turned out to be anything but. 'I didn't know it was evidence. It was a donated clock that had gone missing and suddenly turned back up. I thought it was odd, not critical.'

Dan looked at her, then at Joy, then down at Millie, who seemed bored sitting by Mary's leg, doing nothing. 'When did you realize it might be something I'd like to know about?'

'When the key fell out.' She shifted her weight and looked around. A chair would be most welcome about now. 'That's when I realized what must have happened.'

Dan ran his fingers through his hair and looked at her without expression. Joy, he ignored. 'What do you think happened?'

'That whoever took the clock knew it contained something but not what they found. They didn't know what to do with it, so they just brought it back here and left it.'

'That's one possibility. If you're right, I'm going to further guess there will be only your fingerprints on the clock or the key.' He paused. 'I wonder what they thought they'd find.'

Mary could only shake her head.

'All right.' He stood up straight, laid his hands gently on Mary's shoulders and turned her toward the door. 'You look all in. Go home. I'll take Joy home, then I'll drop this…' he indicated the clock and the key, '…off at the station. Then I'm also going home. It's been a tough day.'

Joy clutched her purse to her bosom. 'In a squad car? I'm not driving up to my house in any squad car.' The horror in her voice would have made Mary laugh any other time.

Right now, Mary was so tired all she could think of was her reading chair and her mug of by now-cold tea. Could you heat up already brewed tea? She planned on trying.

'You'll be in the front seat, Joy,' Dan told her with a straight face. 'I'll even let you turn on the siren.'

Joy didn't seem to see the humor in that statement, but riding in the front seat seemed to soothe her. Dan escorted them both out to the parking lot, making sure the door was locked behind them.

'Seems to me there are way too many keys to this building floating around town.' He looked at Mary. 'You might want to talk to Les about rekeying it.'

Mary nodded. She opened the door of her car for Millie, who jumped in and crossed to the passenger seat. Mary followed her, inserting the key in the ignition. She waited until Dan and Joy had pulled out then followed. All she wanted was to get in her front door and collapse. No phone, no visitors, just her and Millie and, before too long, bed.

TEN

MARY SWIRLED THE tea in the pot. Would it be fit to drink if she heated it up in the microwave? It was worth a try. She had just put the mug in when Millie growled. When Mary turned around, her back door slowly opened. She gasped and grabbed the counter for support. What did she have at hand to defend herself ? The knife caddy was on the opposite end. She'd never reach it. The potato masher? Not likely. Then Millie started to wag and whine. The door opened a little wider and a dark head peeked around it. 'Can I come in?'

'John. Oh, you gave me quite a start. Of course you can.' Mary waited for a moment before she moved, giving her heart a chance to settle before she dared let go of the counter. 'I was just going to have a cup of tea. Would you like one?'

'Thank you, no. I'm only going to stay a second. I thought I'd check on you. I've heard the news and it's awful.' He came all the way into the room and stopped as Millie pranced beside him, demanding he notice her. He did. 'Were you really going to attack me with the potato masher?'

Mary managed a weak little laugh. Luckily the microwave dinged and she was able to turn her back while she picked up her mug. She hadn't wanted to admit even to herself how unnerved today had left her, and she definitely didn't want to announce it to John. 'I guess I'm a little tired. Let's sit down.' She set her mug on the old kitchen table and gratefully sank on a chair, motioning for John to do the same.

'Why did you think you needed to check on me?' She grinned at him over the top of her mug. 'Afraid I would be so done in by all the excitement I wouldn't be able to show up at the pet shop tomorrow?'

John returned her grin a little sheepishly. 'Well, it has been a terrible day. I thought I'd just see how you were doing.' His grin disappeared and the lines in his face tightened. 'You are all right, aren't you?'

'I'm fine. Just fine. I'll be there.'

'Are you going to bring Millie?'

Mary looked at him, surprised. 'I was. Is that a problem?'

He shook his head. 'She's spent a lot of hours in that shop. I think she brings in customers. Just be sure she doesn't go near the dragon.'

'Neither of us is going near that thing. I hope your zoo man comes in early. Did Pat call you about the pet adoption?'

John blinked then chuckled. 'She did, and we're on board. That's only the day after tomorrow. Will you be there to help?'

'I'm not sure what I can do, but I'll be there.'

'You can take charge of the cash register. By Saturday you'll be a pro.'

Mary didn't want to be a pro. The cash register was intimidating and she wasn't looking forward to being left alone with it tomorrow, but she'd manage. She always did. The dogs and cats needed homes. And the hospital needed John's expertise as a surgical nurse. So she'd become a pet shop pro, if only for a few hours. 'I'll be there before ten. What time did you say Krissie would be in?'

'Not before noon. That's her first appointment. But I'm sure you'll be fine. Glen is going in early to feed all the critters and make sure everything is in order. I'll be back—whenever we finish.'

Mary nodded. 'Where are you going to set up the dog adoption? I don't think the city will let you do it on your front sidewalk.'

'In our parking lot, behind the building. Glen and I own it and the other shops that open onto it, so there won't be any fuss about what we do there. We're having our spring sale. People can adopt a dog or cat and buy all the things they'll need at the same time.'

'I hope it works out better than today did. I don't think they placed a single animal.'

'Under the circumstances, I'm not surprised. We're going to put a big poster in the window tomorrow and it will be on the radio. I tried to get it on the local TV station, but they're so full with the murder they can't be bothered with cats and dogs. We'll place some of them, though. I've already talked it up at the hospital and a couple of people are interested in adopting.'

'Wonderful. It breaks my heart to think of all those animals going without a home or even proper care.' She looked at Millie, who sat beside John, looking at him, expecting her ears to be stroked.

John was a longtime friend, and he never failed her. But this evening he seemed distracted, the stroking automatic.

'Mary, all this with Miss Emilie—Glen says you found her. Is that true?'

Mary was a bit taken back by the abrupt change of

subject, but the murder was on everyone's mind. 'Yes. I did.' She paused and took a sip of her tea and a shudder ran through her. A reaction to the bitter taste of tea left to sit too long or a mental picture of little Miss Emilie in that chair. Which, she wasn't sure.

'Glen's taking this really hard,' John said slowly, as if the words didn't come easily. He left Millie and leaned forward over the table. 'He hasn't been president of the bank very long, and he takes his position seriously. I can tell you confidentially a lot of the investment accounts were in a mess, and he's trying to straighten them all out, but the Plym trust is the one that has him the most worried. That Richard Plym isn't helping matters. Do you know…does Dan have any idea who might have done this terrible thing?'

Mary shook her head. She was surprised at John. He must know that even if Dan had told her anything, which was unlikely, she wouldn't pass that information along. John didn't seem to have the same qualms.

'It's all that missing money. No one seems to have the least idea what Miss Emilie did with it, and Richard Plym going around accusing Caleb and Lorraine of stealing isn't helping any. Glen's a wreck. I don't know what to do…' He looked at her as if she would come up with some brilliant idea that would cure everything.

That wasn't possible, especially as Mary had no idea what he was talking about. What missing money? She was about to ask, but John changed the subject again.

'But that's not why I came. I wanted to make sure you were all set for tomorrow. I've pasted a list of instructions on how to work the cash register and other things on the desk, and I've left phone numbers for you if you get in trouble. You won't be able to reach me, of course, but Glen will be standing by. Just in case.' He frowned. 'If you can think of anything else…'

John seemed worried about the shop and Mary's short stint as proprietor, a nervousness which didn't help Mary's anxiety one bit. She wasn't sure of her ability to catch a rat someone might want to take home, and the little net they used to capture the fish didn't look easy to use, either. As for the snakes, she'd already decided if someone wanted one they'd have to come back when one of the men was there. She wasn't going near them. Dog food she could do. Snakes, no.

She smiled at John. 'It's going to be fine, and Glen said Krissie will be there shortly after I open, so I can always ask her if I get stuck.'

John snorted. 'Krissie's a darn good groomer but don't let her near the cash register. She messes it up every time.' He leaned in and patted Mary on the arm. 'You'll do just fine. If you really get stuck, call the bank. Glen will leave and come rescue you.' He stopped and gave her arm a squeeze. 'And Mary, thank you.'

Mary waved him off. 'It'll be fun. After all, Millie knows the shop well, and the customers. She can help.' She laughed, and so did John, but she didn't think he looked quite sure. Mary decided to ignore him. 'You go on and don't worry. Don't worry about Glen, either. Dan will get all this terrible business sorted out.'

She sat for a long time after John left, mulling over the whole day. It wasn't cheerful mulling. What had John meant by missing money? Missing from where? And why had Richard Plym accused the Duxworths of stealing? Could that have a connection to Miss Plym's death? Or was that a coincidence? Mary didn't believe in coincidences, but right now the connection eluded her. She also didn't see how Miss Emilie could have gotten back to the church hall in the middle of the night, let alone get into the locked, dark building without help. And the clock. Who had taken it and then put it back? The only possible explanation was that someone thought something else was in it that they wanted. But what? And how did Gloria Sutherland fit into all this? Or did she? Shaking her head, Mary got up, poured the rest of her tea down the sink and put her soup on to heat. Right now she was going to take two Tylenol and get ready for what was to come in the morning.

ELEVEN

MARY STOOD IN front of the back door of Furry Friends Pet Shop, key in hand, thinking this was too much like yesterday. Only it wasn't. It was halfway through the morning, and the lock showed bright under a weak early spring sun. This door was truly locked and opened easily with the turn of her key. Millie, who hadn't liked what lay on the other side of yesterday's door, was already wagging her behind as this one swung open. Mary sighed as she followed Millie into the back room of the shop. Why did she let herself get talked into these kinds of things, anyway? She knew nothing about pet supplies, electronic cash registers, small rodents or fish. Especially fish. But here she was, and she would do the best she could. She let go of Millie's leash and watched the little dog trot through the back room into the store, head up, ears pricked forward. Mary ignored the contents of the back room, walked through the shop, unlocked the front door, turned the sign over from 'closed' to 'open' and hoped no one would come in anytime soon. She needed to put away her purse, turn on the cash register and make coffee. Coffee first. Thank goodness they had a decent coffeemaker.

With a fresh mug in hand, Mary felt a little stronger, more in control. Yesterday had taken a bigger toll than she'd wanted to admit, even to herself. Millie circled the puppy pen, which was empty, left it to examine the dog crates stacked in one corner and ignored the fish in their tanks as she walked down the aisle to say good morning to the parakeets. They twittered something back, but Mary didn't think it was good morning. Millie stopped next to an elevated wire cage that contained baby rabbits, who immediately hopped over to stare at the dog. Were these bunnies destined as Easter pets for small children? She hoped not. With one eye still on Millie, she walked over to the checkout counter. John had, as promised, taped a checklist on it. She examined it, ticking off each item as she turned on the cash register, made sure the date was correct and the starting amount zero. So far, so good. Then the door opened to the tinkling of a bell. She gave a start that almost emptied her coffee cup on John's list. 'Oh.'

Millie's bark wasn't any more welcoming as she looked up at Mary.

The customer laughed. 'It doesn't seem you two were expecting company.'

'What are you doing here?' Mary sank down in the rolling chair behind the counter, her heart still fluttering.

Millie ran to greet Ellen, knowing she was about to get her ears scratched.

'I need cat food, so I thought I'd pop in and get some.'

'And keep an eye on me at the same time?'

Ellen grinned. 'Something like that.'

'So far, so good.'

'Meaning I'm the only one who's come in so far?'

Mary grinned and nodded. 'Want some coffee?'

'Thought you'd never ask.' Ellen looked around. 'No puppies?'

'No. Also no chicks or kittens. But there are bunnies.

Poor little things. I hope no one buys them for Easter baskets.'

'So do I. However, I think they're destined for a not-too-pleasant life, no matter where they go. Living in a small cage on wire when you're bred to hop around all day in a nice green garden can't be much fun.'

Mary blinked. She hadn't thought of it quite that way and decided she didn't want to now, either. She was on anxiety overload, and the future life of bunnies was one thing she couldn't deal with. At least not right now.

She changed the subject. 'I hope we get good homes for some of those dogs and cats and some good donations for the future shelter. If we can fund the no-kill shelter, it will be wonderful.'

'The rummage sale is usually a huge success, so you should get some money from that.'

'If we ever get a chance to hold it.'

Ellen looked at her aunt in surprise. Gloomy was not usually her mood. 'Dan said they'd be through in a couple of days. I thought you and Les had settled on next Thursday.'

'We did, but you don't always get as good a turn-out when you have to reschedule.'

Ellen laughed. 'You'll whip the radio station and the paper into giving you daily publicity all the rest of the week, every pastor in town will be announcing it from his or her pulpit, every club in town will be sending emails… you'll get a good turnout.'

Mary allowed herself a small smile. Ellen was right. That was exactly what would happen, and they probably would. It was just there were so many things…so many questions…and poor Miss Emilie. She couldn't get her out of her mind, sitting in that chair, looking so pitiful with her furry pink slippers, her robe falling off her shoulders… No, she wasn't going to think about it. She would concentrate on minding John and Glen's shop until they got back, and that was all. Only she wasn't going to get off quite that easily. The little bell rang again.

Mary had never seen the young man who walked through the doorway. Tall, thin, black hair pulled back in a ponytail, his black baseball cap worn backward made it hard to know where his hat ended and his hair began. His jeans were black and so was his half-zipped hoodie. The only color on him, other than his too-white face, was his T-shirt. From what Mary could see it was covered in so many lightning bolts it could have ignited half the town. He looked around the store and studied Ellen for a minute before addressing Mary.

'Hi. I'm Charlie Johnson. I've come for the lizard.' He held up a small animal carrier.

Mary stared at it. So did Ellen.

'You're here for the lizard? Do you mean the Komodo dragon?' Mary couldn't keep her eyes off the carrier. Did he mean to try to transport that nasty tempered dragon in that flimsy carrier? It wouldn't hold a chihuahua safely.

The young man's narrow face creased into a frown. He took his cap off, ran his hand over his hair and slapped his cap back on. 'No one said nothing about a dragon. My mom told me to pick up the lizard. She said it wasn't a little bitty thing so I should take along a good-sized carrier. I did.'

He raised the small box up again and waved it slightly.

Ellen gave a snort of laughter. 'You'll never get that beast into that little carrier, and if you did he'd be out the other end before you got the door closed. Here. Follow me. I'll show you.'

He followed Ellen through the store to the back wall, clutching his carrier close beside him. Mary didn't follow. She'd seen the dragon and was sure she could live nicely without ever seeing it again. Millie didn't need to see it either. She snapped the leash on her little dog and kept her tight beside her. It wasn't long before she heard a sharp gasp.

'That's what I'm supposed to transport?' There was a pause. 'Guess that's why she told me to take the truck.'

Charlie Johnson returned to the front of the store a great deal faster than he'd ambled through it to view the dragon. 'I wouldn't touch that thing with a… I can't take it. I came on my motorcycle.'

Mary thought his face was even whiter, if such a thing was possible, than when he'd sauntered in, and his casual off-hand manner had disappeared. Instead, a very upset young man stood before her.

'My mom is going to kill me, but she didn't tell me that thing was… It spits. How do you go about getting it out of that glass fish tank and into another carrier, anyway? If she thinks I'm going to stick my hand in there and pull it out by the back leg—well, I'm not. I do a lot of things at that zoo but I'm not getting into a fight with a dragon. She said it was just a baby. If that's a baby, what does a full-grown one look like?'

'They can get up to ten feet long and weigh well over one hundred pounds. That one is probably just over three feet and weighs maybe thirty pounds or so,' Karl Bennington said.

Charlie Johnson flinched as if he'd been shot. Mary smiled. She hadn't heard Karl and Pat Bennington come in.

'Hi,' Ellen said. 'Do they really get that big?'

'In the wild, they do. Not sure if they will in a zoo. Charlie, are you sure your mother didn't tell you how to handle it? Or did you just not listen?' Karl's voice was carefully neutral, but there was an undertone of displeasure.

White was replaced by red. 'Ah, she said it was a lizard, a sort of big one and to take the truck. And to call you. Gosh, Doc. I thought I could handle a lizard, even a sort of big one. I didn't know it was a monster. She's going to kill me.'

Karl grinned. 'You're probably in more danger of your mom doing that than the lizard. I believe John and Glen named him Bernard, but I'm not sure that's appropriate. I've never personally examined him, or her, and I'm not sure I want to. Dogs and cats are my thing. However, I've done a lot of work for your mom at the zoo, and I think I can help you get this guy moved safely. But not in that.' Karl pointed to the small animal carrier Charlie still held. 'Let's give your mother a call and see what we can work out.'

He took Charlie by the arm and aimed him toward the front door and the motorcycle prominently parked in the street in front of the shop.

Pat Bennington watched, her smile barely repressed. 'That kid is in for it. Ginger didn't get her name for her red hair alone.'

'What are you two doing here?' asked Mary.

Ellen's grin was a little broader than Pat's, just one step from all-out laughter, but it subsided when Mary spoke.

'So, when are we going to get rid of that blasted lizard?' There was more than a little trepidation in Mary's voice.

'I don't know,' Pat said. 'Karl works with Ginger at the zoo. He swore he'd never treat anything larger than a Great Dane but he's in love with that old brown bear they have. I wonder if it's possible to tranquilize lizards.' She looked at Mary and grinned. 'They'll get it out of here soon. As for why we're here, we're trying to figure out the best place to put the dog crates and portable runs. What's the weather supposed to be like tomorrow?'

'Nice. No reason you can't set up in the parking lot, but I was wondering, can anyone see you back there? Will they come?'

'I was wondering the same thing. It's a great place to have them—lots of room and it's safe. We can set up the adoption application table in the back room. All we have to do is move some of those food bags and those boxes of stuff. We'll ask later. I was thinking we might be able to put one dog in the front of the store, along with a sign, to sort of tell people what's going on.'

Mary wasn't so sure, but they had to do something. Unadvertised events weren't usually very successful. 'Let's see what John says.' She glanced at her cell phone. 'Krissie should be along any minute. Maybe she'll have some ideas.'

'Who's Krissie?' Ellen asked.

'If you had a dog instead of a cat, you'd know,' Mary told her niece, a trace of tartness in her voice. That Millie spent more time at the groomer than Mary did at the hairdressers was one thing Mary hadn't anticipated when she took on the little dog.

Pat laughed. 'That's why short-haired dogs are so popular.' She turned to Ellen. 'Didn't you see the new station in the back of the store? John and Glen just finished it last week. Bring your dog in, get it groomed and shop for dog food, little sweaters and special dog and cat treats all at the same time.'

'Is that what that is?' Ellen gestured toward the back of the store, where a glass partition could be seen. 'I thought that was new but didn't know what it was for. Dog grooming? And this Krissie is the groomer?'

'Yep.' Pat beamed. 'Krissie was a real stroke of luck. She's been working at the Dolled Up Dog Parlor for ages and does all of the show dogs in this area, but she and the owner had some sort of falling out and when the guys heard about it they called her, and here she is. Or she will be pretty soon.'

The bell on the front door tinkled, and a tall man with a blond ponytail, a diamond earring and a small chocolate-brown poodle under one arm walked in. 'Hi.' He smiled. 'I'm early, I see, but I thought I'd drop Fred off. I have to open the library and people get a little testy if I'm not on time.'

'Hey, Luke. Hey, Fred.' Pat reached out and gave the little poodle a scratch behind his ear. He gave her a slobbery lick on the hand. 'Thanks.' She whipped her hand down the side of her pants.

Luke laughed. 'This is sure going to be convenient. I've been taking Fred to Krissie for a long time but it was a thirty-minute drive each way. You don't mind if he hangs out until she gets here?'

'Of course not,' Mary said. 'Millie will be delighted.'

'So will Fred. Just don't let them play chase.' He set the dog on the floor, unsnapped his leash and handed it to Mary. 'I see Charlie Johnson out there, talking with Karl. Surely he didn't try to pick up the Komodo dragon on that motorcycle?'

Ellen burst out laughing. Pat appeared to try to smother her chuckle.

Mary wasn't as amused. 'He drove up here with a carrier that wouldn't have held a small cat. Karl is out there right now making arrangements with Ginger to get the beast properly removed. How they're going to go about doing that is beyond me. Just as long as they get it done.'

Luke watched Fred and Millie get reacquainted for a minute then looked up. 'Is there anything new on who killed poor Miss Emilie?'

Mary shook her head. 'Not that I've heard.'

'Is it true she was in the church hall in her night clothes? That someone strangled her?'

Mary nodded.

'You found her?'

Again, Mary nodded. It was about all she could do. The horror and sympathy on Luke's face made her choke up all over again, and tears wouldn't help an already impossible situation.

'Dan's checking on a few possible leads right now.' Ellen reached over and touched her aunt on the arm.

Mary smiled back and dabbed at the corner of one eye.

'I don't understand what she was doing there, in the middle of the night, or how she got in. Did someone bring her?' Pat looked as if she would start sniffling any minute as well.

'Lorraine says she wanted her stuffed dog. They think it somehow got into one of the boxes of things they donated to the rummage sale. She brought Miss Emilie to the hall on Wednesday when we were setting up, but they didn't find it. Lorraine thinks she may have come back to look again.'

'In the middle of the night?' Luke looked incredulous.

None of the ladies did. They all knew the Plym sisters and had watched as Miss Emilie lost track of night and day, along with other things. 'She'd gotten a little… mixed up.'

Luke's face softened. 'Yeah. They'd both come into the library, her carrying that stuffed dog. She'd ask me every time if it was all right if she brought him in. "He won't make a sound," she'd always say. Miss Eloise would start to grumble but I'd just say don't worry, it's fine. She always went into the children's section or young adults and wandered around, then Miss Eloise would bring a pile of books up to the counter and call for her to come on. What was she doing in that section anyway?' Luke paused and watched the dogs for a minute before he looked back at the women. 'I used to feel sorry for her, but I finally figured out she wasn't unhappy. I'm not sure what world she lived in, but she seemed to like it.'

Mary had to agree. Miss Emilie seemed, if not happy, then content.

'What I can't figure out,' Luke continued, 'is how she found her way to the church hall in the middle of the night. Most days she couldn't find her way home in broad daylight.' He turned to go, pausing at the door. 'Tell Krissie I'll come get Fred around four. I have a short day today.'

He was halfway across the park before anyone said anything.

'He's got a point.' Ellen's voice was thoughtful, as if she was working something out.

'Another thing. Even if she could find her way, even if she knew that's where she wanted to look for that stupid toy dog, I can't see her remembering to bring a key. I can't believe she ever had one or if she did, remembered what it was for. This just doesn't make sense.' Pat looked around as if suddenly some answer would appear, but the door opened and it was only Karl.

'Sorry, Mary. It looks as if your dragon isn't going anywhere until Monday.'

'It's not my dragon, and I won't be here on Monday. The problem now is where are we going to put the dogs and cats up for adoption?'

'The cats will have to come in here, somewhere. Dogs can go in the parking lot, and if John agrees we'll set up the adoption table in the back room. I can get my staff to make a couple of signs this afternoon. We don't have many appointments and no surgeries,' Karl said.

Mary stared at Karl for a moment, not sure what to say. 'We'd just established that…' She looked over at Pat who, with a straight face, nodded at Karl.

'An excellent idea, dear. That's just what we'll do.'

Ellen watched them for a moment then put her hand over her face and coughed, trying to disguise her smile.

Concern creased Karl's face. 'Are you all right?'

'She's fine,' Pat said, still smiling. 'We'd better go. The office will open soon and you really should be there. Mary, you'll fill in John? If there's going to be any changes, let me know. Otherwise, I'll be here before nine in the morning with the dogs in our charge and ready to meet the others. I don't have the cats. The girls from Atascadero rescue are bringing them. Give Krissie my best and tell her I hope to see her soon.'

'Krissie? Krissie who does the wonderful dog grooming? She's coming here?'

'Yes, Karl. She's going to have her own dog grooming business right here in Furry Friends. I wonder where people get these pet store names. Let's go. Mary, don't go near the dragon. Karl's people will take care of it on Monday. See you all. Ellen, you and Dan still coming over tonight? Good.'

Pat steered Karl out the door and around the corner.

'Poor Karl. He had no idea we were way ahead of him on how to set up.'

'He's way ahead of us on how to get rid of that lizard.' Mary's tone was a little cryptic. 'You're going over there tonight?'

Ellen nodded.

'See if Dan's any closer to finding out how Miss Emilie got into the hall and who might have been with her.'

'I'll find that out long before we go visit the Benningtons. I think the clinic's open tonight until six, so we're going to take Chinese over about seven. In the meantime, I have an appointment to list a house—one that's going to be much easier to sell than the Plyms'. I need to go home and shower and change. Can you ring up this cat food for me?'

Mary managed, and she continued to manage the rest of the morning. There was a steady stream of customers in and out of the store, almost every one of whom wanted to talk about the murder. It was close to noon when Joy arrived.

Mary watched her as she wandered around the store. If she hadn't known Joy so well she would have thought she was a potential shoplifter. Joy walked slowly up and down the aisles, picking up one item after another, putting each down, walking on, picking up something else and not seeming to see any of them, all the while clutching a brown paper bag. Mary decided she was waiting for the woman who had been at the counter forever, mulling over which kind of wild bird seed to buy, to leave. The woman finally decided on the one that that was ten cents cheaper than the other, paid for it and left.

Joy immediately joined Mary at the counter. ‘Mary, I have no idea what to do with this so I thought I’d bring it to you. I hope you don’t mind.’

‘Bring me what?’

Joy set her paper shopping bag on the counter. ‘Miss Emilie’s stuffed dog.’

‘Oh, my goodness. What am I supposed to do with it?’

Joy sighed deeply and mournfully. ‘I don’t know, but I can’t bear the thought of throwing it in the trash and I don’t think anyone would want it if we put it back in the rummage sale. Not only is it pretty worn out but everyone in town knows it was Miss Emilie’s. I thought maybe you’d have an idea…’ Joy pushed the paper bag closer to Mary’s hand.

Mary took the bag with great reluctance and stuffed it under the counter with her purse. ‘I don’t, but I understand not wanting to throw it away. I’ll think of something.’

Joy brightened—not a usual look for her. ‘I knew you would. Now, I need some food for my granddaughter’s dog. I don’t hold with dogs in the house…’ She looked at Millie and frowned.

Millie’s tongue rolled out one side of her mouth.

‘But that dog is the best thing that’s happened to the child since she got so sick. The food comes in one of those big brown sacks.’

Mary knew exactly what kind Joy wanted. It was what she fed Millie. ‘Do you want the ten-pound sack or the big one?’

Joy took the smaller bag and left.

John walked in the door, still in his hospital scrubs,

as Joy was going to walk out. ‘How’s your granddaughter’s dog?’

A rare smile creased Joy’s lips. ‘They adore each other. The dog mopes all around the house while she’s in school. Or so my daughter says,’ she added hastily.

Since Joy’s daughter worked the breakfast and lunch shift at the Yum Yum café, did the little dog mope around at her house as well? Joy left.

Mary smiled as John walked up to the counter.

‘How’d it go?’ He looked around the shop then at the floor where Millie had come to sit on one side of him. Fred sat on the other. That they expected ear scratches was not in doubt. ‘Krissie’s not in yet?’

‘Fine and no, she’s not, to the second.’

‘She’s late.’ He frowned, scratched Millie’s ears, scratched Fred’s and advanced into the store.

‘Didn’t you say she’d be here around noon? It’s just a few minutes past.’

As if to prove John wrong, the door opened again and a tall, handsome black woman, her curly hair cut no-nonsense short, her green smock open and flowing around her yellow T-shirt, rushed in. ‘Am I late? There was another accident on the freeway. If this works out, I’m moving up here. Hi, Fred. Hi, Millie. Oh, dear. Millie needs her “do” done.’

Both dogs made a beeline for the woman who must be Krissie. Mary studied the woman as she coo’d and goo’d over the dogs, who yelped and squealed with pleasure.

‘Yes, she does.’ John looked at Millie with undisguised displeasure. ‘You only have a few, so maybe you can work her in. Fred’s first.’

‘Then that’s where we’ll start.’ She gathered Fred up in her arms and finally faced Mary. ‘You must be Mrs

McGill. I'm Krissie. I used to groom Millie for…before…poor Evan.'

Poor Evan, indeed. His murder had been tragic but Mary thought he'd be happy his good friends, John Lagomasino and Glen Manning, were doing such a good job taking care of his beloved shop and that Mary had acquired Millie. She took a look at her. She did look a little shaggy. A lot shaggy.

She sighed. 'I've heard a lot about you, Krissie, but I didn't know you were the one who… She needs her "do" done?'

Krissie laughed and John chuckled. 'Her hairdo. She needs a new hairdo,' he said.

'Oh. I guess she does.'

'I'm not sure I can do her today, but if you want to make an appointment, I'll check the book.'

Having Millie groomed wasn't an expense Mary had budgeted. Krissie could check her appointment book, but Mary needed to consult her checkbook. How much did Krissie charge? Millie didn't like the groomer she'd been using. She was about to ask when John interrupted with other news.

'You'll never guess who was at the hospital today looking for a job.'

'Gloria Sutherland.' Krissie had started toward her grooming area but turned back, Fred tucked into the crook of her arm.

'How did you know?' John looked crestfallen, his interesting piece of gossip apparently not the minor bombshell he'd hoped.

'Sissie called me. She was all up in arms. Said if they hired her and she ended up on her floor, she was quitting.'

'Who's Sissie?' Mary asked. 'And what would she be quitting?'

'My sister, Sybil. She's an RN at Tri-Counties Hospital. Gloria is an RPN so some things she can't do. Gloria does them anyway. She was fired from Trinity Lutheran because of that. The RNs were afraid one day she'd do something really wrong and hurt someone. Since then she's worked as a home health nurse's aide but that's dried up. She probably got caught snooping in people's drawers and desks one too many times.'

John looked like a deflated balloon. This was his story and he wanted to tell it. She was pretty sure he had something to add.

'It dried up because she did more than snoop. Remember that old lady who died last year, the one with dementia? Gloria took care of her. She got the old lady to sign a codicil to her will, leaving a substantial portion of her estate to Gloria. Her kids challenged it in court, and yesterday the judge threw it out. He ruled the old lady wasn't competent to sign it, plus…and this is the good part… the witnesses' signatures weren't valid. Gloria got lucky. The kids won't prosecute. They just want her to go away.'

Mary cringed. She'd known Gloria since she'd been in her seventh-grade class. She hadn't been easy, but children of older parents sometimes weren't. That was true in Gloria's case. Her mother seemed perpetually surprised she was there and her father noticed only his failing business. She craved attention and didn't seem to care if it wasn't always approval. She dominated conversations, pushing herself into groups that increasingly rejected her. The result was Gloria often sat alone at the lunch table, at the library and on the bus home. She hadn't outgrown the need to make herself important, and she still didn't seem to have many friends, but somehow that didn't translate into stealing from an old lady, or going through people's drawers, especially when they were sick and in your care.

'Are you sure about that?' Mary knew her voice was a little faint, but she felt as if the air had been knocked out of her. It was Millie jumping on her leg, whining in what must have been agitation that made her straighten up. 'That's a very serious accusation.' She felt stronger, and strangely, a need to protect Gloria, the last person she ever thought she'd be protecting.

John nodded. 'It seems the brother of the assistant district attorney is another of the operating nurses. He told me. Our Gloria needs money, but cheating old ladies isn't the way to get it.'

'She does? I thought her parents left her in good shape.' Mary was beginning to feel more and more out of her depth.

John shrugged. 'I only know what I told you. There's a real shortage of good home health nurses, but she can hardly get a job. Now, is the dragon gone? Do we know what we're doing tomorrow? How did you get on with the cash register?'

'Everything's fine. The cash register wasn't a problem but the dragon's still here. There was a transportation mix-up. Karl was here and he got it worked out. It leaves Monday. I think they got tomorrow all worked out as well.'

John started to say something, but the sight of Millie, wiggling beside Mary's foot, looking anxious, distracted him. 'How long has it been since Millie's been out? She looks like she needs to.'

'Oh.' Mary looked down; the little dog stood up and

headed for the front door. Mary grabbed her leash and followed. 'We won't be long.'

'Can you come back for about a half hour longer when Millie's finished? I need to go home and change.'

'Yes,' Mary managed to say as Millie towed her through the doorway and out to the tree in the front of the store. When she was finished, she started down the block, sniffing at each tree as they went, dragging Mary after her.

'I promised John we'd go back to the store. Aren't you done?'

Millie ignored that statement and kept going. She had something in mind and it wasn't returning to the store. Mary was watching her so intently, she almost ran into Lorraine.

'Oh, Lorraine, I'm so sorry. I was watching Millie and not where I was going.' She paused and gave an apologetic laugh, but Lorraine didn't seem to notice.

'Millie. Yes.'

Millie no longer tugged at the leash. She sat in the middle of the sidewalk, her head tilted, ears forward, staring at Lorraine, who hadn't moved. She looked pale and more than a little distressed.

'Are you all right?' asked Mary.

Lorraine didn't say anything for a moment, but tears pooled at the corners of her eyes. She tried to wipe them away, but without much success. Mary reached into her jacket pocket and pulled out the pack of tissues she kept there. She handed one to Lorraine, who wiped her eyes, blew her nose and handed it back. With a little surprise and a lot of reluctance, Mary took it and stuffed it back in her pocket. 'What brings you downtown?'

'I had to get away. Caleb wants to start packing. Cassandra is stuffing all of Miss Eloise's clothes and everything else that's left in her bedroom in boxes. What she's going to do with it, I don't know, but I expect she'll start on Miss Emilie's room next. She wants to get the house ready to sell. I guess we'll have to clear out as well.' She sniffed. 'Oh, Mary, that's what's happening to me. I'm going to be stuffed in a box and dropped off with all the other discarded things.' More tears dripped.

Mary handed her back the tissue.

Lorraine was being a little dramatic, but then it had been a hard year. First, Miss Eloise dying so suddenly, then watching Miss Emilie getting more confused month by month and now all this. Mary thought she was probably right about having to move, another trauma to overcome, but their job at the Plyms' had ended.

'Where are you going to go? Have you decided?' She tried to put sympathy in her voice but she was having mixed emotions. Lorraine and Caleb had lived in the apartment above the Plyms' garage for a long time. They'd paid no rent and Caleb had only worked for the sisters part-time. He had a full-time job as custodian of one of the local grade schools and did some yard work for a few people. Lorraine had done just about everything for the sisters—cooked, cleaned and drove them to their appointments or social engagements but still managed to find time to volunteer at St Mark's. They'd known that arrangement would come to an end when the sisters either died or went into a care facility. Surely the Duxworths had made plans.

'Caleb has.' Bitterness practically dripped from those two words. Lorraine's eyes narrowed and the tears seemed to have dried up. Her lips were so narrow Mary was surprised she got the words out.

'What do you mean?'

'We bought a piece of land out in Almond Tree Hills years ago. Put a mobile home on it. We've been renting it out all this time but now the renters want to move to town and Caleb wants to move us out there. I don't want to live out there, and he knows it.' Her face contorted with what Mary thought was rage, or possibly despair, or maybe some of each. Red blotches stained her cheeks, more red lined her eyes and a twitch appeared in the corner of one of them. Her hands twisted together as she looked up and down the street. 'I love living in town. I can walk everywhere. To the farmer's market, to the library, even to my dentist. I love volunteering at the church. Those people are my friends. I can't do any of that if we move out there.' She hiccupped as she tried to swallow a sob. 'But does he care? No. We only have the truck, and he uses that for his gardening. He doesn't like me to drive it, and he won't want to take me into town. I'll be stuck out there. I don't know…'

Mary wasn't sure what to say. She knew the area. The rolling hills used to be covered in oaks but now there wasn't a tree for miles. They'd been pulled out when the land had been planted in barley, but that market had collapsed right along with no rain to irrigate the crops. The farmers had planted almond trees, hence the name, but that hadn't been any more successful. Some enterprising soul had gotten the county to let him subdivide the land into ten-acre parcels and they'd sold cheap. The price was their only redeeming feature. The roads had never been paved and were little more than rutted trails. Water wasn't plentiful and the wells were deep, unreliable and often contained sulfur. Building permits were hard to get—so was electricity—and the septic systems didn't leach well. She wouldn't want to live there either. She tried to think of something to say but Lorraine didn't give her a chance.

'You don't know how lucky you are, Mary McGill. You have that sweet little house right in the middle of town. I'd give anything to have your house.'

Lorraine turned and scurried down the sidewalk in the direction of the bank. Mary watched her go, stunned. Someone was envious of her house? She'd lived in it for over fifty years and had no plans to live anywhere else. She and Samuel had bought it shortly after they married and had never felt the need to move. The children they had both wanted never came, so its small size hadn't bothered her, and the location was perfect. The house was comfortable but not one that would inspire envy.

Millie barked sharply. Mary started then looked down. 'You're right. We need to get back. I promised John. What do you think about Lorraine? I had no idea she felt that way. Do you really think…'

Millie was already on her feet, headed back to the pet shop. What a strange conversation, Mary thought as she allowed Millie to tow her up the street. The last couple of days had been emotionally draining, and now one more sad thing to mull over. It didn't, however, get her any closer to knowing why Miss Emilie had gone to the church hall in the middle of the night and who had been with her, or why she'd been killed.

Sighing deeply, she opened the pet shop door and entered, letting the little bell ring as she called out, 'We're back.'

TWELVE

'ARE YOU TELLING us the key was to a safe deposit box that belonged to the Plyms and it was empty?'

Mary laid her fork down, a small shrimp still entailed on it. She was sitting at the Benningtons' dining-room table with Dan and Ellen Dunham, eating Chinese food. Ellen had called just as she had started to heat up the soup, asking her to come. At first she'd declined, she was so tired, but when Millie was included in the invitation she'd laughed and accepted. She was glad she had. Some of the things John had said bothered her. Now was a chance to find out what he'd been talking about. That was, if Dan felt he could reveal anything, which was by no means a sure thing.

'Not empty, no. It was crammed with stuff. Old insurance policies no longer in effect, birth and death certificates, the twins' mother's wedding ring and some other jewelry, even a copy of the original trust Mr Plym set up years ago, but nothing else. Nothing that anyone but them would find valuable. Well, the rings and things, but...' Dan reached for the carton of fried rice and looked in. 'About one more tablespoon. Anyone?'

He held it aloft but no one replied. He scooped the meager contents onto his plate, mixed in a little sweet and sour sauce and proceeded to eat.

'Ugh.' Ellen pushed her plate away. 'How can you eat it like that?

Mary paid no attention to Dan's plate. Her interest was in the contents of the safe deposit box. 'What about the trust?'

Dan looked up from pushing what was now sweet and sour rice around on his plate. 'What about it?'

'John said...' Mary's face warmed. She was the one who made a point of never listening to gossip. Only this wasn't gossip. This was asking for information.

'John said what?'

She had Dan's full attention. She might as well tell him. He probably knew anyway.

'He said Ed Kavanagh messed up a lot of people's portfolios and Glen was worried about the Plym trust. Only he said it was more about the missing money than anything else. Is money missing?'

Dan studied his plate then pushed it away. He picked up his glass of beer and took a small drink. Stalling for time, Mary was sure, or maybe just trying to think how he should put it. Whatever 'it' was.

'If by "missing" you mean money that's been withdrawn from the trust, money no one seems to know anything about, then, I guess the answer's yes.'

Four pairs of eyes stared at him.

'Would you care to explain that?' Ellen finally said.

'I'll try.' Dan looked around the table. 'I'm sure I don't have to tell you that what I say goes no further.'

Four pairs of eyes looked at him in disgust.

'No, you don't have to tell us that. Now, what is all this about missing money?' John had also mentioned missing money and this time Mary wanted to know what they were talking about.

'I have to go back a little for this to make sense.' He

looked around the table at four interested but slightly puzzled faces, rolled his eyes and went on.

'The Plym twins withdrew money from their trust on the first of the month for years. They always appeared in front of the same teller, Dab Holt, took out a small amount of cash and left.'

'Everyone in town knows that. The trust pays all the bills, including their groceries, so all they ever had was a little for extras. A candy bar, a magazine, something like that,' Pat said.

Dan nodded at Pat. 'That's right. And it seemed to work fine. Only, soon after Miss Eloise died, Miss Emilie went into the bank on the first of the month and presented Dab Holt with a request for money that far exceeded anything they'd taken out before.'

No one said anything; they all just stared at Dan.

'Why would she do that?' Ellen finally asked.

Dan shook his head.

'Was anyone with her?' The look of puzzlement on Pat's face deepened.

'No. She was alone. She had a note all made out, typed as if it had been done on a computer, that said how much she wanted and that she wanted it in fifty dollar bills.'

'Fifty dollars was more than they ever took out between them. Miss Eloise used to say they did just fine on twenty dollars a month. What would she want with more than that?' Mary knew she sounded surprised, but she was. Then something struck her. 'But you said bills.'

'Yes.' The serious look on Dan's face intensified. 'I did.'

'Dan, how much money did she take out?' An ominous feeling crept over Mary. Something was very wrong here, something that just might have contributed to Miss Emilie's death. From the look on Dan's face she was afraid he thought so, too.

'Five thousand dollars.'

A gasp went up all around the table so loud that Millie, who'd been dozing under it, picked her head up off Mary's foot.

'Did you say five thousand dollars?' Pat could hardly get the words out.

'Why didn't Dab Holt get Mr Kavanagh? She shouldn't have been trusted with all that money. And what did she need it for? All her bills were paid.' Karl sounded shocked but also almost angry.

'Dab Holt did. At least, she did the first time. Ed came out, talked to Miss Emilie then told Dab to make out a withdrawal slip for her, that there was nothing in the trust that said she couldn't take out that much. But she couldn't get any more money until the first of the next month.'

'She wouldn't need any until then, or until the end of the year.' That sounded a little more tart than Mary had intended, but she was having a hard time picturing Miss Emilie with all that money. Then something else Dan said penetrated. 'Did she come back for more the next month?' She sounded dumbfounded, but she felt that way.

'She's come back every month since then and every month she's taken out five thousand dollars.'

There wasn't a sound in the room. Millie had dropped her head back down and the only sound was her soft snore. Nothing else. Not even someone sucking in breath, which was what Mary felt like doing.

Finally Pat said, 'Miss Eloise, how long has she been gone?'

'Almost a year.' Mary tried to think how many months—at least ten. Or was it eleven?

'That's...dear God in heaven. That's fifty thousand dollars. Or more. What would she want with fifty thousand dollars? Dan, you said missing money. Are you saying no one knows where that money is?'

'That's exactly what I'm saying.'

'That's the...why didn't someone stop her?' There was no mistaking the anger in Karl's voice now.

'No one dared try, but after Ed Kavanagh retired and Glen came on, Dab approached him. The last time Miss Emilie came in he took her in his office, asked what she wanted with so much money, what she'd done with the other withdrawals but got nowhere. He said she sat there, the stuffed dog on her lap, her big ugly purse under her arm and answered nothing. Just kept saying could she please have her money, she needed to get on home. He had no grounds on which to stop her, so she got her money, but Cassandra got a phone call right after she left.'

'So that's why she showed up so unexpectedly. I'll bet that's why Richard's here, too. They wanted to find that money and put Miss Emilie where she couldn't take out any more.' Mary paused, looked around at the sober faces surrounding her and addressed Dan once more. 'You have no idea where it is?'

'I don't, no, and legally it's none of my business. No one has reported it stolen. But no one seems to know where it is, or if they do, they're not admitting it. Cassandra and Richard have looked, I'm sure, and other than Richard accusing Lorraine and Caleb of stealing it we have no evidence Miss Emilie didn't hide it somewhere that no one's yet thought to look.'

'What did the Duxworths say?' Mary had given up on her dinner, although she loved Chinese. This whole thing was making her a little sick.

Dan shrugged. 'We took both their statements this morning about what happened Wednesday night. I asked about the missing money as well. Caleb looked like he was going to have a coronary when he found out how much money we were talking about. He said when Richard accused him of stealing he thought he was talking about the small amount the sisters used to take every month. He had no idea she wasn't just doing what she'd always done. Lorraine said the same thing. She took her to the bank on several occasions and then either waited for her or ran an errand while she was inside. Evidently, Gloria Sutherland also took her a few times, but she never went inside, either. Lorraine and Caleb claim they went to bed early that night and never heard a thing. They knew nothing about her leaving the house until Cassandra woke them, banging on their front door, saying Miss Emilie was gone.'

'And you believe them?' Ellen sounded incredulous but Dan shook his head.

'It doesn't matter what I believe. What matters is what the evidence proves, and so far I don't have much of that. And until someone reports the money has been stolen, someone who has a rightful claim to it and can prove it's been stolen, my hands are tied.'

'Why haven't you searched the house?' Karl had pushed his plate away and glowered at Dan, as if this was somehow all his fault.

'Because I don't have a search warrant and Richard Plym has made it clear we're not going any farther than our conversation in the kitchen without one.'

'Can't you get one?' The look of surprise on Ellen's face mirrored what Mary was thinking. 'Even if all that money doesn't have any connection to who killed Miss

Emilie, someone had to have helped her, and there may be clues as to who did in the house.'

'So far, I haven't been able to convince the judge of that. He's of the opinion she turned up at the church hall and disturbed someone trying to steal something. He's leaning toward one of the homeless.'

'What would some poor homeless person be after?' Pat's tone was scathing. 'That old toaster, maybe? That would come in handy if you were living under the bridge.'

'I don't think she was killed for a toaster,' Mary said, 'or for any of the other things we have. None of those people would have a key, and there was no sign anyone had broken in. Besides, it's not likely Miss Emilie got down there on her own. She had help, and it wasn't from one of the bridge people.'

Dan picked up his glass and studied his beer, then set it back down and addressed Mary. 'Are you sure? That she had help, I mean. How foggy was she? That note she presented… Did she know the significance of it? Did she really not understand how much money five thousand dollars is? She knew enough to hide it. When she got lost, people took her home. Are you sure she didn't know where she was or did she just want company and a ride? Willis was pretty bizarre but he could have had a real significance to her. Maybe he reminded of her of real dogs she no longer had. Or, wasn't it you who told me she always said that as long as she had Willis she'd have nothing to worry about? Her father told her that. Maybe Willis was her Linus blanket.' He paused as if waiting for someone to say something, but no one did. He took a swallow of his beer. 'Is it possible she woke up and remembered she was trying to find him and where she'd been looking? Put on her robe and slippers and just gone down the stairs and out the door? If the judge is right and someone was already in the church hall, she wouldn't have needed a key.'

Mary knew she was staring at Dan, her mouth slightly open, but she didn't know how to answer. She looked over at Ellen, who seemed equally as stunned, then at Pat.

Pat appeared to be thoughtful. 'I didn't see much of her, but sometimes I wondered. Especially the rides—it was like a little game.'

'Yes,' Mary said slowly, remembering. 'She always seemed so pleased with herself when I took her home, as if she had a private little joke, but I thought that was… her being foggy. But there was one time…just a couple of weeks ago…'

'What?' Dan leaned forward as if to encourage her.

'We were sitting on the side porch. She was in the rocking chair, Willis in her lap.' Mary closed her eyes, trying to re-create the scene, trying to get it correct. 'I forget what we were talking about, but often you started talking about one thing and she'd veer off onto another subject for no apparent reason. I thought this was one of those times.'

'What did she veer off onto?' Ellen's interest was evident as she also leaned forward, her body tight with anticipation.

'She asked me if five thousand dollars was a lot of money.'

'What did you say?' Dan's interest was just as intent, but he kept his voice low and calm—unlike Ellen, who gave a little gasp.

'She caught me off guard and, of course, the question didn't seem relevant to anything. I said something like yes, it was and why did she ask? She just shook her head and went off about something else, I don't remember what.'

'All right.' Dan sat back and looked at each of them in turn. 'You all knew her, some better than others. Any thoughts on how much Miss Emilie really took in? Was she capable of returning to the church hall that night without help? Did she know how much money she had taken out and could she have hidden it?'

The people around the table once more fell silent as they looked at each other.

Finally Ellen spoke. 'I don't know. I drove her home once and visited her from time to time but I have no idea if she knew who I was.'

'None of you are sure, are you?'

They had to admit they weren't.

'Are you trying to say you think whoever killed her somehow knew about the money and killed her trying to make her tell him where it was hidden?' Somehow that idea didn't sit easily.

'It could have been a her.' Pat's voice was grim and her mouth was set in a straight line.

Ellen looked over at her, eyes slightly narrowed with no smile in them. 'Are you thinking what I'm thinking?'

'Gloria,' they said together.

'What makes you think of Gloria?' Dan's voice was still mild, but suddenly Mary saw where this was going.

They were his family, his friends; he didn't want to officially question them, he had no reason to, but they all knew what went on in town. Any one of them might have information that could be useful, information they might not even know they had. Their observations could possibly point him in the right direction. Like now. How cognizant was Miss Emilie of what went on around her? Why did Pat think of Gloria? She had crossed Mary's mind as well, but she wondered what made her cross Pat's.

Pat reddened slightly. 'It seems unfair to accuse her. I don't have one shred of proof, but Gloria was always there. Even after Miss Eloise died, she hung around. Lorraine complained about it a lot.'

Mary nodded. Lorraine hadn't been silent on the subject.

'Go on.' Dan's expression was neutral but Mary thought there was interest in his eyes.

'Well…' Pat didn't seem quite sure what to say next.

Ellen was. 'Gloria Sutherland has the reputation of being a snoop. She's evidently a competent LVN, although I've heard complaints she oversteps her authority there, too, but most of the complaints are that she snoops. She's been caught reading private mail, going through people's desk drawers—even managing to get passwords and logging on to her patients' computers. Can you imagine what she could discover by doing that?'

'I hadn't heard that!' Karl's face also reddened, but not from embarrassment, Mary thought—from anger. 'That's unethical.' Probably, next to murder, it was the worst crime Karl could think of.

Listening to gossip and repeating it as if it was gospel was one of the worst things Mary could think of. 'Are you positive about all that? I know Lorraine was upset with Gloria and I'm sure she had good reason—Gloria is annoying—but to say someone in her position of trust would go through private effects is a serious charge.' But even as she said it, she remembered John and Krissie. Had Gloria gone through Miss Eloise's bank records? Did she know how much money was in the Plym twins' trust account? Had she figured out a way to get Miss Emilie to withdraw huge sums and hand it over to her?

Was that what worried Miss Emilie? She increasingly lived in her own world, that was true, but she wasn't entirely removed from this one. She often didn't know morning from night, but she knew what a bank was for, and she remembered that she and her sister went there on the first of every month to get money. Just how much money, and what they did with it later, might not have had much significance to her, at least not most of the time. But from time to time she came up with statements that indicated she realized more than she let on. Was she beginning to understand that someone was stealing from her? Or suspect that might be true? Even though Mary had spent a lot of time with her, she still wasn't sure how much Miss Emilie understood or how much she remembered. Had she hidden her money because she was afraid of Gloria? And then had Gloria… Mary shook her head as if trying to rid it of these thoughts. She had no real reason to suspect Gloria. She had no real reason to suspect anyone. Yet.

Ellen interrupted her thoughts as she went on with her tale. 'Gloria's been fired from more than one job because she got caught doing just that. The home health agency where she worked won't use her for that very reason. I know because our office secretary's daughter works as an aide for the same agency and she told her mother.'

'Who in turn told you and the rest of the office?' Mary had a low opinion of gossip, as either a reliable source of accurate information or as a decent way to treat people, and it was obvious she considered this gossip, or as good as. But, once again, John and Krissie's story was reinforced.

Ellen grinned. 'Not the whole office. Only a couple of us.'

'And you two think Gloria might have killed her?' Mary looked from Ellen to Pat, with her best steely-eyed middle schoolteacher look. 'That would be a stupid thing to do. Gloria isn't stupid. Annoying, possibly unethical, but that doesn't make her a murderer.'

'Pat didn't say she thought Gloria killed her. Just that she might be…robbing her,' Ellen stated.

A shudder ran through Mary—part distaste and part sadness. She'd never liked Gloria much and her compulsive need to impress people. She succeeded in impressing them, but not the way she wanted. Mary had been surprised when she'd married the easy-going Mike Sutherland and saddened, but not surprised, when it only lasted a few months. Gloria returned home and went to school to become an RPN. As far as Mary knew, there had been no other men in her life. She'd thought her a sad person and more than slightly annoying, but a thief? That was hard to believe. She couldn't picture her as a cold-blooded murderer, either. She turned to Dan. 'Do you think she had something to do with this? How would you go about finding out?'

Dan stared at his plate, but Mary didn't think his frown had anything to do with fried rice drowned in sweet and sour sauce. 'Good questions.' He looked at each one of them in turn. 'I wish I had answers. Right now, I have no idea who was with Miss Emilie Wednesday night, nor do I know what happened to all that money. However…' his voice got softer, but the lines around the corner of his mouth deepened, '…I plan to find out.'

THIRTEEN

MARY STOOD ON the porch, fumbling for the key to her back door. Millie sat beside her, patiently waiting for it to open.

'Drat and blast. I've spent the best part of the last two days trying to open a door and something always goes wrong. Why on earth did I drop my car keys back in my purse?'

Millie didn't even look up.

'You're probably as anxious to get into bed as I am.' Mary pulled her hand out of the purse, keys dangling from her fingers. 'Found them.' She slipped the key in the lock; it turned easily and they were in. Millie checked her dinner dish—empty as she'd remembered—took a small drink and headed for Mary's and her bedroom.

Mary watched her as she set her purse on the kitchen table. The dog would be fast asleep before Mary ever got into the room, and not on her dog bed. She should have known better than to let her jump up on her bed the first night she came, but she was so scared, and Mary was so upset, and it didn't seem to be a terrible thing to do… Oh, well. Maybe she'd fix herself a cup of cocoa before she went to bed. Ellen had offered her a glass of wine with dinner but she'd refused. She'd been afraid that, as tired as she was, she'd fall sleep in the middle of her Moo Goo Gai Pan. She should have accepted. She was still very tired but somehow not sleepy. So many things had happened, there was so much to think about, her mind wouldn't let any of it go. Maybe a cup of cocoa would relax her. She hadn't made cocoa for herself in ages, but she was sure she had some of those little packages somewhere. She bought them for the children down the street, who often turned up at her house on cookie baking day. She'd given up trying to figure out how they knew. There was the box, pushed back on the shelf, almost out of sight. All she had to do was heat the water and… Didn't she still have an open bottle of Bailey's Irish Cream? She did. Maybe she'd add a teaspoon or two to her cocoa. In the meantime, her robe and slippers sounded very good.

The tea kettle was whistling when she returned to the kitchen. Good. The aroma of chocolate and Irish cream was soothing as she carried her mug over to the kitchen table and sat, absently stirring as she thought over the events of the last two days.

She couldn't shake the sight of Miss Plym sitting bolt upright in that straight chair, her head resting against its high back, her jaw slack, arms down by her side, and those ridiculous childish pink slippers on her feet. Why was she there? Who was with her? How did they get in? With a key, that seemed to be a given. She didn't know how many keys were floating around town but it seemed a goodly number. She had one. She did so many things at the church hall, fundraisers like the rummage sale, dinners for the homeless, committee meetings for just about everything, she never turned her key back in. It hung most of the time on her key hanger just inside the kitchen door. It was a line of black cats, their backs facing the room, all with long tails that curled up on the end, ready to accept your car keys or whatever else you wanted to hang. Millie's leash went on a tail next to Mary's key ring. St Mark's church hall key went on another and was marked with a cardboard placard bearing the initials SMCH printed in bright orange. Mary had made it and a number of others so the keys could be easily identified and, in most cases, quickly returned. Les was supposed to check them out and back in, but she suspected he rarely did. The 'why' Miss Emilie was there seemed to Mary to be a little more clear. She wanted her stuffed dog. She'd come to think of it as one of her beloved Shih Tzus. But the dog must have some other meaning if the killer was willing to risk taking her into a dark church hall in the middle of the night to find it. Or was that just an excuse to find something else? The clock? Why? The safe deposit key had been put back and the clock returned to the Plyms. No, there was something about the dog. Now, where was it? She'd brought it home... She looked around the kitchen, trying to retrace her steps when she returned home this afternoon. She'd stuffed it into her tote bag, paper sack and all, hadn't she? She'd set that down to answer the phone. It had been Leigh, giving her a dozen excuses why she wouldn't be able to help this Saturday with the adoption clinic. Mary had hoped her sigh of relief hadn't been heard over the phone. Evidently it hadn't, because Leigh kept talking. Mary had finally managed to cut the conversation short while assuring Leigh they'd manage. Where had she put her tote after that... There it was. Half hidden behind the door leading into the dining room, where she'd dropped it in her haste to get the phone. She pushed back her chair, carried the tote over to the kitchen table and pulled out the paper bag containing Willis. She set him on the table and looked at him. A dingy white long-haired dog with a top knot tied up with a pink ribbon.

The ribbon looked almost new; Willis' fur appeared a little sparse but carefully combed. Mary poked at him but nothing happened. No squeaks, no clunks, no strange noise. She picked him up and gave him a gentle squeeze. His stuffing rustled—a lot of stuffing, but nothing else. No loose seams, no tears or rips, no missing eyes or ears or anything else to indicate he was anything but what he looked like: a well-loved and cared-for stuffed toy dog. She sighed and started to put him back in his paper sack when she noticed a tiny rip in the seam right under his top knot. Her fingers explored it. Nothing. Just a small place where the threads had come loose, no doubt from many combings of that top knot. She finished stuffing him back into the sack. Now what? Bed, that was what. The cocoa had done its job, with perhaps a little help from the Irish cream, but suddenly she could no longer keep her eyes open. She deposited her cup in the sink, ran a little water in it but left it there. She gathered up Willis, sack and all, and carried him into her bedroom. He'd be safe on her closet shelf until she figured out what to do with him. Up he went, and Mary forgot about him in her hurry to finish her nightly ablutions and get into bed.

'Move over,' she told Millie, who groaned and did just that. Mary slid under the covers, yawned once and was asleep almost before her eyes closed.

FOURTEEN

'THIS IS REALLY worrying you, isn't it?'

Ellen sat at Mary's kitchen table, sipping coffee, watching her aunt with a worried frown on her face. 'Lorraine probably didn't mean she was really envious of your house—just that she and Caleb have to move. They've lived in that apartment, I don't know how many years, and living way out there makes her nervous.'

Mary nodded. 'I'm sure that's part of it.' She looked around her kitchen, at the pine cupboards that had been so popular fifty years ago but now looked only dated, at the yellow tiles she'd thought elegant when the house was new but today looked like old tiles that had been re-grouted one too many times. The window above the sink had been replaced; so had the kitchen floor and the dishwasher hadn't been there when she and Samuel moved in, but it was still a small house with nothing to separate it from many other small, old houses scattered around this aging town. 'But I think it's something more.'

'What?' Ellen put her coffee mug down and looked at her aunt expectantly.

'I'm not sure.' Mary paused, trying to put a feeling into words. 'There's an unease, an unhappiness about her that bothers me. I don't want to make this seem dramatic, but…'

'If I was married to Caleb, I'd be unhappy too.'

Startled, Mary sat up straighter and stared at her niece. 'Why do you say that?'

Ellen paused, looking thoughtful. 'He's…crafty. Oh, he's nice enough on the surface. Always smiles and says hello at church, helps with the cleaning up, works hard or I guess he does. The school seems happy with him, so do the people he does yard work for, but…he reminds me of a ferret. Except I like ferrets.'

Mary burst out laughing. 'You mean because he sort of darts around?'

'Maybe. No, I think it's because he slinks. You don't know he's even around and suddenly he appears, right in your face. He makes me nervous.'

Mary, still smiling, nodded. 'He does do that. And, I agree, I wouldn't want to be married to him either. Not because he slinks but because he's so controlling. I don't think Lorraine has had an easy time of it, all these years. I doubt she's made very many decisions.'

'Like Miss Eloise and Miss Emilie?'

Mary hadn't thought of it that way, but now she nodded. 'Probably. Miss Eloise certainly was the dominant twin. Maybe that's why Lorraine was so fond of Miss Emilie. She identified with her.'

Ellen picked up her coffee mug, pushed back her chair and headed for the sink. 'Maybe that's why Miss Emilie always seemed so vague: it was her way of getting out from under Miss Eloise's very large thumb. Are you going over to Furry Friends for the adoption?'

Mary barely heard her over the sound of running water. She waited until Ellen put her mug in the dishwasher before answering. 'A little later. Pat called. Only a few dogs showed up and just two cats so she said not to hurry. Oh. I almost forgot. She sent you a message.'

'Oh?' Ellen turned from the sink to stare at her aunt. She had gotten very still, and Mary thought her expression had turned guarded. 'What message?'

'That three-legged hound dog is one of the ones still up for adoption.'

'Wouldn't you know it.' Ellen let out a deep sigh. 'I suppose she let my husband know as well. He'll be over there, staring at the dog, with the same sad look the dog has. Damn! Jake's going to hate me for this.'

Mary opened her eyes wide and laughter bubbled up. 'Are you going to adopt that dog?' She looked at Millie, who had been asleep, her head on Mary's foot as usual, but who picked her head up and studied Ellen, ears slightly forward as if the conversation had finally gotten interesting.

'We talked about it last night. Or rather, Dan talked about it. I listened. So did Jake the cat. He really wants that dog.' She sighed. 'Dan, not Jake. I guess I'd better make a point of dropping by Furry Friends later this morning. I may be in the market for dog food.' She walked over and dropped a kiss on Mary's forehead. 'See you later.' The back door opened and closed behind her, but Mary sat on.

She kept thinking of what Ellen had said about Lorraine. And Caleb. Which made her think of Richard, rushing in and accusing them of a crime that might not even be a crime. Miss Emilie might have hidden all that money for reasons that only existed in a brain slowly losing its capacity to distinguish between reality and fantasy. She wished she could like Richard. He was the son of her late husband's best friend, but he seemed to go out of his way to make that impossible. Cassandra was as nice as Richard was rude. Or was she? She'd only recently given a thought to what moving to Shady Acres might do to Miss Emilie, and she didn't seem to give much more thought to the family things in the house. Her family things. She hadn't paid any more attention to Miss Emilie's well-being this past year than Richard had until she was informed that Miss Emilie was systematically taking large sums of money out of the trust. Money that would belong to her, as well as Richard, when Miss Emilie died. The more Mary thought about it the more she wondered.

FIFTEEN

Pat was right. There weren't very many people looking at the animals. Several children were tugging at reluctant adult hands and an older lady Mary didn't recognize, who stood in front of a very fluffy gray and white cat's cage, was staring at it, a speculative expression on her face. The cat looked past the woman at the tree on the edge of the parking lot, with no expression on hers. Pat stood beside the woman, silent, her shoulders drooping a little, also staring at the cat, but the expression on her face was more of exasperation than pleasure the cat might have found a new home. She brightened when she saw Mary and Millie.

'That is not a match made in heaven.' She walked close to Mary and indicated the woman who continued to stare at the cat. 'I don't know why that woman is even considering a cat. She's done nothing but say she can't bear hair on her furniture, she hates cat boxes, cats claw furniture and she'd expect any cat of hers to earn its keep by keeping the house free of mice. No halfway intelligent mouse would dare enter her house, and if she decides to fill out an application I've a good mind to tell her we only let people adopt cats who plan on letting them sleep on the sofa. That ought to do it. That's a nice cat. She deserves better.' She paused as if to catch her breath then bent down and gave Millie's ears a rub. 'Hello, Millie. How are you? Are you here to get a haircut?'

'Not today, but soon.' Mary looked at the dog. She really did have to make that appointment.

Millie wagged her rear end but stared at the cat, right along with the strange woman.

'What you need is a nice cup of coffee. How long have you been here? Have you found suitable homes for any of them?' Mary took Pat's arm and steered her toward the back door of the pet shop. Millie followed reluctantly, twisting her head to look back over her shoulder at the cat.

'Don't even go there,' Mary told her. 'I'm not getting you a cat.'

The dog seemed to sigh as she followed them over to the table that held a coffeemaker and white Styrofoam cups.

Pat filled one, handed it to Mary and filled another. 'I think we've only really placed one dog so far.' She smiled at Mary as she spooned powdered cream into her cup. 'Maybe two.'

'What's so funny? Oh, are they going to take that dog?'

'I'd bet money on it. That's a match that really is made in heaven. Dan would love that dog—so would Ellen, and Jake would get used to him. He's a neat dog; missing that rear leg doesn't seem to bother him a bit and he'd fit right into the family. Dan could take him into the station with him sometimes and he'd be fine left alone. Some dogs don't take well to that, but this one is pretty laid-back.'

Mary wasn't as sure of that as Pat seemed to be, but if that was what they wanted… She hadn't planned on getting a dog—it never crossed her mind. A cat had, once in a while, but never long enough for her to act on the idea. Millie had come to her accidently when her previous owner had been murdered, and she hadn't been with her more than one day before Mary realized she wanted her to stay. Evidently the dog felt the same as she'd settled right in. Now, she and Millie were rarely parted. The dog actually seemed to enjoy the committee meetings Mary attended and the events she so often chaired, and everyone who met her seemed to enjoy Millie. Her long, silky black cocker spaniel ears, her pretty face and her effervescent greeting for just about everyone she came across was hard to resist.

'What are you going to do with the dogs and cats that don't get homes?'

Pat sighed. 'What I always do. I've got foster homes lined up for a couple of them. The rest will go home with the rescue workers who brought them and we'll try again. There are a couple of dogs and a cat who haven't been spayed yet. Those we'll keep for a while. Karl will take care of that. We'll get them up to date on their shots and hope we can find homes locally. It's an uphill battle but I'm always thrilled when we get a good placement. Now, that woman over there, trying to stare down the cat, I'm sure she'll… Oh, there she goes.'

The woman gave the cat one last look. The cat looked right past her without acknowledging her. The woman glared at the cat, turned on her heel and walked out toward the parking lot. Pat audibly sighed with relief. Mary thought the cat did also but not as loudly.

'So, do you need help?' Mary asked, secretly hoping Pat didn't.

'Unfortunately, no.' Pat sounded somewhat distracted. Her attention had shifted to a woman who was being dragged forward through the store toward the back room by two children who were loudly proclaiming, 'You'll love him, Mom. He loves us, too. We can tell.'

'I'd better go see which dog those kids have decided is going home with them.'

Mary watched her receding back then turned to survey the store. John was ringing up someone who had a whole stack of dog-related supplies piled up on the counter. Two bowls, a collar, a leash, a bed, dog food and an assortment of dog toys. A small boy stood next to his mother, who held a taffy-colored dog of no particular breed. The boy kept petting the dog's leg while it squirmed in the woman's arms, trying to lick the boy's face. The mother beamed at the boy, who beamed at the dog. The father, who wasn't beaming, put down a charge card in front of John.

Mary smiled at Millie. 'Another dog just found a happy home.'

Millie wagged her behind.

'We might as well go for a walk before we go home,' Mary told her.

The word 'walk' had Millie on her feet and headed for the door almost before Mary could collect her purse, but she followed the dog onto the street. Mary felt at loose ends, a feeling she didn't much care for. However, a good brisk walk might do her good. She hadn't had much time to think—really think—and it was a lovely day.

Spring was doing its best to edge past winter, and today it felt as if it was winning. The trees were showing more than a hint of green; the plants that had looked like dead sticks all winter were studded with tiny nodules proclaiming they were alive and well. The hills on the edge of town, still planted with almond trees, were already dusted with pink almond blossoms.

Mary took a deep breath and let it out slowly. The sky was Wedgewood blue, the clouds fat and white and the breeze warm on her face. She smiled. Spring was almost here. She resolutely turned her thoughts away from the pet adoption, the postponed rummage sale and the reason it couldn't be held. Instead, she'd think of the Easter egg hunt the church was planning for the smaller children and how much fun it would be. Who could she talk into wearing the Easter bunny costume this year? She had almost succeeded in wiping Lorraine's distress at having to move, Caleb's resentment of Richard, Cassandra's rush to clean out the house and Richard's rudeness from her mind when a voice shattered her tranquil mood.

'Yoo-hoo, Mary. Wait up.'

Agnes. Mary sighed and stopped. So much for a tranquil walk. Agnes would want to talk, and Mary was sure it would be about someone. Probably Miss Emilie and the people close to her. Maybe she could sidestep it all somehow.

'Oh, Mary. I'm so glad I saw you. Are you going somewhere?'

Mary looked at Millie, who politely sat when they stopped and now looked at Agnes with, Mary thought, the same lack of enthusiasm Mary felt. 'Just for a walk.'

'Oh, good. Have you had lunch? I'm on my lunch break and thought I'd get a tamale. Juan has really good tamales. Why don't you get one and join me? We can sit on that bench and eat and talk. I have something I want to talk over with you.' She eyed Millie a little doubtfully. 'She doesn't want one, does she?'

'No. I don't think tamales are… Agnes, we're on our way home, so I don't think…'

'Good. Now you won't have to make yourself lunch.

You sit right there and I'll get them. Do you want hot sauce? I like those Mexican sodas. Orange. I'll get you one, too. Would Millie like water? Be right back.'

Mary knew when she'd lost. She and Millie walked over to the picnic bench and Mary sat. Millie lay down, her nose on Mary's foot.

'Drat and blast,' Mary said to Millie. 'I knew I shouldn't have tried to cut through the park.' She looked around at the few stands that had opened for the traditional farmers' market Saturday. Not too many bothered during the winter—there wasn't much produce and fewer customers. Even Juan's tamale wagon didn't come out. If you wanted fresh corn tortillas you could go to his store in San Felipe, a short drive north of Santa Louisa. Spring must really be on its way if he was back at the farmers' market.

'I got chile relleno and sweetcorn. Is that all right?' She put a white paper plate in front of Mary and set two orange sodas on the table. 'There. Now we can have a nice lunch. It's been ages since we've talked. I wanted to ask you, how are you? I know how hard all this must be, finding Miss Emilie like that. I just can't take it all in. Dan and I are working to find out what happened, but it's pretty confusing.' She started to unwrap her tamale, seemingly not noticing the expression on Mary's face.

Agnes helping with the investigation? Mary didn't think so. Agnes worked on the front desk, answering all non-emergency calls, directing people to the correct city office, doing the simplest of tasks. Her dark blue pants along with her light blue blouse were not Santa Louisa police uniform issue. She found them in the Army Navy store in Santa Barbara. She wore a thick black belt but not a single knife, pair of handcuffs or gun hung on it.

Especially not a gun. But she thought of herself as law enforcement and took her position, such as it was, seriously. She would have been taken more seriously by Dan if she'd learn to work the computer reliably.

Mary unwrapped her tamale, picked up her white plastic fork and took a bite. Delicious, as usual. 'What did you want to tell me?'

Agnes set her fork down and took a small sip of her orange soda before she spoke. 'You know the night Miss Emilie died.'

Mary nodded and waited for her to go on.

'I was out patrolling and saw something...actually someone, and I thought it was strange. I thought about telling Dan but...well, that didn't seem like such a good idea, but I need to tell someone, so I thought I'd tell you.'

Mary almost choked on her tamale. It took a moment and a big swallow of her orange soda before she dared speak. Agnes patrolling? 'Does Dan know you go patrolling?'

'Actually...it's not like I take a patrol car. Nothing like that. But we don't have a very big force and I just sort of drive around, making sure everything's all right. A sort of civilian patrol. You know, like the people who work with the sheriffs.'

Mary had heard of the citizens' patrol. The county was large and most of it rural. There just weren't enough sheriff's deputies to cover it all every night, so some of the citizens, mostly older people, took turns checking the ranches and back roads. They weren't allowed to carry weapons of any kind and were instructed to do nothing but call in anything or anyone that seemed suspicious. The incidences of rustling, where the thieves pulled a horse trailer up to a field in the middle of the night and threw a halter on someone's horse or cut a calf or two out of the herd and into the trailer, had decreased by half, according to Dan. He, however, had never seen the need for a citizens' patrol. Santa Louisa wasn't a very big town and, so far, his small force had managed just fine. He wouldn't be happy to hear Agnes had taken it upon herself to 'help.' No wonder she hadn't told him.

'I know.'

'It was Wednesday night.' Agnes pushed her half-eaten tamale aside but kept her eyes on the plate while she seemed to sort out her words. 'I thought I'd drive around here in town, just to make sure everything was all right. No drunks, no one trying to drive under the influence, especially those people who frequent that place.'

She gestured toward a row of businesses that anchored the east end of the park. There were only four—the art gallery, the movie theater, a candy and ice-cream store and, directly in the middle, the Watering Hole, the only place in town that had a full bar.

'The Watering Hole? You came out to see if you could spot someone drunk leaving the Watering Hole?'

'It wasn't quite like that. I've heard tales about that place, letting folks leave that could hardly walk, getting in their cars and trying to drive, serving drinks after hours… I even heard they serve minors. Thought I'd drive by and see for myself.'

What Agnes expected to see, while in her car, Mary wasn't sure, but she had seen something. 'All right. What did you see that's bothering you?'

'Gloria Sutherland.'

'Gloria…coming out of the Watering Hole?'

'No. Just walking down the sidewalk.'

'I don't understand. What was she doing?'

'Walking around the park. Then she walked down the sidewalk in front of that bar. When she got to the parking lot, I lost her.'

Mary shook her head, confused. 'Why shouldn't Gloria walk around the park? Lots of people do in the evening, especially if the weather's nice. Maybe she had gone to the movies and was stretching her legs before going home.'

'It was cold that night and it was after one. What was she doing wandering around the streets at that hour? Nothing was open except that bar. Maybe she had just come from there.' Agnes admitted the possibility grudgingly, 'But I've never thought Gloria the type to go to bars.' Distaste wrinkled the corners of her mouth as she considered the possibility.

'For heaven's sake, Agnes, it's not a den of iniquity. The Wallers run a respectable business. Lots of families go to the restaurant side. They have the best onion soup in town, and their hamburgers are famous. They have live music on the bar side on weekends, and people go to dance, play darts, watch sports and lots of things. There aren't many places around here where you can do things like that. Gloria could easily have gone for a glass of wine or some soup. Why did you think it was so sinister?'

'They may have great soup, but that wasn't what Gloria was after. They quit serving it around ten. She was on foot at one in the morning. All alone. She didn't see me. I was in my car but she was looking around as if scared to death. No. She was doing something she didn't want to be seen doing.'

Mary abandoned her tamale and gave Agnes her full attention. She didn't usually. Agnes was prone to gossip and usually wasn't too interested in getting her facts straight, but this was different.

'Did you tell Dan in the end?'

'I tried to. That man doesn't listen to me. So I thought if I told you, you could tell him. He listens to you. I don't understand it. After all, we work together, but that's the way it is.' Agnes shrugged her shoulders in resignation and rolled her eyes a little.

Millie lifted her head and looked at Agnes, then up at Mary, as if to ask what the woman was going on about. Mary didn't think it took much explanation to know why Dan paid her no attention—not if you knew Agnes.

'I'll talk to Dan about this.' Mary wadded up her paper plate, picked up her half-empty pop bottle and untangled herself from the picnic bench.

Millie was on her feet too, ready to be underway wherever they were going.

'Thanks for the tamales, and thanks for telling me. I don't know what it means but I'll be sure Dan knows.'

Agnes pushed her bench back a little and got to her feet as well. 'I have to get back. My lunch is only a half hour, but I'm sure glad you're going to tell Dan. It bothered me. Now, I'm not saying Gloria had anything to do with Miss Emilie being killed and all that, but she looked downright furtive, looking over her shoulder and all. Mary, are you going to throw that in the trash?'

Mary nodded, reached over and picked up Agnes' paper plate and napkin. 'You want the rest of your drink?'

'I guess. I can drink that at my desk.'

'Then we'll be on our way. Thanks again. See you in church tomorrow?'

'You bet.' Without another word Agnes walked off in the direction of the police department.

Mary watched her for a moment, and so did Millie. Mary looked at the dog. 'Well! What do you make of that?'

They walked over to the trash can, deposited the rest of the lunch and started down the brick path out of the park, Millie sniffing every tree and bush, Mary lost in deep thought.

SIXTEEN

MARY PULLED INTO the church parking lot in no frame of mind for the church service. She was tired, cranky and late. Not like her at all. She'd slept poorly, turning, tossing, dozing a little then waking up, unable to shake the thoughts that kept racing through her brain. Foremost was Dan's reaction to Agnes' extracurricular activities. He actually exploded. Better at her than at Agnes, but it hadn't been pleasant.

'What does that woman think she's doing?' he'd shouted over the phone. 'If I've told her once I've told her a hundred times. She's the office manager, not a cop.'

'Is she?'

'Is she what?' Dan had stopped his tirade.

'Is Agnes the office manager?'

Mary heard the pause with relief. At least he was thinking, not just yelling.

'Not really, but she likes to think she is, and I've never thought it hurt to give her that title. Seemed to make her feel important.'

'Agnes needs to feel important,' Mary agreed.

'She doesn't need to feel so damned important she goes out on patrol without telling anyone. Can you imagine what might have happened if she'd stumbled on a robbery? She could have gotten herself killed, or worse, gotten someone else killed. She's out of control.'

'What about Gloria?'

Another pause. 'Gloria.' A sound came over the phone that Mary couldn't identify. It seemed to be a combination of a groan, a gnashing of teeth and a swallowed curse.

Mary smiled. 'Yes, Gloria. Agnes has a point. That is a strange hour for someone to be out wandering around. Do we know approximately what time Miss Emilie died?'

This time Mary had no trouble identifying the groan.

'You and Ellen watch too much TV. The ME says most likely between midnight and two in the morning.'

'Oh, dear.' It was all Mary could think to say.

Was it possible Gloria could be the killer? Or involved in some way? Dan had gone on for some time, saying it didn't prove anything; it proved so little they had no reason to even ask her why she was out roaming the street, and they certainly didn't have cause to ask for a warrant to look at her bank records. The mention of bank records brought Mary up short. She hadn't thought about that but, of course, if Gloria had set Miss Emilie up somehow and had taken the money she had to have put it somewhere. But in her bank account? Wouldn't that be the last place someone would put stolen money? It would be the last place Mary would put it. But it had to be somewhere. Had Miss Emilie really given it to Gloria? Given Gloria's track record they couldn't rule out the possibility that, somehow, she'd tricked the old lady.

Mary had finally talked Dan out of firing Agnes, an act he'd have regretted but which Agnes probably deserved. She'd spent the night going over everything that had happened, trying to make sense of it. Had Miss Emilie gone back to the church hall looking for Willis or was it the clock she wanted? If so, why? Did it have something to do with the safe deposit key? Again, why? Dan said there was nothing in the box that mattered. However, by that he meant no money. Was there something else in there that mattered to someone? Mary couldn't think what it might be. Had Miss Emilie put something in it recently or taken something out that someone wanted? The bank would have a record of who went into the box and when. But Glen would have checked.

Dan seemed to have dismissed the whole safe deposit thing, so her theory that the key wasn't what whoever took the clock was expecting was probably right. That still didn't answer who took it and what had they expected? Had Miss Emilie hidden the money somewhere and had whoever opened the clock thought there was a clue inside as to its whereabouts? When they hadn't found one, had that same person tried to get Miss Emilie to tell them where it was and ended up strangling her? It was possible, she supposed, but likely? Those thoughts and a lot of others played tag most of the night. Mary had gotten up several times, to the consternation of Millie, to pace the floor, trying to put pieces together, but nothing made sense. The only thing that did was that someone was looking for that money and was determined to find it, no matter what the cost.

Finally, about four in the morning, she fell asleep. The only thing that woke her was Millie, standing on her chest, whining her need to go out. Mary had gotten out of bed in time for a quick shower and an even quicker cup of coffee before she had to be out the door. Millie hadn't been happy when she realized she wasn't included, but the grocery store and church were two places Millie wasn't welcome. Mary found a parking spot on the fringe of the lot, quickly took it and threw open the car door. Another car pulled in right beside her, its occupant appearing just as frazzled as Mary felt.

'Jackie Waller, just the person I wanted to talk to.'

'Mary McGill. You're late. Now that makes me feel better. You're never late.' Jackie smiled her wide toothy smile, grabbed Mary by the arm and started off toward the church at a trot. 'Les won't like it one bit if he's already started the service.'

'I know, and we can't talk now.' That came out a little breathlessly.

Jackie had a brisk trot.

'Are you going to the fellowship gathering after the service? I have something I want to ask you.'

Jackie held the door for Mary to enter. She had just time to say, 'You've piqued my curiosity. I'll see you afterward.'

The first hymn was in progress when they entered and took seats toward the back.

The service was all about Miss Emilie. Les didn't dwell upon the unhappy circumstances of her death, other than saying the police were investigating and if anyone had any piece of information, no matter how small, would they please contact the police department. He then went on to talk about her, about Eloise, about the family and what they had meant to Santa Louisa over the years, how Emilie's gentle ways would be missed and how we had all been blessed to have had her in our lives. He weaved that into a sermon about goodness and kindness and how any one of us could, at some time, need the help of others, how we may have to depend on the generous nature of our brothers and sisters. Mary was certain she wasn't the only one who needed a tissue as they left the church for the informal gathering in the Sunday school building.

Mary had been chairwoman of the hospitality committee that was responsible for refreshments after services for years, but last year, with so many other responsibilities, she had passed it off to Jessica Saunders, who was doing an excellent job. It gave her an unexpected pang, however, to walk into the hall and not immediately check the coffee level in the urn and make sure there were donuts and muffins on the tray, enough juice for the children and sugar and cream out for the adults. She was in the middle of giving herself a stern talking to, telling herself she couldn't do everything and it was good someone else had stepped up when Jackie Waller interrupted her mental tirade.

'Is this a good time or am I interrupting something important?'

Mary looked at her, startled, then smiled. 'It's actually a good time. I was just giving myself a little advice.'

'Something we should all do more often,' Jackie said with a straight face. 'What did you want to ask me?'

'Do you have coffee? Good.' Mary motioned her to follow and led the way to a couple of chairs in one corner that was, at least for the moment, empty. 'Sit down. This won't take but a minute, but I did want to know… Oh, dear. Please don't think I'm being nosy. There is a reason for all this.'

Jackie laughed and sat. 'I promise I won't. What's all this about?'

Mary looked around. There was no telling when someone would come up, wanting her or Jackie's attention. She needed to get right to the point. 'Has Gloria Sutherland been in your place lately?'

Jackie's jaw dropped, along with the hand that held her Styrofoam coffee cup. It sloshed but didn't spill. 'Gloria? Gloria Sutherland? Why on earth…no. I haven't seen her in…oh… I don't know how long. She used to come in for the fish and chips, but not lately. Why?'

'By herself ?' Mary let her shoulders drop. Disappointment? Relief ? She wasn't sure. That Gloria hadn't been in the Watering Hole didn't prove anything one way or the other.

'Yes.' All traces of a smile left Jackie's face. 'By herself. Unfortunately she didn't always stay that way. If there was a table with people she knew, no matter how slightly, she joined them. Just pulled up a chair and joined them. I've had customers walk out because of that. I've never known how to handle it and, I have to admit, I've been relieved she hasn't been in.'

Mary felt a wave of sadness wash over her. To think someone was so inept at social skills…if that was what it was. Hadn't she heard about some sort of personality disorder? Maybe that was Gloria's problem, but it didn't get her any further toward finding out what she was doing wandering around downtown at one in the morning.

Somebody was whistling. Mary looked around to see who it was but stopped when Jackie pulled her cell phone out of her jacket pocket.

Jackie looked at it, tapped in something then turned to Mary. 'I have to go. We have Sunday morning brunch today and Liam says one of the providers didn't show and he needs me. Now.' She dropped her phone back in her purse but stopped long enough to give Mary a long look. 'I don't know why you're asking questions about Gloria but I hope I've helped. One of these days, soon, I want to know what's going on. OK?'

Mary had only enough time to nod before Jackie disappeared through the hall door. One question was answered, but she didn't think it was an important one.

Gloria hadn't been in the Watering Hole that night. So what had she been doing wandering around town? As much as Mary didn't want to admit it, the church hall was in the direction Agnes said Gloria had come from. Was that where she'd been? If so, how did she get in? Had she gone in or had she seen someone else go in? And come out? That still didn't answer why she was out.

Maybe it was a coincidence that Gloria was out prowling around. Mary found coincidences suspicious. Gloria had, at one time, had a key to the Plym house. Did she still? Miss Emilie must have had help, if not getting out of the house then certainly getting into the church hall. Gloria knew the layout of the Plym house as well as she knew her own. She knew exactly where Miss Emilie's room was and could probably get up and down the staircase without turning on the lights… Was there a nightlight somewhere? This was getting her nowhere. The only thing she knew for sure was Gloria wasn't home in bed during the time Miss Emilie was killed. She looked around the room almost from habit, making sure everyone had what they needed, but her eyes came to an abrupt halt. Lorraine was in the kitchen, doing what Mary couldn't see, but Caleb was standing beside Cassandra Brown and her brother, Richard Plym. They were talking with Les and they all looked very serious. Were they talking about the funeral? She'd better find out if they needed any help.

'I didn't expect to see you here this morning. I'm so glad you came.' Mary used her most welcoming tone of voice.

Richard Plym glowered at her. Caleb scowled, but no more than usual.

Cassandra was the only one who smiled and it looked like it took a lot of effort.

'Thank you,' Cassandra said. She sounded as if saying even that was forced. 'We felt we should come and hear what Reverend McIntyre had to say. It was a beautiful sermon.'

The look of distaste on Richard's face seemed to encompass the hall, the people in it, the tepid coffee he held gingerly in one hand and the donut he held in the other. 'There was nothing beautiful about it. There hasn't been anything "beautiful" about any of this. That miserable old woman would have to go and get herself killed and leave all of her accounts in a mess. God knows how long it's going to take to get them straightened out, and that know-it-all banker isn't making matters any better. It's what you get when you have small-town people with small minds in charge of things.'

Mary couldn't have felt more paralyzed if she'd been turned into the proverbial pillar of salt. The smile on her face seemed pasted on, her hand, half outstretched, frozen. Had she heard right? Had Richard really said all those hateful things? He had.

'I can't stand here another minute, trying to drink this pig slop.' Richard indicated his coffee by rolling his cup back and forth. Some of it sloshed on the floor. Richard ignored it. Instead, he turned to Cassandra. 'I'm leaving. Are you coming?'

Cassandra's face was beet red, with rage or embarrassment, Mary wasn't sure. Probably both. She managed to shake her head. 'I'll walk.'

Richard paused for only a moment, then shrugged. 'Suit yourself.' He turned on the heel of his highly polished loafer, pausing only long enough to dump both coffee and donut in the trash container that sat beside the door.

Caleb watched him go without a word then glanced at Cassandra. 'Nice guy, your brother. Real polite and all.' Then he turned on the heel of his unpolished work boot and stalked off toward the kitchen, muttering things Mary was sure she didn't want to hear under his breath. He grabbed Lorraine by the arm and pulled her over to the back of the kitchen. His face contorted, his fist upraised, Mary watched Lorraine shake her head and, for one awful moment, thought that Caleb's fist was going to meet Lorraine's nose. No. He hovered right in front of her, pushed her up against the counter and stormed out the same door Richard had used. Was he going after Richard? Mary hoped not. They'd had enough trouble to last out the year; they didn't need any more.

Les stood beside Mary, also in shock. 'I'd better go see if Lorraine is all right.'

Mary could barely make out his words but she saw the pitying look he gave Cassandra. So did Cassandra. Mary heard the little hiss as she sucked in a breath. They both watched Les as he approached Lorraine, who hadn't moved since Caleb stormed out. Les took her by the arm and led her to a chair right next to the kitchen door. He placed her in it, pulled another up to sit beside her, leaned over and started to talk. Mary took a deep breath of relief as Lorraine answered him. Mary turned her attention to Cassandra, whose face had faded to the color of white bread.

'Oh, Mary. I'm so sorry. Richard is… He's never been easy but… He's gotten so much worse since… He's acting like a pompous ass.'

Mary thought that evaluation grossly understated, but she didn't say so. 'Since what?'

Cassandra blanched. Mary didn't think she was going to answer, but suddenly it all came out. 'Since the furniture stores took a nosedive and his wife took a hike.'

Mary blinked as she stared at Cassandra. That sentence contained more clichés than Mary thought necessary, but she'd gotten her point across. 'You mean his wife left him?'

Cassandra nodded.

'Oh, dear. How awful. Do they have children?'

Cassandra nodded again. 'Josh is about to graduate from college and Annabelle is a sophomore majoring in chemistry, of all things. As far as Tiffany is concerned, it's no loss. She stuck it out as long as the money flowed freely. As soon as it slowed to a trickle, she left.'

Cassandra's face had tightened into a scowl and her voice had an edge Mary had never heard from her before.

It seemed a good time to change the subject. 'He has a furniture store?'

'Stores. Four of them. Very upscale. He sells to the very rich or the people who decorate the homes of the very rich. Only, these last few years, even the very rich have cut back. He's closed one of the stores and has turned two of them into stores for the rest of us. You know, lounge chairs with footrests, sofa beds and coffee tables with never-mar tops. He could hardly bring himself to do it but it was either that or close them. I think he's just holding on until this recovery we're supposed to be going through is complete. But that's no excuse for the way he's acting.' She sighed, a shuddery kind of sigh. 'I don't know why I agreed to let him come with me. I knew he'd make trouble.' There was what sounded like a sob in her voice as she said this. She stood a little straighter and took a deep breath. 'There's some money missing. Glen Manning told me about it. I came out here to see what was going on. That's why Richard insisted on coming. But so far we have no idea where it is and it's driving him crazy.' She sniffed again, hitched her purse up higher on her shoulder and tried to smile. 'I'm sorry. I didn't mean to dump all this on you but I seem to keep doing it.' She blinked rapidly then sighed. 'I'd better go see if Lorraine's all right. Caleb isn't any easier.'

She turned and walked toward Lorraine, who still sat hunched over in the folding chair.

Mary watched for a minute then looked around. The hall was emptying quickly. She started to follow Cassandra but stopped. Cassandra already had her arm around Lorraine, almost protectively. Les said something to them both and went into the kitchen.

Mary veered off and went into the kitchen as well. 'Les.'

He stopped and waited for her. 'This has been a Sunday morning to remember.'

'Is Lorraine all right?' Mary glanced around the kitchen but the only two volunteers left were busy collecting empty cups and crumpled napkins, putting leftover donuts in boxes and washing down the sink. No one was paying any attention to them. Nonetheless, she kept her voice low.

There were worry lines around Les' eyes and an uncertain tone in his voice. 'I think so. Lorraine's been getting more and more edgy for a while now, and I'm not too sure why.'

'Since Miss Eloise had her stroke?'

Les nodded. 'I know she was worried about Miss Emilie, but she really seemed upset when she found out Cassandra and Richard were coming to see for themselves how bad she'd gotten. All that talk about putting her in Shady Acres really bothered Lorraine.'

Mary nodded. 'She told me Caleb wants to move them into the mobile home they have out in Almond Tree Acres. She doesn't want to go.'

'She told me, also, but I think there's something else.'

'What?'

'I don't know. I wondered if it might be something to do with their son. I think he'd like his mother to move to Seattle to be near him, but he can't stand Caleb, so that would be...difficult.'

Again, Mary nodded. 'Difficult, indeed, but if I was Lorraine I'd jump at the chance. Life with Caleb can't have been easy.'

Les laughed—a wry kind of laugh. 'Just what I was thinking. And now she's got two difficult men to deal with. At least Richard's sister seems nice. I think she likes Lorraine, so maybe she can help.'

Mary wasn't so sure, but there wasn't much she could do about it and she wanted to get home to Millie. She glanced at the chair where Lorraine had sat. It was empty, so there was no reason for her to stay. Something caught her eye as she turned to go. There, right beside the kitchen door, hanging on a hook, were two cardboard key holders, the initials SMCH in bright orange letters proclaiming where they belonged and what door they unlocked. 'Les, look.'

'At what?'

'Keys. Right there. Keys to the community hall.'

'Yes. I've asked the ladies to hang them there when they're finished so we don't keep losing them.'

'Do you know who hung those?'

A slight flush crept up Les' neck and over his cheeks. 'Well, no. I guess whoever is going to open up the room for an event just takes one and puts it back when finished.'

Mary looked at him, appalled. When she was head of the hospitality committee the management of the keys was not handled so...carelessly was the only word she could come up with. 'Les, have you told Dan how you handle the keys?'

'I just started this system. I hope we can keep better track this way. It's easier than handing out a key every time someone wants to use the hall or to put something away or...' The worried look in his eyes intensified. 'I know the other way was lax. Do you think...'

'I think this is even more...inefficient. We need to get a locksmith out to rekey everything and then come up with some kind of system where we have control of who has a key and when they return it. There's enough money in the treasury to do that. Let's take it up at the next board meeting.'

Les nodded, a bit sadly. 'I'm sure you're right. Can you call the locksmith?'

Mary started to protest but stopped. As chairperson of the steering committee she would have no problem getting the board to authorize the expense, but she'd have to get some estimates. It was one more thing to add to her list, but the work had to be done and, if she did it, she'd know it had been done. 'As soon as the board agrees. I'd better get home. Millie is all alone and she's not too fond of that. I'm going to see Dan this afternoon. I'll be sure to tell him about the keys. I don't see how it helps much, but he should know.'

Les nodded, still looking miserable, but he turned to thank the last of the volunteers who were also getting ready to leave. Mary checked to make sure she had her car keys and walked out of the hall doorway, pulling the door closed behind her. It was a good thing she had a short drive home through streets that would be largely deserted this time on a Sunday morning. Her mind was full to bursting with things that had nothing to do with oncoming traffic and stop lights.

SEVENTEEN

MILLIE YELPED, HOWLED, barked and ran in circles as Mary came in the door, finally giving it all up to stand as close to Mary's knee as she could get while her ears were scratched.

'It's nice to be welcomed home, but don't you think you're overdoing it a bit?'

Millie didn't. She followed Mary around the kitchen as she put the kettle on for tea, took bread and tuna out of the refrigerator for a sandwich and set a banana on a plate. Mary handed Millie a dog cookie as she pulled out her chair and settled in to eat. Millie lay right beside her, munching her own lunch.

'Too bad they don't allow dogs in church,' Mary told the dog between bites of her sandwich. 'It was a most interesting morning. I'm not sure I learned anything important, but it was interesting.'

Millie made a little growling noise, which Mary interpreted as an indication Millie wanted to hear more.

'Agnes...you remember her, don't you? She works for Dan at the police station... We had lunch in the park with her—she's the one who decided to do a little extra patrolling downtown the night Miss Emilie died. She claimed she saw Gloria coming from the direction of the church and that she was headed home, or at least in the direction of her home. Remember? She wasn't coming from the Watering Hole, which was the only place left open at that time. Jackie says she hasn't been there for a while. Then Richard Plym was unbelievingly rude to Les and mentioned money was missing. Cassandra was appalled, and I don't think it was the first time. She apologized all over the place and said he's been under a lot of stress lately. Business failing, his wife left him… I couldn't help but wonder if he came out here to see how much money he could wring out of the ladies' trust fund. I'm not sure how much is left after Miss Emilie's withdrawals, but there is the house.' She paused, her sandwich halfway to her mouth. 'It seems to me I heard… I wonder if it's true. Now, who told me…why, Sam did! Years ago. I can't remember what we were talking about, but…' She paused to unpeel her banana. Millie looked up, decided she had no interest in bananas and went back to worrying her cookie.

'It must have been about the Plyms because I remember he said the house couldn't be sold while either of the twins was alive or until they had to go into a care facility.' She took a mouthful of banana and chewed thoughtfully. 'Do you suppose that's why they wanted to put Miss Emilie in Shady Acres?'

Millie made faint growling noises while she also chewed. Mary watched her for a moment then got up and took her empty plate to the sink, rinsed it and put it in the dishwasher. She turned, wiping her hands on the dishcloth and addressed Millie once more.

'I wonder if they could have sold the house once Miss Emilie was living in Shady Acres.'

Millie looked up then returned her attention to demolishing the last of her cookie.

'I'm glad you agree with me. It certainly doesn't look good for Richard, but then, it doesn't look very good for Gloria, either.' She walked back over to the table, pushed her chair back, bent down and wiped the floor under Millie's face with a damp paper towel. 'You certainly manage to get crumbs everywhere. I thought dogs licked them up. From now on you're going to have to eat yours in your dish.' She stood, with an alarming creak of her right knee, and headed for the trash can. 'The Duxworths were certainly in a position to steal from her, but somehow… Do you suppose Gloria got all that money? That she's got it tucked away somewhere?'

Millie didn't answer. She watched as Mary started to wipe down the counter. Mary finished, turned and leaned up against the counter and stared at Millie. 'Caleb is a cantankerous old coot. How Lorraine has put up with him all these years, I don't know. But he is a hard worker. He keeps the Plym grounds lovely, Mr Blankenship at the grade school seems pleased with his work and he does several other people's yards. That's a lot. He and Lorraine must have known their time at the Plym house was limited, however. The sisters were old. They were bound to die or need more care. That would mean he and Lorraine would have to find someplace to live that would involve paying rent and utilities. You'd think that would be a good reason to keep Miss Emilie alive and well. Unless Caleb has money put aside. A lot of money.' She stopped as another thought occurred to her. A horrifying thought. 'Lorraine. She wants to live in town. You don't suppose she put Miss Emilie up to giving her that money, that she thought she could buy a house… It was a lot of money but nowhere near enough to buy a house. Besides, she loved the sisters.' She paused.

Millie cocked her head to one side and gave a small bark.

'You're right. She wouldn't.' She pondered this unwelcome thought for a moment until Millie once more interrupted with a series of small barks.

The dog got up, went to the back door and barked again, then looked at her leash and barked a third time.

'A walk? Is that what you want?'

Millie started to turn in circles, barking and whining. She jumped up, trying to grab her leash, then ran to the door then back to Mary, who watched this performance with amusement.

'All right. You haven't been out lately and it's a beautiful day. I think a walk will do us both good.'

A destination was running through her mind. Why, she wasn't sure. Walking by someone's house wasn't going to tell her anything. However, she had to walk somewhere. The phone rang.

'Oh, Ellen. I wasn't expecting to hear from you. You sound… Is everything all right?'

There was a note of something in her niece's voice that Mary couldn't quite place. She was even more surprised when Ellen said she and Dan would like to come over, if that was all right?

'Of course, but I was just about to take Millie for a walk. Do you…' Before she could finish, Ellen interrupted.

'Even better. Can you wait for us? We'll be there in ten minutes.'

'Of course.' Mary hung up the phone.

Millie was dancing in circles and Mary wasn't sure she could restrain the dog that long, but Ellen sounded elated.

Curiosity was stronger than Millie's need for a walk. 'Just hang on, we'll go, but I'm not going walking in my church clothes.'

She was tying her shoelaces when the front door opened and a voice called out, 'Hi.'

Ellen, Dan and a large three-legged dog walked into the kitchen.

Mary and Millie stared at the dog. He stared back.

'He's…big.' It was all Mary could think to say. He was big. His sleek coat was black and white, eyes large and brown. His ears folded over slightly and his long tail had a white tip on the end.

Millie was more direct. She walked over to him, stood under his large head and looked up. The dog looked down at her. Mary held her breath. Both tails started to wag. The big dog dropped his head and sniffed Millie. Her rear end wagged harder. Mary let her breath out with a sigh.

'I think they like each other.'

Ellen laughed. 'I think they do. Now, if we can just convince Jake that Morgan isn't going to eat him, or even chase him and that's it's all right to come down from the bookcase…'

'Morgan?' Mary looked down at the dog, then at Ellen. 'You named him Morgan?'

'He came with that name.' Dan sounded gloomy. 'I thought we'd name him Spot, but he only answers to Morgan.'

Mary thought she heard a small laugh from Ellen. 'I think Morgan is a fine name. He's a good-looking dog and Millie seems to like him. Jake will come round.'

'Eventually.' Ellen didn't sound convinced. 'We thought we'd introduce him to you and Millie and join you on your walk.'

'That's a wonderful idea. But can he walk all right without a leg?'

'This dog can outwalk the three of us.' Dan sounded

as proud as if the dog had just won an Olympic medal. But if the dog really could… Mary decided it was worth a try. She only hoped the dog could climb hills. She hoped *she* could.

'Well, then, I'm ready and so is Millie. I'll just get her leash.'

'Where are we going?' Ellen stood at the bottom of the steps watching Morgan tow Dan down the sidewalk. Mary closed her front door, checked to make sure it was locked, and then she and Millie joined Ellen.

'No place in particular. We'll go up here a few blocks then over a little and then home.' Mary's voice was deliberately neutral.

Ellen looked skeptical but only nodded. They walked on, across Main Street, past the inn, up 12th Street to Elm, then crossed over to Maple and started up the hill. Even the dogs were willing them to stop when they got to the top.

'What a lovely view,' Ellen said.

The town spread out below them, the river that separated it dry this time of year but nonetheless impressive. The almond trees were in full bloom, pink flowers covering the adjoining hillsides. The buds on the oak trees were swelling, ready to burst into leaves, and the grapevines that covered more and more of the hillsides every year showed just the tiniest hint of green.

'I don't know what was wrong with Spot. I had a dog named Spot when I was young. He was a great dog. This one's going to be a great dog, too. Morgan's a dumb name for a dog,' Dan grumbled.

'You don't have to name him Morgan,' Mary pointed out. 'He's your dog.'

'See Spot run.' Ellen smiled.

'What?' Dan looked at her.

'See Spot run. See Dick run. See Sally run. It's what I always think of when I hear a dog named Spot.'

Dan looked at her, then at the dog. 'I suppose you like Morgan.'

'Actually, I do, sort of.'

The dog looked up at the sound of his name, or what Mary supposed was about to become his name. He got up and came and sat at Ellen's feet.

'I give up.' Dan shrugged and looked around then turned to look at the house they stood in front of. 'Isn't that Gloria Sutherland's house?'

Mary had to admit it was.

'Why are we here?'

She didn't answer. She couldn't. She wasn't quite sure why she'd wanted to come, but now she was here, she stared at it. It was a ranch-style house that still had its 1950s heavy shake roof, a rarity in the California fire-prone foothills. The shakes were green with mold. So were the overloaded gutters that hung under the roof. The red paint on the fascia boards was faded and peeling in spots, as was the red front door. The windows were single paned and slid open in aluminum casings. Mary wasn't sure these slid very far. Some of the troughs looked caked with mud. The brick front porch, however, was swept and clean. No pots of flowers decorated it, no flowering plants showed their fresh spring buds in the yard but the shrubs that grew were trimmed almost militarily. The yard had not one stray leaf left over from autumn. The house might not be in the best of shape but the yard was.

Gloria's elderly Toyota sat in front of the slightly sagging garage door. An old grape stake fence could be seen on the far side of the garage, a closed gate in the middle and gravel in front of it. A service yard, but no trash containers were in evidence. There was nothing to show the house was lived in but the car. Mary walked over to join the rest, looking out at the town below. Gloria might be in there. Was she watching them from behind the draperies that covered the plate-glass window, wondering what someone she knew was doing staring at her house? That a group of people and dogs were at the end of her street, staring out over the guard rail to view the town below was probably no surprise. She must be used to it. Her street, her house, was known for its wonderful view. Mary turned to look again at the house. There was no sign anyone was behind the drapes, no faint hint of movement. Gloria must be home, but if she knew they were there she had no intention of acknowledging them. Well, there was no reason she should.

Dan held Morgan's leash tightly as the dog peered down the hill. A low growl grew in his throat and the hair on the back of his neck stood up. 'What's the matter with this dog?'

The leash in Mary's hand tightened as Millie dropped into her attack crouch. She, too, stood at the top of the hill, looking down it through the almond trees, seeing something Mary couldn't. She whined and tried to crawl under the guard rail, but Mary pulled her back.

'Something's down there.' Dan tightened his hold on Morgan's leash. 'Probably a coyote or a fox. Whatever it is they don't need to tangle with it. Are you ready to go?'

Mary nodded and pulled Millie closer to her side. She didn't think Millie was any match for a coyote and had no intention of letting her find out.

Dan tugged on Morgan's leash but the dog continued

to stare down the hill, his throat still rumbling. 'Come on, Spot.'

The dog didn't move.

'Morgan, let's go.' He immediately left his post to walk quietly by Dan's side. Dan muttered something unintelligible as he started down the hill.

Ellen took Mary's arm, her grin threatening to split her face. 'I think his name is Morgan.'

'I think you're right,' Mary said, trying to make sure Millie stayed on her left side. She, also, was reluctant to go.

'Did you find out what you wanted?' Ellen's voice was low and curious.

'Whatever do you mean?'

'You know exactly what I mean. Did you?'

Mary frowned. 'I'm not sure. I found Gloria could easily have walked home that night. It's a bit of a trek to get up this hill but she's probably done it a million times. She grew up in that house. It's not in very good repair, but the yard is. I don't understand that.'

'That's easy. Caleb's taking care of the yard. I know because he complained loudly she was behind on paying him. Said he wasn't going back until she got caught up.'

Mary stopped to stare at Ellen. Millie, caught unaware, also came to an abrupt halt and made her displeasure known with a large yelp.

Mary ignored her. 'When was this?'

'When Cassandra was here for Miss Eloise's funeral. She'd called and asked me to come over and talk about possibly selling the house in the not-too-distant future. She felt even then that Miss Emilie needed more consistent care and selling the house might be necessary. We were in the kitchen, talking, when Caleb came in, practically spitting flames. Said he wasn't going back, Gloria made good money taking care of Miss Eloise and she could sure as… I'll delete that part…pay him. Cassandra asked him to leave, actually told him he was interrupting, and he did. But not before he took a long hard look at me. I think that was the first time it occurred to him that he and Lorraine would have to move.'

Millie tugged at the leash, probably upset the other dog was so far ahead, and Mary started walking again.

'She must have paid him. The yard doesn't look neglected. In fact, it's a yard coming into spring healthy and in good shape.'

Ellen nodded. 'Caleb probably leaned on her pretty heavy. Gloria's not known for letting a penny go easily.'

'Hurry up,' Dan hollered as he tried without much success to reel Morgan in. 'Let's stop by the dog park and let these dogs run.'

Ellen laughed and yelled they'd meet them there. Dan and Morgan trotted ahead but Ellen and Mary kept to a good steady walk. Had Millie ever been to the dog park and, if not, would she be all right? Mary wasn't too sure of her ability to intervene if Millie got into trouble. But then, Ellen and Dan would be there to help if she needed them.

Mary smiled at Millie. 'You'll love the dog park.' She hoped she was right.

Ellen hurried ahead, which was fine with Mary, who was beginning to feel tired. Millie wasn't. She tugged at her leash, head up, stub of a tail wagging. The fence surrounding the dog park was right ahead. Morgan was already in the holding area, waiting for them. A thought, unrelated to dogs, had started to form in the back of Mary's brain but retreated as Millie's ears pricked forward and she tugged at the leash. Mary smiled and walked a little faster. She'd worry it all through later. Right now, her legs felt like they had ten-pound weights on them, and the bench inside the park fence looked more than a little inviting.

She unsnapped Millie's leash and sank down beside Ellen. Not only did her legs thank her but it was safer sitting. The dogs, free of any restraints, were eager to show off how fast they could run to their friends, both new and old. A serious game of chase was on. Dan stood in the middle of the area, trying to direct traffic with little success while talking to another dog owner, someone Mary thought looked familiar but couldn't quite place.

'Tired? That hill was no easy climb.'

Mary looked over at her niece and reluctantly admitted she was. Ellen looked a little winded as well, a thought that gave Mary a small twinge of pleasure. Maybe her tired legs were just a result of not being used to climbing hills and had nothing to do with her seventy-plus years. She just needed to go to her Silver Sneakers exercise classes more regularly.

The dog pack roared past her, yelping and growling, ears flying, eyes glowing with pleasure.

Mary pulled her feet back as far as she could and put her tote bag up on the bench. 'They seem to be having a great time. I'll have to bring Millie again.'

Ellen smiled as she watched Dan try to keep from being run over. 'We'll have to bring Morgan also. Missing a leg doesn't seem to bother him at all. I have to admit, I was worried he'd have trouble, but he more than keeps up.'

'He's getting tired, though.' They watched as Morgan stopped next to the dog-friendly water fountain and took a long drink. He then ducked his head under the flowing water and shook water all over himself and the other two dogs trying to get a drink. They didn't seem to mind.

'Mary, can I ask you for a favor?' Ellen seemed a little hesitant and Mary looked over at her, puzzled. Ellen didn't usually ask for favors and she was almost never hesitant.

'Of course. What do you need?'

Morgan roared past them once more, this time with Dan in hot pursuit. 'We need to get going,' he hollered at them as he tried to catch the dog.

Ellen nodded then turned back to Mary. 'Cassandra texted me. She wants me to come over tomorrow to do all the preliminary things that need doing before we list the house. Would you come with me?'

A start of surprise ran through Mary. 'If you want me to, but why?'

Ellen didn't say anything for a minute. A slight flush started up her cheeks and her mouth twisted into a frown. 'Richard. He'll be there, I know he will, and he makes me nervous. I want someone with me.'

Mary's breath caught in her throat. Richard was rude and difficult, but surely not dangerous. Unless Ellen meant…

Ellen smiled. 'No, nothing like that. It's just I'll have to walk through the house, measuring it, making notes, asking questions, and I'd bet real money he's the kind who'd say later something was missing after I went through everything or that I promised something or gave a value to something that wasn't true. I don't trust the man. Also, I don't think he'll be as rude if you're there. He bullies his sister and I know he'll try to bully me. Somehow, I don't think he'll be quite as obnoxious if you're there.' Almost as an afterthought, she added, 'Bring Millie.'

'He may try to bully Cassandra, but I don't think it works very well. I don't know if I'll be much help, but if you'll feel easier…' Mary quickly ran through her schedule for the next day, Monday, usually one she devoted to household chores and phone calls. She seemed to recall, however, something…the committee meeting for the Easter egg hunt on the church lawn for the preschoolers. What time were they meeting? Early, she thought. While the children were all in preschool at the church and the mothers were available. Nine—that was it. That shouldn't last more than thirty to forty-five minutes. She already had everything planned, she just needed to confirm which volunteer was doing what and make sure they understood their allotted task. She did, however, have a list of phone calls she had to make, the rummage sale had to go off as planned on Thursday and she needed to do a lot of follow-up to make sure the publicity she needed to announce the new date was getting out. She especially wanted to call the radio station. Everybody listened to the local station. She'd also have to be prepared for the barrage of phone calls she'd be getting from people who planned on using the church community room. She'd work with Les and Ysabel on finding them alternative facilities. What was she forgetting? The Friends of the Library book sale committee meeting. No, that was next Monday. This Monday was, all in all, a quiet day. 'What time?'

Ellen grinned. 'How about eleven? We can go to lunch afterward and discuss how it went.'

'I'm not sure about lunch, but eleven should be fine. Shall I meet you there?'

'I'll call you in the morning after I confirm the time with Cassandra.' Ellen stood, stretched and held her hand out to Mary. 'We're both going to be sore tomorrow.'

Mary took her hand and got to her feet. Millie, who'd slowed down to a trot, came over and sat beside her. Mary quickly clipped the leash onto her collar. Dan had Morgan, but barely.

'Are you ready to go?' Mary asked.

Dan nodded. He was the first one at the gate, holding Morgan's leash tight.

The short walk home was slow, even the dogs seemingly content to stroll quietly, sniffing interesting trees and bugs as they went.

Ellen and Dan chatted about how well Morgan was doing as they walked, hoping Jake would accept him soon. Mary listened with only half an ear. Suddenly she was very tired. Her legs hurt and so did her head. She wasn't used to climbing hills, even small ones, and she wasn't used to murder. The sight of Miss Emilie kept creeping back into her memory at unexpected times and she couldn't help thinking of who'd left her sprawled, dead, on that chair. How could anyone? Why would anyone? They were almost home. Millie tugged at her leash. She probably wanted a full dinner dish. Mary wanted to sit down.

'Are you all right?' Ellen had fallen back to walk beside her and looked at her with concern.

'Fine. I'm just tired, that's all. I need to get out and walk more.'

'Good idea. You don't have enough things to do.'

Mary laughed. 'Most of what I do doesn't involve this much walking.'

'I thought you went to that Silver Sneakers exercise class they have at the YMCA.'

Mary nodded. 'Two mornings a week. I think I need to make it three. We do a whole lot of different exercises but we don't climb hills. The backs of my legs are screaming at me.'

Ellen smiled a little ruefully. 'So are mine.' She stopped. 'Here we are. Do you want me to come in?'

Mary shook her head. 'You go on home. Millie and I will be just fine.' She started up her front stairs, not her usual way of entering, but she didn't think she could walk around the house, through the gate and climb the back stairs. Millie bounded up the stairs with seemingly as much energy as when they left the house. Mary glared at her then turned and waved goodbye to Ellen, Dan and Morgan.

'Call me later,' Ellen said.

Mary nodded and unlocked the door. Millie trotted in, through the living room, into the kitchen and sat down in front of the closet where the dog food was kept. Mary stopped in the kitchen doorway, looked at her and sighed.

'All that walking up hills and running has evidently made you hungry, but hold on a minute. I'm turning on the tea kettle first.' That done, she returned to the closet, scooped food into Millie's dish and sat down, waiting for the water to heat.

'We didn't learn a thing, but I'm not sure what I thought staring at Gloria's house would tell us. I wonder where she was. Of course, I didn't expect her to run out and ask us in for a visit, but still, the house looked almost deserted. If her car hadn't been there, I'd have sworn she…' Mary stopped and thought. 'I was going to say left. Now, why would I think that? Where would she go?'

The tea kettle whistled.

Mary took her tea into the living room, set it on the table and sank gratefully into her favorite chair. Did she want to watch TV? No. Millie came into the room and stood in front of Mary, who moved over. The dog jumped up and put her head in Mary's lap. Mary let her hand rest on Millie's head, leaned her head back and closed her eyes. She'd just rest them a minute and let her tea cool off while she thought through a number of things. When she opened them again, her tea was stone cold.

EIGHTEEN

MARY'S KNEE WAS stiff. She limped a little as she wrapped her robe more tightly around her on her way to the kitchen. Millie was already standing at the back door, ready to go out. Mary opened it, watched the little dog bolt down the stairs, closed it again, walked, or rather limped, over to the counter and pushed the button on the coffeepot. It hadn't been a particularly good night. Questions about how to make the rummage sale a success to why Miss Emilie was in the church hall and who she'd been with had refused to leave her alone until early this morning, when she'd finally fallen into a deep sleep, and she was running late. Again. This wasn't like her. Perhaps a good hot shower would help. If she was going to climb hills, or even take long walks, she'd better work up to it more gradually. Millie came back in, looking for breakfast. Mary obliged then headed for the shower, holding a full cup of coffee. It was already seven thirty, and she had to be at St Mark's for her preschool Easter egg hunt meeting by nine. Then she had to meet Ellen at the house and somewhere in there she wanted to talk to Glen Manning. There were some things about the withdrawals Miss Emilie had made that bothered her, but not as much as where the money was now, or how to go about finding it.

She took a look at the weather through her bedroom window before laying her clothes on her bed. It hadn't changed. Overcast with possible rain. The radio confirmed it: unusually chilly for the first of April. Sweatpants and a sweater were called for. Thinking spring couldn't get here fast enough, she turned on the shower.

The meeting was held in a classroom in the Sunday school building. There weren't too many people there. Les, of course, a few young mothers with babies in strollers and more than a few grandmothers. Joy was one of them. She stared at Millie as if she disapproved of her presence. Mary readied herself to defend Millie's right to attend but Joy surprised her.

'Millie needs her "do" done.'

'I'm going to make an appointment with Krissie later this week.'

Joy nodded. 'Let's get this over. I've got bread rising and need to get back to it.'

Why she was so surprised, she didn't know. Joy was the only woman Mary knew, other than herself, who still baked her own bread. Even she didn't as much as she used to. The new bakery down on Walnut made oatmeal bread every bit as good as she did, and all she had to do was take it home and slice it. She sighed. Maybe she was getting old. However…

'All right, everyone. Here's what I've got so far. If I've forgotten anything, let me know. Our biggest problem is keeping the older grade school boys out of the roped-off area while the little ones are hunting. That and who'll volunteer to wear the bunny costume.'

They were done by nine thirty. Mothers volunteered fathers to guard the roped-off area against the young egg invaders. It was unanimously decided each child would have only one adult inside the egg hunting area. All picture-taking grandparents would have to stay behind the ropes, as well as older siblings. Designated egg hiders had been assigned and a committee of three delegated to fill the plastic eggs the committee had purchased with donated funds. They hadn't asked for much money and had collected enough to buy the eggs, the candy that would be inside and have a reserve of baskets for any child whose family couldn't afford one. Evidently most parents decided it was a small price to pay to keep their toddlers from being run over at the town Easter egg hunt held each year in the park. The only question unanswered was who would wear the bunny costume. Mary was sure she could come up with someone and that someone wouldn't be her.

She was gathering up her now-empty folder and checking to make sure she had everything in her tote bag when Ysabel walked in. She looked around the empty room. 'That had to be the fastest committee meeting I've ever heard of. How did you do it?'

Mary smiled. 'I had everything ready and everyone already assigned to tasks so there wasn't much discussion. Besides, they all had things to do, especially those young mothers. They wanted to get to the store, or do whatever else that was easier without the help of a three- or four-year-old. It's a great motivator.'

Ysabel laughed. 'I remember those days well.' Her smile faded. 'This is a wonderful idea, Mary. I watched the little ones get run over in the park last year. The boys aren't mean but the thrill of the hunt overcame them. The babies never had a chance. This way the older children can still have their hunt in the park and the babies can have one of their own. It should be a lot better, and having it on the church lawn works just fine. The Saturday before Palm Sunday is perfect. Holy Week is always hectic—so many church functions. This is a good choice.'

Mary certainly hoped so. She had also watched the carnage at the park. More than one young child had come out of the egg hunt area in tears; more than one parent was ready to throttle someone else's older child who, in the frenzy to find the most eggs, had pushed little ones aside, or worse, snatched eggs out of their baskets. Mary had vowed then and there that this year would be different. She hoped it would also be a success. That would be defined by how much fun the children had and how relieved the parents felt.

'Keep your fingers crossed,' she told Ysabel with a smile. On a more sober note, she asked, 'I've put the word out the rummage sale is this Thursday. It's all over the news and I think we'll have a good turnout. Are we putting a strain on you, tying up the hall all week?'

'Not really. We've been able to postpone or cancel the few things that were scheduled. However, the middle-school dance is Friday night. Will you have everything cleared out by Friday morning so the children can decorate?'

Mary set her tote on one of the small tables. Millie lay beside it, her head on her paws. She looked up at Mary, decided they weren't yet ready to move and dropped her head back down.

'What time do you need it on Friday?'

'Mid-morning would be great. Caleb will clean, no matter how good you leave it, and the kids can start after lunch.'

'We'll have stuff that doesn't sell—we always do. However, Bob, who runs the food bank and the homeless program, is going to take what's left to their distribution center. It will all be gone after we close. All the tables will be put back and the dressing area taken down…we close our doors at four and should be out of the hall by six. We'll come back early Friday to make sure everything is cleared out. Caleb shouldn't have much to do. The children can start decorating by lunchtime. Will that be soon enough?'

Ysabel nodded. 'That should work out fine.'

Mary thought there was relief in her voice as well as a little amusement.

'You evidently don't know Caleb. He acts as if the hall and its upkeep were his exclusive responsibility. He hovers over every event, making sure no one does anything they're not supposed to. He's obsessive.'

Mary thought you could substitute bossy and controlling for obsessive, but maybe it amounted to the same thing. 'Yes. He's very dedicated.' She picked up her tote, pulled out her cell phone and checked the time. If she hurried, she might have time to pay Glen Manning a visit at the bank before she had to meet Ellen. Something was bothering her and she wanted to talk to him.

'I hope all my volunteers are as dedicated,' Mary continued. 'Although I won't need as many as those who turned up on Wednesday. Half the town was in the hall, helping to set up. Gloria Sutherland was the only person I can remember who wasn't there.'

Millie was on her feet and heading for the door. Mary turned toward Ysabel to say goodbye but was stopped by the worried look on Ysabel's face.

'Gloria was there. I remember because I wondered why. Gloria never volunteers for anything. She stood over in one corner, watching Lorraine and Miss Emilie. I was busy and forgot about her, but after they left, Miss Emilie in tears, I looked for Gloria again. She knew Miss Emilie so well, I thought she could help, but she was gone.'

The worried look on Ysabel's face intensified. 'Should I have said something to someone?'

Mary reached out and touched Ysabel on the shoulder. 'I can't think why you should have. Most of the people there were trying to help, but plenty came to get an advance look at what they might want to grab when the doors opened. Gloria wasn't the only one who didn't come to work.'

Once again, relief flooded Ysabel's face. 'I'm sure you're right. Thanks, Mary. Don't worry about locking up. The Quilting Bees are going to use this room for their meeting this morning. I'll come back and lock the whole building after the preschool lets out.' She hurried out.

Mary followed more slowly, Millie by her side. Ysabel had dismissed any thought of Gloria's rather surprising visit to the rummage sale setup, but Mary found she couldn't. Why had Gloria shown up and why hadn't she jumped right in when she saw Miss Emilie was upset? That wasn't like her. Mary was once more lost in thought as she and Millie headed for the bank.

NINETEEN

TSHERE WAS A picture of a person with a small dog on the bank door, a line drawn through them, the inscription underneath stating service dogs only. Millie didn't qualify.

'I wonder what would happen if I took you in there, anyway? Glen knows you well, he loves you, but even if he is now president, he still has to obey the rules.' She glanced at her cell phone. 'It's getting late. I'd better call Ellen. We'll talk to Glen later.'

There was a bench in front of the bank. The placard on its back said it had been donated by the Beautification Committee of Santa Louisa. Mary didn't bother to read the placard. She'd headed the committee to raise the money for the benches and, at the moment, was glad she had. She sank down on it, pulled out her cell and scrolled to Ellen's number. It was busy. Millie, who'd jumped on the bench, lay down and put her head in Mary's lap.

'We'll try her again in a minute. I'm in no hurry to meet Richard again, anyway.' She tilted her head up and let the weak spring sun warm her face. It had been a long winter and, by California standards, a cold one. She hoped her jasmine had made it through the heavy frost in February. She'd know soon enough. What would it be like to live in one of the really cold areas of the country, with all that snow? Spring must be an even more welcome event if you lived in Boston. Or Chicago.

'Mary, are you all right?'

She opened her eyes, startled to see Lorraine standing in front of the bench, a worried look on her face, a quilted tote bag over one shoulder and a large wooden frame held awkwardly under the other arm.

'My goodness, you startled me.' Mary gave a little laugh to cover her embarrassment at being caught woolgathering on a city bench. 'Just waiting for Ellen to get off the phone. I'm to meet her at the house—your house—and was verifying the time.'

'Yes.' The expression on Lorraine's face changed from worry to…what? A combination of things but none of them happy. 'She told me. I've left our door unlocked. I won't be there. I'm going to the Quilting Bee meeting.'

Of course. The wooden thing under her arm was a quilting square. Mary's grandmother had had one. Her quilts had won blue ribbons at the county fair for years. Some of the quilts exhibited were pieces of art. They were all pieces of dedication and fortitude.

'I didn't know you belonged to that club.'

Lorraine nodded. 'For years. Quilting keeps me sane. I'm going to enter the one I'm working on now in the fair. That is if I get it done in time.' Her smile radiated real pleasure, the first one Mary thought she'd ever seen on Lorraine's face.

'That's wonderful. May I see it when it's done?'

Lorraine bobbed her head shyly. 'If you really want to…'

Before Mary could respond, the door of the bank opened and Glen Manning stepped out. 'Mary, did you want to see me?'

'Oh, Glen, yes. I have a question…' Her cell phone rang. It was Ellen. She held up her hand as she answered. 'Ellen, hold one minute.'

Lorraine stared at Glen, her quilting frame clutched to her breast, all traces of a smile gone. 'I'd better go.' She turned and fled.

What changed her mood so quickly? Mary hoped she hadn't been rude. But she had to answer Glen, and she needed to find out when to meet Ellen. 'Just one minute, Glen.' She put the phone to her ear. 'Are we still on?'

'We are; I'm on my way over right now. Where are you?'

'In front of the bank. I'll meet you there.' She clicked her cell phone off and walked over, Millie tugging at her leash to greet him as well.

'You wanted to see me?' Glen repeated as he rubbed Millie's ears and smiled as she wiggled her pleasure.

'Yes. I have something I wanted to ask you but I have to meet Ellen at the Plyms'. I would have come in, but there's that sign on the door…'

Glen stood and smiled. 'I'll be here. Don't worry about Millie being in the lobby. You can come directly to my office.' He paused. 'Unless you need to do banking with a teller?'

Mary shook her head. 'No. I wanted to ask you… I can ask you here.' Suddenly she was doubtful. This was really none of her business, but… 'If you can't answer, I'll understand.'

Glen smiled. 'Good. What do you want to know that I may not be able to answer?'

'It's about Miss Emilie.'

Glen looked a little wary, but he nodded.

'Those withdrawals she made.'

Glen looked even more wary.

'I was told she came in with a note, telling how much

money she wanted to withdraw. Did you ever see one of the notes?'

There was a pause while Glen stared at her, obviously trying to decide how much, if any, information he could safely give her. Finally he shook his head. 'Did John tell you?'

'No.' She didn't volunteer any more.

The relief on Glen's face was almost funny. John had been known to let things slip that he shouldn't have. That he hadn't this time seemed to make Glen's tongue a little looser.

'Only once. The last time she came in to withdraw money.'

'What happened?'

'Dab Holt came and got me. She was worried. By that time, Miss Emilie had taken out…a lot of money, and we had no idea what she was doing with it. Ed Kavanagh didn't think it was a problem but Dab was afraid she was getting bilked. I thought she could be right, but I got nowhere. She wanted her money and I had no right to stop her from taking it.'

'Was that when you called Cassandra?'

Glen nodded. 'I hope I did the right thing. I can't help but feel I'm responsible in some way but don't know what I could have done differently.' Stress lines creased his forehead. 'As far as I know, the money still hasn't turned up. What she did with it…' He broke off and spread his hands out in a hopeless gesture.

'There was never anyone with her?'

'No. Dab says not.'

'Then how did she get to the bank? Miss Emilie got… confused. She couldn't always find her way home. Sometimes she seemed pretty, well, not sharp exactly but as if she knew what was going on. Other times…how did she get herself to the bank so consistently, get her money and go back home without help?'

Glen shook his head. 'I don't know. I'd wondered about that as well, and frankly, so did Dab. Evidently she tried to find out, but she says no one ever came into the bank with her and she never saw anyone meet her outside.' He paused, as if trying to decide something. 'One time, she saw Gloria Sutherland outside. She thought she was watching Miss Emilie but couldn't be sure, and it was just once. Other than that, nothing.'

Gloria again. 'Was it after you took over that you found out how much money she'd removed?'

Glen nodded; an unhappy nod. 'I knew she'd been taking larger sums than usual, but until I started handling the trust I had no idea.' He paused and his eyes narrowed. 'Why are you asking all these questions? You think that money had something to do with her death, don't you?'

'I don't know, but no one seems to know where it is. It's not in her account, I take it?'

'She didn't have an account. Just the trust fund. The sisters paid cash for everything the trust didn't get billed for.' Worry creased Glen's forehead and sounded in his voice. 'Mary, I've been just sick about this. If that damn money was somehow responsible and I didn't stop whatever was going on…but how, I don't know.'

'Whatever happened, it isn't your fault. Quit worrying. Dan will figure it out. I'd better run. Ellen's waiting for me. Oh. One more thing.'

Glen frowned.

'Does the bank send out statements on the trust?'

Apparently she'd surprised Glen. 'Of course. Every month. Why?'

'Just wondered.' She gathered up Millie's leash and started down the sidewalk, giving him a little wave as she pulled a reluctant Millie along beside her. She glanced back once. Glen still stood on the sidewalk, worry still evident on his face.

TWENTY

'WHERE HAVE YOU BEEN?' Ellen stood on the sidewalk in front of the Plym house. She'd been taking pictures with her digital camera. A large and fully stuffed tote bag sat beside her. She had a pencil stuck behind one ear and a nervous look on her face.

'I got caught up talking to Glen Manning. I hope you haven't been waiting long.' Mary was puffing a little. Millie had set a rapid pace.

Ellen grinned. 'Just a couple of minutes, but I wasn't going in until you came along. I'm not going to beard that particular lion in his den without backup. He makes me nervous. Cassandra and Lorraine are OK.'

'You won't have Lorraine. She's gone to her quilting club meeting.'

'I didn't know she quilts.' Ellen looked genuinely surprised but not very interested. She was more interested in the picture she'd just taken. 'What do you think of this? Did I get it all in? It's got so much yard. It's hard to show it all.'

Mary looked at the picture Ellen held up. Digital was certainly easy. You got the picture immediately and if you didn't like it, you erased it. 'You're right. You left out a lot of the property. It's a good shot of the house, though.'

'I think I might get a better one from across the street.'

'Hmmm. You're probably right. Try again when we're done in there.' She glanced up at the sun. 'The light might be better then. The carriage house won't be in so much shadow.'

'Carriage house?' Mary had Ellen's attention now. She turned and looked at her quizzically.

'It was one when the house was built. I'm told they kept two horses and a small carriage. It was a garage by the time I started coming around.'

'That's something we can put in an ad. How interesting. Who'd know more about that?'

'No one still alive.' Mary wasn't sure why a building that had once housed horses instead of cars would be especially interesting, but if Ellen thought it would help sell the house…it would certainly date it.

The large elm tree that had been in the Plym front yard for as long as Mary could remember did a good job of keeping the morning light from flooding the front porch. The afternoon sun would do that. It would lighten up the front of the carriage house as well. Mary had never known it as anything but a large garage, but when the house was new, horses and a small carriage had been the family's only means of transportation. She thought there had been living quarters above it then as well. Who'd lived there, Mary wasn't sure, but probably whoever took care of the horses and perhaps the grounds. The apartment had been remodeled several times, as had the downstairs. What they had originally looked like she had no idea, nor what they looked like today. It would be interesting to find out.

'I wonder if you can see the front door and porch from the carriage-house windows.'

'What?' Ellen had moved back to try another shot and seemed to pay little attention to her aunt's musing. 'Are you ready? Let's get this over.' She tucked the camera in her large canvas tote bag which she slung over one shoulder, leaving her hands free to type on the small tablet she carried.

'What are you doing?' Mary and Millie followed Ellen's slow progress up the stairs, watching as Ellen looked carefully at each stair, wiggled the railing and walked across the porch, pausing to bounce slightly on any board that looked a little loose. She took up-close pictures of the windowsills, evidently looking for dry rot, a problem in homes over a hundred years old and some considerably younger.

'Doing a visual inspection of the house. They have to fill out a disclosure but I have to make my own inspection.'

The front door opened and Cassandra appeared, standing in the doorway, saying nothing but watching Ellen's progress around the porch.

Ellen looked at her and smiled. 'Good morning.'

'Yes, isn't it?' Cassandra smiled back. 'Making sure none of the windows are broken?'

'Not exactly. Trying to see if any have been replaced. It looks as if these are original.'

'Is that good or bad?' Cassandra walked over to stand beside Ellen and stared at the windows. 'They don't look very new.'

'Have you ever tried to open them?' Ellen stepped back, looked at the top of the high windows then down to the sill. They appeared to be stuck to the wood with layers of paint.

'Oh, dear.' Cassandra also peered at them. 'No one goes into the living room much and the draperies… Are the windows going to be a problem?'

'It depends.'

An answer, Mary thought, which cleared up nothing.

Ellen's fingers continued to fly across the tablet. She finally looked up to peer once again at the windows. 'Have any of the windows in the house been replaced?'

'I've no idea.' Cassandra's voice had taken on a helpless tone. 'I wasn't thinking about windows when I was here last year, only about the burial and making sure Aunt Emilie was taken care of. It seemed Caleb and Lorraine had things under control, and that's as far as I went.' There was a long pause as she stared at the windows, but Mary didn't think they were what she was seeing. 'I had problems of my own. My husband hadn't… He'd been diagnosed with cancer. They thought they could treat it but…he died several months after I left here. Aunt Emilie hasn't been a priority for a while.'

Ellen looked stricken and clearly didn't seem to know what to say.

Mary felt much the same. She'd had no idea. As for the windows…

'Are you sure you want us to go through the house today? If you're not feeling up to it we can come back later.'

Cassandra brought her attention back to the front porch with a little jerk of her head. She turned to smile at them but Mary was sure there was a tear in the corner of her eye. Cassandra ignored it, so Mary did as well. She glanced over at Ellen, who cut her eyes back at Mary and started to power down the tablet.

'Please, don't go. I'm fine, really. It's been over six months now and I've gotten myself together. We need to get this resolved. About the windows…' She shrugged. 'I think you're going to have to make a list of questions and we'll see about getting you answers. Will that be all right?'

Ellen, relief written all over her face, nodded. Millie got up from where she had been sitting beside Mary and started for the front door. Cassandra laughed and held the door open wider for her to pass through, followed closely by Mary. They all stopped in the entry and looked around.

'Bleak, isn't it.' Cassandra waved a hand at the oversized hall seat, its high back heavily carved and inset with small mirrors that did nothing to infuse light into the dim hallway. An umbrella stand in the shape of an elephant stood in the corner, still holding two large black and frayed-looking umbrellas. Mary doubted they still opened. The oak floor was dark with polish, and the flowered rug, perhaps originally intended to brighten up the entry, seemed to help drain what light there was.

Ellen audibly sighed and activated the flash on her camera. 'I need light. Can you turn on the chandelier?'

There were two white buttons protruding from a brass plate just inside the door. Mary gave a start of surprise. She hadn't seen a light switch like that since she'd played with the one in her grandmother's house. Cassandra glanced at her then pushed one of them. Dim light tried its best to flow from the small single light fixture hanging high in the entryway.

Ellen looked at it and this time couldn't repress a snort of frustration. 'You might want to ask Caleb about putting in a higher-watt bulb,' was all she said.

She set her tote on the floor, took out her tape measure and handed one end to Mary. They slowly made their way through the downstairs rooms, Cassandra and Mary measuring and Ellen muttering under her breath while making notes on her tablet. Millie showed increasing signs of boredom.

Cassandra kept up a running dialogue. 'I think this old house could be made really pretty. It's just so dim. Most of the furniture is old but there are some beautiful things. If the heavy draperies were gone, or at least pulled way back and everything lightened up…do you think it could be made into a bed and breakfast? Would someone buy it for that? I can't see anyone buying it to live in.'

Ellen made no comment, just nodded slightly and continued to make notes.

The kitchen was the last room on their downstairs inspection tour. Richard Plym sat at the table, sipping coffee from what looked like a bone china cup. There was no sign of welcome on his recently shaved face and no words of greeting.

'Good morning, Richard,' Mary said.

He regarded her with dispassion. His sister and Ellen he ignored. His attention fastened on Millie. 'Does that dog go with you everywhere?'

'Yes.' Mary felt he deserved nothing more than that terse comment.

'Can it…'

'The dog is welcome, Richard.' Cassandra's voice was quiet but tinged with more than a little ice.

What had they been discussing before she and Ellen had arrived to produce this frosty atmosphere? But it seemed, from what she observed the other morning, that the frosty atmosphere between brother and sister was probably nothing new.

He glared at her then turned his glare on Ellen. 'Have you come up with a price, yet?'

He made it sound as if she was purposefully dragging

her feet. How so few words could hold such insult Mary wasn't sure, but she was becoming less fond of the man by the minute.

Ellen's eyes narrowed and her voice sounded even icier than Cassandra's. 'This is an old house. There are a lot of things to take into consideration. After I've collected all the information I need, I'll be able to give you a range of value. Until then…'

Mary thought Richard was going to challenge her again and, if he did, she was almost positive Ellen would walk out. She almost hoped she would, but there were some things in this house Mary wanted to see. She hoped Ellen could stick it out at least until their tour of the house was finished.

There was something she remembered from that terrible morning, but there had been so much going on she'd barely registered…she had to make sure. Yes. There. Right by the back door. A key rack. Not cats, like hers, but a row of hooks. There were keys on three of them. One hung from a cardboard placard marked clearly: SMCH. This must be the key Caleb used when he needed to get in to clean the hall. But why would he keep it here? 'I see you have a key to the church hall.'

Three pairs of eyes immediately swung toward her.

'What?' Cassandra looked blank.

'Where?' Only Richard's eyes had briefly swept the key rack before he glared at Mary.

'Oh. We have to tell Dan.' Ellen's face drained of color as she stared at the key rack. 'Only…'

'Yes,' Mary murmured, agreeing with Ellen on both counts. 'It does seem unlikely, but he'll have to ask.'

'Ask what?' Cassandra didn't have any more color in her face than Ellen did, but she hadn't once glanced at the key rack. 'How do you know we have one? Why would there be one here?'

'Caleb and Lorraine both volunteer at church events. She helps out with the fellowship gathering after services on Sundays and Caleb cleans up after events. According to Ysabel…the pastor's wife…' Mary inserted this for Cassandra's benefit, who looked a little lost, '…Caleb takes his job seriously, checking every event to make sure nothing is left undone or damaged. It's not surprising they should have a key. It is a little surprising it's hanging here, in your kitchen…' she nodded toward the key rack, '…instead of in the Duckworths' apartment. In any case, Dan will have to know.'

Richard started to his feet, his hands clenched into fists, holding his weight as he leaned forward on the table, his face blotchy and his mouth contorted. 'Why? What does that wretched key have to do with us? We had nothing to do with her death or with her wandering around town in the dark, either. If you're looking to accuse someone, where's that Gloria Sutherland? The pushy one who thinks she's family? Ask her if she has a key. Ask her if she took beloved Aunt Emilie's money. Our money.'

All three women stared at him, apparently too stunned for a moment to speak.

Finally Mary broke the spell. 'Richard, for heaven's sake, sit down. No one is accusing you of anything. But there are a lot of keys floating around out there and we need to try to account for them. Someone let Miss Emilie into the community hall the other night, and that someone had a key. There's a very logical explanation why this one is here, but that doesn't mean Dan shouldn't know about it.'

The blotch faded and he slowly lowered himself back into the chair.

She wasn't finished. 'What money are you talking about, and what makes you think Gloria took it?'

His face closed as effectively as if he'd pulled down a shade. He looked at his hands, which lay on the table, fingers now spread out, not clenched, his face pale instead of blotchy red and his voice modulated, not pierced with rage. 'I don't know what you're talking about.'

Mary glanced at Ellen and lifted her eyebrows. They both knew what money Richard was talking about but he wasn't going to discuss it or Gloria.

'Richard…' Cassandra broke off with a hopeless flutter of hands, pulled out a chair and sank into it. 'Ellen brought a bunch of paperwork we need to go through. Inspections we need to get, disclosures we need to fill out. She wants to go over them with us. I think now would be a good time.'

Ellen dug into her tote and pulled out a file. 'Is that all right with you?'

Richard looked at her, then at his sister and scowled. 'No.' He abruptly pushed his chair back and got to his feet. 'You do it. I'm not disclosing anything about a house I know nothing about. I'm going for a walk.' He opened the back door, pulled it shut behind him with a bang and was gone.

For a moment, no one moved.

Finally Cassandra broke the silence. 'That was dramatic.'

For a moment, Mary thought Ellen was going to leave as well, but she placed a folder of papers on the table and turned toward Cassandra. 'Do you want to continue? We don't have to.'

Cassandra shook her head. 'I want to know what we have to do when the time comes. Let him walk out his frustration. I'll explain it all to him later.'

Mary was certain Richard hadn't planned on mentioning missing money. The possibility Gloria helped herself to it wasn't open for discussion either, but what made Richard think she might have? No, he seemed sure of it. Was he planning something? The look on his face when he accused her and the quick way he got himself back under control made her nervous. Richard made her nervous.

'Would you like me to go upstairs and…look around?' Mary turned toward Ellen. 'I could check the windows, make notes, take some pictures and save a little time.'

Mary had no desire to sit in on their conversation regarding forms, but a lot of interest in seeing the upstairs.

The smile Ellen gave her aunt said plainly, 'Save a little time, ha!' Aloud, she said, 'That would be great.'

Mary smiled back and fished in her purse for her phone.

'The back stairs are over there, off that little hallway.' Cassandra pointed toward a small opening to the right of the back door. Mary nodded. She was familiar with what lay beyond it. The morning room where she had often visited Miss Emilie and her sister opened off it, and farther down the corridor was the laundry room, a half bath and the back staircase. She tugged a little on Millie's leash and they headed for the stairs.

TWENTY-ONE

It was dark in the little hallway. The door to the morning room was closed, and so was the door into the laundry room. The door to the half bath was slightly open but its high window let in little light. The staircase, steep and treacherous-looking in the dim light, started just beyond the bathroom door. Mary stood at the bottom, looking up. Surely there was a light somewhere. There. Two buttons on the wall beside the bottom step. She pushed the top button and a weak light came on. Enough to stop her tripping, at least she hoped so, but certainly not enough to see much detail. And the electrical system…she needed to have a talk with Ellen. Those push button switches had been phased out years ago. How did the system support modern needs, such as the television set that sat on a cabinet at one end of the small dining area of the kitchen? Or the computer and printer she'd glimpsed on the very old mahogany desk in Mr Plym's library? It was something to look into.

She climbed the stairs slowly, Millie tight by her side. The dog looked all around, seemingly somewhat nervous. Mary didn't know if she was frightened but she clearly was not happy. Her usual brisk trot was missing, her stub of a tail limp.

'I don't like them either,' she told Millie, 'but we need to take a look upstairs. You'll be just fine.'

They'd come to a landing that ended in a closed door,

the stairs continuing upward just beyond it. Up to the attic? They looked narrower and darker than the ones she was on. The decision not to climb higher wasn't hard. The landing was fairly large, at least Mary thought so, but it was difficult to tell. The bare bulb light that hung from the ceiling left a large portion of it in shadow. The cut-glass door handle, however, was easy to find and turned readily in her hand. She pushed the door open but, as she stepped through, something flickered. A red light. It lasted only a second but she was sure she'd seen it. She looked around. Nothing. She pulled Millie back and closed the door, leaving them once more on the landing. Millie whined and pawed the door. She'd seen escape from the dark staircase when the door opened and she wanted to be on the other side.

'Just a minute.' Mary tightened up on the leash and pointed at the floor. The dog sat, but not happily. 'What was that flicker? I know I saw something. It came from up there.' She looked at the door, letting her eyes run up to the top of the door frame. Nothing. Cautiously, she opened the door and scanned the inside frame. Something was up there. A thin white thing with what looked like glass in the middle that emitted a red beam. It reminded her of the beam of light that operated her garage door opener. What on earth... She stepped through the doorway once more, watching the white box intently. The flash came again as soon as she and Millie passed in front of it. She backed up once more, closed the door then opened it, this time letting only Millie go through. The dog happily obliged. Nothing happened. Mary passed through and there was the flash again. She turned to face the door and closed it slowly, watching the top where the door met the jamb. She opened the door once more but this time stayed where she was. No flash. The little white box was a motion detector and as she hadn't moved through the doorway, it had nothing to detect. It hadn't detected Millie either. The beam was set too high. But it would have detected Miss Emilie.

She stared at it a moment. 'Caleb's alarm system? It has to be. I wonder which other doors have one.'

Millie sat calmly in the middle of the hall, waiting for Mary to quit playing with the door. The motion detector held no interest. She got up, stretched and started down the hallway.

'Wait,' Mary told her. 'I need a picture of this.' She wasn't sure she would get anything worth keeping, but she could try. There should be a zoom…there. And the flash. The picture wasn't very good, but you could at least see there was something at the top of the door. 'OK,' she said to Millie, 'let's see what else is up here.'

The hallway was long, wide and gloomy. She looked around but didn't see a light switch. There must be one and next to the stairway door seemed logical. Yes. The same white buttons. She pushed the top one and a hanging fixture glowed. One lightbulb.

'If I lived in this house, the first thing I'd do is put in bigger light fixtures.'

The doorway they'd just passed through was at the extreme end of the hallway next to a large stained-glass window. The top of the main staircase was at the far end. There were four doors on either side, spaced unevenly down the hallway and all closed. She took a picture.

'I'll get a picture of the stained-glass window when we're done with the rooms. The garden scene is actually pretty.' She started toward the door diagonally across the hall from where they stood but stopped.

Millie looked at her.

'Isn't that the most hideous wallpaper you've ever seen?' She allowed herself a shudder as she examined it more closely. 'Whoever buys this place has a lot of work ahead of them. Come on. Let's see what's in here.'

She stopped in front of the door, admiring the glass door knob, but not the Oxford brown paint on the solid wood-raised panel door. How much work would it be to sand the door down and paint it white? Immediately she dismissed the thought. That would be someone else's project. She let her gaze travel up the door to the top of the doorjamb. No sign of a motion detector on this door. She pushed it open, stepped in and stopped. The room was large enough to make the kingsized bed that sat against one wall look lost. There were two windows that looked out onto…what? She walked over, pushed aside the lace panels and looked out. There was the elm tree and the stretch of well-tended lawn. The daffodils that crowded the flower beds were in full bloom, iris were heavy with buds ready to explode and tall foxglove filled in the back, their lethal but lovely bells taking form and showing the first hint of the vibrant flowers that would soon appear. She must be directly over the covered porch off the dining room. She had noticed the flower beds when she looked out the locked French doors, thinking how pleasant it would be to breakfast on that porch. So, the carriage house and the driveway must be on the other side of the house.

She turned to survey the room. Large, maybe once two rooms? There were two windows and two doors leading into the hall but only one old fireplace in the far corner. No ashes, the firebox small, cold and empty. It had probably warmed a much smaller room with coal many years ago. The mantel held a wide variety of objects: a pewter candleholder and small etched-glass vases designed to hold only one rose and a pile of books. The massive dresser was covered with family pictures in silver frames, more books, jewelry, a lovely tortoiseshell hand mirror and old-fashioned personal items that had probably belonged to Miss Eloise, or perhaps her mother, all haphazardly tossed together on top of an embroidered table runner. A pile of bed linens, neatly folded, lay on the stripped bed, ready to be placed in one of the empty boxes that littered the floor. Several other boxes sat next to the open closet, taped shut. The closet was empty. Cassandra had been busy. What did she plan to do with the full boxes? Did she have a criteria for what to keep and what to give away? Millie poked her head into one of the empty boxes, decided it held no interest, sat and looked at Mary.

'We didn't come in here to poke our noses into personal stuff,' Mary told her. 'We came to look at the layout of the house and to see what kind of condition it's in, so that's what we're going to do.' She took another look at the windows. 'They certainly haven't been replaced. Judging from how many layers of paint are on here they probably don't even open.' She snapped a couple of pictures and moved on toward a door that seemed to lead into a bathroom.

'I'll bet this was a sitting room or a night nursery at one time. Someone's turned it into a bathroom, and not recently. It's a nice size, though, and claw-foot bathtubs are pretty popular, at least according to the decorating magazines at the beauty shop.' She got a picture of it and moved on to the large white freestanding sink. No cracks, but the bowl showed the wear and tear years of scrubbing had inflicted. So did the white porcelain handles on the tall faucet. The mirror had silvered but the frame was still beautiful. The light above the sink hung from a black chain, the shade was amber glass and the bulb couldn't have been more than twenty watts. Mary shook her head and took another picture. 'At least they upgraded the heating system. There are vents in here and the bedroom. I hope they have A/C. I'll bet it gets pretty stuffy in here in the summer.'

Millie yawned.

'Let's move on.'

They left what had been Miss Eloise's room and her parents' before her to examine the other rooms. There was nothing that wasn't expected. The closed door next to what was now Miss Eloise's was another bathroom. Mary was sure it hadn't started out as a bathroom, but it had been turned into one some time ago. The tiles on the floor had been out of date for years, and the shower was small and dark. She didn't even try to get a picture. The last door on this side opened into what must be the guest room where Richard was staying. It held a double bed with a black iron headboard, with a handmade quilt pulled neatly across it. The quilt was pretty but not unique. The pattern was one she'd seen before, but if it had a name she didn't know it. The edges were a little puckered, the corners a little bunched, but the stitches uniform and straight. As an old home economics teacher, Mary wondered if this was one of Lorraine's first attempts. If so, she'd done a good job.

The oak dresser was about the same age as the house and still had what Mary, a dedicated *Antiques Roadshow* watcher, thought were the original drawer pulls. Mary pulled out one of the drawers and hastily closed it. Richard's personal belongings were in it, neatly put away. She took pictures of these windows, pushing back the sheer panels that covered them, then turned to look more closely around the room. It had been Richard's father's room while he was growing up. Had this been his furniture? Had he slept in this bed, kept his books and treasures on the long and largely empty oak bookshelf that covered much of the far wall? Did Richard know and, if so, how did he feel about it? Angry, probably. That seemed to be the way he felt about everything. She looked around to see if there was anything else she should photograph and decided no, they needed to move on but not before she looked closely at both the inside and hall side of the door. There was no little white box.

She was at the other end of the hallway, facing a door directly opposite Richard's, the main stairs leading to the entrance hall on her right. The stained-glass window at the end of the hallway was on her left. Mary took a picture. She looked down at Millie, who stood at the top of the staircase, staring down with apparent interest.

'The door at the very end by the window is where we came up. The landing is behind it, so let's go back and look in the room next to it.'

She walked back along the hall, followed by a reluctant Millie, looking at the outside of each door frame for a sensor box. There didn't appear to be any more, just the one on the stairway door. She opened the door next to the one she'd come through. A linen closet, but bigger than any linen closet she'd ever seen. It was as big as some bedrooms in the new tract houses that were going up on the outskirts of town. There was an odor, not unpleasant, but familiar. She sniffed then breathed deeply and smiled. Cedar. Shelves and built-in drawers lined both sides of the room. A long rod stretched across the back. Only one long, black lady's coat, badly out of date, hung on it. She supposed the room would have held bed linens, blankets, towels and hat boxes. Out-of-season clothes of all kinds would have hung on the rod across the back of the closet; all the things a family living in a late nineteenth-century home used would be stored here. Now the shelves were almost empty and only a vacuum cleaner and a mop and a pail remained. 'This is huge for a storage room. Having a whole room cedar lined would be nice.'

Millie sneezed.

The last two doors must be the connecting bedrooms, but she wasn't sure which was which. Neither had a little white box on the outside frame. Maybe on the inside? She opened the door closest to the staircase she came up. This must have been Miss Eloise's bedroom before she moved into her parents' room. It was the room Cassandra was using. Mary walked in, followed closely by Millie, and stopped. The room was large, sunny and looked as if it had been hastily furnished out of attic rejects. The Jenny Lind bed was old, its finish rubbed thin in spots, its covering a faded green chenille bedspread that fell to the floor. It was pulled up over what appeared to be two thin pillows. Mary walked toward the bed to get a better look. She shook her head slightly. They had better bedspreads go through the rummage sale than this one.

She turned to look at the rest of the room. A bow front oak dresser sat on the opposite wall. The mirror that was mounted on top of it tilted forward to reflect the cosmetic case and the neatly folded hand towel that lay on top of the chest. It had, at one time, been upright to reflect the owner. No longer. Mary stood by the bed for a moment, taking it all in. A bookcase that sat against the wall next to what must be the closet door held nothing but a somewhat battered volume of the King James Bible.

The small gateleg table beside the bed held a white ginger jar lamp on a slightly yellowed embroidered doily and a paperback mystery. That and the cosmetic bag on the dresser had to be Cassandra's. Nothing else was that new. The room had the look of being hastily put together with whatever was to hand. Was that what happened? Had this room sat empty for the last few years, all of the things Miss Eloise prized moved to the big room she occupied until her death? How had Miss Emilie felt about that? The twins had slept next door to each other all their lives and Miss Emilie didn't adapt well to change. She wouldn't carry any purse but the old black one, and sat in the same chair in the morning room. You could tell what day of the week it was from the dress Miss Emilie wore. Probably the first time in her life she'd had a little privacy, but Mary wasn't sure she'd felt safe without her sister next door.

Not a very welcoming room for Cassandra. Had it been hurriedly assembled for this visit or the one a year ago, when Cassandra was here for Miss Eloise's funeral? In either case, Miss Emilie had spent close to a year up here all alone.

The door directly opposite it must lead into Miss Emilie's childhood room. Had she kept the connecting door open to Miss Eloise's empty room? Or had she felt more comfortable keeping it closed? It was closed now. She looked up to examine the top of the inside of the door. Nothing was there. That didn't surprise her. There would be no need for one in an unoccupied room but there should be in the room next door. She motioned to

Millie, who had decided one of the braided rugs was a good place for a nap, and walked back out into the hall.

This had to be Miss Emilie's room. The door opened at the touch of her hand.

Mary stood in the doorway for some time, looking into the room but made no move to enter it. This was a girl's room, a very young girl. The layout of the room was a mirror image of the one next door, but there the resemblance ended. This Jenny Lind bed was white, the bedspread pink plaid. The ruffles on its side hung limp and tired. So did the double ruffled white curtains. The wallpaper was tiny pink rosebuds and the molding around the windows and door was a darker pink. Fluffy pink rugs lay matted on a bare wood floor. There was only one chest of drawers in the room, a long, low one, also white with pink roses on each drawer. It was a room a twelve-year-old girl would have delighted in, a twelve-year-old in the forties. Mary wasn't sure the room would appeal to girls of today, who she'd heard all had posters of rock stars on their walls, but the girl who had delighted in this room had ceased to be one decades ago. Somehow, she'd kept the room the same her whole life. She'd never had a husband, or children, nor a career, just this very pink room, the stuffed animals on the bed and the bookcase filled with books Mary suspected girls didn't read anymore. *Pollyanna*, *Little Women*, *Lad: A Dog*, more books about animals and what looked like a full set of Nancy Drew. Not one adult book. What had gone on in Miss Emilie's mind all those years as she watched the world pass her by?

But that wasn't why Mary was here. She took a step into the room and, out of the corner of her eye, saw a flash. She looked up and there it was. Sitting above the door, tilted down slightly so the beam would be broken by someone not very tall, like little Miss Emilie. She'd broken the beam. She must have. There was a red light on in the middle of the glass. She lifted up her hand and waved. There was the flash. So, if someone was monitoring it, they'd know she was in this room. Or at least they'd know someone had broken the beam. Could that someone tell if she was still here or if she'd left? She had no idea. She didn't know how these things worked and she couldn't think who might be watching. Lorraine was at her quilting meeting and Caleb was, she supposed, at work at the grade school. So if no one was home to monitor the system, why was it on? This whole thing gave her a creepy feeling, like she was being spied on. No wonder Richard told Caleb to turn the system off the night Miss Emilie was killed. However, it was too bad they did. If Caleb had known she was gone…but someone knew. A shiver ran down her spine.

She stood in the middle of the room and slowly turned around, taking it all in. Millie walked over to one of the rugs and lay down.

Everything in the room was worn but clean and well taken care of. The bed was made, three stuffed animals resting comfortably on the pillow. Mary stared at it for a minute. Why was the bed made? Cassandra had said the covers were partly on the floor when she looked in and found Miss Emilie gone. Had Lorraine come up and taken care of it, placing the small animals where they probably rested daily as a sort of tribute? Mary doubted it but would have to ask. Another odd thing among several.

The door on the wall opposite the bed must be the closet. The door swung open without a protest. The closet was small and it, too, smelled faintly of cedar. It held very few clothes, all of them dresses, all neatly hung. Two pairs of shoes sat on the floor, carefully arranged. Several shoeboxes were on the shelf, ends facing out so their contents were easily read. There was an empty hook on the back of the closet door. Where a bathrobe usually hung? Mary sighed. Miss Emilie's black purse sat next to the shoeboxes. Mary reached up and took it down.

She walked over to the white chest of drawers that matched the Jenny Lind bed, set it down and looked at it. Should she? No, but she was going to. The large clasp wasn't hard to open. The purse held very little. A small white handkerchief with lavender pansies embroidered in one corner, a dog biscuit, a square of white paper folded into fourths and an old-fashioned coin purse which held two one-dollar bills and some change. Mary put it back into the purse and took out the paper. Was this the note she presented to the teller each time she went to the bank? Carefully, she unfolded it. Miss Emilie's name in bold print, her address and a phone number was all that was on it. Mary stared at it then looked back into the purse. There was no note. Shouldn't there be? Maybe Glen had taken it. She closed the purse and set it back on the shelf. It was all so sad. It was also painfully tidy. That must be Lorraine's doing. Miss Emilie was sweet but not tidy. If she'd hidden her money, it wasn't in the closet. Lorraine would have found it.

A window on the side wall, like the one in the adjoining bedroom, looked out over the driveway and the carriage house, giving a view of the staircase leading up to Lorraine and Caleb's apartment. Mary walked over to examine it more closely, Millie by her side. The curtains covered enough of the window so that no one could see in during the day, but you could see out. Millie had her front feet on the windowsill, the ruffled curtains draped over her head, staring intently at something. What, Mary couldn't see. Instead, she took her picture. Ellen wouldn't want it, but it was adorable. Should she get one of the closet? No. The size of that closet wouldn't do anything to help the sale of the house. But she could get one of the connecting door.

Getting the shot to make sense was harder than she'd thought. She backed up, then one more step right into something sharp.

'Ouch.' Then, 'Oh, dear.' Something had fallen.

Mary wheeled around. She'd backed into a corner of the white dresser. Had she broken anything? No. She heaved a sigh of relief and set the white wood lamp with the pink checked shade upright. Was there anything else? A wooden box, also white with little rosebuds painted all over it, had been pushed to the side but it hadn't fallen. Mary stared at it. A box. A good-sized box. The kind stationery used to come in when people wrote notes instead of emailing everything. Did it still contain stationery? No, and it never had. There was no need to lock a stationery box.

Millie, whose front feet were still on the windowsill, turned her head to look at her, decided nothing important was going to happen and resumed staring out the window.

'You're not much help,' Mary told the dog. Her hand went out and touched the top then slid over the brass plate. There was a small keyhole but no sign of a key. The lid didn't budge under the pressure of her fingers. What could have been so valuable Miss Emilie kept it locked? Keepsakes of some kind? She picked it up, letting it rest in her hands. It was large enough for her to need both of them to hold it, but it wasn't heavy and it didn't make any noise when she tilted it slightly. Maybe it was empty. No. Something shifted, but whatever it was made no sound.

Voices sounded in the hall. 'Where are you?'

'I'm in Miss Emilie's room.' She was still holding the box when Cassandra and Ellen walked in.

'You've got her precious box.' Cassandra smiled. 'Another thing I've got to figure out what to do with. Some little girl would love to have it but I can't find the key.'

'What?' Mary looked at the box then back at Cassandra. 'The key?'

'She used to keep it in that little dish.' She pointed to a small white bowl with, of course, tiny pink rosebuds painted on it. 'It amused me that she'd lock it and put the key in plain sight right beside it, but I guess that way she always knew where it was.'

'What's in it?' Mary's interest in the box had suddenly sharpened.

Cassandra shrugged. 'Not much. Old pictures, Valentines, birthday cards, things like that. She showed them to me when I was here before but I'm afraid I wasn't paying much attention.' A rueful look passed over her face. 'I was a bit distracted.'

'Yes. I imagine you were. Have you seen the key since you've been here this time?'

Cassandra shook her head.

Mary dropped the subject and put the box back on the dresser.

Ellen turned slowly, taking in the room and shaking her head. 'This looks like something straight from a nineteen forties' home decorating magazine.'

Mary agreed, but she had another question for Cassandra. 'Did Miss Emilie mind you staying in her sister's room?'

'She didn't seem to.' Cassandra smiled as if remembering something pleasant. 'She came through several times, wanting to talk. At first she seemed surprised, but after that… I don't think she ever figured out who I was, though.'

'What did you talk about?'

From the look on Cassandra's face, Mary thought she was increasingly uneasy with the direction of this conversation.

'I'm not entirely sure,' she finally said. 'It was hard to tell if she was talking about things happening today or years ago.'

Mary nodded. She, too, had had trouble following Miss Emilie's ramblings. It was easy to just let her rattle on, nodding and smiling and mentally putting together a grocery list. But sometimes… 'Did she talk about Lorraine? Or Caleb? Or Gloria Sutherland?'

'Lorraine. She seemed to love Lorraine, and it was plain she relied on her. She only mentioned Gloria Sutherland once. I think she was a little afraid of her. But it was Willis she talked about the most. I should have known…'

'What did she say about him?'

'The same thing over and over.' Cassandra finally smiled. 'I'd only been here a few days but she kept telling me her father, my grandfather, told her if she ever got in trouble, Willis would take care of her. What a stuffed toy dog could do, I have no idea, and I don't think she did, either.'

Mary nodded. 'The morning she…that you discovered she was missing. Didn't you say you looked in here, found she was gone and the covers were on the floor?'

There was obvious hesitation before Cassandra answered—that and discomfort. 'Yes. When I realized she wasn't in the bathroom either, I grabbed my bathrobe and ran to wake up Richard.'

'Did you come in the room?'

Cassandra looked at her blankly, then at the bed. 'Yes. It was dumb but I was afraid she'd fallen out of bed, so I picked the covers up to make sure she wasn't under them and checked the closet.'

Mary thought her next question was easier to answer. 'Richard was asleep? Was his door closed?'

'Yes, to both. Why?' Cassandra was starting to seem wary of all the questions. It was time to back off a little.

Mary turned toward Ellen. 'You're going to want to go through these rooms yourself and make notes. Cassandra and I can measure, if you'd like.'

Ellen beamed at her. 'Thank you. That would be wonderful.' She took Mary's phone and scrolled through the pictures. 'You got some good ones.' She handed it back, the picture of Millie in the window displayed. She pulled her tablet out of her tote bag along with a tape measure, a yellow legal pad and a pen, which she handed to Mary. 'I assume you'd rather use these.' She smiled.

Mary took the tape measure and handed one end to Cassandra. 'I've learned to use my cell phone but I don't think it's up to measuring rooms. At least, that's not an app I've discovered yet.' She walked across the room, the tape playing out behind her. Millie immediately decided this was a game and pounced. It took a minute to convince her the tape wasn't a toy. Mary looked at the dog, eyes expectant, ears forward, ready to attack the yellow enemy again, sighed and raised the tape waist high.

They finished, in spite of Millie, and headed into what used to be Miss Eloise's room. Mary looked around at the mismatched furniture, the worn-out bedspread, the lack of any personal interesting touches and asked, 'Was it like this when you were here last year?'

Cassandra read the measurement off the tape, recorded it then nodded. 'Lorraine told me Gloria used to spend the night sometimes, and so did she. I guess Aunt Eloise couldn't be left without someone close by. They went up in the attic and brought down whatever they could find.' She looked around and shrugged. 'That's what it looks like—something thrown together—but it's a nice room. It could be really pretty. So could Aunt Emilie's.' She moved over to the window, pushed aside the curtain and looked out. 'The grounds here are beautiful, and I think the house could be as well. It needs someone who has some imagination and is willing to do the work.'

'A lot of money would help.' Mary looked at the single lightbulb hanging from the ceiling, covered by an amber etched-glass shade. She thought of the electric system in the house, the amount it would cost to heat and air condition it, the need for new and double-pane windows and shuddered. It wasn't a project she would want to tackle.

'Yes.' Cassandra looked around thoughtfully, ran a finger over the windowsill then held up the old lace curtain, made a face and dropped it. 'It would take a lot to get this place back in shape, but it could be beautiful.' She turned to Mary with a briskness Mary hadn't seen in her before. 'Ellen said she's going to find out about zoning. I do think this could be a wonderful bed and breakfast, and as the wine industry has brought in so many tourists…'

A jolt of surprise ran through Mary. Wine industry? Tourists? Cassandra was right. Their little town had grown a lot in the last few years, and the demand for accommodation more interesting than the Bide-A-Wee motel had boomed right along with it. However, Mary hadn't expected either Cassandra or Richard to know anything about that. They lived on the other side of the country, far removed from what was happening on California's central coast. Or had Cassandra been doing her homework? After all, she was going to inherit, right along with Richard. It made sense she'd want to know something about the town where she was soon to own property. Didn't it?

'She said something about that, yes. Shall we get this finished?' Mary handed Cassandra the end of the tape, holding her end high above Millie's reach, read off the latest measurement and recorded it on the legal pad. But she tucked Cassandra's interest in bed and breakfast possibilities away for future consideration. Cassandra had something in mind, and Mary wondered what it was.

Ellen was in Richard's room, examining paint. She scraped the windowsill with her fingernail and made another note. 'Lead,' she murmured. 'I'm almost sure of it.' She turned toward Cassandra and Mary as they walked in and held up one paint-flaked finger. 'A complication we could have lived without.'

Santa Louisa was an old town and had a fair amount of old houses, many of which had lead-based paint. Ellen had told her horror tales about getting rid of it. Another problem she, luckily, didn't have to deal with.

'I'm going to have to get Larry, the paint-scraper guy, out,' she said, disgust in her voice, 'and then we'll have to send samples to the lab. I'll bet it's in a lot of rooms.'

Mary turned to hand Cassandra her end of the tape, but she was sitting on the bed, staring at the few personal items Richard had left on the bureau, all neatly arranged. His bed was made as well. Mary wondered who'd made it. Lorraine? Or did Richard prefer privacy to maid service?

The handmade quilt was spread neatly, the pillows set evenly against the iron headboard. The white-and-gold Hurricane lamp sat precisely in the middle of a heavily embroidered doily in the middle of a freshly dusted bedside table. Richard was a tidy man. They'd have to make sure the quilt was smoothed again when they left, but it didn't seem that was going to be anytime soon.

'I need to apologize to both of you for Richard's behavior.' Cassandra looked at her hands, which were tightly clasped in her lap. She took a deep breath and glanced up just once before she went on. 'Richard isn't an easy man at the best of times, but he's been impossible on this trip. I think I owe you both an explanation.'

'Oh, no. You don't, and you don't need to apologize,' Ellen said.

Cassandra didn't look as if she'd heard Ellen or had taken in her diatribe about lead paint. Mary had expected her to at least ask what it meant, wanting to know what removing it entailed, but staring at Richard's rigidly neat room seemed to have once again triggered the worry and fear.

'What do you mean?' Ellen's frown was full of doubt and not a little suspicion. She pulled a tissue from her tote, wiped her finger, looked around for a trash can and finally dropped it back in her tote. 'He's been a…bit difficult, it's true, but it's not up to you to apologize. You haven't been.'

Cassandra looked from one of them to the other and sighed, evidently trying to decide where to begin. Millie jumped up on the bed and lay beside her, putting her head in Cassandra's lap. Certain Richard wouldn't appreciate a dog on his bed, Mary started for her but stopped. Cassandra's hand dropped on Millie's head and she started to stroke the dog. She relaxed, her breathing settled down and the tension in her face eased. Mary let the dog stay where she was. She'd pick every dog hair off by hand before they left, if necessary. In the meantime…

'We were brought up to resent our aunts. It never bothered me much, but Richard's felt they cheated him all his life.'

'Why?' Ellen had apparently forgotten all about the paint. The shocked look on her face was testimony Cassandra had her full attention.

Mary wasn't quite as shocked. Saddened, but not shocked. After all, she'd known Cassandra's father well and heard tales of Richard Plym Sr's attitude toward his children, about the disparity between what he expected from his only son and what he didn't expect from his twin daughters. She was about to hear more.

'My grandfather put my father through college and that was all. He expected him to go out and make something of himself. That was the phrase my father always used when he told the story, which he did frequently. He did, too. He established the furniture store chain my brother now owns. My grandfather assumed his daughters would need to be taken care of all their lives. If not by a husband, then by him, and he was right. Why they never married, I don't know, but when he died they got the house as part of the trust and all the money. My father was instructed to care for them if need be, but other than his college education, that was it. He never forgave my grandfather or his aunts, and he made sure his son, my brother, felt the same way.' She took a deep breath and lifted her hand off Millie's head.

Millie looked up, surprised.

'He also made sure I didn't expect to be treated like

my aunts. I wasn't. I went to college, worked after I graduated and married a man who was as far removed from the way my father and brother think as possible. Richard feels he…we…are finally getting what's owed us, and he came out here to make sure to collect it. Whatever that may be.' She gave Millie one last pat and stood.

Millie, visibly disappointed, jumped down.

'I want you both to know I don't share Richard's feelings.' She blinked hard a few times, as if trying to hold back tears, and forced a smile. 'OK. Let's get this measuring finished.' She turned to Ellen. 'Are you going to need to measure the attic?'

Ellen looked at her cell, then at Mary. 'It's getting late. What's up there?'

Cassandra shrugged. 'I've only been up there once. There's what used to be a playroom in the tower, then two small rooms that could be bedrooms but are empty. The rest is just…attic. Finished off, sort of, walls and carpet, lots of old furniture and some old trunks.'

'I'll eventually have to get up there, but for now I can estimate square footage. The rest won't lend value to my market analysis.'

A feeling of relief swept over Mary. She didn't want to go up there but she was torn. Could Miss Emilie have? She must have played up there as a child. Did she feel comfortable going up those stairs? Mary wasn't going to find out today.

The only conversation for the next half hour was about paint, worn carpeting, old-fashioned plumbing and other assorted house details. Neither Richard nor the Misses Emilie and Eloise were mentioned. They ended once more in the kitchen, Ellen seemingly all business, Mary upset but thoughtful.

Richard hadn't returned. Neither had Lorraine.

'All we have left is the carriage house and the grounds. I'll need to know where the property lines are...'

The look on Cassandra's face left Mary in no doubt Ellen would have to consult someone else on that subject.

A ghost of a smile passed over Ellen's face. 'After taking a look at the grounds and going through the carriage house, both the apartment and the garage, I'll be ready to go back to the office and see what I can put together. I've already got some ideas but I want to be sure before we decide how to proceed. I also have to talk to Glen about when we can get this on the market. We'll need to have some repairs made, and I want to talk to the planning department about zoning. Advertising this as a potential bed and breakfast is a good idea, but I have to be sure it can be done.'

'Do you think it's possible? To get the zoning, I mean. What will the city require?' Cassandra watched Ellen with a worried look on her face.

Mary was beginning to think it was a permanent fixture.

'Parking, for one thing, and that you have. This is probably three city lots. Then the other people who live on the street would have to agree. I think the city would like to see this whole street commercial in some way. It's quaint, it's historic and it's right around the corner from the park. However, some of the homeowners might not feel that way. I'll talk to the city manager tomorrow and see where we stand.'

'I don't think Richard is going to want to stay around much longer. But I can. I don't have any ties at home. My boys are away at college and my husband...' She turned to Mary. 'Maybe I could help you with one of your projects while I'm here.'

It wasn't actually a question and it wasn't quite an offer, but Mary made a practice of taking help wherever she could find it. Well, almost everywhere. There were some people…like Gloria Sutherland. She'd lose more volunteers than she'd get if Gloria showed up on one of her committees. But Gloria didn't volunteer unless it got her something she wanted. Briefly, she wondered why Gloria hadn't shown back up at the Plyms' with an offer to do something. Maybe Richard was too much for her. If so, it would be a first.

'I think I can put you to work,' she told Cassandra. 'Right now, however, I think Millie would like to go outside, and I'd like to go home. So, if we can get the rest of the measuring and pictures done…' She looked at Ellen with a 'let's get this show on the road' look.

Ellen nodded, put her cell phone, tape measure and the legal pad with all the measurements written beside the name of each room in her tote and headed for the door. 'This shouldn't take long.'

Cassandra followed, her face starting to look tired and drawn. Mary paused. Millie was pulling on the leash, but she had one more thing to check. Sure enough, there was a little white box right beside the kitchen door. There was probably one guarding the front door as well. Hopefully she could check before they left, but she doubted there were any others. There were two other outside doors—the French doors in the dining room, which were locked with a sliding bolt across the top, and the sliding glass door that opened out from the morning room onto the same lovely veranda the dining room did. It had a broom handle in the trough the door slid in. The two patios were separated by a low privet hedge. There would be no need to put a motion detector on either door. How the lock on the front door worked, Mary didn't know, nor did she know if it had a motion detector, but it shouldn't be hard to find out. Millie strained at the leash and gave one sharp bark. Maybe she'd take Millie through the front door to find her tree.

'You two go on to Lorraine and Caleb's. Millie and I will be there in a minute.'

Ellen laughed and walked out the kitchen door, Cassandra following slowly behind.

TWENTY-TWO

'WHY, THIS IS NICE.' Mary walked through the front door of the apartment and stopped in surprise.

Cassandra held one end of the tape measure for Ellen and turned to smile at Mary. 'Yes, it is very nice.'

A large window looked down on the side yard of the Plym house. The kitchen porch was at the back of the house and was barely visible through the trees that provided privacy for the Plyms but did nothing to block the view of the brick driveway and the street. The dining-room veranda and the morning room were on the opposite side of the house, but the front porch… Mary stood at the window, wondering if she moved back just a little… you couldn't see the front porch but you could plainly see the front walk. There was a streetlight almost directly opposite the walk, right where it joined the sidewalk. Anyone who came out of the Plym house by the front door would be visible, day or night. She turned back to examine the room.

The staircase ran up one side of the carriage house, so the entry to the living room opened directly into a large, well-lit and comfortable room, a dining alcove at the far end. The kitchen must be behind it, forming an L. A small hall opened immediately to the left as you entered, leading to a bath and at least one bedroom. The rooms seemed good sized, the windows large, the overall effect one of compact but comfortable living. The furnishing didn't give quite the same impression. Clean and serviceable, there was nothing attractive or interesting about the beige sofa or the two brown recliners. The lovely quilt thrown over the back of the sofa and the quilted pillows that sat in the recliners stood out in sharp contrast. Lorraine's work? If so, Lorraine was indeed talented. Mary walked over for a closer look.

Mary didn't quilt. She had quite enough projects to fill her time, but she remembered her grandmother sitting in her chair, her quilting square in her lap, bags of scraps of material stacked on the dining-room table. Quilting had been an obsession with her, and Mary had learned at an early age to appreciate the artistry involved, even though she had no desire to follow in her footsteps. Lorraine seemed to be in her grandmother's category. 'These pieces are beautiful. Did Lorraine do the quilt in Richard's room?'

Cassandra looked blank. 'I didn't even know she quilted.' She started toward the dining area, looked out the windows, examined the pine floor and entered the kitchen. 'This is nice and sunny. Oh. Look at the appliances. They're almost antiques, but there's a nice laundry room…'

A door opened. A door? What door? She looked at Ellen, who raised an eyebrow. They walked into the kitchen, Millie at Mary's heel. Cassandra had disappeared.

The laundry room was large, with lots of cupboards, another large window and an open door. Millie headed for it. Mary grabbed her leash just as she stepped onto a porch. A stairway descended from it and ended in a service yard below. Assorted garbage cans sat neatly, and cleanly, on a concrete pad at the base of the staircase, a newly planted vegetable and herb garden on the far side of it.

'My, my.' Mary stood at the top of the stairs and watched Cassandra wander through the neat garden rows. 'That must be Caleb's project. He's the gardener. At least, he does all the yard work.' She called down, 'I had no idea all this was here.'

'No one else would, either.' Ellen stood on the little porch, also watching Cassandra. 'You can't see this staircase from the street, but I don't think you can see it from the Plym house or the other houses, either. It's totally private back here. It would make a really nice patio.'

'Hmmm.' It was indeed private. 'Let's go take a look at the rest of it. It's getting late and I'd rather not be here when Caleb comes home. I know he gave permission, but still…'

Ellen grimaced. 'Good idea.' She called down to Cassandra, 'We're going to take pictures of the rest of the apartment. Do you want to come back up or should we meet you back at the other house?'

'I'm coming.' Cassandra headed for the staircase, with only a quick look back at the garden and the large old California oaks beyond it. 'It's nice here.'

Mary and Millie were already back inside. Mary examined the kitchen appliances with a dubious eye. Millie sniffed the floor in the forlorn hope Lorraine might have missed a crumb.

Ellen's opinion of the appliances wasn't any better than her aunt's. 'The Plyms weren't much on updating, were they? Poor Lorraine doesn't even have a dishwasher.'

Mary thought there were worse things you could be without but didn't say so.

Ellen, her tablet once more in hand, addressed Cassandra as she walked into the kitchen. 'Are the appliances the Duxworths' or did the Plyms supply them?'

'I have no idea.' Cassandra stared at the stove with distaste, walked over, opened the freezer door and shuddered. It was as full of ice as it was food. 'Does it matter?'

'It does if the Duxworths bought them and plan to take them when they leave. I'll add it to my list of questions for Lorraine. The cabinets are all right. The drawers seem to pull on runners… What's this?'

'What's what?' Mary was caught by the tone in Ellen's voice. She walked over to peer into the drawer Ellen had pulled out. 'What are you looking at?'

'That.' Ellen pointed at a key lying in the drawer, a piece of cardboard attached bearing the initials SMCH. There was no mistaking Mary's handiwork or what the key opened.

'That's a church hall key.'

'Seems to be.'

'They have two of them?'

'Seems so.'

Mary didn't say anything for a moment. She just looked at the key. Finally she looked at Ellen. 'They might each have a key, but what's one doing hanging in the Plym house?'

Ellen, her mouth thinned out to a straight line, shrugged. 'I think we just added another thing to ask Lorraine.'

A soft chirping sound interrupted Ellen. She looked around, and so did Mary.

'It sounds like a bird is trapped in here, but I don't see one.'

'Or a smoke alarm that needs a new battery.' Ellen made another note.

Cassandra looked up from her investigation of the stove. 'It's the motion detector. Richard must be back.'

'Motion detector?' Ellen looked around, confused. The noise seemed to be coming from a white monitor on a small desk beside the counter. There was a row of green lights and one that was blinking red. 'Is it that thing?'

Mary walked over to it and watched the light blink. The chirping she ignored. Or tried to. Millie didn't. She was beside Mary, head cocked, staring at the monitor, then started to howl. At first softly, then louder, as if trying to drown out the chirping.

'Hush,' Mary told her. Millie howled on.

'Caleb wasn't supposed to have this on while we were here.' Cassandra reached over and hit a switch, a deep frown of displeasure on her face.

The machine fell silent. So did Millie.

'What is that thing?' Ellen stared at the machine, which now showed nothing but green lights. 'Why does Caleb have a…oh. Miss Emilie. Is this the motion detector?'

Cassandra nodded. 'It's the monitor. I was worried about leaving her in that big house all alone every night, especially since she didn't seem very…' She broke off and shook her head slightly.

'Reliable?' Mary suggested.

Cassandra smiled and nodded. 'Lorraine said she'd sleep over there, but Caleb didn't like that idea. He said he could get an alarm set up and they'd put the monitor here. That way they'd know if she tried to wander at night. It seemed like a good idea. I told him I'd pay for it so to get a good one. He did and set it up before I left. He and I discussed where to put the monitors and he showed me how this thing works.' She motioned to the now-quiet box. 'You can set the alarm to go off like a fire bell or to chirp or have a different sound for each zone.'

'Where did you put the devices?' Mary had seen a few, but there were more green buttons on the box than devices she'd seen. Had she missed some?

'Let's see if I can remember.' Cassandra's brow furrowed as she stared at the box. 'There are six stations possible, but I think we only used five. The front door, of course, and the kitchen door. That's the one Richard must have come in just now. One on the doors leading into the back staircase, another on Miss Emilie's bedroom door and… I think we put the last one on the morning-room door. She loved that room and often sat outside on the little porch.'

'Not one on the attic door?'

Cassandra hesitated. 'I don't think so. I asked Caleb about that, but he said she never went up there.'

Mary found herself wishing she'd gone up the stairs and looked at the attic door, but she only nodded. She'd glanced into the morning room before she and Millie had gone out front but hadn't seen one and, by that time, she'd been looking for them. So, where was the sixth one? 'Can they be moved around?'

'Oh, yes. This operates on batteries, so you can put the devices wherever you want.'

'Let me get this straight.' Ellen looked from the monitor to Cassandra, then to her aunt. 'You set the house up so you could spy on Miss Emilie?'

'It wasn't spying. We wanted to make sure she didn't go outside in the middle of the night and get lost or hurt.'

There was a defensiveness in Cassandra's voice that was tinged with a little guilt, at least Mary thought so. Leaving that old lady all alone in the house with no one to help her didn't seem a good idea, devices or no devices. 'What about locks on the doors?'

'The only ones she hadn't managed to unlock were the French doors in the dining room, and that's because the lock at the top is hard to slide. There are dead bolts on both the front and back doors, but they were no challenge. I had Caleb put on chain locks but I think they only used the one in front. They needed to be able to get in the house if she needed help. The monitor alerted them more than once when she was at a door, or through it. She never got off the block before he found her and brought her back. Except that last night.' She made a little choking sound.

Mary thought Cassandra was going to break into tears. She didn't.

She gathered herself together and went on: 'If only I hadn't taken those blasted sleeping pills.' She blinked rapidly, looked at Ellen and said in a brisk manner, 'Are we finished here?'

'As soon as I measure the bedroom and see the bathroom.' Ellen took one last look at the monitor, gathered up her materials and headed out of the kitchen, back into the living room.

Mary and Cassandra followed. Millie was still looking for crumbs but followed when Mary called out to her.

'Nice and sunny.' Ellen stood in the doorway to what appeared to be the only bedroom. There was a window at the far end of the room, overlooking the back stairs and the grove of oaks; another was at the side, just beyond the main staircase with a good view of the Plym house and the driveway. The double bed and highboy dresser left plenty of room for the large quilting frame set up on two sawhorses. A quilt in progress was stretched out on it and a stack of quilt squares sat ready to be stitched in place on a low table beside it. Needles, thread, padding, scissors—all the equipment needed by someone making a work of art out of scraps of cloth was neatly arranged on it. Mary saw nothing else but the quilt.

'Will you look at this! Every stitch done by hand…and the stitches! Just beautiful. Oh, it's all birds. How lovely.'

The bag of fluffy filling looked hardly touched but it wouldn't be needed until the back went on. Lorraine had several squares stitched together but there were a number still waiting their turn. It appeared she'd finished the individual squares and had only the construction of the quilt left to do. Lorraine would use every bit of the padding in that package and, Mary was sure, a lot more before she finished. She touched the perfection of the stiches: so even, so carefully spaced, maybe she should try…what was she thinking! She had more to do than she had hours in the day as it was. She'd admire Lorraine's. There was another quilt pinned to a pants hanger hanging on the back of the closet door. It was folded over so only part of the pattern was visible. It looked as if it had a different wildflower on each square. The lining around the main body of the quilt was smooth and even, and the corners were square and precise. Truly the work of a master craftswoman. If Lorraine had made the quilt on Richard's bed, she'd come a long way.

'We're done. If you're finished looking at the quilts, let's get out of here.'

Mary turned quickly, gathered up Millie's leash and, with one backward look at the quilts, followed Cassandra and Ellen down the stairs.

TWENTY-THREE

ELLEN SLOWED AS she made the turn out of the Plyms' street, made sure the child on the too-big bike wasn't going to fall off in front of her and eased the car forward. 'You haven't said a word since we left. What's bothering you?'

'It's more like what's not.'

'Would you care to explain?'

'There are too many odd little things and they're all pointing in different directions. I can't figure out what matters and what doesn't.'

'Like?'

'Like that motion detector.'

'That seemed pretty straightforward. They could go home and go to bed and still know if Miss Emilie got up and went outside. What's wrong with that?'

'Besides the fact she was all alone up there? What if she'd fallen? Or gotten scared in the night?' She shook her head, thinking how no machine could take the place of nurturing care, but that was no longer a concern. Why she left the house the night she died was.

Ellen came to a full stop at a yellow light, much to the disgust of the man behind her. He let her know his displeasure by honking loudly.

She twisted in her seat to stare at her aunt. 'We know the detectors were off that night. We also know Cassandra took sleeping pills and Richard slept with his door closed. We also know Emilie went looking for her toy dog and someone saw her and went after her. What else?'

'We don't know any of those things. We surmise. Caleb says he turned off the detectors, Cassandra says she took sleeping pills and that Richard closed his door. Someone could have gone into Miss Emilie's room, got her up, told her they were going to look for her dog and taken her to the church hall.'

'And made up her bed before they left? Why?'

'That someone came and got her, or who made her bed?'

'Both.'

The light turned green. Ellen eased the car forward, evidently not fast enough for the man behind her. He pulled around her and headed down the street.

'That man needs a ticket,' Mary observed. 'This is all about the money. It has to be. Miss Emilie might have gone back to the church hall looking for Willis, but I think whoever killed her was looking for the money.'

Ellen turned the corner onto Mary's street, then into her driveway. She shut off the motor and clicked off her seat belt before turning to face her aunt. 'If that's so, then the killer didn't take her money.'

'Maybe no one took her money.'

'What are you talking about?'

'Maybe she hid it.'

Ellen was momentarily speechless. 'How could she… the note…she wouldn't have known when the first of the month was…someone had to have helped her. You don't think that person took her money?'

'I don't know, but someone's looking for it, and it can't be the same person who robbed her.'

Ellen stared at her aunt. 'That's true. If someone took

her money, they'd know where it was. So, why kill her? But, if you didn't know where it was and thought she may have hidden it...only, who?'

'I wish I knew.' Mary undid her seat belt and opened the door. 'Go do whatever you're going to do for Richard and Cassandra. Millie and I aren't going to do one more thing today.'

'Good. It's been a rough couple of days and you've got the rummage sale later this week. Do you need anything?'

Mary smiled and shook her head. She held the door for Millie, who jumped out and headed for the back gate. She closed the car door and stood in the driveway, watching Ellen back out, then opened the gate, waited for Millie to go through and closed it behind them.

TWENTY-FOUR

THE NEXT MORNING was bright with sunshine that actually seemed to warm the air. Mary took her coffee outside to walk around the yard while Millie sniffed the bushes. The roses were starting to put out tender red shoots. Spring really was here. She let the sun warm her while she waited for Millie, and thought. It was really a continuation of the thoughts that wound through her head all last night like a swarm of bees. They still buzzed this morning, but so far, that's all they were doing.

Millie was still meandering through the flower beds when the phone rang. Mary started up the stairs in no hurry. The answering machine would pick up the call if she missed it, and she didn't really want to talk to anyone this early anyway. The last few days had been horrific and this morning was, so far, peaceful and pleasant. A phone call at eight in the morning meant someone wanted her to do something. Mary didn't want to do anything, at least not until she'd finished her coffee.

The phone was still ringing when she entered the kitchen. She must have forgotten to turn the answering machine back on last night. She sighed. If whoever was on the other end needed her so badly they'd let the blasted thing ring a dozen times, she'd better answer it.

It was Ellen. 'Are you all right?'

'I'm fine. I was outside, looking at the rose bushes, and it took a minute. What's the matter? You sound upset.'

There was a tone in Ellen's voice that Mary rarely heard. She might have wanted to know how her aunt was, but that wasn't why she'd called. The little choking sound that came over the phone convinced Mary that, once more, something was wrong. 'What is it?'

'You know how yesterday you were commenting we hadn't seen Gloria Sutherland for a couple of days? That you were surprised she hadn't shown back up at the Plyms'?'

Mary was filled with dread. She took the phone and what was left of her coffee over to the kitchen table and sat down. 'Yes. I remember.'

'They found her.'

The dread got stronger. 'What do you mean, found her. She wasn't missing, was she? She just hasn't turned up… where is she?' A shiver ran through her, strong enough to make her put the half-full mug of coffee on the table. This wasn't going to be good.

There was a quiver in Ellen's voice. 'You know that steep hill across from Gloria's house, the one that ends up in that little ravine? We looked down it the day we took the walk up there. Do you remember how the dogs wanted to go down there? Well, they found Gloria at the base of it this morning, up against a tree, dead. She's been there a couple of days.'

It took Mary a minute before she could say anything. 'Do they know what happened?'

'Dan says it could have been an accident. She could have fallen and rolled down the hill. I guess she was pretty banged up, so…'

Mary wondered if Ellen felt as sick to her stomach as she did. She'd never much liked Gloria, even as a child, but this! 'Are they sure it was an accident?'

Again, a pause. 'No.'

'Oh.' She wasn't surprised. It wasn't that she'd expected this, but somehow… Agnes. She'd seen Gloria the night Miss Emilie had been murdered, walking through the downtown around…what time had Agnes said? Somewhere between one and two. She was coming from the direction of both the Plym house and the church. Had she seen something? Someone? If so, what had she done with that information? Something that had gotten her killed? Poor Gloria. 'Who found her?'

'The people who live on the hill across from Gloria. Their property ends in the ravine somewhere but they never go down there. The only reason they did this morning was because their dog was down there, barking, and wouldn't come back up.'

'What does Dan say?'

'Lots, none of it fit to repeat. He's on his way down to San Luis Obispo to meet with the coroner. He wants an autopsy done, now. He's going to get a court order to go through her house and will be back here in a couple of hours.'

'He's going through…does he think she was killed in her house?'

'I think he wants to look through her bank records.' Ellen's voice was stark. 'I think he's going to be looking for the missing fifty thousand dollars.' There was a pause then Ellen resumed, her voice still a little shaky. 'I've got to go. We have an office meeting and I really should be there. Look, I'll call you later after I talk to Dan.' She paused again. 'Are you going to be all right?'

'Of course.' Mary realized that came out a little tart. She hadn't meant it to, but if Ellen thought she'd be overcome with grief, well, she wasn't. Shocked, upset and more than a little worried, but sadly there was no grief involved. 'Call me on my cell. I have some things to do.'

Millie ate her breakfast with pleasure. Mary finished another two cups of coffee, forced down a piece of toast, did a little housework that could no longer be put off and answered the phone. Several times. The news was out, the local radio and TV stations not only were reporting it but embellishing the story with every grizzly non-fact they could dream up. Gloria might not have had the recognition in life she would have liked, but she was getting plenty in death.

TWENTY-FIVE

AT EXACTLY TEN O'CLOCK, Mary and Millie walked into Furry Friends Pet Shop. John stood behind the counter. Krissie, a small hairy dog under one arm, leaned against the front of it, talking to him intently. They both looked up when the bell rang.

'You've heard the news?' John asked after he'd scratched Millie's ears. 'Of course you have. So has everyone else in town. I can't believe it. How could she fall down the hill and break her neck?'

'Break her neck? Where did you hear that?' Mary stopped short to stare at John. 'Is that what they're saying on the news?'

'Isn't that what happened?'

Krissie shifted the dog to her other arm.

She glanced from John back to Mary. From the expression on her face, Mary thought they'd been discussing how Gloria had fallen down the hill and if someone had helped break her neck. She sighed. 'Last I heard they didn't know what happened. Dan's in San Luis. He wants an autopsy right away.'

'He also wants bank records.' John's face was an interesting combination of pleasure that he had a good piece of gossip to report, and sadness. For Gloria? Mary didn't think so. He barely knew her and hadn't seemed to like her much.

'How do you know that?' Krissie was more than willing to take the bait. 'Why would he want her bank records?'

John reddened. 'Glen said…that is, don't the police always want them?'

'Not unless they think you're selling drugs, embezzling from someone or forging checks. At least, that's why they want them in the mysteries I read.' Krissie narrowed her carefully plucked eyebrows at him. 'Do they think Gloria was doing one of those things?'

'No one thinks anything right now,' Mary inserted firmly. 'It could very well have been an accident. It's slippery on the side of that bank.'

'How do you know?' John looked taken aback.

'Millie and I took a walk up there a few days ago. The view is beautiful but that bank is really steep. If she walked out on it she could have slipped.'

'I can't see Gloria walking out on the edge of a cliff.' John sounded certain.

Mary was inclined to agree with him but they didn't know that for sure. They didn't know anything for sure, except that poor Gloria was dead. However, the absence of facts would in no way stop the rumors flying. That they were already aloft, she had no doubt, and that served no one well.

'We'll have to wait and see what the police say.' Mary's voice was firm. The conversation about Gloria's death had ended. She turned toward Krissie. 'I came in to see if you had any time to groom Millie on Thursday. That's the rummage sale day, and it's going to be hectic. I don't want to leave Millie at home but I don't want her in the church hall, either. I thought we might combine events.'

Krissie's eyes shifted to Millie. She appeared to be mentally clipping and shearing as she stared at her from the front then walked around to view her from the side. 'Thursday. That's the day after tomorrow. Let's look at the book. She sure does need grooming, poor little thing.'

Mary didn't think Millie needed a haircut that badly, and she certainly wasn't a 'poor little thing.' She brushed her daily and, since she wasn't going to a dog show soon, or ever, a little long hair didn't seem so bad. But she probably would be more comfortable, and it would be a safe place for her to spend Thursday. Mary followed Krissie to the grooming room, John trotting along behind. Krissie placed the little dog into a crate, telling him she'd be with him shortly, then pulled a book out of a drawer in a counter along the back wall. Millie immediately stuck her nose in the grill on the crate. Commiserating with the dog? Mary wasn't sure, but that thought was interrupted by Krissie.

'I can take her at ten.'

'Oh.' Mary's face fell. 'I'll never be able to leave and get her over here at that time. Can you take her earlier?'

Krissie shook her head. 'I have two at nine and I can't get here any earlier. I'm sorry.'

'I'll come get her. How about if I pick her up at the community hall about eight? I'll be in the shop by then, anyway. I don't open till ten but I'm always here earlier, feeding, cleaning, that kind of thing. Would that work?'

'John, you're a saint.'

He turned a rather becoming shade of red. 'I somehow doubt that.'

Mary smiled. 'How about a really good friend.'

John laughed. 'I can go along with that.' He paused. 'What time does the sale end?'

'We open the doors at eight and close them at three. Why? Is that going to be a problem?'

'Hmmm. Let's see. Krissie leaves about two; I have to be at the hospital no later than three. They have a surgery scheduled I've done a hundred times and no one else seems to know what to do. I'll leave here about two thirty and will have to lock the shop for a while. Glen can't get here until four. Do you still have the key I gave you?'

Mary nodded. 'I meant to give it back but forgot.'

'Good. Then when I leave, I'll put Millie in one of the crates until you can get here. Come in the back way so no one will think you're opening the store. That will save you some grief.'

Mary laughed. 'That's perfect. Thank you.'

The bell on the door rang. Millie lifted her head, left the dog in the crate and started out toward it.

'Oh, no you don't. John doesn't need any help.' Mary gathered up Millie's leash and motioned for her to sit. She did.

The bell rang again, indicating the customer had left. 'Oh, dear, I hope I didn't lose you a customer.'

'It was Mrs Duxworth. The one who makes the beautiful quilts. She came in, did a quick look round and left. Odd. They don't have any animals, do they?' From where Krissie stood, behind the grooming table, she had a clear view of the front door. Puzzled, she looked from John back to Mary. 'What do you suppose she wanted?'

John shrugged. 'Poor thing. She always looks so sad. She was in here one day, petting a kitten. You could tell she really wanted it. Her husband came in…you know, the one who works at the grade school, and reamed her out good. I guess he does it on a regular basis. If Glen treated me that way…'

'Glen never would.' Mary smiled at John, who smiled back, a tender and confident smile.

'No. He never would.'

'Is it true he sells off her quilts and doesn't give her any of the money?' Krissie sounded personally affronted that anyone would do such a thing.

Mary thought it had happened to many women over the years and, in some areas, still did, but that didn't make it less disgusting.

'I hadn't heard that,' Mary said slowly. She surprised herself by how readily she accepted that it might be true. Caleb acted as if he thought Lorraine's opinion didn't matter or that anything she did didn't have much value. Evidently he'd found value in something, but if Krissie was right, it didn't sound as if Lorraine would get much credit for it, let alone any money. 'How do you know that?'

'My mother quilted before her hands got so bad. I still know some of the Quilting Bees. One of them was telling me after church a while back.'

John snorted. 'That's only half of that story. Her husband has a couple of accounts at the bank but her name isn't on them. He gives her an allowance. What a guy.'

Krissie and Mary both stared at John, at a loss for words.

'In this day and age, can you even imagine?' Disgust was in every word Krissie uttered.

Mary couldn't. It would never have occurred to her, or to Samuel, that she wouldn't have been an equal partner in their marriage, in every way. 'Are you sure?'

John nodded. 'I'm sure.'

Krissie knelt down and lifted the little dog out of the crate. 'I don't want to seem rude but I've got to get Poochie done. What with the radio telling about Mrs Sutherland's death and then John and me talking, I'm way behind. Don't worry about Millie. I'll make sure she looks beautiful for you.' She smiled at Mary, wiggled her fingers at Millie and set Poochie on the grooming table. She was crooning to him, laughing and running her fingers up and down his little spine as John and Mary walked back to the checkout counter.

'What do you think really happened?' The expression on John's face was a mix of worry and vexation. 'I can't believe any of this. First Miss Emilie, the sweetest thing that ever lived, and now Gloria.' He paused then lowered his voice to almost a whisper. 'Do you think there's a connection?'

'For heaven's sake, John. We don't know what happened to Gloria. We're not completely sure what happened to Miss Emilie and we definitely don't know why. Right now we have to wait and see what Dan finds out.'

'What about the money?' He spoke so low she could barely hear. 'We know Miss Emilie took out a whole lot of money the last few months and it's gone. Do you think Gloria took it?'

Mary wasn't sure she hadn't, but she wasn't going to speculate about it with John. There were all kinds of odd things going on. Mary had no idea what was important and what wasn't, and as fond of John as she was, he loved to gossip. Rumors might be flying but she wasn't about to lend any of them wings.

'Millie and I have to drop in on Luke,' she said, picking up her tote bag and gathering up Millie's leash. 'Are you sure you don't mind picking her up Thursday morning? It will be such a help. I won't have to worry about her and she'll come home nice and clean.'

'Also beautiful. I don't mind a bit. Why are you going to see Luke?'

'The Friends of the Library book sale is almost upon us and I haven't done one thing. I need to get it organized. As I'm not scheduled this afternoon, I thought I'd have a look at the books already donated.'

'Tell Luke I said "hi."'

The bell over the door sounded and a young man walked through, holding a little boy of about three by the hand. 'We wondered if you have any of those little turtles for sale.'

'Oh, dear.' The worried look on John's face was back, intensified as he looked at the child. 'For this young man?'

The father nodded.

John took a deep breath and let it out slowly, while trying to smile. 'Turtles are very fragile. Perhaps something a little less…'

Mary smiled as she and Millie left. She couldn't imagine what animal John could substitute that would make the child happy and continue to live. Three-year-olds weren't known for their gentleness. A goldfish? Probably not.

'Mary.'

The voice sounded loud, clear and very upset. Lorraine stood across the street, hailing her. Mary stopped, startled. It was almost as if Lorraine had been waiting for her, but why would she do that?

'Wait up, can you?'

Maybe she had been. Mary stopped and waited for Lorraine to get to her. 'Are you all right?'

Lorraine didn't look all right. She looked frazzled. Her hair was combed but it looked as if she'd run one through it without looking in the mirror. It lay at odd angles on her scalp, with little wisps swaying slightly in the light mid-morning breeze. Her cardigan sweater wasn't buttoned over her long-sleeved T-shirt. Instead, she clutched it around her as if it was a shawl. Her blue eyes were tinged with red as if she'd been crying. Mary sighed. Lorraine had heard about Gloria.

'No…yes…oh, Mary, I don't know. Is it true? Did someone kill Gloria too?' Lorraine moved in, so close Mary stepped back a little, barely avoiding Millie.

The dog sat close to Mary's leg, as usual, looking at Lorraine with obvious curiosity and not a little trepidation. Millie wasn't used to seeing people on the edge of collapse.

Mary tried to keep her tone as soothing as possible for both their sakes. 'It's true Gloria is dead, but killed? That we don't know.'

Lorraine stared at her, mouth going but no words coming out. Finally she whispered, 'What happened?'

'I don't know for sure. She was found this morning down in the ravine across the street from her house, dead. She had…a lot of bruises and a head injury. From what I heard, nothing that wasn't consistent with losing her balance and falling down the hill. The police are looking into it now.'

Lorraine didn't exactly relax but her hands didn't clutch the edges of her sweater as tightly, and her lips no longer seemed to be drawn over her teeth in as tight a line. 'It might have been an accident? She might not have been murdered?'

'No one I've talked to has used the word murder.' Mary said this with a firmness based on truth. No one had used that word. That it was implicit in every word Ellen uttered was another thing altogether.

Lorraine eased a little more, her eyes calmer, but her

forehead was still creased with what had to be worry. ‘So we wait until the police say what happened?’ Her voice sounded a little stronger.

Mary nodded. ‘That’s all we can do. That and not listen to rumors. They’re flying around here thicker than flies at a barbeque.’

Lorraine took a breath that sounded like it might have been the first one she’d taken all day. ‘All right.’

Mary took a step but Lorraine put out her hand. ‘There’s something else.’

Oh, Lord. What else could there possibly be? Mary smiled slightly and waited.

‘The dog. Willis. Miss Emilie’s stuffed dog.’ Lorraine’s slightly wild-eyed look was back. ‘Do you know where it is? Did it ever turn up?’

Mary almost blurted out that she did indeed know where the dog was, but stopped. ‘Why?’

‘Miss Emilie loved that dog so, and I thought no one else would want him. I thought if you knew where he was, I’d wash him up, you know, repair him if he needed it, and we could bury it with her.’

It wasn’t often someone left Mary McGill without words, but Lorraine Duxworth had done it this time. Bury a stuffed animal with a woman well into her eighties. It was ludicrous. Of course, Miss Emilie didn’t seem to realize he wasn’t real, and she did love the blasted thing. Maybe…

Mary would have to think about it. She’d also have to think about how to put this without lying. ‘I don’t think it’s in the community hall,’ she said slowly, ‘but it may turn up. I’ll keep my eye out for it and won’t let it be sold on Thursday if it does.’

There. That was all true, but it didn’t seem to make

Lorraine feel any better. She still looked as if she was going to break back out in tears any minute. She didn't move, only stood clutching her sweater and blinking her eyes. Finally she said, 'I have to go. Caleb's coming home for lunch and he likes it on the table when he gets there. I have to get something for Cassandra and Richard, too.' She looked around, as if making sure no one but Mary could hear her. Her whisper was loud and raspy. 'I hated Gloria Sutherland. She was a conniving and deceitful woman.' She turned as if to leave but swung back to face Mary. 'If you find that dog, you will let me know?' The anxiety in her voice and in her eyes was palpable. 'I keep thinking of her, lying in her coffin without that dog, and it just breaks my heart.'

This time, shoulders hunched as if trying to withstand a strong wind, she walked away.

'Millie, do you have any idea what's going on? Because I sure don't.' Mary sighed as Lorraine disappeared around the corner. 'Bury the dog with Miss Emilie? Breaks her heart? She doesn't make any more sense than anything else around here. Except that she hated Gloria. I'll bet she did, but I can't quite see her pushing Gloria over the bank and watching her roll down the hill. I don't know. Come on.' Mary hitched her tote securely on her shoulder and started forward, Millie on her feet, trotting beside Mary. 'It's time we got some real information. We're going to the police station. Luke and the books will just have to wait.'

TWENTY-SIX

'THE CORONER THINKS she was probably dead when she rolled down the side of the gully, and there's no sign of the money. Unless she hid the cash somewhere, she didn't take it.'

Mary sat in a heavy brown chair with uncomfortable arm rests across from Dan in his overcrowded office. Millie lay on a big new dog bed that had been placed under the one window, close by Morgan's side. Dan had just returned from San Luis Obispo when she walked in the station. He hadn't waited for her to ask him questions but had volunteered answers.

'When will she be sure?'

'Couple of days. However…'

Mary didn't like that 'however.' It usually meant she'd end up doing something she didn't want to. 'However… what?'

'Gloria was an only child.'

'There's nothing I can do about that. Oh, no.'

'Oh, yes. She has relatives—we're trying to find them now—but it looks as if none of them live close by. Hopefully they'll take care of whatever services they want to have. I've already alerted Les and have passed on the phone number for an aunt. In the meantime…'

'You're going to go through her house before the aunt or anyone else arrives. Well, that's your job, but it's not mine, and I'm not going with you.'

Dan smiled. 'I haven't asked you.'

'Not yet.'

'You sound reluctant.'

'I'm more than reluctant. I'm not going to go near her house. If you need someone, get Agnes.'

Dan laughed out loud. 'Let's hope the aunt arrives and takes care of everything.' Then his face changed. Laughter was gone. 'But I do have a court order, and I do need to go through the house. That she was killed seems certain, and we have to treat it as a potential crime scene. I've already put the wheels in motion.' Fleetingly, the grin was back. 'You don't have to do a thing.'

'Good.' She looked at Dan, who'd turned to watch Morgan and Millie, but she didn't think he really saw them. He was probably thinking of something else, and she was sure it had nothing to do with dogs.

'Dan, do you think the same person who killed Miss Emilie killed Gloria? I thought Gloria might have stolen the money and, for some reason, killed Miss Emilie, but I guess that theory no longer works.'

Dan shook his head. 'It's about the only thing I can rule out right now. I don't have a shred of concrete evidence that points to anyone, but it would be a stretch to think I had two murderers running around. I was also looking hard at Gloria, and it's still possible she may have taken Miss Emilie's money, but I think there may be another reason Gloria died.'

'You think she was trying to blackmail someone and that's why she was killed?'

'I don't think we can rule it out. Agnes is sticking to her story that she saw her in town the night Miss Emilie was killed, so it's possible she saw something she wasn't supposed to. But what, or who, I don't know. If I had to rely on fingerprints we picked up from the church hall, I'd have to arrest half the town.'

'What about the white clock? Did you get anything from it?'

This time Dan's grin was wide. 'The best fingerprint we got off that clock was yours.'

'I guess that wasn't much help.'

'Nope. Not much.'

'So, now what do you do?'

'See what the crime lab turns up at Gloria's house and see if there's any sign of money in her accounts that shouldn't be there.'

Mary didn't say anything for a minute. Morgan gave Millie's ears a bath.

Mary turned back to Dan. 'Do you think it's possible Miss Emilie didn't turn the money over to anyone but hid it somewhere herself?'

Several expressions passed across Dan's face, none of them happy. Finally, he said, 'Possible, yes. Probable, I just don't know. It's almost impossible to know what went on in Miss Emilie's mind. Going to the bank and taking out money was part of her program, had been for years, but I don't know if she realized just how much she was taking out. It worries me she asked you if five thousand dollars was a lot of money. Makes me think she might have started to question things. If she took it out for some reason of her own and hid it, she's done a darn good job. I'm sure Richard and Cassandra have gone through the house and, as far as I know, they haven't come up with anything.'

Mary was equally as sure neither Richard nor Cassandra had found the missing money. At least, Richard hadn't. He'd probably be on his way back to Baltimore, the money hidden in his suitcase, if he had. He'd consider it his and going through legal channels, or possibly even sharing it with his sister, would never occur to him. If it did, he'd brush the thought aside quickly. But if Cassandra had found it, what would she do? Mary wasn't sure.

'It's too bad Caleb's motion detectors don't tell us who is moving about, not just that someone is.'

Dan stiffened. 'What?' The thoughtful man, pondering pieces of a puzzle he couldn't seem to solve was suddenly a bloodhound that had just picked up the scent. 'What motion detectors?'

'The ones in the Plym house. Cassandra had Caleb install them when she was here for Miss Eloise's funeral. It has little white things you mount on the wall, and if someone breaks the beam it rings at the monitor. In this case, it chirps like a bird. Didn't Ellen tell you?'

'No. A motion detector.' Dan let the words roll around in his mouth as if getting used to the idea. 'Why not just lock the doors?'

'A couple of reasons. At least, I suppose so. Most people with dementia are pretty good at unlocking doors. Why, I don't know, but they often seem to feel the need to move, walk, go someplace. You can lock them in with padlocks or bolts, but if you do, you'd better be darn sure you can get to them in a hurry in case they fall or set the house on fire. In this case, no one was going to be in the house with Miss Emilie, so no one would know if she escaped or hurt herself or tried to make breakfast and forgot to turn off the stove. But with a motion detector system, they'd know if she moved through the designated doorways. The little blinking light indicates which room the person went in or out of, just by watching the lights.

Caleb said it wasn't turned on the night Miss Emilie died. Richard's instructions.'

Dan closed his eyes and started to shake his head back and forth, muttering something under his breath. Finally he opened them. 'I employ two full-time detectives plus half-a-dozen patrol officers and an office manager who picks up gossip like dogs pick up fleas but can't manage to keep the files straight. Do you know where most of my factual information comes from? You. How can that be?' He turned to his computer, muttering while he brought up the file he wanted, scrolled down, scrolled up, scrolled down again and said a word Mary thought expressed his sentiments but didn't bear repeating.

'There's no mention of a motion detector. Not one word.' He glared at her.

'What are you looking at?'

'The file on the Plym murder, that's what. I sent Pete Nugent, my new guy, over to the Plym house the day we found her. His report's right here. Agnes typed it up. Now I'll have to go through the paper file and see if he mentions it in his notes. If Agnes didn't think it was important, it's not beyond belief she simply wouldn't have included it. However, he might not have noticed it. I don't think he ever got out of the kitchen. So, unless one of them mentioned it… Dear God, I wish we had a bigger budget.'

'What would you do if you had one?'

'Hire someone who can type.'

'Would you fire Agnes?'

Dan gave her one of the gloomiest looks she'd seen in ages. 'Probably not.'

She couldn't help the laugh that escaped. But this was serious business and this time she had a real question.

'So you sent someone else out to the Plym house? You didn't go?'

Dan shook his head. 'I was tied up with the crime-scene people. I didn't think we'd get much from the house but I needed a statement from each of them. An official statement. Pete brought them back, had Agnes type them up and they all came down to the station last Saturday to sign them and get their prints taken. You and Ellen gave me impressions of how they took the news, but I needed statements. It seemed pretty unreal that she could have gotten out of the house and no one knew she'd gone. If I'd known about the motion detector…you said it was off. How do you know that?'

'Caleb said it was when Ellen and I went to the house that morning and they had just realized she was missing. He was furious with Richard, which I didn't understand at the time, and said Richard told him to turn it off—he and Cassandra were there and they'd take care of her. But they didn't. Dan, another thing. Cassandra told Ellen and me she took sleeping pills the night Miss Emilie disappeared. That would account for her not hearing her. I don't know why Richard didn't.'

Dan's fingers started to drum lightly on the desk, a sure sign he was trying to work something out. Mary reached across and put her hand on his.

He grinned, but then he stopped. 'It drives you nuts, doesn't it?'

'Yes. Did Pete get the note?'

'What note?'

Mary couldn't hold in her exasperation any longer. 'The note Miss Emilie had in her purse. The one she always gave to the teller at the bank, Dab Holt. It isn't in her purse. I assumed you had it. Or Glen kept it.'

'I don't. How do you know it's not in her purse?' There was no trace of humor on Dan's face now. Instead, his blue eyes had taken on a steely gray hue and his mouth was clearly pinched under his salt-and-pepper mustache.

'The purse is on her closet shelf. There's nothing in it but her change purse, a handkerchief, a dog biscuit and a piece of paper with her name and address on it.'

'I suppose it just happened to fall off the shelf at your feet and you noticed what was in it while you put it back.'

'Something like that. Why didn't your guy find it?'

'I told you—he didn't have a search warrant and Richard politely but firmly told him he'd have to have one before he did anything other than take their statements. I still haven't been able to get one and I haven't pushed it.' He stared at her a minute, his forehead creased in a deep frown. 'Maybe I should have. OK. What else did you find at the Plym house that's suspicious?'

'Miss Emilie's bed is made.'

The expressions that ran across Dan's face, one after another, were a wonder to behold. Surprise followed quickly by the start of laughter, followed by awareness. Slowly, he leaned forward on his desk and stared at her. 'Are you telling me Miss Emilie got up in the middle of the night, put on her bathrobe and slippers then made her bed? That's a little hard to picture.'

'Probably because I don't think that's what happened. I think someone made it after she was dead. Sometime in the last few days. When, or why, I have no idea.'

Dan leaned back, closed his eyes and rubbed his temples. 'You read way too many mystery novels.' He opened them and sat up straight. 'However, if her purse happened to have Gloria's fingerprints on it…' He smiled, but Mary didn't think it was a very comforting smile.

'What are you going to do now?'

'Wait for Gloria's autopsy report and see if I can get the court to let me have the purse.'

'What about searching Gloria's house? I thought you were going to do that.'

'It's already in progress. My department is too small to have a lot of the forensic equipment we need, so I asked the CSI guys from San Luis Obispo County to take a look at Gloria's house and the ravine. They're there now.'

Mary's hands tightened on the armrests. 'Are they looking for the money?'

'Blood, mainly.' The look on his face was solemn, his voice tight. 'There's almost none where they found her, and if she was alive when she fell down that hill, there should be. They're going through the house and yard to see if…'

'If she was killed somewhere else and thrown down the hill?' Mary's voice was a little shaky.

Millie lifted her head and stared at her, almost as if to ask if she was all right. She wasn't, but she had to go on. 'What about the money?'

Dan sighed. 'Glen Manning's already looked. She hadn't made any large deposits lately, but she could very well have had an account somewhere else. We're starting to make inquiries. Then, when the CSI team is finished, we'll go through her house. See if she might have hidden it somewhere. I can't let the aunt in until we're finished but, according to Les, she didn't sound eager to come.'

How sad. But maybe the aunt really was grieving. Maybe she just needed a little time to come to grips with what happened.

She could certainly sympathize with that—murder was always a shock. But it brought up another thought.

'Dan, how big a bundle would fifty thousand dollars make?'

'Good question.' He leaned forward and picked up his pencil, which started twisting in his fingers. 'Depends on the denomination. According to Glen, she always took it out in fifties. If the amount she's taken out is really fifty thousand dollars, that's one thousand bills. That's got to be several good-sized stacks.'

Mary tried to picture that many bills but couldn't. How would you go about hiding that much money? Where? 'The clock. You don't think…'

Dan shook his head. 'That thing was barely big enough for the safe deposit key. No. Whoever has that money needs a much bigger space than that.'

'Then why did someone steal the clock from the rummage sale and return it with the back half off?'

Dan again shook his head. 'I'd say offhand, whoever took it wasn't expecting what was in there. What they thought they'd find, I don't know. Yet.'

'So you really don't know anything, except that I picked it up.'

'There were a bunch of smudges but nothing that helped. Besides, everybody in the Plym house might have handled it at some time, even Gloria, plus who knows how many people helping at the sale.'

'How about on the key?'

'That was suspiciously clean.'

'So that's no help.' Mary hadn't expected the clock, or the key in it, to tell them a lot.

'Not much,' Dan agreed without enthusiasm. 'Go home, Mary. We're working on it and I know you've got a whole lot of other things, like the rummage sale, to worry about. We're done in the church hall so if you need to get in there before Thursday, feel free. It's still on, isn't it?'

'Yes. I was going to ask you… I'll go over there directly. I'm sure your people left it in good condition, didn't move anything around or leave any of their fingerprint powder on anything. I know you took fingerprints there. I saw them doing it.' She raised one eyebrow at him.

Dan laughed. 'If they didn't, you let me know and I'll send someone over right away.' He looked over at Millie and Morgan, laying close together, watching them. 'What are you going to do with Millie while you're gone all day?'

'I just booked her into Furry Friends for grooming. John's going to come get her at the church hall early and they'll keep her most of the day. I don't like leaving her all alone. She's a good girl, but the last time I left her—and it was only for a short time—one of my sofa pillows was in shreds. I think she got bored.'

'Have you tried getting her some toys? If she has her own she might not tear up your things.'

'She has toys but she's chewed them up.' She covered up her surprise with a broad smile. 'I'll get her some new ones on Thursday when I pick her up.' Her expression changed; a little suspicion crept in. 'Where did you learn so much about dogs? You never had one as a child.'

'It's amazing the information you pick up as a police chief. You and Millie go on. Either Ellen or I will stop by later to see how you're doing.'

'And to tell me what the CSI people found at Gloria's?'

Dan smiled. 'Maybe.'

Mary snapped Millie's leash back on but the dog wasn't eager to leave Morgan. 'You'll have plenty of time to visit with him later,' she told her. 'We need to get moving.'

When they were on the sidewalk in front of the police station, Mary paused. She took out her cell phone and checked the time. 'I don't know where the day has gone.'

Millie sat and looked back at the door of the police station. She didn't seem concerned about time, but it was evident she'd rather return to Morgan than do whatever Mary had in mind.

'We're not going to the library.' Mary's tone was definite. 'The Friends of the Library sale is still weeks off. The rummage sale is the day after tomorrow, and I think we'd better see what kind of condition the sale items are in.' With a destination firmly in mind, she started walking briskly across the park toward St Mark's.

TWENTY-SEVEN

THE SIDE DOOR was open. It sounded like a vacuum cleaner was going full blast. Mary walked in and abruptly stopped. The room was not at all as she had last seen it. Well, a lot of it wasn't. The big items hadn't been moved but the baby cribs were in one corner, the racks holding the clothes were pushed up against them and the tables that had been lined up through the center of the room, items neatly folded and displayed, had been pushed to one side. The items were no longer neat. Toasters sat on jackets; baby clothes were mixed with dog food dishes. It looked like a hurricane had gone through. The makeshift curtains that had hidden Miss Emilie were gone. The back wall was once more bare.

Caleb was vacuuming up white powder from the floor with the church's commercial vacuum. He stopped when he saw her, turned it off and walked over to her. 'Thought I'd come over and see how much damage those cops did. Not too bad, for cops. I'm trying to clean up what they didn't. Took down those curtains, too. Don't think any of the ladies would want to try on clothes in the same place Miss Emilie died.'

'No,' Mary said a bit faintly, wondering how Caleb knew how cops usually left things. 'You're probably right. What's the kitchen like?' For the first time, it occurred to her that probably no one had cleaned out the coffeepot.

She hoped it had been turned off. If not, they'd have no coffee anytime soon.

'Wasn't too bad. Someone dumped the grounds and put the pot in the sink. I'll get to all that after I finish this.'

'Caleb, this is wonderful. I can't thank you enough.' She was already going through her list of volunteers, thinking who she could call to come over and re-do all the tables, put up some kind of dressing area and make sure everything was ready for Thursday morning. 'Will you be able to push those tables back where we had them or do you want to wait until I can get some help?'

'I pushed them over there. Guess I can push them back. Don't know why the cops had to mess up these tables like that. They must have been looking for something, but I don't know what. They vacuumed up where she…you know…pretty good, I can understand that, but they left the rest a mess.'

She had to agree. Dan would get a phone call. She was so absorbed in trying to think how they'd get everything back together she almost missed what Caleb was saying.

'You heard about Gloria Sutherland, I guess.' Caleb's eyes had narrowed to almost a squint. He stared at Mary with an intensity she found a little unnerving.

'Yes. It's hard to believe she could lose her footing and fall like that. A real tragedy.' Why she was avoiding the word 'murder,' she didn't know. Everyone in town thought Gloria had been murdered, or did they? 'Poor thing.'

'Poor thing, my foot. She wasn't a nice woman.' He paused and an almost-calculating look passed over his face. 'Lorraine hated her.'

'What?' Mary didn't know what startled her more, Caleb's disregard for Gloria's fate or his willingness to, by innuendo, implicate his wife. 'What are you talking about?'

'Gloria was a snoop. Lorraine found her in Miss Emilie's room, going through her things on more than one occasion. She found her going through Miss Eloise's bank books, too. She kept that kind of stuff in a desk in her bedroom, and Gloria was thumbing through it one day like it belonged to her. Plus, she ordered Lorraine around like she was a servant. "Bring me tea… This soup is cold… Miss Emilie shouldn't eat beef." She was on her back all the time. Lorraine couldn't stand that woman.'

Mary didn't know what to say. The only thing surprising about any of this was Caleb's willingness to talk. 'What did you think of Gloria?'

'Hardly knew the woman. You want me to put up new curtains? We could put them in that corner. I'll put the tables back in the middle and if I move those old wicker chairs I can set up a real nice area for the ladies.' He started to say something more, closed his mouth then opened it again. His eyes shifted to the jumble of stuff on the long tables. 'Lorraine's been looking for that little dog Miss Emilie carried around. She thinks it ought to be buried with her but it doesn't seem to be around. According to Mrs Brown it got put in one of the boxes she donated to your sale. You wouldn't know where it got to, would you?'

What was there about that pathetic stuffed dog? Why was everybody so concerned about it? Mary decided she'd have another look at it before she turned it over to anyone. 'I'm sure it will turn up. Now, I'm going to make some phone calls and see if we can get help putting this all back together.'

'Yeah.' Caleb kept his squinty-eyed stare on her for a

moment then drifted down to Millie, who sat close beside Mary, not stirring, not wagging, but returning Caleb's stare. Caleb blinked first, grabbed his vacuum cleaner and headed for the wall socket to unplug it.

Mary watched him for a minute, thinking about their conversation, then took out her cell phone and scrolled down through her contacts, looking for someone to call to come and help them.

TWENTY-EIGHT

Two volunteers turned up almost immediately. That Joy came didn't surprise Mary. But Leigh came with her. Mary swallowed what she almost said and thought they could give her a nice safe job that didn't require much initiative. Caleb had pushed the tables back into the middle of the room and they started circling them, Joy muttering and Leigh outright complaining.

'It took us two days to sort all that stuff and get those tables arranged. Why did the police have to mess it up so? It looks as if they were searching for something and just dropped anything they didn't want. We're going to have to start all over. Look at that. Someone dumped a nightgown in a canning kettle.' Leigh picked up the offending garment and draped it over her arm. 'I don't know where to start.'

'We'll start by deciding how we're going to categorize these things. Kitchen things on that back table. It still has a lot of them. Baby and toddler things on this front table, and so forth. Joy, you had all these things priced. Did the tags get taken off ?'

Joy had been examining different items. She held up a bunch of gently used kitchen towels, safety pinned together, a price tag dangling from the pin. 'We got lucky. Looks like all the tags are still on. Woulda been some job if we had to do it all over again.' You'd never have been able to tell, from her expression, that she was pleased.

'This won't take too long.' She picked up a toaster, a spatula and a pair of men's work pants and started down the aisle of tables. 'Let's try to get things on the right tables, then we'll worry about setting them out again. Order won't last more than five minutes after we open the doors, anyway.'

Mary looked around for Millie. The end of her leash disappeared around the corner of a large box in the children's toy section. 'Millie. Where are you going? You can't…'

Millie had discovered a treasure trove of used stuffed animals. Her head was already in the box, which sat on the floor at about her level. Her rear end was wagging, and she surfaced with a gray plush one-eyed elephant in her mouth.

'I guess Dan was right. You want a toy. Maybe more than one. Here. Let me see how much… Joy?'

Joy came around the corner of the box, pen in one hand, a faded yellow hand mixer in the other. The mixer only had one beater. Mary looked at it and blinked. 'Are we selling that?'

'We're going to try. I marked it fifty cents. Someone would probably have bought it for a dollar but I'd a felt like I cheated them.' She paused and looked at the dog, the elephant still clasped in her jaws. 'Looks like Millie found something she wants.'

'Can you see how much you marked this one? I don't think she's planning on going home without it.'

'That's the beat-up stuffed toy box. I marked them all a quarter. People won't buy them for their babies but other people buy them for their dogs.' She looked at Mary and almost smiled.

'Do we have the cash box out yet?'

'Not unless you brought it. I think we can trust you. But you better go see what Caleb's doing. He says he's putting up a dressing room for the ladies but all we need are a couple of curtains and a mirror. He's building something Macy's would be proud to offer.'

For the first time, Mary was aware of hammering. What was he doing? She'd better go see.

Millie was right at Mary's heels, elephant feet flapping out of each side of her mouth as she hurried over to the corner where Caleb stood on a stepladder, nailing a pole to the wall.

'Oh. Caleb, I don't think Les… Reverend McIntyre… will like us putting holes in the wall. He's always said he didn't care what we did as long as we didn't…'

Caleb removed a nail from his mouth. 'He won't like it much if a curtain falls down and some lady is caught in her all-together, now will he.'

Her what? 'No, of course not, but…'

'Don't you worry. I'm the one who has to fix any holes I put in the wall, and fix them I will. I'd never forgive myself if one of these nice church ladies got embarrassed.'

'That's very considerate of you, Caleb, but…'

His scowl deepened. 'Just do as I say and run along. I know what I'm doing. That one you had fixed up before was never going to make it through a whole day. One yank and it woulda been on the ground. Go on now.' He made a shooing motion with the hand that held the hammer. Apparently he wasn't finished. He used the hammer to point to the floor behind her. 'That little dog of yours is going to have stuffing all over where I just vacuumed. Do something about it.' He put the nail back in his mouth, raised his hammer and started pounding again.

Mary wasn't sure how to react. What she wanted to

do was kick the ladder out from under him. Arrogant know-it-all. Where did he think he got the right to… She took a deep breath. Caleb was being helpful, or thought he was. Caleb talked down to Lorraine like that all the time. Caleb was sexist.

When she was a girl, her mother would have referred to him as a SOB, at least when her father wasn't around. He probably thought he was doing her, doing all of them, a favor. And in a way, he was. The price they paid for his help was putting up with his condescending attitude. She wasn't sure it was worth it, but they were going to have a nice dressing area and the curtain probably would stay up. No one would get caught in their 'all-together.' If Caleb thought any woman under seventy who actually tried on anything would be embarrassed if a little extra skin showed in public, he hadn't been to the beach lately.

She looked at Millie, who lay beside her, systematically removing the stuffing from her elephant's stomach. He'd been right about the stuffing, though. Damn the man! She grabbed Millie by the collar, removed the remains of the elephant from her mouth, picked up as much stuffing as she could, re-stuffed the poor animal and looked around for a sack. She'd come back after the sale was over and check on those holes, and if he hadn't filled them in, well, she'd think of something.

'Mary. Can you come over here?' It was Joy, motioning to her emphatically. 'I need you.'

Still bristling, Mary tucked the elephant under one arm and, holding on tight to Millie's leash, walked over to where Joy stood, a mixture of emotions still roiling through her.

'I thought I'd better get you away from Caleb before you took his hammer and used it on his head.' There was amusement in her voice but anger as well. 'How Lorraine puts up with him, I don't know. I've never yet heard him say one thing to her, or any woman for that matter, that wasn't dripping with condescension.'

'I wonder if he knows how offensive he is. Maybe he doesn't care. But I'm glad you called me over. One more sneer and I probably would have set Millie on him.'

Joy looked over at Caleb then down at Millie. Her expression lightened a little as she looked at the dog. 'Millie's a nice dog, but I don't think I'd count on her in a fight. Come see what you think of the tables.'

Mary thought Millie might be more protective than Joy thought. Look what she'd done to the elephant. She didn't say anything, just followed Joy to where Leigh stood, looking at the tables of items that would soon be rummaged through and, hopefully, sold.

'It looks great,' she told them. 'It sure didn't take you long.'

'Nothing was destroyed, just moved around.' Joy shrugged off the compliment but reached over and moved the set of gently used dish towels closer to a not so gently used frying pan. 'Now, where do you want us to set up the cash table? Usually we do it right by the door. That OK?'

The conversation continued, sacks for merchandise and Millie's mutilated toy were found, the payment table set up and preparations for the sale were almost complete when Caleb's voice stopped them.

'I want you ladies to come here and look at what I've done.'

The ladies looked at each other, sighed and walked over to view the new dressing area. It did, indeed, look sturdy. Mary thought if she'd wanted to open a dress shop it would do very well. However, for one day…

'Now, watch how you move this curtain. See, I got some of those curtain clips you had up there and used them. The poles won't come down but the clips might not hold this old bedspread too well. Lorraine uses them to put up her quilts but she doesn't slide them around, so you've got to be careful. Here. I'll show you.' He proceeded to carefully slide the bedspread back and forth, making sure the slide was gentle and the clips didn't get tangled. 'See? Make sure you tell all the ladies how to do it and it'll be just fine.'

They all nodded but said nothing.

'Well, if you think you've got that, then I'll be going. I've got other things to do.'

No one said a word.

Finally, Mary said, 'Thank you for all your help, Caleb. We'll see you Thursday afternoon?'

He nodded, scowled and looked at his handiwork again. 'Make sure nobody yanks on that.'

He was gone.

Mary sighed, reached out and pulled gently on the bedspread. It came loose from the clips and hit the floor.

Leigh started to laugh.

Joy didn't. 'That thing won't last through one woman.'

'Especially if the woman is Penny Cooper. Can you see me telling her to be gentle on the bedspread? Penny's never been gentle with anything in her entire life. And she doesn't take direction well.'

Leigh laughed harder. 'You mean she doesn't play well with others?'

'She plays fine, just rough. We're going to have to change that. Why that man thinks he's the only one who knows anything, I don't know. Poor Lorraine.'

'What is there about the men at the Plym house? I

heard Richard Plym last Sunday talking to Les. That was the rudest performance I've ever heard.' Leigh's laughter ended. She had a serious, almost pained look. 'I know Les didn't want to make a scene, but he should have. There was no excuse for that.'

'Richard Plym. I think I remember his father. Wasn't he the younger brother of the twins? He was ahead of me in school but I remember my sister saying he thought pretty highly of himself.' Joy's frown was more pronounced than usual. Evidently she didn't remember Richard Plym II with much pleasure.

Mary nodded. 'He was a friend of Samuel's. I never completely understood that. Richard, his son, is here with his sister, Cassandra, taking care of their aunts' affairs. And Joy, you're right. He's not very pleasant but his sister is.'

'Does he have dark hair, tall and looks like his father?'

There was a look on Joy's face Mary didn't like. Puzzled, worried. 'Yes. Why?'

'Because I think he might be the man Gloria was having lunch with the day she was…she died. I was in the Yum Yum, buying a quiche for dinner, and noticed them.'

Leigh interrupted with a snort. 'You, buying someone else's baked goods?'

'Hers are all right—not as good as mine, but passable and I was tired.' There was a defensiveness in Joy's tone that Mary understood. If you have a reputation as a good cook, people seemed to think you never relied on others' efforts, no matter how good they were or how tired you might be. But right now, she wasn't interested in the Yum Yum café's quiche. 'Gloria Sutherland was having lunch with Richard Plym?' She thought back to the morning at the Plym house when Richard threw her out—well, sort of threw her out, and wondered what had happened to put them on a lunching basis. 'Are you sure it was Richard Plym?'

'I remember thinking the man looked a lot like the Richard Plym I knew years ago and wondered. Gloria didn't look happy. As a matter of fact, I thought she looked scared to death, which made me a little uneasy, but I certainly didn't think it would be the last time I'd ever see her alive.' Joy gave a little shudder that seemed to run through her from head to toe. 'Do you think he had something to do with it?'

Mary looked at Leigh, then at Joy. Richard and Gloria. 'I don't know.' But it was interesting. Very interesting.

TWENTY-NINE

Mary stood on the sidewalk in front of the community hall and watched Leigh and Joy drive off. They had offered her a lift home but she'd declined. It wasn't a long walk, and Millie needed to stretch her legs, she'd said. Only, she wasn't going home. She was going to the Yum Yum. She was getting tired and a slice of quiche or maybe some of Ruthie's soup to take home seemed a good idea.

It was a quiet time for the Yum Yum. The lunch crowd was finished and the dinner patrons hadn't yet arrived. Ruthie should be able to talk, and Ruthie liked to talk.

'I have Millie with me. Any chance I can bring her in?'

Ruthie looked around the empty café and nodded. 'Are you looking for something to eat or just a cup of coffee?'

'Both. Do you have any quiche left? Or soup? It's been a long day. The last few have been exhausting and I don't feel like going home and fixing anything.'

Ruthie beamed and nodded her head emphatically. Her tight yellow curls bobbed metallically with each nod. 'My dear, you've come to the right place. Let's go in my office and have some coffee, then I'll fix you up with a good dinner and all you'll have to do is put it on a plate.'

Mary and Millie followed her through the restaurant, which Mary knew well, through the swinging door, past the kitchen and into a storage room. A back door stood open with a great view of the alley. Ruthie headed for a rickety table in a corner that held a stack of thick white mugs, a large sugar dispenser and a Mr Coffee full to the brim with what looked and smelled like fresh coffee. Ruthie picked up two mugs, filled them with a practiced hand, gave one to Mary and motioned her to the one chair. Ruthie filled hers with a generous amount of sugar and perched on top of a tall white plastic tub.

'OK. What happened to Gloria Sutherland?'

Mary didn't answer right away. She made sure Millie was beside her and looked around. 'Is this your office?'

Ruthie laughed. 'There's a phone back here, and the coffeepot. I use them both when I need to place orders, find out where my orders are or just plain want to escape. I brought you back here because if I took Millie into the kitchen, even when it's empty, the Health Department would find out somehow and come after me, howling and frothing at the mouth. We're safe here. Now. About Gloria.'

'She lost her balance, fell down the cliff and broke her neck.'

Ruthie didn't say a word, but the look she gave Mary over the top of her coffee mug spoke volumes.

Mary sighed. Ruthie had owned the Yum Yum for years and knew almost as many people in this town as Mary. The mayor, half the planning commission and Dan and Ellen were regular lunch customers. There was very little Ruthie didn't know about what went on in this town, and whether she heard details about Gloria from Mary or someone else, she'd know them sooner rather than later. 'Dan thinks she had help rolling down that hill.'

Gloria set her mug down, her face solemn. 'I thought so. There was something going on with Gloria, had been for a while, but I didn't know what. That last day, when she came in with Richard Plym, she looked worried.'

Ruthie picked her mug back up but didn't drink. 'No. She looked scared to death. I took their order myself, I was that concerned…' She looked over at Mary and grinned, '… OK, curious, but she hardly spoke. Just said she'd have the special, but I don't think she took more than three bites.'

'Did you hear what they were talking about?' Tension built in Mary as she leaned forward, wanting to hear what Ruthie had to say yet dreading it.

Ruthie peered into her coffee cup, lifted it to take a sip then, holding it with both hands, set it on her knee. The breath she took was deep, and she let it out slowly, as if trying to control an emotion that didn't want controlling. 'Gloria and I are about the same age. We were in school together but we weren't friends. Poor Gloria. She was sort of short on friends. I never thought she had a very happy life. Nothing ever seemed to work out for her. No brothers or sisters, no family in town, her mom always looked sort of surprised to see her and her attempt at a marriage didn't last more than a month. I guess she was pretty good as a home health nurse, partly because it gave her someone to talk to, to manage. About the only time she had either. But she didn't seem too unhappy, and I'd never seen her look scared.'

'Richard Plym seems to delight in that. Do you know why? Did he say anything?'

'They both shut up when I came by.' Ruthie looked at Mary, her frizzy blonde curls bobbing around her face. She brushed them back. 'But I heard one thing. He said—I may not have the words exact but they're darn close—"I want to know what you've done with it. It belongs to me, and you're going to give it back."'

A stillness crept over Mary. Ruthie's face receded,

so did all sound and, for a moment, her head swam. But only for a moment. 'You're sure?'

'As sure as you're sitting there.'

'Then what happened?'

'Nothing. At least nothing I could hear. Gloria pushed her plate away, they talked for another minute or so—well, he talked, she just kept shaking her head, then she got up and left. I think he swore, it sure looked like it, but he waved me over, demanded the check, paid and left as well. But not before making sure I knew he thought his club sandwich was substandard. Nice man.'

There was only one thing Mary could think to say. 'Have you told this to Dan?'

Ruthie shook her curls again. 'No. It was a piece of a private conversation. I hear them all the time and make it a policy to repeat nothing. Ever. But then, one of the participants doesn't usually end up murdered.' She paused, worry creasing her forehead. 'Do you think I should?'

'Yes. Just this once. It may mean nothing—probably doesn't—but if Gloria didn't slip and fall, well, Dan needs to know everything. He'll keep it quiet.'

A young girl wrapped in a black apron, her long dark brown hair pulled back in a tight braid, appeared in the doorway. 'We need you. We're starting to get some early birds.'

'Thanks, Marta. I'll be right there.' Ruthie got up from her tub, put her hand on her back and stretched. 'If you'll take Millie out the back way, I'll meet you in the front with your dinner. It won't take but a minute to put together.'

'You'll talk to Dan?' Mary didn't want to sound anxious, but that was how she felt. This put Richard solidly in the middle of whatever was going on. Did he think Gloria had stolen the money and wanted it back? Only, how would pushing her down into a ravine help him get it?

Ruthie nodded but not very happily. 'I'll tell him. I don't like this, but I will. Poor Gloria.'

'Poor Emilie Plym.' Mary's face was grim as she gathered up Millie's leash. 'I'll meet you out front, and Ruthie…' She turned back toward her and smiled—at least, she tried to make it a smile. 'Is it all right if you put the bill in the bag? I'll drop by tomorrow and pay you.'

'Of course.' Ruthie waved it off as if it was nothing.

'Thanks.'

'I don't know what for.' Ruthie hurried off in the direction of the kitchen.

Mary and Millie walked slowly down the alley.

THIRTY

GOING HOME PROVED harder than walking into town had been. Mary's tote kept slipping and she struggled to hold both her purse and the sack containing whatever it was Ruthie had given her for dinner with her left hand and Millie's leash with her right. Millie seemed determined to get home quickly. Mary was equally as eager but not quite as quick.

'Need a lift?'

A car pulled up beside her.

'You're an angel in disguise,' she told Ellen. She opened the passenger door and Millie obligingly jumped in, then into the backseat. Mary handed Ellen her dinner and her tote and settled herself in the passenger seat with a grunt of relief. 'I wasn't sure I was going to make it. For some reason, walking into town was easier.'

'You hadn't walked over half the town yet, and I'll bet you're carrying more home than you started with. Something smells good. What is it?'

'I bought dinner at the Yum Yum. I'm not sure what Ruthie gave me but it does smell good.'

'You don't know? How did that…never mind. It'll be good, whatever it is. You should do it more often. You don't have to cook all the time.' Ellen pulled into Mary's driveway.

Mary didn't dignify that with an answer. 'Can you come in?'

'I really should be getting home. Dan may actually be home in time for dinner tonight and I thought…what?'

Disappointment must have shown on Mary's face, so she immediately smiled. 'Nothing. You and Dan deserve a nice dinner together. I appreciate the lift. Millie and I will be just fine.' Mary got out of the door and held Millie's leash as she jumped down.

Ellen looked doubtful. 'I'll help you get all this stuff inside. That tote is heavy. What do you have in here, anyway?'

'Notebooks, files for different committees, Millie's water dish, things like that.' Mary opened the back door and stepped inside.

Millie elected to stay out, but that wouldn't last long.

Mary set her dinner on the drain board, her purse on the table and turned toward Ellen. 'Tell Dan I need to talk to him. Maybe sometime tomorrow.'

'What about?' Ellen set Mary's tote by the yellow buffet and turned to face her, a suspicious look on her face. 'What have you found out you think Dan should know about?'

'I'm going to have a cup of tea. Would you like one?'

'I really can't, but I'll make yours. You look tired. You've been up to something again, haven't you?'

Mary set the tea kettle on to boil and brought out the teapot, which she set on the counter. She opened the canister where she kept the tea but was interrupted when Ellen took it out of her hands.

'Stop that. Go sit down and tell me what's got you so jumpy.'

Mary sat. She felt unaccountably weak. This whole thing had taken a bigger toll than she'd thought. 'Richard Plym and Gloria Sutherland had lunch together at the Yum Yum the day Gloria died.'

Ellen stared at her aunt for a moment, her mouth slightly open, as if she wanted to say something but couldn't. Finally she said, 'I think I'll stay for tea after all.' She pulled out a chair and sat. 'What did Ruthie hear?'

Mary couldn't help but smile. Curiosity was a powerful thing. 'She said Gloria was scared, or seemed that way. Then, when she brought their order, Richard was telling Gloria she better give something back, it was his and he wanted it.'

'Good Lord, the money?'

Mary shrugged. 'That's all she heard.'

The tea kettle announced the water was hot.

Ellen got up. While the tea was steeping, she turned toward her aunt. 'It sounds as if Richard thought Gloria had the money, that she was the one who stole it from Miss Emilie. Do you think he murdered her for it?'

'I don't know. Murdering her wouldn't get him back the money, if she even had it.'

'No,' Ellen said. She tested the tea, poured two mugs, set one in front of Mary and sat. Immediately she was back on her feet, opening the back door at the insistence of several sharp barks. Shutting the door behind Millie, she sat back down. 'Richard has a terrible temper. At least, he seems to. If she didn't give it to him, or couldn't because she didn't have it and he didn't believe her, he may have attacked her in a fit of rage.'

Mary couldn't rule that out, but it didn't seem right. Richard was cool, not hot. 'He doesn't seem the type to lose his temper like that. More the kind that would let something simmer and act quite deliberately. He still might be capable of murder, but he'd think it out. This all seems so…out of control.'

'But he knew about the money.'

'Oh, he knew all right. That's why he's here, and I think it's the reason he hasn't left yet. Glen Manning called Cassandra to let her know Miss Emilie kept withdrawing such large sums. She told Richard. They came out here to find what Miss Emilie had done with it. I'm sure he was determined to take control of what was left by putting Miss Emilie somewhere she couldn't get her hands on any of it ever again.'

'But you heard Cassandra. She was having second thoughts about moving Miss Emilie to Shady Acres. I'll bet you that's what the argument was about the night Miss Emilie died, when Cassandra decided she needed sleeping pills.'

Ellen sipped her tea. 'Would Richard have known she took the pills?'

Mary shrugged. She thought about the arrangements of the bedrooms. 'Richard's room is right across the hall from Miss Emilie's. He could easily have heard her get up.'

'If his door was open.' Ellen set her tea back down on the table and frowned. 'I have a hard time seeing Richard leaving his bedroom door open.'

She had a point. Richard would want his privacy.

Mary thought about it. 'It really is possible neither Richard nor Cassandra heard her get up. The Duxworths wouldn't—the motion detectors were off. She could have gotten up, remembered she wanted her dog and left without anyone knowing.'

Ellen had just picked up her mug but set it back down

to stare at her aunt. 'Then who killed her, and why? She didn't strangle herself.'

'It brings us back to Gloria, doesn't it? We know she was at least in the vicinity of the church hall that night, and at about the right time.'

'All right. Who killed Gloria?'

'Someone who thought Gloria had the money and was determined to get it?' Mary suggested.

'Richard?' Ellen didn't sound very surprised, nor very upset by the idea.

Mary took a large sip of her tea before she answered. It seemed as if every time she'd tried to make a cup the last few days, something had happened. This time, she was finishing it. 'Possibly. Or Cassandra. Or Caleb. Or Lorraine. It almost has to be one of them.'

'Not Lorraine.' Ellen set her mug down with a bang. 'She was devoted to the sisters. I can't really see Caleb, either. He's a jerk but not a homicidal one. No, my money's on Richard.'

'We don't really know anything about Cassandra,' Mary said slowly. 'She does seem nice, but we don't know much about her. Until the other morning I didn't know her husband had died or that she has two sons in college. She seems embarrassed by Richard's behavior, but that doesn't mean she hasn't the same goals. I keep thinking about the clock. She would have known about that clock. She was here a couple of weeks when Miss Eloise died. The clock was in Miss Emilie's room and Cassandra must have been in there. You could hear something moving in it. She's also the one who donated it, so she knew where it was. Why she'd suddenly want it back, I don't know.'

'Richard.' Ellen got up, put her empty mug in the sink and gathered up her purse. 'She could have told him about the clock, that there was something in it, and he made her get it and they pried the back off. When they saw it was a safe deposit key, they tried to put it back.'

'How did they get it out of the church hall?'

'The key. There's a key to the hall hanging on the key rack in the kitchen.'

Mary put her own tea down and frowned at Ellen. 'We're jumping to conclusions. We don't know anything, really, except two women are dead and there's a whole lot of money missing. Tell all this to Dan and see what he says.'

Ellen pushed her chair back, walked over to the sink, set her still half-filled mug in it, picked up her purse and stood at the door, her hand on the knob. 'What are you going to do the rest of the day?'

'There's not much day left. I should go to the library, but I think I'll stay here, feed Millie and watch the news. I can always count on that to take my mind off things.'

'Why? You want to get more depressed?'

Mary laughed. 'Let me know what Dan thinks.'

'I will. Promise me you won't go out tonight, sleuthing, asking people questions…that you won't do anything more about any of this.'

'I promise.'

Ellen threw her a kiss and was gone.

Mary got up, filled Millie's dish and poured herself another cup of tea. She sat back down and stared into her mug. She'd promised Ellen she wouldn't go out or do anything more about the murder. That was easy. What she could do she had no idea. However, she hadn't promised she wouldn't think about it. And that she planned to do.

THIRTY-ONE

THE MORNING DAWNED warm and clear. A breeze barely ruffled the new leaves on the old oak in the corner of Mary's backyard and did nothing to disturb the plump pink buds on the Cecil Brunner rose that covered the back fence. Mary stood at the sink, kneading dough on the breadboard she'd inherited from her mother. Millie sat across the kitchen, watching the banging, pounding and muttering with a wary eye.

'None of this makes any sense.' Bang went the dough as Mary slammed it onto the board. Flour went flying. 'Did Lorraine and Caleb really not know how much money Miss Emilie was taking out when Richard accused them of stealing?' A punch landed right in the midsection of the dough. A handful of flour dusted its wound. 'I don't blame Caleb for being angry, but someone knew.' *Plop.* The dough was folded in half, and the heel of her hand made indents down it. 'Gloria?' *Smack.* The dough landed back on the breadboard again. 'Gloria. Unfortunately I can believe that. I can picture her going through Miss Emilie's purse, taking money out, counting on her not to realize some was missing.' Mary stared at the dough, pinched it and shook her head. Flour flew and the dough turned white once more. 'Only, Gloria's dead. What did she do to make someone kill her?' The dough gave way under the onslaught of her hands, flour disappearing as it began to take on a shiny look. 'More than one person has probably been tempted to kill Gloria over the years but decided it wasn't worth the price, so it must have been something…blackmail of some sort seems the most probable. Something she saw the night Miss Emilie died? Or was Ellen right? Did she have the money and someone wanted it back badly enough to kill her?'

Mary sighed, a rather exaggerated sigh, and pulled her biggest mixing bowl out of the cupboard.

Millie crept out of the corner, where she had retreated. She sat beside Mary and whined.

'I'm glad you agree. If she didn't kill Miss Emilie, she must have seen something. Only, why was she roaming the streets at that hour? And…' Mary looked at the dog, who looked up, an expression of anxiety on her face, '…two more questions. Why was Gloria having lunch with Richard Plym? He hated her, and I think she returned the favor. And where is the money?'

Millie whined again.

'This isn't getting these hot cross buns finished.' Mary buttered her bowl, plopped the dough in it, turned it so the whole surface was nice and buttery, covered it with a fresh dishtowel and set it on the kitchen table to rise.

'I hope I can get these baked and in the freezer before anyone drops by. I'm planning on them for Easter breakfast, but every year they seem to disappear before Easter arrives.' She stepped over Millie, who was staring at the breadboard as if waiting for it to spring into action again. 'I think I'd better double-check I have everything I need, then I'll get the kitchen cleaned. We'll go into town later, just to make sure everything is ready for tomorrow. I do hope we get a good turnout. It's been on the radio enough, we should.' She opened the pantry where the dog food was also kept. Millie was instantly by her side.

'You've already had breakfast.' Mary moved packages around and cans were pushed to the side.

'Don't tell me…' She closed the door in Millie's face and headed for the cupboard by the stove. 'I'm out. How can that be? I know I had…the chocolate cake. I used the last of it for the frosting.' Clearly exasperated, she stared at Millie. 'I'm out of powdered sugar. I'm going to have to go to the store, and I'd better do it now while that dough is rising. You'll have to stay here. I won't be long.' She looked down at herself and smiled. 'I'd better get dressed, though. They frown on bathrobes in the grocery store, almost as much as they do dogs.'

Millie followed Mary into the bedroom, jumped on the bed and watched as she took down lightweight slacks and a voluminous peasant top.

'It's almost spring. The sun is shining, the air is warm and I'm going to take advantage of it.' Mary laid the clothes on the bed, admonished Millie not to lay on them and returned to the closet for her shoes.

The shopping bag with Willis in it sat on the top shelf. Shoes forgotten, she stared at it. It seemed to be calling her name. Fiddlesticks. Paper bags didn't call out anything. Neither did stuffed animals. The only thing calling her was the grocery store, and she'd better get going if she was going to get back in time to finish the hot cross buns.

The call was too strong. Berating herself for having a weak will, she lifted the bag down, pulled out Willis and walked over to the bed and sat on the end of it. She turned him over and ran her fingers down his paws, over his tail and down his ears, but there was nothing out of place. Except for the tiny rip under his ribbon, he was intact. He even had both his eyes and the little red felt tongue that stuck out of his mouth. If there was any clue to be found involving the stuffed dog, she couldn't find it. She stuffed Willis back in his paper bag and set him just inside her closet. She quickly finished getting dressed, pausing only to hang her bathrobe on the hook in the closet before she gathered up her purse and car keys. Millie was already at the back door, ready for whatever adventure riding in the car would bring.

'Not this time. I won't be long, though. You be a good girl.' With a more than small pang, she shut the door on Millie and left.

The grocery store wasn't only crowded; it seemed she knew everyone in it. She had decided, as long as she was there, to pick up a few more items, but her progress was slow. She couldn't get down an aisle without someone stopping her, asking for information on the rummage sale, if any progress had been made on what happened to Miss Emilie and now to Gloria Sutherland. They all had some story to tell, the ones about Gloria not uniformly complimentary. But all thought how she died was horrible. However, the facts seemed to vary from person to person. There were a few questions they all asked. 'Was Gloria really murdered?' No one questioned that Miss Emilie had been. 'Was there a connection between the murders?' 'Does Dan have any idea why?' And, of course, 'By who?' It was easy to answer the last three questions honestly and quickly. She didn't know.

By the time Mary entered her kitchen again, her dough had risen to perfection. She hurriedly washed her hands and, leaving her grocery sacks on the counter, started on the dough. It was quickly rolled into balls, which she placed onto baking sheets, where it would rise once more.

She made the cuts that designated the cross on each one, set the trays on the table then put her groceries away. The powdered sugar stayed on the kitchen counter, ready to go into the glaze she'd make when the rolls had baked and were cool.

In the meantime, she had other things to do. Tucking the phone under one ear, she made the phone calls she needed as she proceeded to clean the kitchen. She didn't go back into her bedroom until the middle of the afternoon.

She gasped as she stood in her bedroom doorway. A much-reduced Willis sat in the middle of her bed, and the white cotton stuffing that used to be inside him littered the room.

'Oh. Oh, Millie. How could you!'

Evidently, easily. The dog stood beside Mary, also peering into the room, and didn't seem one bit contrite.

'What a mess. It'll take an age to clean up all this.' She walked over to the bed where the remains of Willis lay. Should she just scoop up all the stuffing and throw it out or try to re-stuff the dog? Muttering under her breath, she picked him up to see how much damage Millie had inflicted. It wasn't as bad as she had first thought. One leg dangled by a couple of threads. The tail would never hang straight again, and the ribbon around his neck was beyond salvaging. Never mind. She had ribbon and would make Willis a new bow after all of his insides had been returned and the leg sewn back on. If Lorraine thought he should be buried with Miss Emilie, she guessed she wouldn't care. But he couldn't accompany Miss Emilie to her final resting place like this. She started returning Willis' stuffing to him.

She was on her hands and knees, peeling the last of the

cotton off her carpet, when she saw it. A small gold key sitting by the leg of her dresser. She picked it up, held it up to the light and looked around the room. 'Where did this come from?'

Millie lay on Mary's bed, her head resting on her front feet, watching Mary's every move. Or maybe it was the resurrection of Willis that kept her attention. He lay on top of Mary's dresser, out of Millie's reach, looking plumper all the time.

'Was the key in him?' Mary held it up.

Millie declined to answer, but she didn't need to. Mary had never seen the key before, she had no idea what it was meant to unlock but she felt sure it had been inside Willis when she left for the grocery store. She straightened up, one hand holding it, the other the small of her back. She stuffed Willis, along with any stray pieces that still needed to go inside him, into the paper bag and this time returned the whole thing to her closet shelf. Everything but the key. That she carried into the kitchen, where she deposited it in a small dish which she placed on the windowsill. 'These rolls are ready to go in the oven,' she said to Millie. 'I shouldn't even be speaking to you, but I should have been more careful. I know you love to chew up things. Poor Willis. I can fix him, but you're going to have to stop this.'

Millie didn't look motivated to quit tearing up soft toys. Instead, she sniffed the door to the closet where her dog food was kept.

'Don't even think about it. It's not time, and I have other things to do.' Mary set the timer on the oven and slipped in the trays, finished filling the dishwasher and started the glaze for the rolls, all the while stealing glances at the key. It must have been in Willis. She thought about the small tear right under his ribbon. Had that been made so someone, presumably Miss Emilie, could slip it in him? What did the key open important enough that someone would take such pains to hide it? She stopped, dustpan in one hand, broom in the other, and thought. What was in Miss Emilie's room that might need a key to open it?

The box.

Mary almost dropped the broom. Of course, the white box, the ones with the flowers painted on it. She could almost see it, a good-sized box that felt light but had something inside. Whatever it was moved from side to side when she held it. Was it the money? Was the box big enough for all that money? Maybe Miss Emilie had been more lucid than they'd thought. Or maybe she just liked to hide things and Willis seemed to be a good place to hide the key. He certainly didn't hold any money. Millie had proved that. She glanced at the clock. Eleven thirty. The timer on the oven said the rolls had another fifteen minutes. She propped the broom in a corner, dustpan against it, and reached for the phone.

'Ellen? Are you meeting Dan for lunch today at the Yum Yum? No, nothing's wrong, but I need to tell him something. Do you mind if I join you? I have to stop by anyway to pay Ruthie for yesterday's dinner.' She paused. 'No, I can't tell you now. It's too complicated. Besides, I have to take my hot cross buns out of the oven and… no, I won't bring you any. They're for Easter breakfast, and no, you won't pass out from hunger. I'll see you at twelve thirty.'

She hung up and put her glaze to one side. She'd take out the rolls and let them cool on the counter while she was gone. She'd also close her bedroom door. Millie was definitely getting some more dog toys tomorrow. She picked up the little key, carried it over to her purse and put it in the change compartment. It would be safe there until she could turn it over to Dan. Was there some way she could be there when the box was opened? A tingle of excitement ran down her spine. Were they about to find the money? Would they find out who killed both ladies at the same time? She hummed a little as she took the rolls out of the oven.

THIRTY-TWO

DAN SAT IN a back booth, Ruthie opposite him, white coffee mugs in front of them. Ruthie was talking intently. Dan seemed to be listening equally as intently.

Mary hesitated a moment but she was sure she knew what they were talking about so she wouldn't be interrupting. She stood beside the booth, waiting for a lull.

'Where's Millie?' Dan looked at her then at the floor, as if he expected to see her sitting beside the booth.

'At home and not happy about it. Where's Morgan?'

'Ellen's dropping him off at the station. Agnes is going to dog-sit while we have lunch.'

Mary couldn't repress a laugh. 'That should be fun for both of them.'

'Yeah, well…'

'Who's Morgan?' Ruthie's head bobbed back and forth like she was watching a tennis match. 'And, Mary, will you please sit down? My neck is going to give out any minute now.'

'Dan and Ellen's new dog.' Mary dropped onto the bench next to Ruthie, who looked incredulously across the table at Dan.

'You got a dog?'

Dan smiled and nodded. 'He's a three-cornered dog. Some kind of hound. His name's Morgan.'

'What kind of name is that for a dog?' Ruthie was still shaking her head when the dark-haired waitress from yesterday slipped a mug of coffee in front of Mary. She smiled at Dan and held the pot aloft. He shook his head.

'I used to have a dog named Morgan.'

Dan looked up at her, surprise written all over his face. 'You did?'

She nodded. 'I read a book about a dog with that name, so when I got a puppy for my twelfth birthday, that's what I called him. It's a great name.' She smiled again and walked off.

Mary snatched up her mug and held it in front of her face. Dan wouldn't appreciate it if she started to laugh, which was a distinct possibility. That dog was never going to be called Spot. 'Are you two talking about Richard and Gloria's lunch?'

Ruthie nodded.

'I was asking Ruthie if she was sure Richard threatened Gloria. Did he say what with?'

'What do you mean?' Ruthie looked at Dan with a blank stare. 'Like, did he say I'll bash you over the head and roll you down the hill? No.'

'What did he say?' Dan looked at Ruthie's face, which had begun to take on a stubborn look, and hastened to add, 'As close as you can remember.'

'He said, "It's mine and I want it back."'

'What was Gloria doing? Did she answer him?'

'She didn't say anything that I heard, just shook her head. When she saw me she stopped doing that. He didn't say any more, either. But he must have said something after I went because it was no time at all before Gloria just up and left.'

Dan leaned forward, arms on the table, no expression on his face or in his voice. 'What did Richard do?'

'I don't really know. I had another order to get out and

when I turned around, he motioned for the check. I went over—their plates had hardly been touched—and asked if he wanted a doggie bag. He looked at his sandwich and shook his head as if the very sight of it made him ill. He said he'd pay for both lunches. I gave him the check, he laid money on the table and left. And that's what I've got to do. Is Ellen coming? You all going to have lunch? Let me know when you're ready to order.'

Ruthie made shoeing motions at Mary, who slid out, waited for Ruthie to leave and seated herself again.

'What do you think?' Mary asked.

'About what? Richard and Gloria not having lunch? Someone bashing Gloria Sutherland over the head and throwing her body down the hill? Or Miss Emilie's missing money?'

'You don't have to sound so sarcastic about it.' Mary pushed Ruthie's coffee mug out of her way and set hers in its place.

'Sorry. I'm getting frustrated. The CSI guys didn't come up with a thing in Gloria's house. They've got a few stray fingerprints they're running, but that's all. No blood, nothing to show anyone searched the place, nice clean kitchen, bed made, nothing to show what time she was in the house last. She must have been killed somewhere outside, but so far we haven't come up with where. And before you ask, we don't know what she was hit with, either. Probably a rock and whoever did it probably threw it down the hill after her.'

'She was hit, first?'

'The coroner confirmed it. She was dead when she took her tumble down the hill.'

'You haven't found any trace of the money?'

'Not in her house, not in her bank accounts, nor any

other place we've looked, and believe me, we've looked.' By the look on his face, Mary didn't think he was going to enjoy his lunch very much. He looked as if he needed a Pepto-Bismol more than whatever was on special today.

'Maybe I can help.'

'How?' That single word came out guarded, hopeful and suspicious all in one.

'I've found something. A key.'

Dan simply stared at her for a minute that stretched out to two minutes. Finally he asked, 'A key to what?'

'I think it's the key to a box in Miss Emilie's room, one she evidently kept all her secret things in for, I guess, much of her life. It's locked. I don't think anyone much cared. They thought it was full of old birthday cards, letters from friends, things like that. She used to keep the key in a little dish on her dresser, but according to Cassandra no one's seen it in ages. They thought she lost it. She didn't. It was in Willis, and I think the box might be full of money. The money she withdrew.'

Dan sat like a statue, not moving, not blinking, just staring at her. Finally, in a choked voice, he asked, 'You found this key where and why do you think the money is in the box?'

How did she explain it? She'd known Miss Emilie for many years, had watched her slip into another world. One where none of them could follow. Hiding money, hiding a key, might have seemed a good idea to her. The key would be safe in Willis, the dog who her father always said would keep her safe. Her money could have seemed more secure in a box where she'd always kept her treasures. 'The key was in her dog, Willis. I left him on the floor, which I never should have done, and Millie got him. She tore him apart, and there was the key. It took me a while, but then I remembered the box and knew this had to be the key that opened it. As for the money, it's the only place I can think where she might have put it. It fits, the whole thing. I'm sure it's there.' She sat back and looked at Dan, who didn't seem capable of speaking. 'So, now, what are we going to do?'

'Have lunch.'

'And then?'

'I…don't know.' Dan picked up his mug, brought it up in front of his face and held it there. 'How did you come to have the dog, Willis? And, why is this the first I've heard of it?'

A fair question. She explained about Joy, how she'd found the dog in a box of donations, had recognized him as Miss Emilie's and put him aside to give back then forgotten him. How she'd brought him to Mary, where he'd ended up in her closet until Millie got her teeth into him. Which was how the key happened to be on her bedroom floor. Which was when she remembered the box, how she'd handled it and realized it was locked and made the connection.

Dan's eyes looked a little glazed over when she'd finished, but at least he nodded. 'Where's the key, now?'

Mary pulled her wallet out of her purse, opened the change compartment and laid the key on the table. 'What are you going to do?'

Dan picked it up, held it for a moment then wrapped it in a paper napkin and slipped it into his shirt pocket. 'I'd love to think this might have fingerprints on it that would point us to something useful, but I strongly doubt it. However, I need to have a talk with Richard Plym about several things. So, while I'm at the Plym house I guess I'll have a look at that box. In the meantime, we'll have lunch.'

'Not me.' Mary slid out of the booth and stood. 'I need to get back. I have hot cross buns to ice and a million other things to get ready for tomorrow. Besides, I don't like leaving Millie alone. Let me know what you find, will you?'

Dan grinned. 'I'll stop by if you promise me a hot cross bun.'

'You're on.' She looked around. Ruthie was bearing down on her, carrying another white bag and a check.

'You need lunch, and I knew you wouldn't take the time to eat it here, not with the rummage sale tomorrow, so here's a sandwich. I'll bring over a tray for the volunteers tomorrow, like I always do.' She waved her hand as Mary started to rummage for her wallet. 'Pay me later. Right now, get going.'

Mary thanked her and left.

It was a long afternoon. She finished the rolls, keeping a few out for Dan and Ellen, made sure she had everything she needed for the morning, called the radio station to make sure the last-minute announcements would be made, double-checked her volunteers knew when to turn up and that they'd actually be there, and did some housework. The entire time the questions surrounding the deaths of the two women never left her, nor did the mystery of the missing money. What had Dan found in that box? If the money wasn't there, where was it? She was certain if they found the money they'd know the identity of the murderer. Although an idea was beginning to take shape, its image wasn't sharp, at least not yet. Nor was how she'd go about finding out if she was right. This whole thing was about motivation. Unfortunately there was plenty of that to go around. Money, a lot of money, always provided someone with motivation to do the wrong thing. This time the wrong thing had gotten badly out of hand. She was beginning to expand on that thought when the back door opened and Dan walked in, Morgan at his side.

Millie had been dozing under Mary's chair but was instantly on her feet, barking with what Mary thought was unrestrained joy. Morgan joined her, doing his best to balance on one hind leg while he pawed the air with his front feet, making happy growling noises.

'For goodness' sake, put them out!' Why she'd taken a young dog…

Dan laughed, opened the kitchen door once more, and shut it as they charged through. 'OK. It's safe to get up. Where's my hot cross bun?'

Mary put a plate in front of him along with a mug. She filled it with fresh coffee and topped off her own.

'All right, you've got your bun—where's my information? What was in the box?'

Dan finished chewing the bite of bun he'd taken and swallowed. 'You make the best hot cross buns I've ever had. I don't like those little pieces of hard fruit but the raisins are great.'

'Citron. The hard fruit, it's citron. It's used in fruitcake, too, at Christmas. What was in the box?'

'You were partly right.' Half the bun sat on the plate but Dan ignored it. 'There was money in the box, but not nearly enough.'

Mary put her mug down and frowned at him. 'What's not enough?'

'Miss Emilie took five hundred and fifty thousand dollars out of her account over the last eleven months. There were exactly eleven fifty dollar bills in the box—a total of five hundred and fifty dollars. They were in one of those envelopes the bank gives you when you take out cash.'

Mary had been afraid that would be the case. 'What else was in the box?'

'Nothing that's going to be of help. Old birthday cards, theater programs, a few photographs of the twins with a couple of young men, one of her with one of the men. That kind of thing.'

Another wave of sadness washed over Mary, much like the one she'd experienced the first time she saw Miss Emilie's room. Who was the man, and what had happened to end their relationship? If, indeed, there had been one. But feeling bad for Miss Emilie because she might have missed a lot of rewarding things in her life didn't solve how she died and what happened to the rest of her money. 'That means almost the whole amount is still missing.'

Dan nodded and reached for what remained of the hot cross bun. 'It was a pretty interesting afternoon.'

'I'm sure it was. Tell me.'

'I thought Richard and I had better have our little talk about Gloria before we got to the grand opening.'

Mary smiled. 'That must have been fun.'

'I thought it was, but I don't think he enjoyed it much. The very idea I could suspect him… I had quite a time getting him to stop threatening me with a lawsuit, getting me fired, which, since I'm the chief, might prove to be difficult, and listen. When I finally convinced him he wasn't going out in handcuffs, at least not right then, he started to protest how Ruthie was eavesdropping and he hadn't said anything like that to Gloria—

merely wanted to know if she knew anything about the withdrawals. Says he didn't say anything to her about how much money, just asked if she knew anything about them. He says Gloria got mad—he has no idea why—and stormed out. He then paid for what he called an inferior sandwich and also left. Says he never saw Gloria again. As for where he was on Sunday afternoon, he says he helped Cassandra pack up some things. Earlier, right after church, he went for a walk and doesn't know where. Says he has no idea where Gloria's house is and didn't walk up any hills.'

'Probably to cool off. He was rude to Les, to everyone within earshot of him. He is an angry man.' She paused, thinking. 'Are you sure Gloria was killed on Sunday? We were all up by her house that day. We didn't see anything. Oh.'

'Yes. We didn't see anything, but the dogs smelled something. I think what they wanted to investigate wasn't a fox. I think Gloria was already at the bottom of the hill. It fits with what the coroner said.'

Mary's stomach churned. Richard had stomped out of church that morning and she had no idea where he'd gone, but he was alone. Caleb left right behind him, but he'd gone home. Had Richard…but he didn't know where Gloria lived. She immediately rejected that. Finding Gloria's address was a matter of minutes either on the computer or by looking in the phone book.

'Ellen and I went through the Plym house on Monday. Richard went for a walk that day, too.'

'Did he? Richard seems to like to walk. Do you remember how long he was gone?' Dan sat up straighter and put down his untasted coffee.

'It had to be way more than an hour. He stormed out

when Ellen started to explain some forms they needed to fill out. Then we finished measuring the house. He came home while we were in the Duxworths' apartment.'

'How do you know that? Did you see him?'

'Not exactly. He tripped the motion detector.'

'He did what?'

'The monitor thing is in the Duxworths' apartment. It started to chirp and we all looked at it. Someone had come in the kitchen door. Cassandra said it must be Richard. He was there when Ellen and I left but no one else was, so it must have been him.'

'So, Richard was gone more than an hour, and you don't know where Lorraine or Caleb were?'

'Caleb should have been at the grade school and Lorraine was at a Quilting Bee meeting. Why? Could Gloria have been murdered Monday morning?'

'It's possible. Sunday is more likely, but the weather's been mild and the coroner gave us a pretty wide range.'

Neither of them said anything for a minute, and neither of them made any move to get up to let the dogs in, who were banging at the kitchen door.

Finally Mary asked, 'What did Richard say when you told him about the key and that you wanted to see what was in the box?'

Dan's smile this time was broad. Mary thought it held a trace of something that wasn't humor. 'He got downright chummy.'

'Did he ask how we knew the key was in Willis?'

'No. At this point Cassandra came in and Richard told her about the box and the key. We all went upstairs and opened it.'

'What did they say?'

'Cassandra just kept saying, "poor thing" over and

over. Richard was all set to scoop up the money and got a wee bit testy when I told him it and the box were evidence and that I'd have to take them with me. Almost as bad as when I told him he had to have his fingerprints taken.' Dan smiled. 'If his show up in Gloria's house, well, Richard and I will have another little talk.'

Mary's hand jerked and her coffee sloshed on the table. She reached for a napkin and mopped it almost automatically. 'Why would you think… I thought you said…'

'They aren't all Gloria's.'

'You think Richard might have…'

'I think whoever bashed her over the head and threw her down the hill may have been in her house. If we find Richard's, it will make the conversation even more interesting.' Dan's face was twisted with anger.

Mary had only seen that expression a couple of times before, and it had never been good news for whoever had engendered it.

'Gloria wasn't the most popular person in town but she didn't deserve to be treated that way, and Miss Emilie certainly didn't.'

'All for some money,' Mary said softly.

'It looks that way.' The scowl was retreating but Mary didn't think he was any less angry, just under better control.

'Dan, where were Caleb and Lorraine when you opened the box?'

'Never saw them. Richard said there was no reason to involve them.'

'Hmmm. Did you get into any of the other rooms upstairs? Richard's, for instance?'

'No.' That she had surprised him there was no doubt. 'Why?'

'Just wondered. So, where does this leave us? Any further along?'

'Not a lot. We know Miss Emilie kept some of the money, but not much, put it in her box for safekeeping and that she hid the key in that stuffed toy she carried around. But who took the rest of it and what they did with it we still don't know. Whoever has that money has it well hidden. Probably has it under the bed in a cigar box.' He pushed his chair back, picked up his plate and mug and set them in the sink. 'I've got to get home. I'll drop by the rummage sale tomorrow to see how it's going. In the meantime, get some rest.' He dropped a kiss on her cheek, let Millie in as he let himself out, grabbed Morgan as he followed Millie and left.

Mary sat for some time, thinking. Under the bed? In a cigar box? She didn't think so, but what if…it was possible. The idea that had been forming in the back of her head started to take a more definite form. Where could someone hide a large sum of money other than in the bank? She didn't think under the bed would work, but the money had to be somewhere. Who had known Miss Emilie took money out of the bank the first of every month just as she'd done for years? Half the town. But, who had known she'd taken out so much? Glen Manning, of course, and Dab Holt, the teller. Could Dab have been shortchanging Miss Emilie? She rejected that idea immediately. Dab had brought the withdrawals to Glen's attention. If she'd been helping herself to some of it, she wouldn't have. Lorraine? She said she didn't know and there was nothing to say she did. Caleb? He had seemed genuinely shocked when he found out. What was it Dan had said? That he looked like he was going to have a heart attack. Cassandra and Richard? There was no way they could have known until Glen called them. Who else could have known? Gloria was the most obvious. Gloria the snoop. Gloria who was always around to 'help' Miss Emilie. But if Gloria had helped herself to the money, where was it? Who killed Gloria, and why?

Or, was she coming at this from the wrong end? Had Gloria died not because she had the money but because she knew who did? That would require a lot more thought.

MARY WOKE AT two in the morning. She knew where the money was. Why she hadn't realized it before…and because she knew where it was, answers to the other questions fell into place. She thought about Miss Emilie, her room, her dog, her need to go to the bank on the first of each month, even the route she took when she wandered downtown. None of those things had changed. When something did, that was when she seemed to fall apart. None of this would have happened if Miss Emilie had been a little bit more flexible. It took Mary some time to be convinced she was right, that she really did know who took the money, where it was, who murdered both Miss Emilie and Gloria and why. Thinking back on what people had said, or not said, what they had done, thinking who had motives, motive and needs, convinced her she was, if not at the truth, at least on the right track. But she didn't have a shred of proof and getting it might prove difficult. The question now was what did she do about it?

THIRTY-THREE

MARY AND MILLIE pulled into the church parking lot at seven. A couple of cars and an old truck were already there. Mary sat and stared at them for a moment before making any attempt to get out. The sun was still asleep and she wished she was too. The night had not gone well. She hadn't returned to sleep until close to five, the pieces of the puzzle she thought she'd put together refusing to leave her alone. But that was all she had—a certainty things had happened as she imagined them, but no proof. Sometime during what she thought was going to be a long and difficult day, she needed to corner Dan, tell him what she thought and see what he wanted to do. In the meantime, the church hall door was open, the lights were on and the rummage sale would soon be in full swing.

Caleb was on his ladder doing something to the curtains he'd strung up before. This time he had two shower curtains made of some heavy nubby material that had seen better days and was hanging them from plastic shower curtain holders on the round rod he'd installed.

Mary and Millie walked over. The curtains were opaque. No one would be able to complain they didn't have privacy while trying on clothes, and she didn't think they'd come off the hangers with even the roughest treatment.

'Good job, Caleb. I'm sure the ladies will thank you for this.'

He glared at her, the malevolence in it taking her be surprise. 'You promised me if that toy dog showed up, you'd give it to me. So, instead, you went and turned it over to the police. And after you promised!'

'I did no such thing.' Mary was on the defensive, a place she certainly didn't want to be. 'Lorraine wants to bury it with Miss Emilie. That can still be done. I'll see to it.' She returned his glare.

He dropped his eyes. Unfortunately he wasn't backing down, only changing the subject. 'You going to keep that dog here all day? It'll be a confounded nuisance, barking and getting under people's feet. You should know better.'

Mary's jaw dropped. Anger such as she had not felt in years came surging through her, bringing with it a bushel full of furious statements she wanted to let loose. However, this was neither the time nor the place. With a huge effort, she beat them down and only said, through clenched teeth, 'John Lagomasino is picking Millie up shortly. She'll be spending the day at the pet shop, and what business it is of yours, I fail to see.'

That last escaped her. She simply couldn't keep it in. But she'd said enough. Millie evidently felt the tension because the hairs on the back of her neck started to rise and a low rumble came from her throat. Mary tightened the leash, turned on her heel and she and Millie headed for the kitchen.

'Were you having fun?' Pat leaned up against the counter, Styrofoam cup in her hands, grinning at Mary as she stormed in.

'That man is…'

'Rude.' Joy finished the sentence in a tone that left no doubt of her opinion. 'Did you bring the money?'

'Who's rude?' Leigh turned from filling her cup from the coffee machine to look from Joy to Mary.

Pat laughed.

Mary took a deep breath, willed herself to forget Caleb and told Leigh, 'Never mind.' She set her tote bag on the floor, pulled out the cash box they'd be using and a zipped bank bag. 'Here's the change. I have the breakdown of the cash in it. Put the checks in here, as usual, and the cash in the box. Are you going to act as cashier?' This last she addressed to Joy.

'To begin with. Pat's going to help. We'll need at least two of us. Let's get the table set up. It's already well after seven and we'd better get that door closed. Early birds will be pulling in here any time now.'

John arrived for Millie shortly after eight. The first onslaught of customers had come through and more people were pouring through the door. Mary had time only to hand over Millie, tell John she'd be at the store to pick her up a little after four and get in one last question. One she'd been wanting to ask for days but somehow hadn't. But now that Millie would be in the shop all day… 'John, is the Komodo dragon gone?'

He laughed, patted her on the arm then tucked Millie under his. 'He left Monday. I don't know who was the most relieved. The dragon, because he's going to a great natural habitat, or Glen and me. And, of course, Krissie. She hated that thing.' He paused and shifted Millie to his other arm. 'Don't worry about her. If the shop's locked, just go on in and get her. I have no idea when I'll be through, and Glen said he might be a little later getting there than he thought. I'll leave the bill on the checkout counter. Have a great sale.' He was gone, Millie peeking out from under his arm, looking back at her.

'She's scared.' Mary turned toward Pat, regret already taking hold, but Pat, and the press of people already at the door waiting for their turn to enter, pushed it aside.

'Millie will be fine. We won't be if we don't get these people checked out.'

Sometime mid-morning, Mary came up for air. Why had she worried whether the sale would be a success? Half the town had already been through, their stock of items was seriously depleted and it wasn't even lunch-time.

She was in the storage room, getting another stack of paper bags, when Dan arrived.

'There you are. Here, let me take those. It looks as if the sale is another success.' He took the bags and grinned at her. 'Where do you want these?'

'Out by the checkout table. Dan, I'm glad you're here. I've got something to tell you.'

Dan was already in the hallway, heading back into the hall. He evidently heard her, though, for he turned, his expression serious. 'What?'

'I can't tell you now, but I need to talk to you. We close this down about four and we have to clean up, then I need to get Millie. Can you come over about six or so? I'll explain then.'

They were in the hall, not a good spot for privacy. People were coming in from the parking lot; a man carrying parts to one of the baby cribs edged past them and a woman carrying two loaded shopping bags glared at them on her way out. Mary thought the door of the men's room started to open, but no one appeared.

'You sound anxious,' Dan said, apparently oblivious to the people coming and going. 'Are you all right?'

'I'm fine. It's just that... Dan, I think I know where Miss Emilie's money is hidden.'

The look on Dan's face was enough to make her smile, but this was no smiling matter and she had no time right now to explain.

'Where?'

'It's just a theory, but I was up half the night and I think I'm right. I think I know what happened to Miss Emilie and Gloria, as well, but I don't have any proof. Come over later, please. I'll tell you then what I think, and why.'

Reluctance wouldn't begin to describe Dan's reaction to leaving, but Pat was at the end of the hall, calling for the bags, Leigh right behind her with a question only Mary could answer. He handed the bags to Pat, who hurried away. Mary and Leigh followed her back into the hall.

THIRTY-FOUR

THEY EXCEEDED THEIR expectations by quite a lot, and there wasn't much to clean out. Bob, from the Food Pantry, was there with his truck and a couple of other men, loading up what was left, while several husbands of Mary's most faithful volunteers were putting tables back and sweeping the floors. Pat was in the kitchen, dumping coffee grounds and rinsing out the sink. Joy was on her way to the bank with their money. Leigh was nowhere to be found. Neither was Caleb.

Pat put Mary's car keys in her hand, her tote bag in the passenger seat of her car and ordered her to leave. 'There's nothing left to do but clean up, and we can handle that just fine. Go get Millie and go home. It was a huge success. You pulled if off again. I don't know how you do it, but you do. Now, go rest. I'll see you later.'

Mary pulled into the parking lot behind Furry Friends, exhausted but pleased. She hadn't realized how tired she was until she got into the car, then all she could think of was getting Millie and going home. The first thing she was going to do was take off her shoes and put on her bedroom slippers. Her feet felt like two slabs of raw meat.

The lock on the shop's back door opened easily. She shut it behind her and turned on the light in the back room, hoping it would be enough. She didn't want to turn on the store light. They were supposed to be closed, and she wasn't planning on staying any longer than it took to get Millie. John had pulled down the shades over the two front windows and the one over the front door. The shop was dark. Shadows made mountains out of what she was sure were ordinary displays and traps out of the paper-filled puppy and rabbit pens. She flipped the switch and, with relief, the shadows in the shop disappeared.

Millie's high-pitched bark sounded as soon as the lights went on. Mary smiled. Millie would be glad to get out of that crate. She'd probably…she did. Millie wiggled with delight, barking and whining about how awful her day was, how she had a bath and a haircut and had bows put in her hair and where had Mary been… Could they go home now?

Mary laughed and examined Millie closely. She barely recognized her. She looked like one of cockers on TV at the Westminster or Crufts dog shows. Well, maybe not quite, but close. To Mary, Millie was better. When Mary got through hugging her dog and Millie finished covering her with kisses, Mary clipped on her leash and they started for the front of the store. 'Just let me write a check for Krissie and we'll get out of here. No. Wait. I was going to get you some toys. Let's look.'

The rack with dog toys stood right outside the grooming area, next to a shelf filled with food dishes. The large glass tank that had held the Komodo dragon was pushed back against the wall. Empty. Mary heaved a sigh of relief and, while Millie nosed through the toys, she looked at the water dishes. Millie's was a small plastic one. She kept stepping in it and turning it over. Mary was tired of mopping up the kitchen, so something bigger and heavier…one caught her attention. A large ceramic bowl, with a label that guaranteed the bowl wouldn't tip over, spilling water all over the yard or kitchen. Mary picked it up. It was heavy. Something solid in the base seemed to give it weight, making it hard for the most eager drinker to flip it.

'I think I'll get you this,' Mary said. 'Do you know which toy you want?' She looked down, but Millie was gone. Looking for another toy? Mary started to walk around the shelf, the water dish in her hands but came to an abrupt halt. Caleb blocked the aisle way, feet slightly apart, holding each end of a thin leather leash looped over each upraised hand, the leather loose and swinging slightly between them. Mary sucked in her breath and took a step back, almost falling in her shock.

'I thought I'd find you here,' Caleb said.

Mary didn't say anything. She couldn't do anything but stare at the leash. It swayed as Caleb moved it closer to her.

'Picking up your dog, but there's no one else here, is there? That's nice. Means we can have a quiet little talk, just you and me.' He took a step closer.

Mary took another one back but could go no farther. She was up against something. Something glass. The dragon tank.

'What do you want to talk about?' That came out more like a croak than words, but fear seemed to have done something to her vocal chords.

Caleb smiled. 'Why, about the little toy dog, of course. You were supposed to give him to me, but you didn't. I heard you telling Chief Dunham you know where Miss Emilie's money is. 'Course you do—you've got it. You gave Richard back the key but you kept the money that was in him, and I want it. It's mine. I've earned it. I worked like a dog for those old ladies, and what did they do for me? Nothing. I thought it would be at your house, but it's not. At least, I can't find it. But it's there, somewhere, isn't it? That's where we're going, so you can give it to me.' He raised his hands, the dog leash swinging a little between those strong brown hands that could do so many things: push lawn mowers, fix sinks, paint rooms, strangle little old ladies and even throw one down the hillside. It would take nothing for him to flip that leash over her head, around her neck and pull…he meant her to know he could, he meant her to know he would… wait. What had he said? He'd been to her house? Looking for the money? In her house? Terror built but now it was mixed with anger.

'You went to my house? You broke into my house?'

'Yeah. I found the dog, too, but not the money. Where's the money?' He stepped closer and raised the still-swaying dog leash higher.

'I don't have it. I've never had it.' She took another step back. 'I have the dog, yes, but there's no money in him. There never was.' If she backed up any more, she'd be in the tank. What could she do? Keep talking, if she could. She hadn't taken her eyes off the leash, almost mesmerized by its sway, wondering if he managed to get it around her neck if she could get her fingers underneath it, keep its pressure off her throat until she could get help. Where would help come from? Nowhere. Caleb came in closer and pushed her up against the tank. The leash swayed, and, quick as a snake, he flipped it over her head, around her neck and tightened.

'Tell me where that money is and I might let you live. I've already wasted time tearing your house apart looking for it and I'm not wasting any more. So make it easy for yourself.'

Mary couldn't move, couldn't speak. Her back pushed

against the tank. The leash tightened. Lights flashed and she started to choke. Her knees started to go and she staggered. She brought up one hand and clawed at the leash around her throat. Could she get her fingers under it? One finger. The pressure eased a fraction. Could she still get the words out? She had to. 'All that was in him was the key to that box. I gave it to Dan. You have it all wrong. I don't know anything about the money.'

'You're lying.'

How odd it seemed that Caleb was so calm when all she felt was panic and sheer terror. The 'no' she uttered wasn't much more than a squeak and about as convincing, even to her. She pushed her back into the tank a little more, braced her feet and thought hard. She raised her hand, trying to tell Caleb she wanted to say something. The pressure eased a little more. 'Don't push me. The dragon's in this tank.'

Evidently Caleb understood her. The pressure eased just a fraction more, enough so the lights quit flashing and she could catch her breath. Caleb looked past her into the tank. His hands lowered and his eyes shifted. 'What dragon?'

'He was in this tank just the other day, but the lid's off.' The pressure relaxed a little more. She could get her words out without croaking and instead of clawing at the leash, which was her first instinct, she let her hands hang loose by her sides. She still had the water dish. If he backed off, just a little, if he was distracted by the idea of the dragon… 'Do you suppose he got out?'

Caleb hesitated, searching on each side of him, then his expression changed, and not the way Mary had hoped.

'That ain't going to work. Dragon, huh. There's no such thing and, if there was, there wouldn't be one here.'

All she could do was nod, as vigorously as the leash around her neck would let her. 'Oh, yes there was. It's a large lizard with huge sharp teeth. It's a horrible creature. Scares me to death.' She tried to shift her weight, moved one foot just a little, then her hips. If she could get him off balance, maybe, maybe raise her hand…no.

Caleb's smile seemed to consist of as many teeth as the dragon had and, while they might not be as sharp, the sight of them made her heart beat faster, and not with pleasure.

'We're going to your house, and you're going to give me that money.' Caleb leaned forward, tightening the leash as he did. Mary screamed and tried to drop sideways, sliding on the glass. She almost made it, but her foot slipped. She tried to catch herself, to break her fall, but all there was behind her was glass and, in front of her, floor. She screamed again as the leash tightened, then heard another, more piercing scream. Caleb.

The leash loosened, then fell on her shoulders as Caleb swung away from her, clutching at his pant leg and hollering. At first she couldn't understand him, or his panic, but the words came out with another scream. 'The dragon. It's got me. Do something.'

She managed to get back on her feet, not an easy task as Caleb thrashed and screamed. Why? The dragon was gone, but Millie wasn't. Her teeth were planted in Caleb's calf, her growls fierce and intent, and she held on as he thrashed and yelled. Finally, he made one mad whirl, swinging the dog and beating at her with his bare hands. Millie let go and flew across the aisle, landing in the stand that held the dog dishes. Her howl of pain and protest sent a wave of anger through Mary, stronger than any she'd ever felt before.

'You beast. You horrible man. You hurt my dog.' She was screaming as she struggled to free herself to get to Millie, trying vainly to land a kick on his shins.

Caleb pushed Mary aside. His rage seemed entirely focused on Millie. With a roar, he lunged past Mary toward Millie.

Mary threw herself across the aisle to where Millie lay, trying to get between her and Caleb, the water dish still somehow in her hand. Without conscious thought, she raised it and brought it down on Caleb's outstretched hands, smashing them hard against the display stand. Caleb screamed again, but his hands no longer reached for either of them. Instead, he stared at his bashed fingers.

So did Mary, but just for a moment. Millie was whining and hadn't moved out from under the wreckage of the food bowl stand. Mary gasped and pushed at Caleb to get to her.

'No, you don't.' He grabbed her with one hand, the other hanging limp by his side, blood dripping from his fingers. 'Hit me, will you. You're a dead woman, now. I don't need you. I'll go back and tear your house apart until I find the money, and by the time anyone finds you I'll be long gone. You and that rotten little dog.' He grabbed Mary by the front of her shirt and swung her around so she was facing the dragon tank. 'Lucky you, it's empty.' He thrust her, her head pointed right at the glass side of the tank, and her feet came off the floor. She tried to kick but couldn't get any traction, and then she was on the floor in a crumpled heap. Caleb once more gave a terrified howl. Mary heard a dog growling and snarling, a dog that couldn't possibly be Millie, but was. She heard something else. A man's voice, loud and concerned.

'What's going on in here? Who's in here? You'd better show yourself. I've called the police. They're on the way. What the…' Glen Manning stood in the aisle, seemingly unable to move, as he stared at the scene. Mary on the floor and Millie doing her best to chew off Caleb's leg, who was beating at the little dog while bleeding all over the floor.

'What…' Glen grabbed Millie, who didn't want to release Caleb. She came away with a large piece of his pants in her mouth and, it appeared, some of his skin as well. Caleb stared at Glen, touched the bleeding open wound on his leg with his good hand, glared at Mary and raised it as if to strike her, but stopped.

'Shit.' Caleb charged at Glen who, arms full of dog, staggered backward. Caleb brushed past Glen and headed for the back door.

'Stop him!' Mary struggled to her feet and started after him.

'Where are you going?' Glen, still holding a wiggling Millie, tried to follow. 'What's going on around here?'

'Caleb is the murderer. He killed Miss Emilie and Gloria, and he's getting away. Stop him.'

'I don't need to,' Glen said calmly.

He set Millie down, who immediately ran to Mary, jumping up on her leg, making little whimpering noises. Mary sank back down on the floor, not because she wanted to, but because her legs no longer cooperated. Millie climbed into her lap, sniffing her all over, trying to lick her chin, making sure she was still in one piece. Mary responded by holding the little dog close and burying her face in her fur.

Finally, she looked at Glen. 'Why don't you need to? He's getting away.'

'He won't get far. I really did call the police. I couldn't imagine what was going on in here, but it didn't sound good. I imagine that's them, pulling him over right now.'

Sirens. Police sirens. They hadn't registered, but Mary finally heard them. They were close—in the parking lot in back of the store close.

'I imagine they'll be in here any second.' Glen squatted beside Mary and looked at her closely then up at that tank. 'He was going to throw you up against that tank, wasn't he?'

Mary nodded and closed her eyes. 'It's a good thing that dragon's gone. I wouldn't have liked sharing a tank with him.' She opened her eyes and looked at Millie. 'It was Millie who saved me.' She hugged the dog tighter. Millie laid her head on Mary's shoulder and sighed.

Glen patted the dog. 'Did Caleb really kill them? Why?'

Mary buried her face once more in Millie's neck then looked up. 'It's a long story, and not a very happy one. It's not over yet, either.' She sighed. 'This whole thing, it's such a tragedy.'

The sounds coming from the parking lot suggested one piece of the play was coming to an end. Sirens had halted; voices, a voice that had been screaming at her only minutes before, was quiet, and the drone of another suggested someone was being read their rights. Mary pushed Millie off her lap and held her hand out to Glen.

'You sure you're all right to get up?'

The look she gave him made words unnecessary. She was on her feet, Millie beside her, when Dan walked in.

He nodded to Glen then stood in front of Mary, evidently examining her for injuries. Deciding she wasn't injured, at least not seriously, he nodded. 'OK. We've got

Caleb, we've read him his rights, the medics are fixing one thoroughly smashed hand and another well-chewed leg right now, but I need to know.'

'Know what?'

'What I'm supposed to charge him with.'

Mary took a deep breath and let it out slowly. 'Two counts of murder and one count of attempted murder.'

Dan waited, but Mary said nothing more.

'Not grand larceny?'

Mary shook her head. 'What Caleb stole was a couple of lives.'

'Then where's the money?'

'The only place Lorraine thought she could put it where Caleb wouldn't find it. In the quilt on Richard's bed.'

THIRTY-FIVE

LORRAINE SAT AT the end of the kitchen table in the Plym kitchen, not moving, not making a sound—nothing to show she heard what anyone was saying or that she understood the meaning of the quilt spread out over the table, except for the tears that dropped slowly down each cheek.

Mary didn't offer her a tissue or even a napkin. She was exhausted, sore and still recovering from the terror Caleb had inflicted on her and Millie. She wasn't sure if that had worn her out or if it was the terrible anger she'd experienced when she found out Caleb had broken into her house and then when he'd tried to stomp on Millie. That Millie had torn a hole in his leg didn't count. He deserved it. Mary took a sip of the coffee someone had set in front of her and felt the heat, and the caffeine, revive her. The EMTs had said she'd be sore for a couple of days but she wasn't badly hurt. They'd wanted her to go to the emergency room to be checked out, but they refused to take Millie, so she declined. They hadn't even wanted to look Millie over, but Mary had insisted. She'd known them both all their lives, had them both in her Sunday school class and wasn't taking no for an answer. They'd laughed, said Millie would have some tender ribs for a while but nothing was broken. Then they'd left with Caleb strapped securely to a gurney, swearing like a…well, swearing, followed by a patrol car. Dan had put both her and Millie in his car and they had headed for the Plyms', where they all sat in the kitchen, waiting to hear what Lorraine had to say for herself. So far, she'd only cried.

Glen Manning sighed and laid the last stack of fifty dollar bills on the table beside the other stacks. 'It's all here. Counting the money in the box, every penny Miss Emilie took out is here.'

Mary broke down and handed Lorraine a tissue. She handed one to Cassandra as well. Her eyes looked as if they'd overflow any minute.

'I don't understand.' Cassandra took the tissue, dabbed her eyes and leaned forward onto the table. She picked up one end of the quilt, looked at the edging where the careful, even stitches had been taken out and let it drop. 'You were taking our money? You?'

Disbelief, and Mary thought grief, was in her voice and on her face. The sense of betrayal she was experiencing right now must be overwhelming but, to some extent, it was mixed with relief. Mary was certain Cassandra had suspected her brother. Not of stealing the money. She wasn't sure who Cassandra thought had done that, probably poor Gloria, but of killing both women in his relentless pursuit of it.

Lorraine looked at Cassandra, ignoring everyone else in the room. 'I'm sorry.' Her voice was barely above a whisper. 'I had to. I had to be ready to leave as soon as Miss Emilie didn't need me anymore. I kept thinking she might need it, but if she died or went somewhere like Shady Acres and didn't need it, or me, anymore…' The tears flowed harder. She didn't seem to notice. The tissue stayed in her hand, which stayed on the table, without moving. 'I thought I was protecting her. Instead, I killed her.'

The start of surprise that went through Cassandra was visible. It seemed to almost render her incapable of speech. 'But… I thought…' was as far as she was able to go. Not so, her brother.

'I knew it. You and that thieving husband of yours were in on it together. You're going to jail, my girl. If not for murder then for grand larceny.'

Dan had been strangely silent since they'd arrived, bearing an emergency warrant to search the house. The only thing they'd searched so far was the quilt. 'You're getting a little ahead of yourself, Richard.'

Richard's head snapped around at the use of his first name, his chin went up and his eyes blazed. 'Ahead of myself? She just confessed to murder as well as theft. That sounds like jail to me.'

Dan gave Richard a disgusted look and turned toward Lorraine. He sat next to her and he covered her hand with his. 'Did you, yourself, participate in the murder of Miss Emilie Plym?'

'No. But if I hadn't lied to him and hidden the money from him, he never would have taken her to the church hall that night, and she wouldn't have died. It's all my fault. Everything's my fault.'

The sobs took over and she started to shudder. Dan removed his hand and looked at Mary, as helpless a look on his face as she'd seen on anyone.

She got up, motioned Dan to move, which he did with haste, sat down and gathered Lorraine up against her and let her cry, all the time patting her on the back as she would a small child, murmuring, 'There, there, it's going to be all right.' She wasn't sure that was true, but Lorraine was partly right. A lot of what happened was because of what she did. Mary sighed. She'd had a lot of provocation.

Gradually the sobs lessened. Lorraine sat up straight, accepted the glass of water Cassandra offered and was silent.

Mary straightened up. 'It was Caleb's decision to kill her. Even if he didn't mean for her to die, just to rough her up so she'd tell him where the money was, the entire blame for that is on him.' She gave Lorraine one more pat and settled back into the chair.

Cassandra sat rigidly upright in hers, stress lines digging furrows around her eyes. Mary watched Glen, who still sat at the end of the table, his hand shaking a little as he put a rubber band on the last pile of money and logged the amount into his tablet without looking at anyone.

'Just how did you lie to Caleb?' Dan's voice was still mild but there was no doubt it was time for Lorraine to tell what had happened.

'I didn't start out to steal anything.'

Richard snorted. Everyone at the table turned and glared at him. He subsided.

'Miss Emilie…' She paused, looked around the table then at her hands, which were clasped tightly in her lap, 'Change made her nervous. She never let us change anything in her room, she had the same thing for breakfast every day, she carried the same purse and she went to the bank.' She gave a shuddery sigh then went on. 'Soon after Miss Eloise had her stroke, Miss Emilie wanted to know if it was the first of the month. I took her, she made her withdrawal and we went home. She put her money in her box and put the key in the dish, like she always did. That was when I got the idea.'

She stopped, sighed again and shuddered.

'Why?' Mary tried to make her voice encouraging. A tall order, but even though she thought she knew the answer, Lorraine had to tell them.

Lorraine looked up for a moment, met Mary's gaze then looked back at her hands. 'I wanted to leave. I've wanted to leave for years, but I don't have any money. Caleb took it all. I thought if I could hide some, when Miss Emilie was gone, or somewhere safe, I could get away.' She paused again. 'It worked for a while. Caleb knew she went to the bank, but I told him she only took out her little allowance.'

The silence in the room was absolute. Even Richard seemed to hold his breath.

'Then Richard and Cassandra came and Richard accused us of stealing. Caleb thought he meant the little bit the twins used to take out. When he found out how much money was involved he almost went insane.'

'He thought you had the money?' Mary had her hand on Lorraine's, hoping it would help her keep going.

Lorraine nodded. 'I told him I didn't, that I thought Miss Emilie had hidden it, but I had no idea where. He almost tore the attic apart, looking for it. He even took the motion detector off the morning-room door and put it on the attic door, thinking he'd know if she went up there.' Again she paused. 'She never did.'

'What about the little white clock?' Mary squeezed her hand lightly. 'It was Caleb who took it, wasn't it?'

Lorraine nodded. She finally looked at each of them in turn, but it seemed to be Cassandra she addressed. 'Caleb wasn't always very rational. He thought he knew everything, and when he got an idea in his head no one could talk him out of it. When he couldn't find the money anywhere else he decided it was in her box and she'd hidden the key in the clock.' She almost smiled. 'I kept telling him she hadn't. The key had been in that clock for years. I didn't know what it was but I knew there was something. I think Miss Eloise put it there years ago. But Caleb wouldn't listen. When he found it had been donated he was determined to get it back.' She paused, took a shuddering breath and went on. 'I saw it in the garage on Thursday morning when we were looking for Miss Emilie. Later that afternoon, it was gone.'

'Tell us about the night Miss Emilie died.'

It seemed obvious that Lorraine would rather walk on hot coals than tell Dan about that night, but she didn't have much choice. 'Richard told him to turn off the motion detector but he didn't.' Her words came out stilted and forced, her eyes back on her hands in her lap. 'We both knew she'd go looking for Willis as soon as she woke up. She might not remember she'd been in the church hall but she'd know he was missing and she'd be in a state.'

She paused again.

Dan urged her on. 'Did she? Wake up?'

'Yes. Caleb didn't think I'd hear the monitor. He'd fallen asleep on the sofa, or thought I'd think he was asleep, but I heard it. He got up then slipped out the door. I watched him through the window. He went around the back then pretty soon I saw Miss Emilie go down the front walk. Caleb caught up to her. I waited and waited, but they didn't come back. I didn't know what to do so I went back to bed and waited. Finally, he came back. I was afraid to ask him anything. His face was… I'd never seen him look like that, so I pretended to be asleep. I don't think he slept. I know I didn't. Then, in the morning, Cassandra came knocking on our door, saying Miss Emilie was missing and we had to come help look for her.'

'For God's sake, woman, why didn't you tell the police right then?' Richard's face was turning beet red again, his scathing boardroom voice back.

Lorraine looked directly at him, her face as white as his was red. 'I was afraid to.'

Finally Mary spoke. 'And you've been terrified ever since.'

Tears appeared again in the corners of Lorraine's eyes. She blinked them away.

Dan turned to Mary. 'Just when did you figure all this out?'

'Last night.'

'The answers just came to you, like a bolt from the blue?' Richard's tone wasn't any less demeaning than it always was.

Mary sighed. Richard was about to learn a thing or two.

'The morning Ellen and I came, exactly one week ago, Gloria came rushing in, saying she'd heard about Miss Emilie when someone at the church hall called her. Then Caleb came in saying it was on the radio. They both lied. I checked with the radio station yesterday. They didn't release the information about Miss Emilie until Dan told them they could, and that was much later in the day. All Caleb could have known at that hour was there'd been an accident. That Miss Emilie might be involved was certainly possible, but that wasn't what he said. He knew she was dead, that she'd been murdered. It was possible he hadn't done it, but if he hadn't, he knew who did. Gloria's lie was more obvious.'

'Why?' Cassandra's puzzled look said it plainly wasn't obvious.

'You had to know Gloria.' There was sorrow in Mary's

voice as she went on. 'No one who was at the church hall that morning would have thought to call Gloria. Only a close friend would have done that, someone who thought Gloria had a connection to the Plyms that went beyond once caring for someone who's been dead for close to a year. Gloria didn't have any friends.'

There was no sound in the room except that of Lorraine's quick intake of breath.

'Go on,' Dan said.

'I didn't believe Gloria but had no evidence. There was only one other way I could think of that she'd know about Miss Emilie, and I couldn't believe she'd murdered her. I also didn't think she had a key to the church hall. I wasn't sure about Caleb. The radio could have let the information slip before they were supposed to. It didn't make sense they'd tell the same lie. Not then, anyway. I didn't know about the money. That changed everything.'

'Yes, it did.' Dan nodded at her.

'I thought from the beginning the only person who could have taken that money was Lorraine. As much as I didn't want to admit it, I didn't see who else it could be. Miss Emilie didn't like Gloria, Caleb scared her and Cassandra and Richard weren't here. She loved and trusted Lorraine.'

There was a loud sob from Lorraine's end of the table. Mary felt Millie, who was under the table, pick her head up off of Mary's foot. The sob subsided and Millie's head dropped back down.

'Why didn't you think Lorraine and Caleb were in it together?' Cassandra's eyes looked as if they would overflow any minute, but she seemed determined to hold it together.

Lorraine wasn't. A steady stream of tears ran down

her cheeks. 'I'd never hurt Miss Emilie,' she whispered. 'Not ever.'

'I believe that.' Mary's voice was soft. She put her hand on Lorraine's arm and patted her gently. 'The more I heard about your life with Caleb, the more I thought I understood why you took the money. Caleb obviously didn't know where the money was. He would have if you were scamming together. For a while, I thought Richard was responsible. He was...'

A roar of protest came as Richard rose out of his chair and leaned on his hands. 'How...' His cheeks were bright red, his eyes almost bulging. 'How could you possibly...'

'You made it easy.' Mary's middle schoolteacher voice left no doubt he had, and he was about to be told why. 'You gave us all ample reason to suspect you. Bullying, lying, thinking of no one but yourself and how you could get your hands on the money. It was hard not to consider you, and seriously. Even your sister thought you might be responsible. She made Miss Emilie's bed back up after you trashed it, to protect you.'

For the first time since Mary met him, Richard Plym was struck dumb. His face went from red to white in seconds, and he turned to look at his sister as if he'd never seen her before. Mary was pretty sure it wasn't with gratitude, but shock.

'How did you know...' Cassandra looked equally as shocked.

'You said Miss Emilie's bedcovers were on the floor when you looked in on her the morning she disappeared. She wouldn't have pulled them off the bed. Neither would anyone who might have gotten her up. That had to have happened later, and the only reason I could think of was someone looking for something.' She paused and grinned at Dan. 'Like someone looking for a cigar box hidden under the bed. Only, I think this person was looking for money hidden under the mattress. There were only two people who could have done that.' This time she looked directly at Cassandra and there was no grin. 'You or Richard. I had no doubt which of you had done what.'

Cassandra's mouth formed a small 'Oh.' She glanced at her brother, but he seemed to have nothing to say.

'You need to thank your sister. She was trying to protect you.'

'When and why did you decide it was Caleb and not Richard?'

Mary was certain Dan had reached the same conclusion she had, with the exception of where the money had been hidden, but he wanted to know what had convinced her. 'Caleb lied too much. The first lie was the most damning, but until I checked with the radio station I wasn't sure. They didn't announce it was Miss Emilie dead until the afternoon. Then we were in the church hall and Caleb told me the police had messed up our sale tables. It did look as if they'd been searched, but I didn't think by the police. There was nothing to be learned from searching them, but someone had. Caleb had a key to the church hall. It would have been easy for him to take the clock then put it back. He was in the hall, putting up new dressing-room curtains when I arrived, and he was alone. He asked me about the stuffed dog, Willis. Said Lorraine was worried about it but he seemed overly eager to find him. I couldn't help wondering if he'd gone through everything looking for it.'

Mary stole a glance at Lorraine before she went on. She'd stopped crying. Instead, she stared at her hands that were clasped together on the table in front of her.

She seemed to have retreated into herself, where nothing that was being said could reach her. Mary sighed. 'He sounded almost gleeful when he talked about Gloria's death. He told me how Lorraine hated her but he hardly knew her. Gloria practically lived here for two months while she took care of Miss Eloise and Caleb had done her yard for at least a year. Of course he knew her. So, why did he tell such a stupid lie? Because he wanted to distance himself from her? Gloria hung around the house a lot, even after Miss Eloise died. She also knew something was going on.' She turned toward Lorraine, who sat very still, hand in her lap, so tightly folded the tips of her fingers had turned red. She was almost comatose.

'Lorraine, did bank statements come to the house?'

Lorraine looked up, startled. 'What?'

'Bank statements. Did the sisters get them?'

'Why, yes. I guess they were bank statements.' Lorraine raised her head to look at Mary and blinked once.

'But the sisters only had one account. The trust fund. Were the statements for that?'

It took Lorraine a minute, then she shook her head. 'I have no idea. I put all that kind of thing in Miss Eloise's desk.'

'What did you do with them after she died?'

'The same thing. I put everything in her desk.'

Lorraine's blank look was replaced by something else. Fright.

'Did it occur to you the withdrawals would be on the statements?'

Mary didn't think it possible for Lorraine's face to get whiter, but it did.

'No.'

Mary sighed. Lorraine didn't handle money. Her name

wasn't even on Caleb's accounts. Had she ever written a check?

'I'll bet Gloria knew what was on those statements, and she knew it was being depleted. I'd thought all along she wouldn't have spent so much time with Miss Emilie, for free, if she didn't think there was some way to make it pay. She'd seen Miss Emilie pitch a fit that afternoon, trying to find her dog. She probably saw the clock at the rummage sale and recognized it. Anyone who'd ever handled it couldn't help but know something was inside. I don't how much Gloria figured out, but she knew a lot of money was involved. I think she was watching the house that night, knowing Lorraine would give Miss Emilie a sedative and that when she woke she'd likely try to find the dog again. She planned on being ready to step in and rescue her. Just how, I don't know, but she had a key to the house. She didn't have to go in. Miss Emilie came out. Then Caleb took charge of her. Only, they didn't go back in the house. I think Gloria followed them and watched them go into the church hall. Caleb came out alone. I think she thought Caleb had the money so, instead of telling the police what she saw, she tried a little blackmail. It didn't work out so well for her.'

Mary turned toward Richard. 'You thought Gloria had the money. That's what that lunch at the Yum Yum was all about. It must have come as quite a shock when you learned you'd been sleeping under it all this time.'

The red was back on Richard's face, but he didn't say anything.

'How did you know Lorraine hid the money in the quilt?' Dan asked.

'That took me longer than it should have.' She looked over at Lorraine, who ducked her head, and sighed. 'I used to watch my grandmother quilt. She'd tell me stories while she sewed. How the slaves hid things in the quilts they made—money they weren't supposed to have, fake passes or papers that said they were free. Pioneer women did also. So did women in the south when Sherman made his march to the sea. They hid money, jewelry, important papers. Women have been doing it for a long time. I should have suspected as soon as I saw Richard's quilt. The edges were bunchy, the edging not smooth. The rest of it was Lorraine's neat, exacting stitches.

'I really didn't think Miss Emilie had hidden the money. She might have once, but not eleven times. Whoever took it did. Hid it eleven times. Someone made out the note she carried to the bank, and someone she knew and trusted helped her put some money in her box every month while taking the largest portion themselves. That same person took the note out and destroyed it. There was only one person who could have done that. Lorraine.'

'Why?' Cassandra spoke for the first time. She looked at Lorraine, who seemed to have retreated back into her shell, so she turned to Mary. 'Why destroy the note?'

'Because Caleb was looking for the money everywhere and Miss Emilie's purse was one of the first places he'd look. Lorraine convinced him she didn't have it, but if he found the note he'd think she wrote it. Miss Emilie didn't know how to type, let alone work a computer. By this time, Caleb was convinced Miss Emilie had put the money in her box, but he couldn't find the key. I wondered why he didn't just break into the box, but he couldn't. Too many people knew about it to pry it open. So, where was the key? In the clock. Only, it wasn't.'

Lorraine finally spoke. 'He was furious when he found out it was an old safe deposit box key.' There was a trace of a smile but it didn't last long. 'And when the real key showed up and he heard the box only held a small amount of money, he went ballistic. That's when he decided it was in the dog.'

'Yes.' Mary thought about the chain of events that had led Caleb to the wrong conclusion, one that had almost gotten her and Millie killed. 'He knew I'd given Dan the key to the box, and I guess he overheard me tell Dan I knew where the money was. To him that meant I had the money and the dog. He was badly mistaken. Lorraine, where did Caleb go after church on Sunday? He left the community room right after Richard did. Was he home when you returned?'

Lorraine shook her head. 'Poor Gloria. But she shouldn't have tried to blackmail him.' She turned to Dan. 'What happens now?'

'If you mean to Caleb, he'll sit in jail until he goes to trial. You don't get bail if you're accused of murder.'

'What about me?' There were a lot of questions in those three words, and Mary didn't think Lorraine was going to like any of the answers.

'You're going to jail.' Richard sounded adamant, but not quite so arrogant.

'You won't be going right away,' Dan said, while glaring at Richard. 'I don't have a warrant for your arrest, and that may take a while.'

'There won't be a warrant. I'd have to bring charges against her, and I'm not going to.' Cassandra's voice was soft but emphatic.

Richard started to sputter, but Cassandra coolly cut him off. 'Richard, we have an agreement. I'll buy out your share of the house, and that will be in cash. You'll get half of whatever is in the trust fund and half of the money Lorraine…safeguarded. If you even think of trying to press charges, I'll hold up anyone getting anything out of this house or the trust fund for years in court, and I can do it. So, for just once, shut up.'

Richard's mouth was going in and out like a fish out of water, but he was silent.

Dan addressed Cassandra. 'You're not going to press charges?'

'No.'

'Well, if you're not, neither am I. Caleb is a different matter. I've already charged him with two cases of first degree murder and one of attempted murder, so I guess I'm no longer needed here. Glen, let's get all this money back in your bank.'

Richard started to sputter again but Dan stopped him. 'This money is the property of the trust. After it's settled, I suppose at least half of it will belong to you but, in the meantime…' He turned to Cassandra. 'Is that agreeable with you?'

She didn't suppress her smile. 'It's just fine.'

'Ellen says you're going to keep the house and turn it into a bed and breakfast.'

Cassandra nodded again.

'You're going to do what?' Mary wasn't completely surprised. She'd thought Cassandra had something in mind.

'Turn it into a bed and breakfast. I've already been to the city council and it looks promising.' She turned to Lorraine. 'I'm staying on for a little while. If you want to stay in the apartment until you can find a place to go, you can.' She paused. 'You were going to use that money to go where?'

Lorraine's expression was guarded. She probably hadn't expected this. 'I didn't really know. Maybe to

Seattle to be near my son. I haven't seen him in years and I've never seen my grandkids. You're really not going to press charges?'

'I'm really not. We'll call your son tomorrow. Do you have any money? I won't charge you rent but a salary…'

Glen had all the money stuffed in his briefcase and now stepped in. 'Lorraine is legally entitled to half of whatever is in Caleb's account. This is a community property state. She won't starve.'

Lorraine hadn't expected that either. 'There's money?'

'Quite a bit. Caleb was many things, among them loath to let loose of a dime. There are quite a few of them in his bank accounts. Come into the bank tomorrow and I'll go over it all with you.'

Glen headed for the door.

Dan pushed back his chair, getting ready to go as well. 'Mary, your car is in back of the pet shop. Want a ride?'

She did. Millie seemed ready to leave as well. After all, dinnertime was getting close.

Mary had one last question for Cassandra. 'Did you mean it when you offered to help on one of my events?'

Cassandra broke into a smile for the first time in… had she even seen her smile? 'Every word.'

Mary smiled back. 'Good. I'll call you tomorrow. The Friends of the Library are having a book sale in a few weeks and we need to get started on it. The Parks and Rec people are raising money for a new soccer field, and we're having an organizing meeting next week. I'll count on you.' She smiled, gathered up Millie's leash and followed Dan out the door.

* * * * *